"You said someone slashed some girths?" asked Sarah. "And squirted you and put sand in your coffee. What was it all about?"

"I thought that might rouse your detective instincts," said Julia with satisfaction. "You're building a reputation for being in the wrong place at the right time, or is it the other way around?

"Is it just from insatiable curiosity like the elephant's child, or does crime attract you? Have you really solved something?"

"I detest violence—only sometimes it happens in a perfectly normal place like a shop or a library and I'm there." Sarah turned her gaze away and sighed. "Okay, Aunt Julia, tell me about it."

"It's a sort of epidemic. Little things. Annoying, but so far not dangerous."

"Out with it because I'd hate to think we're just going to have a dull old time watching me fall off a horse every day."

"Well then," said Julia firmly, "I shall begin at the beginning...."

St. Martin's Paperbacks by J. S. Borthwick

DUDE
ON
ARRIVAL

J.S. BORTHWICK

ST. MARTIN'S PAPERBACKS

Rancho del Gato Blanco, Cat Claw Ranch, the town of Lodestone, Buzzard Mountain, Buzzard Creek, and all events and characters described in this book are imaginary.

DUDE ON ARRIVAL

Copyright © 1992 by J. S. Borthwick.

Text illustrations copyright © 1991 by Alec Creighton.

Library of Congress Catalog Card Number: 91-22970

ISBN: 0-312-92955-2

Printed in the United States of America

St. Martin's Press hardcover edition/January 1992
St. Martin's Paperbacks edition/November 1992

10 9 8 7 6 5 4 3 2 1

For Dotty Gurney, who has rescued more animals than I can count, and for her daughters, Susie and Nancy

Thanks again to my medical back-up team, Mac and Rob; a salute to Sandy Nevens, master of the perfect pun; and a grateful nod to certain guest ranches in Arizona where nothing happened to me and my family but kindness and hospitality.

Cast of Principal Characters

Sarah Deane. . . . Teaching fellow at Bowmouth College
Julia Clancy. . . . Aunt to Sarah Deane
Alex McKenzie. . . . Doctor of internal medicine
Judy Steiner. . . . Head clerk, Rancho del Gato Blanco
Cookie Logan. . . . Clerk, Rancho del Gato Blanco
Fred Arco. . . . Manager, Rancho del Gato Blanco
Maria Cornish. . . . Actress
Blue Feather Romero. . . . Boyfriend of Maria Cornish
Senator Leo J. Hopgood. . . . Junior senator from Alaska
Maud-Emma Hopgood. . . . Wife of Leo
Artie Hopgood. . . . Son of Leo and Maud-Emma
Lily Farnsworth. . . . Secretary to Senator Hopgood
Mr. Owen and Mr. Yates. . . . Aides to Senator Hopgood
Morty McGuire. . . . Head wrangler at Rancho del Gato Blanco
Todd Logan. . . . Assistant head wrangler and husband of Cookie
Peter Doubler. . . . Head chef at Rancho del Gato Blanco
Heinz Simmons. . . . Owner of Rancho del Gato Blanco and
    president of Blue Sky Ranch and Ski Resorts
Esty Simmons. . . . Wife of Heinz
Mr. and Mrs. Howell. . . . Friends of the Simmonses'
Laddie Danforth.. . . . Entertainer at Rancho del Gato Blanco
Harvey Wallow. . . . Sheriff for the town of Lodestone
Shorty Fox. . . . Chief of homicide, Phoenix
Solly Jackson. . . . Forensic pathologist and chief medical
    examiner, Phoenix
Douglas Jay. . . . Special agent, FBI

ONE

"What a location for a ranch! Then on the instant, cold and sickening, came the thought that this spot might be his grave."
    —Zane Grey, The Fugitive Trail

THE envelope from Julia Clancy to her niece, Sarah Deane, had unusual bulk. Opened, it revealed three pages of news and gossip in Julia's spiky handwriting. Concealed underneath these sheets and accounting for the bulge in the envelope was a glossy brochure which showed decorative people eating decorative food and sporting against a backdrop of western splendor.

Sarah, home from her afternoon teaching stint, looked out through her kitchen window at the gray, snow-filled scene beyond, shivered, and then turned to the opening paragraph of the brochure.

Welcome to Arizona's newest and brightest star. Come to RANCHO DEL GATO BLANCO and be part of the Romance of the Old West. Play our eighteen-hole championship golf course, enjoy tennis on one of our six all-weather courts, or ride a gentle horse with our experienced cowboys along breathtaking trails on Buzzard Mountain or along the flowing waters of Buzzard Creek. Splash in our Olympic swimming pool, shop in one of the fashionable boutiques in the old mining town of Lodestone, and sing along with Laddie Danforth and his guitar at our Saturday Campfires. Come and vacation with the discriminating and distinguished people who spend their holidays at Rancho del Gato Blanco.

Sarah noted with interest the presence of sunlight in a photograph of blue and purple mountains, gave a slight shudder at the idea of singing along with anyone called Laddie Danforth, and picked up her aunt's letter. It began with the ritual inquiries about the weather back East, Sarah's academic struggles as a teaching fellow at Bowmouth College, and the state of the medical practice of Sarah's live-in companion, Alex McKenzie. These courtesies over, Aunt Julia plunged in.

Well, this so-called ranch isn't quite what I expected because it's more resort than ranch—really too much of a good thing, and where, I ask you, is all the water coming from to keep the golf course looking like velvet? I suppose all the surrounding countryside is completely sucked dry. I will write the Wilderness Society and ask. Anyway, thank heavens for the horses. I've been riding every day trying to pretend I'm not an arthritic old biddy who hobbles around at home clutching a cane. Fortunately the horse does most of the work and I sit there and bounce.

I haven't really made friends because I don't mix into the bar and pool scene and I go to bed right after dinner. But the passing scene is fairly distracting because of this perfectly dreadful senator from Alaska, Leo J. Hopgood—he's the one that spiked the Save-a-River Bill when he was in the House representing Texas, and how did he manage that switch, I'd like to know. He's here for Thanksgiving and is spending all his spare time kissing babies and waitresses and horses because the rumor has it that he's going to run in the Republican presidential primaries, at which I say God help us all. He's followed around by a couple of aides in silk suits and pointed shoes while a rather depressed southern wife and an appalling son, Artie, lurk in the distance.

And if the excitement of Senator Hopgood wasn't enough, along comes—hold your breath—Maria Cornish. The Maria Cornish. She must be closing in on fifty? sixty? but you'd never know it because she is remarkably preserved. And busy, all those talk shows and miniseries and a movie once a year, playing lady spies or sinister widows.

As you know, I arrived the first of November and I must say things were rather slow—empty rooms, empty 'tables at the dining room, the staff hovering too much—but you can see that a senator who's talking about running and a glamourpuss movie type are just the juice the place needs. Everyone is sitting up and taking notice, the place has filled, and the manager—a Fred Arco, who looks and acts like the Emperor Napoleon—is rubbing his hands. He spends most of his time chewing out the staff when he thinks the guests aren't listening and worrying about PR and the ranch image. The actual place is run by two invaluable women, Judy Steiner and Cookie Logan, without whom the place would fall to bits overnight.

That's all for now, but I'm going to make you an offer you can't refuse—not your old auntie. Think Arizona for Christmas. It's on me because I want company, some friends to cheer me in my dotage. It will be my Christmas present.

Love, Julia

Well, well, thought Sarah, folding the letter. Arizona. Warmth, dryness, food cooked by others, a swimming pool. Mountain vistas. Lone cowboys. Cactus. Tumbleweed. Canyons, campfires, and desert sands. She looked again through the kitchen window. The wind had come up, the snow had turned to hard little nuggets and was rattling against the windowpane.

Why not? Aunt Julia could be rather overbearing, but the wide open spaces of Arizona would probably dilute her powers. And Alex? Alex, who in irritation referred to Aunt Julia as "the Widow Clancy," also felt she came on a bit strong. Okay, bringing Alex around would take management. Sarah would wait until even he, a lover of Northeast winters, felt that a temporary transfer to a warmer climate would be a positive move. Sarah took the ranch brochure and tucked it in her briefcase. She would bide her time until the weather turned even colder, gloomier, and more generally vile.

Julia Clancy was right on the money when she suggested that the arrival of a senator and a movie star at Thanksgiving would revive the fortunes of the newly refurbished Rancho del Gato Blanco. In its present guise, the ranch represented the metamorphosis of White Cat Ranch, a modest working and guest ranch, into its present form as a trendy upscale resort with an upscale Spanish name to match. All it needed to kick it from red ink to black was the arrival of two high-profile guests.

On the Friday after Thanksgiving, Cookie Logan—on the front desk and always ready to chat—called out to her co-worker, Judy Steiner, who was working behind the scenes on the reservation charts.

"It isn't," said Cookie, "as if we shouldn't be grateful for all these big names, but I'd say that Senator Hopgood is almost more trouble than he's worth. All that room shuffling and extra telephones and cleaning out Sombrero Suite for his aides."

"We can't choose our celebrities," Judy reminded her. "One big name attracts other big names. And little names with big incomes."

"Like flies on flypaper," said Cookie. "That senator tried to ruin Texas and now he's in Alaska making shit."

"He's safer in Alaska than in Washington," said Judy. "Cross your finger he gets shot down in the primaries. Now, no more talk, I've the Christmas reservations to work on."

Judy, essentially a straight arrow as far as business hours were concerned, bent her head over the chart. She was a cheerful redhead built for action. Big. Big forehead, full mouth, strong chin, wide shoulders, and thighs of steel. She could wrestle an inebriated guest into quiescence, catch hold of a runaway horse, or change the wheel on the largest pickup truck. She also had managerial talents of no mean order and kept the resort ranch on track and rolling forward.

The day shift clerk, Cookie Logan, seemed the opposite of Judy in that she was a fragile-looking, fuzz-headed blonde whose tiny hands seemed designed only to give a manicurist pleasure, but her spirit and sinew were as tough as Judy's. Cookie, who dressed on the job in western square-dance cotton flounce style, broke her own horses and two years before had won the Lodestone barrel race against all comers. Now, being not so committed to the work ethic as Judy, she tried to keep the conversation going. She switched to a more interesting object: Maria Cornish.

4

"You know, she's really something," said Cookie.

"Who is?" said Judy, still deep in her Christmas chart.

"Maria Cornish. She autographed her menu for me. She signed it 'Edith LaGrange' because I told her I'd followed that soap she was in, *The Loves of Our Lives*. Remember, Maria played Edith LaGrange who came out of a coma after thirteen months and found her husband a quadriplegic and her pregnant daughter on drugs."

"Concentrate on Christmas. We're almost completely booked."

"Maria Cornish," sighed Cookie. "Think of her coming here all by her lonesome, not even with a maid. Only that boyfriend, Blue Feather, who if you ask me is just a muscle-bound scum ball."

But Judy had now turned her attention to a stack of notes and memos. She waved a rose-colored sheet of paper at Cookie. "It's a message from your favorite movie star—to the boys in the corral." Judy sniffed the paper appreciatively. "I'd know that perfume anywhere. Western Passion Rose."

"What about the boys in the corral?" demanded Cookie. Her husband, Todd, was the assistant head wrangler, and so anything to do with the corral interested Cookie.

"Maria Cornish's own horse," said Judy. "Coming by van today. He's called Diablo Bravo and he's to have his own stall. A Paso Fino, one of those four-gaited things from South America. I wonder how our horses will take to him."

"Not to worry," said Cookie. "Our horses will have him for lunch."

Thus it was that Thanksgiving weekend at Rancho del Gato Blanco as well as the week that followed passed in a flurry of celebrity-related events.

Every appearance of those two notables, Senator Leo J. Hopgood and Maria Cornish, had been entirely satisfactory. The junior senator from Alaska handled the hearty-good-fellow scene with just a touch of the rude and crude as if he were already halfway through the primaries. He posed in the lobby and was photographed in the kitchen in a chef's hat and beside

5

the corral on a horse. Maria, besides graciously autographing menus, also made several interesting appearances during her stay. Three times she came poolside swathed in huge robes topped by a hat of Ascot proportions and was seen to dip a shapely ankle into the water and with a tiny shudder return to her chair. Twice she had been descried as a silhouette against the landscape astride her Paso Fino, Diablo Bravo, accompanied by her companion, Blue Feather Romero.

It is from this period of time that we find the following documents:

From the tooled-leather scrapbook kept by manager Fred Arco and left open in the ranch living room under the legend THANKSGIVING WEEK AT RANCHO DEL GATO BLANCO, a clipping from the *Arizona Highland Gazette*:

SENATOR LEO J. HOPGOOD TAKES TIME OFF

Senator Hopgood of Alaska, rumored to be an early runner in the presidential marathon, turned up booted and spurred at the popular new resort Rancho del Gato Blanco—known to old-timers as White Cat Ranch. Mrs. Hopgood, pictured above, accompanied her husband and on Thanksgiving Day presented the trophies in the third annual junior barrel race. The senator's son, nine-year-old Arthur, placed second in the buckaroo division.

From a postcard mailed by Arthur "Artie" Hopgood to a school friend:

Hi, Joe.
Almost won the barel race but the girth on the sadle held on the stupid guy's horse who won it after I cut it in haf when he wasn't loking. This place sucks.

See you, Artie

From a second letter sent by Julia Douglas Clancy to her niece, Sarah Deane:

Dear Sarah.
You have not answered my letter so here's another to shame you into it. No real news except I suppose my arthritis is better. Tell Alex that the new low dose is

6

working pretty well and that I'm taking it easy, only riding out two or three hours a day. As I expected, everyone is gaga over Maria Cornish and her hunklike boyfriend, Blue Weather or Feather, who if you ask me is not Indian by more than I am but is milking the idea for all it's worth. Maria Cornish wears enormous sunglasses and a complete bra system under her bathing suit. Now, I expect you and Alex here so I've gone ahead and made reservations—we'll have adjoining cottage units.

Love, A. Julia.

P.S. There's a poltergeist or a vandal working in the stable cutting girths.

Memo from Judy Steiner to Manager Fred Arco:

Okay, we're booked solid for Xmas with repeats from the senator who wants a room for his secretary—his wife and child are going elsewhere—and maybe Ms. Cornish so I'll put her suite on hold for now. Chef wants okay for double meat, veg, fruit, and some staples thr. New Year's.

Note left by head wrangler, Morty McGuire, for Cookie Logan:

Let me know how many horses you'll want over the Christmas time. Also am sending a bill into the office for ten slashed girths. Some joker came along and just slashed through those strings like they was spaghetti. I'm betting on that Hopgood kid.

Memo from Manager Fred Arco:

To all members of the Gato Blanco staff: I have heard insinuations that Arthur Hopgood, the senator's son, was responsible for the ten slashed girths in addition to the one damaged during the junior rodeo. There is no evidence to support this and the management wants it understood that even if there had been evidence, we value the senator's presence at the ranch and want no discourtesy or unpleasantness. Thank you for your discretion in this matter.

TWO

IT was an early December Saturday sometime after one o'-
clock on the coast of Maine. The local weather person, a jolly
lady called Billie Bright, had just demonstrated with pointer
and diagram that the weekend would be windy and cold with
mixed precipitation, adding cheerily that life in the great outdoors would be entirely foul.

Sarah Deane snapped off the radio and studied the December sleet slicing against the kitchen window. The time had
come. She passed Aunt Julia's second letter to Alex McKenzie.

"Arizona sounds like heaven," she said.

"So does a hot bath and it's a lot cheaper."

"Not really. Aunt Julia wants to give us the vacation. Join
her in Arizona. As a Christmas present, which is really very
generous because she loathes Christmas. She wants friendly
faces."

"It's too much to accept," said Alex. "Besides, she'll make
friends. The Widow Clancy is a powerful lady, she'll attract a
retinue before she knows it. People who love saying 'Yes,
Julia.' "

"She doesn't want a retinue, she wants us. She and Uncle

8

Tom didn't have children—as you know—they had horses instead, so now that Uncle Tom's gone, our family is it. And she may hate Christmas but she gives wonderful presents. Last year it was this table. Remember?" Sarah made a circular sweep with her arm over the satin walnut surface of the large handsome table. "You've been eating off it for almost a year. Sometimes," she added, "you have to accept gracefully. It will give her pleasure."

"I have a conference on December twenty-first, and I'm on call Christmas week. Everyone gets sick at Christmas."

"Switch. Trade with someone. Say you'll do Easter and Valentine's and the Fourth of July."

Alex in his turn examined the icy outdoor scene. The building, a yet unimproved farmhouse purchased by both in a moment of frustration with their previous two-family lodging, trembled in each gust of wind, the windows rattled, and a steady ping sounded from a metal pail set under a leak by the back door.

Sarah, knowing Alex's greatest weakness, now played her top card. "Rancho del Gato Blanco is right next to a wildlife refuge. The birding should be terrific, all those oddball hummingbirds. And cactus. We could study cactus and desert vegetation."

Before Alex could answer, Sarah marched over to her briefcase and fished out the ranch brochure. "Look this over. Warm by day, cool by night. A heated pool, riding the range, cookouts under the stars, tennis, golf."

"You don't play golf and you hate riding."

"No, I'm afraid of riding. I'm chicken about horses, but the ranch probably has quiet ones, so I might try it."

Alex opened the brochure and examined it. "My God," he said, "it's a resort, Palm Springs, not a dude ranch." Then he frowned, pointing at the photograph of the golf course. "When will people learn not to put golf courses in the middle of the desert? It isn't as if there's enough water for the next billion years."

On most occasions Alex, a tall lean man with a hungry look, could be considered handsome in a dark, chiseled-rock way, but when in a state of disapproval, he always seemed to Sarah more like a highwayman whose horse had lost a shoe at a critical moment.

Sarah examined him from across the table and thought, This is a man who needs to get away from both the weather and the practice of medicine. "I suppose it *is* a resort," she said, *"and* a ranch. I mean there are such places, but they're not all completely evil, or un-American. Maybe," she added doubtfully, "they recycle the golf course water."

Alex looked up briefly. "Recycle? In the desert? Be real." He picked up Aunt Julia's second letter. He nodded at the first paragraph. "I cut down on her medication and she's apparently doing fine." And then, "Oh Lord, a movie star."

"And a senator. Celebrities probably need a vacation, too. Come on, Alex, let's go for it."

"The last time you talked me into taking a trip it ended with two murders. We needed a vacation to recover from the vacation."

Sarah ignored this detour. "Exams finish on the eighteenth. I should be able to get my grades in by the twentieth. I'll fly out then and you can join me when your conference is wound up."

But Alex had now come to Julia's postscript. "What's this about a poltergeist in the stable, the horses' girths being cut?"

"Are you trying to scare me about riding? More than I am already?"

"No, but it sounds as if Aunt Julia is."

"I read that, but she's probably just being chatty, coming up with the latest gossip. If it really happened, it's probably someone's nasty little child."

As it happened, someone's nasty little child was at that moment the subject of a family dispute. Maud-Emma Hopgood, spouse of Senator Hopgood, wanted her husband to take Artie with him on his return visit to Rancho del Gato Blanco.

"Please, Leo. He'll be bored stiff in Alabama. All that visiting back and forth and shopping. And boys like Artie make Granny Forrest nervous."

The senator looked up from the suitcase open on the king-sized bed. "Artie makes a lot of people nervous, me included. And this is a working vacation." He returned to his packing. Shirts were piled on the pillows and neckties hung from the headboard.

The senator himself was a large-shouldered man with a smooth ovoid face. His fine head of graying hair and florid complexion suggested life in the outdoors or too much time spent hoisting whiskey and branch water. But there was about him that admirable combination of assertiveness and self-centeredness which, helped by a booming bass and a push-button smile, had made his climb up the political ladder smooth and fast. But now there was no smile, just a familiar—to Maud-Emma—look of determined meanness. He put down a stack of bikini briefs in a tiger pattern and addressed his wife.

"Look here. If Artie hadn't fucked up that last visit to the ranch, if he'd even been a normal, high-spirited kid, but hell, no. He had to sneak around playing cute little tricks, slashing that boy's girth in the barrel race and then probably cutting all those other goddamn girths. Well, I don't need that kinda shit. Not from my own kid. It's final. Artie goes with you. Besides, I'm full up. I'm taking Owen to handle the PR and Joe Yates to run interference and work on the speeches. Going to rough in some campaign strategy. Business and pleasure."

Maud-Emma, a plump blonde woman with the sort of face that was meant to be cheerful but now more resembled a faded cushion, gave in. "But," she added wistfully, "I would have come with you because families should be together at Christmas, but not if you're going to be doing politics the whole time." She reached for a pair of socks and began rolling them with an expert hand. "Besides, it's Granny Forrest's turn for Christmas."

The senator, seeing that he'd won this round, was hearty. "Right. Can't disappoint Granny Forrest. And, you know, I'd be mighty glad to come to Talladega, but this is a chance to feel out the Southwest. Besides, honey"—the senator could now afford the luxury of "honey"—"as you know, I may have the chance later to buy an interest in this little old ranch, and I like to keep an eye on the place. Everyone there seems plenty glad to have me visit and I give them their money's worth."

"You surely do," said Mrs. Hopgood in a somewhat acid tone. She ran her hand over the top shirt in a stack of senatorial shirts, cream silk with a monogram on the pockets. They had just come from Paris and Mrs. Hopgood resented every stitch. She still waited for the sales before buying off the better dress rack. And then, because it had been a matter of contention, she said, "Artie swears up and down he did not slice those girths. He said he wouldn't do something stupid like that."

"Artie," snorted the senator "would do something exactly like that. That stunt has his brand on it. He's the smartass who cut the baggage tickets off the luggage when it came off the claim chute. Now, let me finish packing because I've gotta pick up Lily by four."

"Lily's agreed to go?" said Mrs. Hopgood. "At Christmas?"

"I can't keep a campaign moving without a secretary. And thank God the press boys can't make any mileage out of Lily."

Mrs. Hopgood nodded, fitted the senator's socks into a space beside the tiger briefs, and departed. There had been some near misses with the susceptible senator and his secretaries, but now Lily Farnsworth represented safety from scandal. She had all the necessary secretarial abilities, but more important, she had the face of a middle-aged mustang. An intelligent, capable mustang.

In the choice of Lily, Senator Hopgood congratulated himself that he had outfoxed the press. And his wife. Leo Hopgood believed, along with legions of liberated women, that beauty of face is irrelevant. He was a sensual man and cared not a whit about Lily's looks—in fact, her equine features may have endeared her to this man of the West. In bed Lily was a creature of passion and imagination. She'd get a real kick out of his new tiger briefs, and he looked forward to her careful unbuttoning of his new silk shirts. Fortunately, his aides knew how to keep their lips buttoned, and the senator was looking forward to his Christmas holiday with happy expectation. He ran an appreciative finger over the silken surface of one of his new shirts and then crammed the lot into the suitcase and snapped the lock. He stood up, braced his shoulders, and smiled. Christmas with Lily: it sounded like the title of a good country-western. He whistled softly a few bars of "My Cheatin' Heart" and picked up his suitcase.

The Saturday following Senator Hopgood's declaration of independence—December sixteenth to be exact—found Judy Steiner and Cookie Logan already in place at the ranch reservation desk at the commendably early time of 6:30 A.M.

"The good news," observed Judy, "is that Fred Arco can relax. We're booked two weeks past New Year's."

"So what's the bad news?" asked Cookie, who stood by Judy's side looking over the big reservation chart.

"None," said Judy. "Senator Hopgood's secretary, Lily Farnsworth, has confirmed that he's coming without his wife and kid. Just Hopgood, his secretary, and his aides. So it's just good news today because Artie Hopgood is a horror."

"Well, you're wrong about today," said Cookie, looking up. "Bad news just came through the front door."

It was Julia Clancy. She hit the front desk in the shape of an elderly tornado. A tornado still wearing a flannel nightgown imperfectly covered by an ancient and somewhat damp-looking blue wool dressing gown.

"Why, good morning, Mrs. Clancy?" said Judy, putting on the face she used for unpredictable guests—and Julia Clancy had been proving herself such since her arrival before Thanksgiving.

Julia stamped her foot—an ineffective gesture since she was wearing sheepskin slippers. "It's not a good morning. It's a terrible morning and I need help. Right now. You're going to go into my room and mop it up. And wash my clothes. And fix my bed."

"Something is wrong?" asked Judy.

"What's wrong is I'm soaked. My room, my bed, my clothes, everything drenched. Some fool turned the hose on my window."

"An accident," said Judy in her best bedside manner. She had always found that once you put a label to an incident, it could be dealt with appropriately.

"An accident! It had better be an accident. Because I don't suppose one of those birdbrained men you have squirting water at all hours of the day on a lawn that shouldn't have been planted in the first place would have actually wanted to aim at my window and get rid of a guest who has not yet paid her bill."

Judy ventured a reassuring smile. "Of course an accident. We have a schedule for watering the cottage shrubs. Was your window open?" Toss the ball back, thought Judy, let her think she was asking for it.

"Of course it was open. Do you think I live in a hothouse? I took the first spray full in my face. A shock. I was up, about to dress. I get up at six at home. I get up early here even if it is dark. I was going on your breakfast ride and now my boots have an inch of water in them."

"I'll call for a house aide immediately." "House aide" was a unisex all-purpose term for maids, porters, cleaning persons, and general slaves.

"You do that," said Julia Clancy, planting herself in a leather-thonged barrel chair next to the desk. "I'll wait until they come, and I would very much like a cup of coffee and a roll to keep me going, because I can't go into the dining room like this." Julia indicated her person with a sweep of her hand.

Judy pushed a kitchen intercom, ordered coffee and a selection of hot rolls, pronto, to the front desk, and from this vantage point studied Mrs. Clancy.

Although the popular picture of the accomplished horsewoman, eastern style, was that of a tall female in classic costume of a black velvet hard hat, white stock, black jacket, with broad shoulders and lean shanks, Julia Clancy probably fitted another acceptable stereotype: the stubby woman with a weathered face and brindle short-cut hair that stood up in moments of agitation like the bristles of a dandy brush. At home in her riding arena, Julia habitually stood with legs apart, hands on hips, skewering some unfortunate rider with the sort of eye associated with the Ancient Mariner. Her voice could freeze the blood of a careless student, and her resounding "Ho!" could stop a horse in its tracks. Her softer side was most manifest in the dark hours of the night when one of her mares was straining to deliver a foal or when she was working with a horse that threatened colic. Then Julia Clancy was patient, tender, and long-suffering.

"Why," Alex had asked Sarah, "does your Aunt Julia want to go to a guest ranch when she can bed right down at home with a complete herd?" But Sarah reminded Alex that he himself had suggested Arizona as a proper winter retreat for someone in arthritic misery. "She's sixty-seven and can't ride much in the winter, it hurts too much. And she's got a stable manager, so everything goes right along without her. In fact, I'll bet Patrick is delighted to see the back of her."

Judy Steiner was also delighted to see the back of her. Julia Clancy marched off with a house aide, José Codero, and Cookie Logan. Cookie to assess the damage and continue the work of mollification, José to the mopping and cleaning.

The room was a mess. Water splashed everywhere, the plaster walls spotted, bedclothes sodden, puddles on the floor, and the imitation Navajo rug squelching when walked upon. The room belonged to a four-apartment adobe-style complex called Agave Cottage, Julia Clancy's being Agave Four. This cottage stood at the top of a row of like buildings and commanded a view of two other cottage rows set below. Beyond the cottages ran the circling ranch access road, Camino Rancho Grande, and falling away to yet a lower level lay several holes of the golf course, the object of Julia Clancy's disapproval.

Every cottage opened to a small low-walled patio with two gates: one from the small parking space by the cottage side door, a second which gave out on a narrow gravel drive separating the next tier of cottages. The identical brick-paved patios of each cottage had an edging of greenery and small shrubs. Each had its own water faucet, and a long hose with nozzle hung on a metal loop next to it.

"There," said Mrs. Clancy triumphantly. She walked to a

glass sliding door and pointed to a serpentine loop of hose in the middle of her patio. The nozzle still dripped into a damp patch in the middle of the bricks. "Why would anyone deliberately spray inside a bedroom? A hard well-aimed spray kept up for almost a minute."

Mrs. Clancy moved back into the room and addressed Cookie, who was assisting José by collecting bedclothes into a bundle.

"I'm here for my arthritis, for quiet exercise, and everyone to date has been most accommodating, but somewhere on the property there is a lunatic who decided to have a good time and give an old lady a bath." Julia Clancy was given to describing herself as an old lady when she felt at her strongest. It made a good position from which to launch a power play.

"I shall put this in writing," she said, "and I shall expect my clothes to be laundered and returned by noon and to have one day's charge subtracted from my bill."

Sometime later, Julia, dressed in her version of a western riding costume of jeans, flannel shirt, chamois vest, and a sort of Australian bush hat, arrived at the corral for the breakfast ride. Her horse, a big bay with a white blaze, Pecos Bill, was already saddled. She noted that the head wrangler, Morty McGuire, was standing at Pecos Bill's head and that only one other rider was assigned to what was termed the "intermediate ride": a young woman named Christy on vacation from Wisconsin, who would be riding a quarter horse called Copper. Julia always signed up for the intermediate ride knowing that it was not a popular choice, so she would not be riding out with something looking like a cavalry brigade. The "fast ride" was for speedballs who wanted to gallop, the "slow ride" for beginners who wanted to cling to their pommels and move like snails in a long nose-and-tail procession.

From long habit, Julia checked her tack, ran her hand under the girth, and then, with her joints protesting, she climbed onto the mounting block and slowly swung herself into the saddle.

The morning ride was a pleasant one, up and down the milder foothills of Buzzard Mountain, and it ended in a saucer where numbers of guests had assembled, either by horse or by the ranch bus. Todd Logan, Cookie's husband and assistant head wrangler, met them, helped Julia and Christy dismount, and tied their horses. But Julia, as she walked toward the breakfast center, became aware of a mutter, a rising sound that threatened to turn into a mass grumble. This sound rolled down the lines of guests who moved slowly with plate in hand for servings of scrambled eggs, bacon, pancakes, hot rolls, juice, and coffee. By the time that Julia made it to the end of the line, the mutter had become articulate. In good clear English from many mouths it said, "No coffee."

"What do they mean, no coffee?" demanded Julia.

"That's what they said," returned the man in front of her.

"None?"

"What they said." The man, a large fellow in a red gingham shirt, addressed the woman standing next to him, obviously a member of his family. "Go on up, honey, and see if you can see what this is about. They gotta have coffee. I've been riding for two hours for a goddamn cup of coffee."

"I'll go," said a young man farther up the line. He slipped out of place, made his way to the lines of tables where the ranch kitchen staff was dishing out the breakfast. He returned at once.

"Coffee's spoiled. Some joker put mud or sand in it. Had to throw it out. They've sent one of the trucks back for more."

Julia washed down her scrambled eggs with a second dose of orange juice and considered the ill-tempered scene. There is something about an open-air breakfast following exercise that demands a hot bracing drink. Caffeine is needed, or at least something that used to have caffeine: a good dark decaf. But now quantities of sand apparently had been mixed with both these fluids, which had been brought in huge kettles from the ranch to be heated on the fire before serving. Tea and the children's cocoa were for most of the guests a poor substitute.

Julia, who at least had that early morning cup under her belt, found herself sitting next to Cookie Logan. Cookie always went along on these affairs to help organize the serving and to mix with the guests, and she had just put in a good three quarters of an hour soothing and promising replacement. Julia suggested a parallel between the hose incident and the spoiled coffee.

"Oh no, Mrs. Clancy," said Cookie. "This is very unusual, but of course, you know, the staff, well, they're human. Or maybe someone wanted to play a joke. One of the children."

"That boy, Artie what's his name, the senator's child. He's not here, is he?"

"No," said Cookie. "And his father's coming for Christmas without him, for which we're all pretty grateful. I know the senator is a VIP but that kid was too much."

Julia Clancy agreed and returned to her eggs. The arrival of fresh coffee some thirty minutes later improved her view of the day, and afterward she mounted her horse with anticipation of an enjoyable return to the ranch.

The return ride was without incident, but Julia could not help returning in her mind to the ruined coffee, the hose soaking, and the ten cut girths. One event might be an accident, two a coincidence, but three?

THREE

THE remainder of that December Saturday was spent by manager Fred Arco seeking heads to roll, hashes to settle, and tails to blister. Fred Arco was, as Julia Clancy had written to her niece, a physical reincarnation of Emperor Napoleon I. It was a resemblance that the manager milked for all it was worth. He was short but stood straight, as if braced for any emergency; his dark hair receded and the forelock was brought forth in the Napoleonic manner. He walked briskly and at times appeared to strut. He dressed in the western-Spanish style in loose trousers, high gleaming black boots, a snow-white ruffled shirt and a bolo tie that was held closed by a slide featuring the ranch logo in silver and turquoise. When he went forth on his horse wearing a black Stetson, his trousers tucked into his high boots, one could almost hear the rumble of the French artillery behind him. Fred Arco was only forty-two, but in employee exploitation, manufactured charm, and general oiliness he was ageless.

First Fred hit the kitchen and chef Peter Doubler on the subject of the coffee. Peter explained that the coffee containers had contained coffee without sand and after they had been loaded on the equipment truck they were out of his jurisdiction.

"The buck stops here," said Fred Arco, indicating with a sweep of his arm the long kitchen with its gleaming kettles, its zinc-covered table, its multiple butcher blocks and pastry tables.

Peter, in the middle of early dinner preparations, folded his arms across his chest. "No way, Fred."

"Mr. Arco." Fred indicated the interested crowd of subchefs and kitchen help who were hanging on the scene. "It's 'Mr. Arco' to you, Pierre." This name was all part of a difficult charade that Fred was trying to force down the gullets of the house staff. Peter Doubler had been born and bred in nearby Lodestone, the town that served Rancho del Gato Blanco as well as other neighboring ranches. In fact, Peter was a cousin of Cookie Logan's which made him marriage kin to Cookie's husband, Todd. And certainly everyone for miles around knew Peter Doubler was no Pierre Doubler—pronounced "Dooblay" by Fred Arco in an attempt to display the fact that Peter had spent two years in France learning the finer points of French cuisine. Further, lanky Peter Doubler with his red hair and freckled face defied the public's idea of a French chef.

But Fred Arco never gave up, and with the breath of Heinz Simmons—ranch owner, mover, and shaker—always on his neck, he pushed for the continental-resort western-style ambience. The White Cat Ranch's transformation to Rancho del Gato Blanco, the Spanish Colonial look, the landscaping, the sports facilities, the installation of a gift shop with top-grade Indian jewelry and pottery, were all part of the struggle to be number one. Number one in Arizona, or better—the owners thought big—number one in the Southwest.

But Peter Doubler was made of strong stuff. "Listen, Mr. Arco, if you want to sling blame around, go hit the drivers. You imported those birds. You didn't even try Lodestone for staff. Now, get off my back, man, because that coffee left here like coffee. Clean to the last drop."

But Fred never sounded retreat; he just walked away and

regrouped. "If it happens again . . ." and he again swept the kitchen with a menacing palm. And departed.

He then spent a bracing half hour rattling Judy Steiner and Cookie Logan's cage. He demanded an inventory of hoses, diagrams of outdoor faucets, and the schedule for watering, and then he stomped outside and discovered a hapless John Wong working on a petunia bed—a flower Fred Arco felt combined the right sort of western colors with eastern familiarity. John was hauled in and grilled about his watering habits and those of the outdoor staff. His salary was reviewed and his family was threatened with loss of lodging. In vain, John pointed out that the chief landscape gardener, Logan Younger, supervised the groundspeople and arranged the watering schedule and that he, John, had been nowhere near Agave Cottage Four when the incident took place.

Feeling better, Fred returned to Judy Steiner. He became confidential. "Judy, you see a lot of Morty McGuire, don't you?"

"No more than you do, Fred." Judy had not given in to the order to call him Mr. Arco. She did it in front of guests, but not alone. "I ride, my horse is in with the herd. Sometimes in the evening when I'm off duty, Morty and I ride out. We check the trails, try some of the new horses. Do what I'm not paid to do and what I should charge you for if I had any sense."

"What I mean about Morty," said Fred, "is that he's really out of it. Not guest-oriented. An old-timer. Guests don't like *old* cowboys and we're in business to please guests. They like Robert Redford types, cowboys like Stevo." Stevo was a new blondly handsome cowboy who was much in demand by the younger female guests. He rode with panache and took the fast-ride groups on wild and sometimes thoughtless trail gallops.

Judy spoke through her teeth. Strong teeth that could chop her western drawl into bite-sized pieces. "Morty cares about the horses. And the guests. You're plenty lucky to have Morty."

"And Todd," said Cookie, leaving her computer and entering the combat ring. "Those two guys hold the trail-riding program together. Stevo and some of the other new cowboys are so full of their own riding and roping and steer wrestling that guests come second. They blast around, lather up the horses, and cut the guests' rides short. They're always trying to steal time to work on competition because the big rodeos will be coming up."

"We need our cowboys to do well in the rodeos," said Fred. "It's good publicity. Morty isn't even trying to run a class operation. And about the horses, well, I'm going to be talking to Todd and Morty. I've sent to Montana for fifteen head. Appaloosas—all broke and sound—because I think Morty's running an old-horse nursing home. The bottom line is that some of those animals he's using are dog factory material. I want to see a few loaded and transported next week. We'll start with six and then cull the rest of the herd after Christmas. Pecos Bill and that runty Copper and Lollipop and some of the others will make out just fine as Alpo."

Here Cookie broke in with great indignation. "Those horses . . ."

But Manager Arco cut her short. "Sentiment doesn't pay the bills, and, Cookie, I've told Todd that any ideas he has about the riding program will be mighty welcome. Ideas Morty hasn't thought of. Morty's been here a long time, so he may be pretty fed up with doing the same job day after day. I've been expecting him to quit for quite a while. What do you think, would Todd like to be head wrangler? Big salary increase and you could have Morty's cottage. Why don't you feel out Todd on the idea? And Morty, we'll give him recommendations and a chunk of cash. Morty'll make out just fine. Lots of guest ranches could use him. He's a real character."

And Fred withdrew, leaving confusion and spleen in his wake.

"Damn him," said Judy under her breath.

"What he's going to do," rejoined Cookie, "is get Morty and Todd by the balls and twist. Natch, Todd would love to manage the riding program, and Morty is never going to play the resort business by the book or bring in guys like Stevo. And you can bet Morty's not going to let any horses be shipped out without his say-so."

Judy sighed. "Well, you can't keep some of those animals on forever. I hate to say it but Fred's right on that score."

"All right, all right, but they get rid of Pecos Bill over my dead body. He's got a lot of good years left. And Copper, I saw him foaled." And Cookie slammed her fist on the desk.

Herewith memos and documents circulated Saturday, December 16.

From the manager's office, December 16:

ATTENTION: Pierre and kitchen staff: The coffee incident of today will not be repeated. You will each be held individually responsible for this and any further incidents. Our breakfast rides are an important part of our ranch program and we expect them to go absolutely without a hitch.

F. Arco, Mgr.

To Todd Logan, Assistant Head Wrangler:

Just had productive talk with Cookie about future. You come to my office after dinner tonight for discussion of new plans for trail-riding program, personnel changes, and innovations.

Fred Arco, Mgr.

To John Wong:

You are no longer member of the garden staff. Please turn in your uniform and cap at the equipment office and report to Mr. McGuire at the corral to assist with saddlery and corral-cleaning program. Effective immediately.

The Manager.

To Mrs. Julia Clancy, Agave Cottage Number Four:

We have received your letter. Please be assured that the unfortunate incident of this morning will not be repeated. We regret any discomfort and inconvenience to you and will of course make an adjustment on your room charges for today. Our wish is to provide the finest vacation experience in the Southwest for each of our guests.

Sincerely yours, Frederick G. Arco, Manager, Rancho del Gato Blanco.

And a letter from Julia Clancy to Ms. Sarah Deane and Dr. Alexander McKenzie:

Dear Sarah and Alex:

The poltergeist has been busy again. Early this A.M.—I still seem to be getting up on eastern time—I was squirted by a hose stuck into my window and then our breakfast coffee was full of sand. Sarah, your mother tells me that you and Alex have been mixed up in some rather disagreeable incidents, so perhaps you both can keep a wary eye out when you arrive. It will distract you from the awful Christmas preparations. I'm ready to meet Sarah in Phoenix, 12:05 Thursday the twenty-first, and expect Alex Christmas Eve. I ride a wonderful horse called Pecos Bill who is an absolute lamb. We'll find something safe for you, Sarah, because as I remember you were absolutely hopeless on a horse.

All my love, Aunt Julia.

To Fred Arco, Manager, from Heinz Simmons, President, Blue Sky Ranch and Ski Resorts, Inc. Keystone, Colorado. Memo.

Am bringing Mrs. Simmons and two guests arriving Thursday, Dec. 21, approx. 12:15 in company plane. Have ranch van meet us and have owner's house and guest cottage ready. Tell McGuire to have my horses ready and Blaze and Patches for guests set aside for their exclusive use.

To Southwest Horse Transport, Inc., Phoenix, Arizona, from Judy Steiner, Office, Rancho del Gato Blanco, Lodestone, Arizona:

Please arrange our shipment fifteen horses from Flying Box Ranch Montana to arrive here by end of year. Also put us on your schedule to pick up six horses for delivery next week to Bonzo Pet Food stockyards. Call ranch office and leave the exact dates and times of pickup.

The next day, Sunday, December 17, began with manager Fred Arco on his predawn patrol, which was in fact a jogging tour of the paths, cottages, and assorted buildings of the ranch complex. A morning never began properly for the manager unless he had circled his kingdom and saw for himself that all was well. Or not well. Usually the latter meant wheelbarrows not properly stored, vegetation not tended, pool chairs not lined up. However, on this early Sunday all was in order with not the slightest hint of the visiting poltergeist. Julia Clancy, as usual up with the birds, watched the progress of the manager with mild interest; his regular jogging appearance had become a feature of her morning.

And this morning continued in a peaceful vein. Some guests took the ranch bus to church in nearby Lodestone, others attended a nondenominational service conducted in the main lounge. Also, despite the warm weather, the tropical plantings, the desert vistas, Christmas was on track. Fred Arco had spared no effort to make sure that Christmas smote the guests hard between the eyes the minute they made it into the lodge. Straw wreaths with red ribbons hung from the casement windows, tiny poinsettia plants had replaced the usual table flowers, and the female staff wore red aprons and the males featured red waistcoats and red bolo ties. In a bay window of the main lounge appeared a tall Douglas fir circled with wrapped presents, Cookie Logan and Judy Steiner having spent several hours Saturday night wrapping empty boxes.

Christmas had actually made its first official appearance at the Saturday night sing-along led by the popular (or as Cookie called him, that over-the-hill) cowboy entertainer, Laddie Danforth. Laddie, a dyed-blond relic of TV westerns, had been hired to stroll among the guests during and after dinner with his guitar and give out with such favorites as "Goodbye Old Paint" and "The Old Chisholm Trail." Last night, after a rousing group effort of "Don't Fence Me in," Laddie had switched to "Jingle Bells," and with a small child on each buckskin knee, wound up with a throat-rattling "Frosty the Snowman."

Julia Clancy, who, as was her custom, had gone to her room soon after dinner, heard the first notes of "Jingle Bells" from the open windows of the dining room across the lawn. She had immediately risen and closed the window of Agave Four and returned to her crossword puzzle in blessed silence.

But now on this Sunday the threat of Christmas shone round about. Julia returned from a pleasant morning walk along one of the nearby ranges to find at the corral that one of the big ranch chuck wagons, used to take nonriding guests for trips around the ranch's perimeter, had been fitted with sleigh bells. Undoubtedly Santa Claus—some unlucky staff member encased in a red suit and beard—would be making his appearance before long.

"Fools," murmured Julia to no one in particular as she returned to the sanctum of her cottage. Here she changed to an ancient cotton and patched shirt kept exclusively for private moments in the sun and collected a copy of *The Chronicle of the Horse* in order to catch up on the doings of her own equine world. Christmas, she thought, has really run amok. She remembered from a favorite British novelist, Angela Thirkell, the expression "the dread season of Christmas," smiled to herself, and made her way to her little walled terrace, pulled the aluminum lounge chair into a patch of partial sun, and sat down. And through. Directly through the seat to the hard flagstones beneath.

Actually the whole movement from the act of sitting to the final resting place on the stones was a slow-motion event. First, Julia's bottom touched the interlaced strips of plastic and finding them slashed, continued downward while the entire apparatus collapsed around its victim, leaving her in a jackknife position.

Ten minutes later, after rolling around on the flagstones, encased in the clutch of the chair, Julia wriggled herself out of its grasp, rose, and headed for the front desk, her progress somewhat modified by a slightly wrenched shoulder muscle.

Twenty minutes later, Julia returned to her room, holding—figuratively speaking—the scalps of Fred Arco, Cookie Logan, and Judy Steiner, as well as the promise of the heads of the entire ranch staff. And except for the threatened condition of her shoulder, Julia felt that the whole scene had been worth it. She hadn't felt this exhilarated in years. It took her back to the days when she broke and schooled all her own young horses and thought nothing of a ten-mile gallop over meadow, fence, and hill.

Of course, someone at the ranch was clearly out to get her. But why? Julia reviewed the cast of characters at the ranch but could come to no conclusion. The entire place was peopled by apparent strangers. Naturally it was possible that some guest here, unknown to her, had at one time or another been a student of hers at High Hope Farm and had been reprimanded ungently or tossed from one of her horses. Or Julia in her capacity as a horse show judge had affronted some rider. Something like that. Anyone can make enemies, she thought, and perhaps she had been better at it than most. But here at this ranch? At Christmas, season of goodwill? Maybe that was it. Christmas did bring out the beast in some people. It brought things to a boil that had simmered safely for months. Well, she would have to look over the guest list. And the staff list, too. See if someone from her past had turned up here in the sun of Arizona. Thank heaven only four more days until Sarah arrived. Someone to talk to. Someone whose seemingly blameless life as a college teaching fellow had been interrupted more than once by fraud and felony. Sarah would understand.

Fred Arco had not enjoyed his scene with Julia Clancy. In the first place, she had arrived at the front desk wearing a shirt he wouldn't have allowed to be used as a duster; it lowered the tone of the entire lobby. Then Mrs. Clancy had used a voice that reached into every cranny of the main building and brought the curious from as far away as the kitchen.

When she had retreated, Fred spent a few moments revolving around the interested spectators, explaining and soothing. He not only managed to insinuate that Mrs. Clancy was eccentric and old, but hinted at instability, drink, and forgetfulness. "We must all make an extra effort with our senior citizens," he said.

The manager chivvied back to their stations the staff members who had turned up in the outskirts of the lobby, and when all was at peace, he slipped off his Dr. Jekyll mask and became Manager Hyde.

"Okay, Judy. Anything more happens to that old lady, I have your next week's salary. You, too, Cookie. The whole damn lot of you. Just lucky Mr. Simmons isn't coming until Thursday. We'll have who's responsible hanging by his thumbs by then."

"Since it's happened twice to Mrs. Clancy, maybe you should check and see if someone here knows her," said Judy.

Fred Arco cheered. "Right. July, you check through the

guest list and see if anyone else is from Maine. Or New England. Eastern people make a lot of enemies. They have a snotty way about them, acting know-it-all. Like Mrs. Clancy."

"Oh, she's all right and she knows horses," said Cookie defensively. She rather liked Julia Clancy, who spent time chatting with the staff and seemed interested in their lives and jobs.

"I don't want to hear her name or see her at the desk until she checks out," snapped Mr. Arco, "so Cookie, send one of our VIP bouquets, the ten-dollar one, to her room, and a new patio chair and a complimentary copy of *Country Inns* with our recommendation marked. That should cool her down. And," he continued, "let me know when you hear from the transport people. I'm going to make sure the riding program is cost-productive or else."

"Such a nice guy," murmured Cookie as Manager Arco moved to the double glass doors to welcome two new guests who were just pushing through the main lodge entrance.

"Do you want this job or don't you?" said Judy. "Send those flowers to Agave Four and be glad Arco didn't transfer both of us to the laundry detail."

"Any more of these little events and it's him that's going to be job hunting," said Cookie with satisfaction.

"You hope." Judy then opened her reservation ledger and smiled on two new guests, a Mr. and Mrs. Torquay from Chicago. Fred Arco was winding up his welcoming speech by larding it with the side references of visiting stars.

"Maria Cornish, she's a regular visitor but she's asked to be just another guest. Like anyone else. Although she often eats just in her suite, really very shy."

Shy like a fox, thought Judy, putting on her welcome look and pushing the registration card across to Mr. Torquay. "Mr. and Mrs. Toquay, welcome to Gato Blanco. You have one of the new cottages, Arizona Poppy number three."

"And Senator Hopgood," continued the manager. "No fuss at all. You'd hardly know that he's thinking of running."

"What on earth for?" demanded Mr. Torquay, returning the pen to its holder.

"Well, it's just a rumor, but they say the presidency. In the primaries. He was here at Thanksgiving and is coming back with his staff for Christmas. Of course, it's very hush-hush."

"Then you'd better hush," said Mr. Torquay, a dark-visaged man with a thrust-out jaw.

But Mrs. Torquay, a floral type, was of more impressionable material. "Maria Cornish," she said. "What fun. And I know all about Senator Hopgood. I think he was blacklisted by the Wilderness Society."

"One thing in his favor," said Mr. Torquay. "Come on, Phyllis, we're not here to get autographs. I hope," he said over his shoulder, "that my letter made it clear that we want golf starting times every day at a reasonable hour. That's what we're here for, the golf." And Mr. and Mrs. Torquay passed out of the lobby followed by a sweating house aide carrying three suitcases.

"He's one of those golfers who make a fuss if everything isn't perfect," said Cookie. "Do you think we should introduce him to Julia Clancy? She'd give him an earful." Cookie adjusted the frill on her blouse and patted her curly hair, hair that bloomed over her head in a pattern of tight curls. "The Orphan Annie look," she always lamented. Now she lifted the phone, rang the greenhouse, and ordered the twenty-dollar VIP bouquet for Mrs. Clancy.

"Why'd you do that?" demanded Judy. "Fred said ten bucks. And he'll check."

"It'll all even out in the December accounts. I'll give Senator Hopgood the ten-dollar one, he won't know the difference."

Judy looked at her coworker with disapproval. "Cookie Logan, you watch it. I don't want to start protecting your butt."

"Save your strength for saving Pecos Bill, Copper, and Lollipop, and the rest from the meat wagon. Let me know right off when you hear from the transport company."

"Cookie, you can't save all the old horses in Arizona."

"No, but I can try. Arco's sending six and I've called my mother at Cat Claw and she's willing to take three for their trail rides. That leaves three to rescue."

"You won't get away with it," said Judy, and she marched back to the inner office to confront the ranch computer.

"Well, I damn well will," said Cookie softly. The telephone rang and Cookie lifted the phone. "Good afternoon, Rancho del Gato Blanco, may I help you?"

FOUR

THE stretch of time from Monday the eighteenth of December to Thursday the twenty-first was pockmarked by a series of small events that, each taken alone, might have been considered in the nature of harmless practical jokes. But added to the previous disturbances, they began to suggest to the staff and guests, and to the irritated mind of Fred Arco, an entirely sinister sequence.

Monday shone bright and clear, the temperature comfortably in the low sixties. Perfect for golf, tennis, riding, and hiking. It was the golfers that were hit first. The first foursome off the tee at seven-thirty, two businessmen from Dallas and their wives, had a smooth progress—if the balls sliced and hooked into the mesquite are ignored—until the fourth tee.

The fourth tee introduces the player to a long dogleg left par-five hole with patches of natural desert vegetation interrupting the green sweep of the fairway. The drive itself offers no problem. The first two hundred yards are straight ahead, but unless the player drives the full distance, the second shot is a blind one.

In the matter of this early-bird foursome, the male members

took their second shot at about two hundred yards and the ladies took three shots before their balls disappeared around the corner. But turning the corner brought a marvelous sight. The fairway, the rough, the scattered sand traps, and the green itself were peppered with balls. Hundreds of golf balls. Old balls and practice balls rimmed in red, clearly balls from the practice driving range. The Dallas foursome stopped their carts, swore, and began a series of futile circles. They were joined shortly by the foursome coming up behind them. This foursome, which included the newly arrived Mr. and Mrs. Torquay of Chicago, had actually driven into their midst, not seeing that their predecessors had stalled ahead of them.

And so it went. The fifth, seventh, and ninth holes were heavily sprinkled with alien balls, and the remaining holes, all the way to the eighteenth, had just enough vagrant balls scattered on each fairway to make each search for a player's legitimate ball a nightmare. Even after the golf shop had been alerted and sent out a crew with ball-pickers, at least seven sets of players had quit in noisy disgust, and golf pro Tommy Brass's and Fred Arco's phones rang off the hook for the large part of the morning. Calm eventually settled: tickets for a complimentary eighteen holes were issued to disgruntled golfers, together with a new package of balls, and Fred Arco made plans to spend the luncheon hours in the Driver's Den Grill Room, making friends and smoothing feathers. Golfers deprived of their anticipated games are not easy to deal with, and it was not until well after three that Monday that the manager felt the golf program was back on track.

Tuesday found the golfers at peace and the tennis players featured. No nets. Sometime before the earliest players arrived for their scheduled hour, before early riser Fred Arco went jogging on his rounds, the ranch vandal—as he was beginning to be known—had spirited the tennis nets away, along with two reserve nets kept in the equipment shed. Fred Arco, making copious notes, was able to add sixteen more irritated guests to his growing list.

Judy Steiner and Cookie took a good deal of the brunt of the discontent. Guests came to the front desk for mail, for telephone messages, and to pick up the day's program. And now to unload grief on the two women's heads.

"You know," said Judy as one family, tennis rackets in hand, retreated grumbling, "we're full capacity after today, one hundred twenty guests. Wanna bet we've made at least sixty of them hopping mad and ready to try another place next time?"

Cookie shrugged. "So it goes, good days, bad days."

"Not quite this bad," said Judy.

But Cookie didn't answer. She was struggling with Wednesday's schedule, which called for a trail ride to Buzzard Flats, a cookout, and a sing-along.

Judy wasn't finished. "We're the ones getting the heat. And Fred. I never thought I'd feel sorry for that man, but he's sure being dumped on."

"Good for what ails him," said Cookie.

"Well, me, I'm getting an ulcer. Okay, have you got Laddie set for the trail ride and campfire? And Todd to keep an eye on him?"

"Todd says he's had it playing nursemaid to that lush. It's bad enough seeing that he doesn't fall off his horse, but trying to keep him away from the sauce at a cookout—well, it's easy to find booze in the dark, and Laddie is a real pro at sneaking the stuff."

"Laddie can sing with a skin full but we don't want him falling into a canyon, so he can go back in the chuck wagon, and I'll ride his horse," said Judy. "Almost a full moon, so no problem."

The next day, Wednesday the twentieth, went by without incident. Golfers golfed, riders rode, skeet shooters shot, swimmers splashed in the heated pool and lounged in deck chairs in the warmth of a beneficent sun. And the tennis players enjoyed a game with new nets rushed from Phoenix. In short, it was the sort of day that brought the smile back to Fred Arco's face.

Indeed, Wednesday outdid itself. Maria Cornish, media star, arrived at midafternoon in the best of all possible moods. She had just completed a series of appearances on a well-known talk show, and there had been speculations in print about the possibility of her return to prime-time TV in a drama series. She made a proper star entrance, sweeping up the long curving drive to the main ranch office in her cream Jaguar and directing her boyfriend, Blue Feather Romero, to the heaps of luggage that crammed the boot of the car. Blue, having been sent away from her presence the previous week without a cent to his name—or a joint for his pocket—had come back in a penitent state and was now ready, for the Christmas period at least, to play fetch-and-carry in return for being kept in comfort.

"Darlings," cried Maria to Judy and Cookie and Fred Arco, all drawn up in a welcoming trio by the front desk. "Merry merry Christmas! Cookie, darling! Judy, do I have my suite, my same adorable suite? Mr. Arco, how marvelous to be back and have Christmas with such good friends. But Mr. Romero and I are just the teeniest bit tired so we'll have dinner in our rooms. My home away from home. And Diablo, has he been behaving himself? Tell Morty McGuire that I'm planning a morning ride tomorrow."

And Maria Cornish with Blue Feather Romero at her side turned the Jaguar around the corner of the main lodge to the wing containing the Desert Star Suite. Maria had not wanted a cottage separate from the main establishment, because "you never know just who's out there waiting and I am so well known."

Wednesday evening's cookout at Buzzard Flats almost restored Manager Arco to well-being. Laddie Danforth remained fairly sober, and to his usual repertoire added five well-known carols beginning with "Adeste Fideles," in which he was joined by the entire cookout crowd. Laddie, seen by the campfire, was impressive. Blond, six foot three, the lines of his face, the bags of his eyes masked by the firelight flicker, he was everything a showtime cowboy should be. His tenor voice was still pleasant, he was usually on key, and his memory of lyrics went one or two verses beyond that of his audience.

"Back on track," repeated Fred Arco as he watched Laddie being loaded into the chuck wagon.

"Knock on wood," said Cookie, climbing in beside Laddie and fending off a reaching arm.

"An efficient operation doesn't need to knock on wood," returned Fred Arco, "so let's keep it that way."

"Certainly, Mr. Arco," said Cookie, detaching Laddie's hand and stamping on Laddie's instep with the curved heel of her boot.

Thursday's weather was on a par with Wednesday's: bright, warm, and favored by a slight breeze from the north. Julia Clancy checked her eastern wristwatch for the estimated time that her niece Sarah would spend in the air. When traveling into foreign time zones, Julia always wore two watches—one for the time she considered real home time, in this case eastern standard, the other set now at western mountain time. After subtracting two hours she discovered there was time for a morning ride before she left for the Phoenix airport.

But when she arrived at the corral, she found only Stevo and an older cowboy, Bruno, in attendance. The group was small. Five beginners now being mounted on Dakota, Stormy, Flash, Bucket, and Harpo, and only the girl Christy waiting for the intermediate ride. Christy was not sitting on the reliable Copper, but on a large paint with a suspicious eye. Pecos Bill was nowhere in sight.

Julia Clancy marched up to Christy. "Christy, why aren't you riding Copper? He's a very good horse for you. You should ride the same horse until you know him, and then you can relax and begin to pay attention to your riding. I will talk to Morty."

Christy stopped Julia in mid-flood. "Copper isn't available. Either is Pecos Bill. They're being looked at by the vet to make sure they're okay."

"Okay? Why shouldn't they be okay? Has something happened since yesterday?"

"No, it's just that . . . well, Stevo said they're both being checked out before the transport picks them up. That they're being cut from the riding herd. They're too old, or not suitable. Or something."

"Transported. Transported to where? And why?"

"Well, I'm not sure, but Stevo, I heard him say something about the dog food factory, that the order had come down from the manager, and that those horses were finished. I guess the factory wants to make sure they aren't sick. Lollipop is going too. She's the one who can jump over barrels, but she's supposed to be too hot for any guests to ride."

Julia's face, which had begun darkening with the beginning of the recital, now contorted. "I am damned," she said, crunching each word out, "if Pecos Bill is ready for dog food. Or Copper. Or Lollipop. I've been around horses all my life and they have years left. Where's Morty McGuire? Or Todd, because I am damned . . ."

But Morty McGuire cut her short. He came around the corner of the corral, a lead shank in one hand at the end of which walked Pecos Bill. Morty's face was darker and angrier than Julia's.

"You want to ride Bill, Mrs. Clancy?"

"Of course I want to ride him. But I've just heard the most outrageous nonsense. About a dog food factory."

"None of my animals are going into dog food without my saying so," growled Morty. "Damn interfering people who don't give a . . ."

"Shit?" suggested Christy.

"Yeah," said Morty. "You can come down off Banjo if you want, he's a little much for you. I'll have Copper saddled right away. Stevo!"

"Morty?" Stevo thrust his handsome leading-man head around the door of the tack shed.

"Stevo, you saddle Copper and take Banjo yourself today. He needs work but not with Christy."

"What about the vet? He's waiting to go over those two horses."

"He can look at Clipper—he's gone lame in his left fore. And send the vet bill to management. Damn sorry, Mrs. Clancy, about this, but I'm mad enough to spit nails."

"Morty, I agree with you. And now I've got time for a nice ride before I go to the airport to meet my niece. I want a quiet, bombproof horse for her. Something to build her confidence."

"I'll put Pokey on hold starting this afternoon. Okay, you can mount Bill. We'll ride out by Buzzard Creek this morning. It's a nice distance. Okay, Christy, all set with Copper? Let's head out." Morty reined Spider, his roan horse, in a circle and headed for the gate, and Christy and Julia Clancy fell into line behind him. Julia could hear from the distance of two horses muttered "Nobody's gonna mess with my horses."

Morty McGuire was a picture cowboy, the sort labeled on postcards as "Old-time Cowpoke" or "End of the Lonesome Trail." He was built like a barrel and had a handlebar mustache, heavy brows over squinting blue eyes, a black hat with a beadwork band, leather cuffs and chaps, evil-looking Spanish spurs, and a huge silver buckle on his belt. He looked like one tough character, and he was. But a character with a soft heart, particularly as far as his horses went. Humans, particularly in the shape of ranch guests, Morty was mindful of, but they came a distant second after horses. Unlike many cowboys who take their animals without sentiment—lose one, buy one, sell one, put one down—Morty hung on as long as possible to his old-timer horses and suffered much when they came to grief through old age, sickness, or a misstep. He and Julia Clancy made a good pair.

Besides sharing this life view, Julia liked going out with Morty the best of any of the cowboys. There was no nonsense, no ingratiating little speeches, no sense of being bored taking an old lady on a quiet ride—just honest pleasure in riding out into the desert, seeing the mountains, and pointing out the sights. Today, except for the shadow of the knacker hanging over their horses, Christy and Julia Clancy enjoyed a fine morning outing that included two long lopes on the flat, a walk through a sunny wash, and a placid climb above Buzzard Creek.

Morty reined in his horse and pointed out the snakelike turns of the creek. Only a small trickle marked its progress.

"Used to be pretty full," remarked Morty.

"The golf course?" suggested Julia.

Morty shrugged. "Maybe. Likely the ranch is sucking up any water they can tap into. Buzzard Creek's available. It runs right along this ranch and divides up the two ranches."

"Gato Blanco and what else?" said Julia, moving her horse away from a paloverde that Pecos Bill was beginning to reach for.

"Well, I still call this one White Cat Ranch because it's hard to change names after all that time. Twin ranches. White Cat and Cat Claw divided by Buzzard Creek. Two brothers, and the one sold out to Mr. Simmons. He's coming in today with guests."

"And Buzzard Creek?" prompted Julia.

"Water level's so low I've heard tell that Cat Claw has to truck in water for their range animals. I suppose it doesn't make for good feeling. White Cat—Gato Blanco—gets first crack at the water, since Buzzard Creek comes into its land before it winds around and borders Cat Claw."

"War? Family feud?" suggested Julia, interested. It sounded like a real western script.

But Morty put a damper on the idea. "No, just some griping now and then. People here accept Gato Blanco. The resort employs a lot of people in Lodestone and around. Hell, without this ranch resort setup, half the population would have moved out, gone down to Phoenix for jobs."

"You mean all those little gift shops and restaurants?" put in Christy.

"Yeah. Those and three gas stations now and a chain supermarket. New school building, a twenty-bed hospital. Most folks'd say this ranch was the shot in the arm the county needed."

"Do you say say so, too?" asked Julia.

But Morty had clammed up. "I got a job, house for my family, health benefits, so I'm not complaining. But they can't fool around with my horses. I'm still head wrangler, and I'll make decisions. It's a misunderstanding. I'll straighten it out when we get back."

"And Copper and Pecos Bill. And Lollipop?" demanded Julia.

"They ain't going anywhere . . . except out on their range tonight."

Julia leaned over to pat her horse's neck and then turned to Morty. "If the management gets tough about this, call me, will you, Morty? Agave Cottage number four. I know guests aren't supposed to mix in ranch business, but call me."

Morty didn't answer. He neck-reined his horse in a circle and gestured down at the spread of buildings and the green of the golf course which ran around three sides of the ranch layout. "Time to head back if you're going to get to the airport on time."

Julia tried again. "So you'll call me?"

But Morty had moved off at a jog, his back stiff, his gaze ahead. Julia knew that she had tried to breach an age-old code: guests and staff do not interact on a personal level. And Morty had suddenly remembered that and reminded her. She put Pecos Bill into a trot that made her body thump up and down like a sack of potatoes. For a moment all Julia could do was curse the length of western stirrups, and then in defiance of western custom and to save her spine, begin to post up and down.

Presently Morty, probably feeling that he had made his point, slowed Spider to a walk and pointed out to his guests the dark shape of a Harris hawk soaring above them.

Julia and Christy nodded with appreciation, and the three made their way down the trail to the ranch corral.

FIVE

SARAH Deane, still in her postflight state, hands wet, knees infirm, made her way to the baggage claim center. This anxious condition which had caused her to refuse lunch had also prevented her from relishing thoughts of her coming ranch adventure.

Even now she avoided looking out of the big airport windows and so was unable to admire the sun or speculate about the temperature. Furthermore, by keeping her head deliberately away from any view of the runway or of arriving and departing planes, Sarah missed a small welcoming drama that was taking place near one of the departure points. A Learjet had landed with the words "Blue Sky Ranch and Ski Resorts" writ large on its flank, and now Heinz Simmons, Mrs. Estelle Simmons (known to friends as Esty), and their two guests were being loaded into one of the ranch vans for the trip to Rancho del Gato Blanco. Manager Fred Arco himself did the honors as chauffeur, luggage person, and door opener.

Aunt Julia was at the baggage claim counter as Sarah worked her way into the area. She knew from past experiences of shared travel that her niece would be in a less than healthy state. This being so, Julia took charge.

And Sarah let her. Even if she had not been weakened by her flight nerves, it was sometimes easier to let Aunt Julia take hold. Her aunt was an elemental force with more energy than was good for someone half her age.

Sarah smiled, waved, and then kissed Aunt Julia in greeting. Today, as usual, there was a faint whiff of barn about Mrs. Clancy—not remarkable since after her ride she had only changed her shirt before going to the airport. Sarah saw that her relative's vacation garb differed only in being somewhat fresher and newer than her accustomed at-home costume of corduroy riding breeches and a repellent pullover.

"Sarah, dear, good, you made it. You look a wreck. I think you should spend a week on a plane, you know, flying from airport to airport and you'd never be afraid again. When someone falls off a horse, I make sure she gets right back on and spends an absolutely tedious hour just trotting round and round until she's bored out of her mind and not afraid. It's the only way."

"Yes, Aunt Julia, you're probably right, but it would be expensive. Flying around for a week like that."

"Worth it. Money well spent. Now, where are your bags? We'll have to hurry to be in time for the two o'clock trail ride."

Ten minutes later, Sarah, trying not to think about the two o'clock ride, shouldered her duffel, picked up her suitcase, and followed her aunt out of the airport sliding doors. Reviving slightly, she began to have second thoughts about letting Aunt Julia take charge. Did she want to spend her entire Christmas vacation yielding to someone, no matter how beloved, who combined the personality of a headmistress and a drill instructor?

Settling into Aunt Julia's rental Chevy Corsica, Sarah listened as Julia began a comforting description of Sarah's mount-to-be, Pokey. "As mild as milk, wouldn't spook at a flying saucer. Morty says a six-year-old went out on him last week."

Sarah leaned back against the car's headrest and through

half-opened eyes began to take in the details of the highway leading out of Phoenix, while Aunt Julia moved from praise of Pokey to the probable fate of Pecos Bill, Copper, and Lollipop.

"Copper and Bill aren't young but they're perfectly sound and going nicely. Lollipop is another matter. She's a bay quarter horse, but somewhere along the line a thoroughbred got mixed in. She's too rangy for a quarter horse. She's a handful just now, only six, but she'll settle down if she's managed properly. The cowboys have been jumping her over barrels and that hasn't improved her as a trail horse, but it's shown me she may make a jumper."

Sarah was used to her aunt's enthusiasms and had once been with her when, driving past a pasture, she slammed on the brakes, hurtled into the driveway, and two days later—after heavy negotiations—became the new owner of a seventeen-hand Percheron-thoroughbred cross named Mickey Mantle who proceeded to clean up at the local shows for years to come.

"But Aunt Julia, you can't try and rescue this Lollipop just because she *might* be a jumper. And look out for that truck, you're over in his lane."

"He's in *my* lane. I had my turn indicator on." Julia swung her car around the truck, stepped on the accelerator, and moved ahead of the immediate crush. Then, collision avoided for the moment, she glanced sideways at her niece.

Sarah, always thin, today had a transparent quality, although perhaps this was the effect of a bright Arizona sun on the pale winter cheek of an overworked Northeast resident. Julia knew that the Douglas family's skinny genes had bypassed Julia herself and settled in Sarah—those high cheekbones and deep-set eyes. Julia always thought that Sarah, and other members of that branch of the family, looked as if they had just arrived as refugees from some stringent climate that provided little in the way of fodder. Today, Sarah's hair, normally a neat dark cap, was spiking every which way—a sign of her agitation, no doubt. She had a strong chin, long arms that ended in restless hands, and a very straight way of sitting, even when unnerved and tired, reminiscent of certain doughty Victorian ladies.

Julia, returning her attention to the highway after a close blast from an angry horn, decided that Sarah had horse potential. She had the build and probably the grit if this unnatural fear of planes and horses could be eradicated. Julia would start with fear of riding. A week of trail riding twice a day should do wonders in the way of confidence and skill.

Unaware that her aunt had already planned her future riding career, Sarah looked about her and took in Sun City and its dreary sequence of matching roofs passing on their right, and decided to make an effort at conversation. And find out something about the ranch. The poltergeist, for instance.

"You said someone slashed some girths? And squirted you and put sand in your coffee. What was it all about?"

"I thought that might rouse your detective instincts," said Julia with satisfaction. "Your mother says you're building a reputation for being in the wrong place at the right time, or is it the other way around? Is it just from insatiable curiosity like the elephant's child, or does crime attract you? Have you really solved something?"

"I wish Mother would be quiet," said Sarah crossly. "I detest violence—only sometimes it happens in a perfectly normal place like a shop or a library and I'm there." She turned her gaze away from Sun City and sighed. "Okay, Aunt Julia, tell me about it."

"It's a sort of epidemic. Little things. Annoying but so far not dangerous."

"Out with it because I'd hate to think we're just going to have a dull old time watching me fall off a horse every day."

"I shall begin at the beginning," said Julia firmly, "and describe it all." Which she did, ending with the possible fate of Pecos Bill, Copper, and Lollipop.

"I shouldn't think that was one of the tricks," said Sarah. "It sounds like the sort of thing a practical hard-hearted ranch manager would do to keep the budget straight."

Here Julia reluctantly nodded her agreement and returned to the matter of those tricks directed at herself.

Sarah for a moment was quiet, enjoying the disappearance of Sun City and its replacement by western vistas of ridges covered by mesquite and an occasional saguaro cactus rising up against the sky. Then she shook her head. "It doesn't make much sense. Why you? You don't know anyone out here, do you?"

"Anything," said Julia Clancy darkly, "is possible. I had a stable helper once who dropped a bale of hay on me." She paused to point out a route sign. "We turn toward Lodestone now. It's off past Wickenburg toward Congress and Prescott."

"But," Sarah persisted, "you don't know anyone at the ranch."

"I don't think I do. But then, I've batted around. You never know who's lurking. Some student who didn't want to be told she was ruining a perfectly good horse. Like Lizzy Blastowe last year. I sold her that nice six-year-old gray gelding and she let herself get kicked. Obviously wasn't paying attention. Perfectly sweet-tempered animal. Of course," added Aunt Julia, "it might be someone from Chuck Fiddler's family. He's still on crutches. None of them knows a horse from a cow. And then," she concluded bitterly, "they blame me."

"So it might be someone who knew you at High Hope Farm," said Sarah, sidestepping the idea that her aunt might ever be at fault in these cases. "Someone who saw you here and decided to get even. You can look over the guest list, but it's probably a practical joker and you got caught twice by coincidence."

"I suppose you're right," replied Julia Clancy as, in her role as a free automotive spirit, she zipped past a cattle truck. It was strange, thought Sarah, because Julia, when mounted on a horse, was a person of sensitivity and judgment, while behind the wheel of a machine she was a positive menace. But then she saw Julia crane her neck and flick a hand toward the side of the road.

"Look, there's the ranch van. Just ahead. The way things are going, someone has probably put glue in the distributor. I'll see if they need a ride, because I suppose we could stuff whoever they have in our backseat."

Julia swung the car into the shoulder lane and swooped up behind a long handsome maroon van with the large letters "Rancho del Gato Blanco" on its door. The hood was raised and Manager Arco was peering into the van's entrails. A tall blond man in lemon-colored slacks, a blazer, and an open shirt stood at his side, arms folded, an expression of annoyance fixed on his face. Inside the van Sarah had the impression of females in pastels and a white-haired male, and as Julia switched off the ignition, the occupants began to debark: an elderly woman in pale blue, a younger woman in two-piece aqua, both nicely coiffed, and a white-haired male, rather stout, in his shirt sleeves.

"I'll investigate," said Julia, opening her car door.

Sarah decided to stay put. Five people plus Aunt Julia were too many. She watched from the car window a pantomime indicating that the ranch van had mysteriously come to a halt. Then she saw Aunt Julia indicate her own car, saw relief and agreement expressed, and her aunt return with four of the party in tow.

"We can scrunch," announced Julia. "Three in the backseat and three in the front."

"How lucky we are," said the older woman in a doubtful voice. "You coming along like this and staying at the ranch, too."

"I'm Heinz Simmons," said the man, extending a manicured hand. "My wife and the Howells. Our guests. We are very grateful. As soon as we get to the ranch I'll have a car sent back."

"You mean you don't have a telephone?" demanded Julia.

"It was supposed to have been installed. An oversight," said Mr. Simmons.

Aunt Julia started the car and swung into traffic, and Sarah, as they passed the ranch van, had the impression of the driver watching them with a face contorted with rage and mortification.

"He looks absolutely wild," said Sarah.

"I expect Fred is," said Mr. Simmons. "I make a point of emphasizing a smooth operation, and the minute I get to Arizona the van breaks down."

"Oh, you're the owner, aren't you?" said Julia. "I'd forgotten the name. Well, you can't expect Mr. Arco to look happy. He's had a difficult week, what with the cut girths, the tennis nets, and the golf balls." Generously, Sarah thought, Julia did not mention her own grievances.

Heinz Simmons from the rear seat expressed interest, and his wife echoed it, adding, "You see, Heinzie, what happens when you're not here to crack the whip." She was a rather brassy, sharp-nosed person, and her aqua dress was studded with little silver nails which, since she was squashed between Sarah and Julia in the front seat, scratched Sarah's bare arm every time she turned to address the rear seat population.

Julia warmed to her work. "It's just a series of odd things, practical jokes perhaps. I think the golf ball business must have been rather funny. But your staff has been wonderful about it all. And I'm very impressed with your wrangler and his crew. The horses, too. They seem well cared for and in good condition."

From the rear seat Heinz Simmons expressed gratification and finished by saying that he hoped all the ranch guests felt they could be frank about any little problems or discomforts.

Here it comes, thought Sarah. The squirting and the broken chair.

But her aunt had more important things in hand. "I will be perfectly frank about the horses. Copper and Pecos Bill are not ready for the dog food factory, they're sound and useful. As for Lollipop, I am thinking of asking you if she's for sale."

There then followed a rather detailed discussion of horses—age, soundness, performance, suitability—which ended with a promise by Mr. Simmons to look into the matter. Mrs. Simmons vouchsafed that Copper was "cute," that Pecos Bill was "very cute," and that Lollipop made her nervous. Then the passengers, wedged warmly together, fell silent, and they swept down Route 89 toward Lodestone.

Sarah, gradually recovering from her flight, closed her eyes and for a while let her mind drift back to her house and life in Maine. And to Alex. She had left him preoccupied with several medical problems, an eruption of temperament in the hospital staff, as well as the loss of a resident to hepatitis. Alex would love Arizona. Sarah opened her eyes briefly. All that space, those mountains rising in the distance. Even horses. Alex expressed confidence when the riding was brought up. And Christmas was coming. Sarah had presents to buy, for Alex, her family, Aunt Julia. She would try in Lodestone tomorrow. Perhaps a cowboy hat and one of those funny ties that looked like shoelaces. Something to remind them of the trip. And she might look for a Mexican wedding dress because they were going to be married in the spring—May, or June—medical and teaching schedules permitting.

"Lodestone," announced Julia, slowing the car and pointing to the thirty-five-mile-per-hour sign. "Wake up, Sarah. Here's Lodestone and there's Buzzard Mountain ahead."

Sarah, turning her head to see past Mrs. Simmons's considerable bust with difficulty, saw the buildings of Lodestone slide by. The archetypal western town with its wide streets and low flat-topped buildings had been infiltrated here by a series of trendy-sounding boutiques and restaurants. Sears, Runty's Auto Parts, and Parker's Western Saddlery jostled with Gemstones Unlimited—Contemporary Indian Designs, the New Wave Art Gallery, a shop called Milady's Wardrobe, and the Sierra Vista Café.

"Poor old Lodestone," yawned Mrs. Simmons. "They keep trying but I wouldn't be caught dead eating in that café."

"You won't have to," said Heinz Simmons in a cross voice. The backseat squeeze was probably getting to him. "I'm glad Lodestone is trying to get into the act. I've eaten at that café and it's very, very good. I have my eye on the cook. We need an assistant chef in the kitchen. Now, tell me, Mrs. Clancy, what do you think of our meals? Pierre Doubler studied in Paris."

"Very good," said Julia absently. She seldom paid much attention to what she was eating. "He probably wasn't responsible for the sand in the coffee on the breakfast cookout."

"The what?" demanded Mr. Simmons.

"Didn't I mention that?"

"You didn't," Heinz Simmons said in a grim voice.

"It was this way," began Julia, and as she brought the car up to speed she entertained the ranch owner with the story of the spoiled coffee. "Probably a poltergeist," she finished, "a sort of malevolent spirit, the ghost of someone you fired, do you think?"

"I do not think," snapped Heinz Simmons. "But I will find out."

Mrs. Simmons turned toward her husband, again scraping her studs across Sarah's arm. "Heinzie, that's just what the ranch needs. A ghost. A lonesome lost cowboy. A real legend. Someone who was 'done wrong' like in those old movies. You know, he comes back as a ghost and tries to revenge himself. We could say we hear him, his spurs jingling. We could get a tape and play it at midnight through a loudspeaker. A ghost," she finished happily.

Heinz Simmons glared at his wife. "You can forget that idea right now. A ghost is exactly what we don't need."

SIX

HEINZ Simmons, wife, and guests having been duly delivered to the owner's house and guest cottage complex—Saguaro One and Two—Julia Clancy kindly allowed Sarah fifteen minutes to unpack, get a snack from the buffet, and dress for riding.

Still somewhat dazed by the sudden transition from sleet, freeze, and icy blasts to semitropical warmth, Sarah presented herself to the corral and Morty McGuire for her horse experience.

"Okay, Miss Deane," said Morty. "Here's Pokey. He's just a little old pinto pony a hundred years old and smart as they come. Smart enough not to spend any energy he don't want to. You mount from this side, the horse's left, unless you're somewhere you can't or have a broken arm."

"Should I expect a broken arm?" asked Sarah. She eyed the stubby black and white horse who was busy whisking his tail at some unseen insect.

"Listen, Pokey's not goin' anyplace. Pokey, if he had his way, he'd just stand still and eat. This little pony lives to eat."

"Pony?" said Sarah, now mounted and peering at the

ground from her saddle. It seemed quite a good distance down. Her experience with ponies had been at county fairs sitting on little shaggy creatures not more than waist-high.

"A pony is fourteen two or under. In hands, that is. You measure in hands," put in Aunt Julia. "Now sit up, Sarah."

"Mrs. Clancy, if you'd please hold up on the instruction. I'm responsible for Miss Deane's safety. And forgive me, but you haven't quite got the hang of riding western yet. You don't sit into your jog."

Julia, silenced for once, let Morty get on with a briefing. He gave Sarah a quick run-through of neck reining, halting, and sitting up, and tied a knot in her reins. "Mostly we ride with 'em untied, two separate reins. If we come off, the horse is trained to stop, but I can't have you losin' a rein every five minutes. If you feel good holdin' the saddle horn, go ahead. Or Pokey's mane. So if you start slidin' around, grab hold. Later on I'll tell you to cut it out, but for now it's okay."

Sarah leaned over her saddle and for good measure tried out a handful of Pokey's stiff mane. It seemed substantial and Pokey made no objection.

"Now," went on Morty, "we'll get along on a nice easy trail ride. I can teach you more out riding than I can sittin' here in the corral. Mrs. Clancy, you come last. Miss Deane, bring that Pokey—yeah, give him a little jab with your foot, wake him up—move him in behind me. Okay, that's good. Not too close to Spider. Spider, he don't mind Pokey nibblin' his tail but some horse's gonna to kick the bejeezus out of you if you come up like that. It's unsafe and bad manners to crowd the horse ahead of you. Okay, now, I'll get the gate."

And Sarah rode forth—or rather, Pokey in the manner his name implied—went forth. Sarah felt small, chastened, and back to kindergarten. But after ten minutes she suddenly came to and found she liked it. Pokey ambled along, and although Sarah found herself unable always to stop him grabbing at bits of greenery, she wasn't afraid. She and Pokey were a team. She felt they were bonding. The scenery, the mountains, the rising cliffs fading into hazy blues and purples, the little rocky gullies that Pokey almost took at a jog, the sun on her neck and shoulders—it was glorious.

And Morty McGuire, riding ahead, shoulders square, so solid in the saddle, his hat pulled over his brow, his spurs literally ajingle as the song said—well, Morty's very stalwart presence made Sarah think of riding as a perfectly natural way of life. Now positively daring, she turned in her saddle and called back to Julia. "This is great. I love it. Maine was so dreary, poor Alex."

"Good," said Julia. "I think you'll have a good seat. I'll work with you when we get home. Make a rider of you."

"Don't push your luck," said Sarah. "Let's just get me back to the ranch in one piece." And then, seeing a great series of green loops below them—they were riding along a ridge—she realized that they had ridden in a huge semicircle. She called out to Morty, "Why, that's the golf course."

"Yeah," said Morty, looking back. He reined in Spider, and Pokey, always willing to stop, came to a halt. "That's the ninth, the tenth, and the eleventh, which is a water hole. You play golf?"

"No," said Sarah. "It's always seemed sort of silly, hitting a little white pill up and down a lawn and into trees. But that water hole, is it natural?"

"Nothin' about that golf course is natural," said Morty in an even voice. "But guests love it. It's what brings most of them here, not the riding and the horses. That's what attracts business groups, meetings, conferences. All that stuff," said Morty.

Julia brought Pecos Bill alongside of Sarah and swept the golf course with her free hand in a wide gesture. "Those golf carts. Now, that isn't sport. Sitting in a little machine and getting out just to take a swipe at the ball. Really. At least golfers used to have to walk. There was some reason for the game."

Sarah nodded. "Those carts look just like mushrooms, planted along a field. Little white blobs. I thought people doubled up and rode with each other, but there're at least six on that one hole."

For a minute Morty stayed staring at the green fairways below them. Then he shook his head. "None of 'em moving," he said. "Not a blessed cart. See over back by the tenth green, it looks like a convention. I count eight."

Julia's face suddenly lit up. "I think the things are stalled. Dead. Look over at the eleventh fairway. Sarah's right, they're like mushrooms. They've stopped and taken root."

"Jeezus," said Morty softly, almost to himself. "Another snafdoogle."

But Julia heard him. "Snafdoogle?"

"Polite way of sayin' something else," said Morty. "Shall we move along? Miss Deane here's dying for some action, aren't you, Miss Deane?"

"Be my guest," said Sarah as Pokey put himself into a slow-motion walk behind Spider. "And," she added, "my name is Sarah."

"Okay, Sarah, we'll have you doing a lope by Christmas," said Morty. "If we can talk Pokey into it."

But Julia ignored the chitchat. Even as she reined her horse in behind Pokey, her head was turned toward the golf course with its complement of stalled carts. She was adding. Cut girths, one; hose, two; chair, three; coffee, four; golf balls, five; tennis nets, six; ranch van stalled by airport, a possible seven; golf carts stopped, eight. Very interesting. She began counting days. Today was the twenty-first; four days until Christmas. Did the ranch poltergeist have a bigger, better Christmas surprise in store for them all? Or would he wait for New Year's? Or try for a doubleheader? "Come on, Bill," she said aloud to her horse, which had whirled in a half circle, having caught sight of two deer standing on an adjacent rise of ground. She brought the reins across Bill's neck and pressed her legs into his side. "None of that nonsense, you're letting Pokey get ahead."

The golf pro shop was not a happy place. Foursome after foursome had stalled out somewhere between the ninth and fifteenth holes and had returned on foot, their round unfinished. Even those players who might have wanted to continue on their own legs found that all the holes ahead were littered with stopped carts forming new and unplanned hazards.

Tommy Brass, the pro, did his best. He soothed and sympathized and hoped to hell that the newly arrived owner, Heinz Simmons, was not somewhere on the course with important guests. Or worse, with investors or shareholders in the ranch.

But that was exactly whom Heinz Simmons had in tow—although fortunately not on the golf course; they were all revolving in the private swimming pool behind the Simmonses' Saguaro One. Orvis Howell and his wife, Corla, Christmas guests of the Simmonses, had sunk what used to be called a fortune, and now was referred to as a considerable investment, into Rancho del Gato Blanco. Orvis had met young Heinz among the oil fields of Texas during those exciting volatile days in the seventies when oil was oil and men were men in the Lone Star State. Orvis and Simmons, with the active encouragement of that eclectic politico, Senator Leo J. Hopgood, had for a happy spate of time splashed around in the black gold and then, with remarkable foresight, taken the money and run. Orvis Howell to the financial marts of Chicago, Simmons to the high-rise traders of New York and Denver, and Leo J. Hopgood to the political fields of Alaska, where a man interested in government could still swing a free arm and make a promise he couldn't keep.

The telephone rang; and Tommy Brass extricated himself from the mob, slipped into the office in the back of the pro shop, and picked up the receiver. It was Fred Arco yelling his head off.

Tommy defended himself. "Someone unplugged the bloody things. The morning carts went out just fine."

"So what the hell happened?"

"We keep 'em in order," persisted Tommy Brass. "Like the first ones back from yesterday are plugged in first and the last ones in are plugged in last. So the first ones are charged and ready for the morning rounds and the later ones go on charging until they're set for the afternoon rounds. Only," he added unhappily, "someone unhooked the afternoon ones and they stalled. All over the g.d. course."

There was a silence on the other end of the line and then Fred Arco exhaled slowly. "Well, Christ." And another pause. "Listen, Tommy, it's your ass. But it's mine, too. So listen. Give all the golfers who had their game loused up drinks on the house. And free carts tomorrow. If someone's going home today, give 'em a souvenir. Glasses with the ranch logo, T-shirts. You figure it out. And keep track of what you're taking out of inventory, you hear?"

Tommy Brass heard. He went forth into the arena, shoulders squared to do battle. At the rate things were going golf-wise, he thought, there wouldn't be an inventory or a job left by Christmas.

Back at the ranch office, Judy Steiner and Cookie Logan conferred.

"We can't keep the lid on this one," said Judy. "No matter what Fred says. I mean how can you shut up a hundred mad golfers?"

Cookie Logan shrugged and pulled at the shoulder of her embroidered Russian blouse—a special effort for the arrival of the ranch's owner, who had laid out guidelines for ranch personnel dress—Mexican and Spanish and western flavoring being the approved fashion. Cookie believed in making her statements of independence in little displays of disobedience.

Judy pointed over her head toward the open window. The red-tiled roof of the manager's cottage—Saguaro Three—could just be made out beyond the cactus garden. "Fred's already in a lather about the van breaking down. Things are supposed to be super smooth for these Howells. I sent over the big hospitality package for their cottage this noon, and Simmons wants a wine and cheese basket in place by five o'clock—only make it champagne, not wine. And the use of a golf cart if they can't struggle over here to the dining room on their own feet."

"You mean a golf cart that works. Did you know who gave Simmons and the Howells a ride to the ranch after the van broke down? Who would you pick? What one lady would you pick?"

"Not?"

"On the nose," said Cookie, and she sounded almost happy. "Mrs. Thomas Clancy. Julia Clancy. I'll bet she filled Simmons's ear. She's not the type to hold back."

"She's not afraid of losing her job like we are," said Judy.

"Well, I know one thing. That trip to the pet food factory is on hold. The one for Pecos Bill and Lollipop and Copper—I told you Mother's promised to take the other three. Morty blew his stack and Simmons put a call through to the corral. Someone maybe got to Simmons. Like Todd told me Julia Clancy rides Pecos Bill."

"We can't mix ourselves up with the riding program," said Judy. "It's bad enough us sitting here in Mission Control taking the flak, but we should keep our noses clean as far as the horses go. And you shouldn't listen in when someone makes a call."

"I didn't listen in," said Cookie virtuously. "I put Mr. Simmons's call through from our switchboard. All I heard him say was something like, 'Todd, what the hell's this I hear about shipping horses out for dog food?' and I hung up."

"Listen, Cookie Logan, Santa Claus is going to leave a load of coal in your stocking if you fool around with the switchboard."

"Never mind," said Cookie, "The way things are going, we may not even stay open until Christmas."

But Judy was on her feet, her face fixed in its special welcome expression, ready to deal with two red-faced men in golfing attire.

Back in Agave Three, Sarah, mindful of a stiffness settling into her lower limbs, took a soaking bath and then joined her aunt for predinner drinks in the sitting room of Agave Four.

"There's no point in spending money in the bar when I keep perfectly adequate supplies right here," said Julia, who sat by a low table made in the shape of a Navajo drum, spreading cheese on Wheat Thins. She was wearing a dress apparently inspired by the Franciscans—an above-the-ankle garment with a hood and a rope at the waist. Julia indicated her costume. "All-purpose. Now, what will it be, an honest whiskey or my special rum swizzle?"

"The swizzle, please," said Sarah. "It sounds exotic."

"You look exotic. I like that Chinese jacket. I expect you're feeling sore after your ride. It will be worse tomorrow but we'll have you right back in the saddle. Hair of the dog and all that." Julia leaned back on the bamboo settee and took a long swig of what appeared to be undiluted whiskey. "Now, what I'm thinking is this. That there's someone around who wants to make hash. Hash of the whole ranch operation."

"Does there seem to be any pattern?"

"The only thing in common seems to be a sort of childish mentality behind it all. Maybe it's an environmental group angry about the water this place is guzzling. As for me, I'll get hold of the ranch guest book and see if I can find any familiar names."

Sarah took a long satisfying sip of her drink and then nodded. "I agree, the whole business sounds childish, so if you don't find some old student of yours in the guest book, let's just settle down and enjoy. Alex says to tell you—"

But Julia was never to hear Alex's message. Through the partly open window of Agave Four came the most blood-chilling screech that Sarah had ever heard outside of the theater or cinema.

The scream rose, stayed on pitch, and then, like an expiring siren, descended and ended in a series of whoops.

Sarah and Julia sat like statues, Julia with one hand on the cheese knife, Sarah with her drink halfway to her lips.

Then somewhere a door slammed, feet ran across a paved walk, and at the same time the nearby doors of Agave One and Agave Two burst open and the screen doors slapped shut.

Sarah lowered her drink to the table and Julia dropped her cheese knife. They looked at each other blankly, stood up, hesitated, then at a run followed each other out of the cottage's front door and onto the paved walk that led to the main lodge. There, every light was on, a group was clustered at the lodge door, and from every side guests poured out of cottages.

Then Sarah saw her. "Look, that woman."

Julia looked. There on the lighted patch of lawn that divided the guest wing of the main lodge stood a woman. She was clasping her hands and now making a softer moaning noise, and a tall man bare from the waist up was reaching ineffectually for her hands. Ineffectually because as she moaned she snatched her hands away.

"Who is it?" demanded Sarah. "She looks like a ghost." She did. A Roman ghost, to be more exact. Sarah saw that the woman was wearing a pale draped garment that flowed and fluttered in the night breeze, even as she resisted the man's attentions.

"Maria Cornish. I think," said Julia Clancy.

"Shouldn't we do something?"

"No, here come the troops." Julia indicated the front door from which emerged at double time the solid figure of Judy Steiner and less solid of Fred Arco, followed closely by Cookie Logan and several unknowns.

And Maria Cornish, if it was indeed she, was suddenly quiet. A white arm came across her brow, the voice crooned to a stop, and she sank gracefully onto a bench, her pale dress subsiding around her like a parachute. Here she was immediately circled by a solicitous group, while on the fringe the tall man with the bare torso leaned against a tree and watched.

"The show's over," announced Julia. "Let's go back and finish our drinks. I think we need them."

"But," protested Sarah, "shouldn't we find out . . . or ask?"

"At dinner. We'll find out. Everyone will find out. If my guess is correct, Maria Cornish, if she's all right and hasn't been poisoned or bitten by a vampire, will get some dramatic mileage out of this. I mean, what do actresses live for?"

"It was quite a scene," admitted Sarah. "Very effective."

But, settled back in their chairs, neither Julia nor Sarah could revive interest in the cocktail hour or in domestic conversation. Maria Cornish intruded.

"She was here at Thanksgiving," said Julia. "With her boyfriend, that fake Indian, Blue Feather something."

"How do you know he's a fake?"

"He overplays his part, lays it on with a shovel. Indian details of dress, grunting, looking off into the hills. I'd say he's some sort of second-rate actor she picked up to carry her luggage around. She has a horse called Diablo Bravo. A Paso Fino."

"A what?"

"It's a Spanish. Quite an interesting animal, a natural four-beat gait . . ."

Sarah interrupted what threatened to be an equine-centered flood. "Wait about Diablo and tell me what Maria Cornish is like."

"I've only had the briefest of words. Vintage Hollywood and stage type. Can be ever so charming. Joins the peasants at dinner and laughs with her waitress. Blue Feather hangs around, looking surly, but he dances a mean sambo, or mamba—or whatever it is—when we have music. There's a little combo that does oldies as well as very mild rock. I usually go to bed."

"Is she given to having little scenes?"

"Not that I've noticed. But who can tell about actresses? Temperament is all, no doubt. Now, Sarah, let's have dinner."

"Where all will be revealed."

"We trust so."

Judy Steiner was doing the hostess job for the evening, wearing a black satin jumpsuit with a bright red scarf and her evening footgear, gray snakeskin cowboy boots. She escorted Julia and Sarah to a large round table.

"Well," said Julia as Judy handed out the dinner menus. "What was that all about?"

"Just a little upset. Miss Cornish was frightened, nothing serious," said Judy, lighting the candle in the table's center.

"That was *not* a little upset," insisted Julia.

But Judy just smiled and said, "Have a pleasant evening."

"I'll get something out of Cookie Logan. She's an easier nut to crack," said Julia. "And maybe I can find out about Copper, Pecos Bill, and Lollipop at the same time."

Sarah nodded. She was busy looking over the dining room scene and taking stock of her fellow diners—all ranch guests, she presumed. A dressy bunch, she thought. Very few could she picture hanging over the cookout fire, holding out tin plates for the campfire stew. And there were children, boys in little suits and girls in pseudo-Victorian flounces. That there were children was to be expected, because it was, after all, Christmas vacation. And grandparents, too. Extended families sat at large oval tables and talked with animation. Only one or two singles and not many couples. Ordinary holiday resort scene, Sarah decided: a stylish mix of old and young.

The surroundings were expensive. The long dining room was finished in a variation on the Spanish Colonial with Spanish artifacts, oil paintings of dark-visaged conquistador types mixed with sepia western landscapes—these ranged along the plaster walls—and over an enormous mantel in the center of the room hung what Sarah thought might be a genuine Remington. And everywhere the hand of Yuletide. Wreaths, swags, red candles.

Julia pushed away a tiny poinsettia. "It's a communicable disease," she said, plunging a fork into a shrimp. "A yearly epidemic. Fortunately I am immune."

"I don't believe it. Didn't you ever get into a lather over a dollhouse? Or skates?"

"Never. My parents, your Grandmother and Grandfather Douglas, believed in educational presents. A new history book, Bible stories for young people, a sewing basket. But once, once, they lost their grip. They gave me a pony and I was hooked for life. Eighteen years old, a little gray Welsh pony. Glennie—as in Owen Glendower—and I had him for ten years."

Sarah smiled. She had heard her Aunt Julia's tales of Glennie and she was ready to listen again. After all, Christmas was the season of goodwill, and Sarah had not yet suffered complete burnout. But Julia broke off in the middle of describing her first experience of taking Glennie over a fence. "She's here."

"Who?"

"Maria Cornish. In all her glory. She's making an entrance."

Maria Cornish was indeed present. She stood in the dining room archway, a luminous presence in layered white and gold, flanked by no less a person than owner Heinz Simmons. Leaning in a willowy way on Simmons's supporting arm, she allowed herself to be drawn toward the private alcove, a space circled by a wrought-iron filigree partition leading off the main dining room.

In the warm glow of wall-sconce lights and the flicker of the table candles, Maria was magnificent, every feature rounded and smoothed and radiant. Heavy gold earrings, gold chains, and a gold belt made of interlocking coils distracted the eye from any imperfections of figure. And Heinz Simmons, with his smooth features, his brushed blond hair, and his immaculate dinner jacket, was a fitting complement.

"I suppose," said Julia, "she's worth the price of dinner."

"I think so," said Sarah, admiring. "You don't have it any better on the screen . . . or the tube."

"And here comes the supporting cast," said Julia, inclining her head toward the dining room door. "Two by two."

These proved to be the Howells and behind them Mrs. Simmons and Blue Feather Romero, both looking as if they wished they could disengage from each other. Esty Simmons, in gray silk, looked second-rate after the passage of Maria Cornish, while Blue Feather—in tight white jeans, a silver concha belt, and an open-neck shirt—wore an expression more like a sulky teenager than a romantic lover.

This expression explained itself when Blue Feather, having delivered Mrs. Simmons to the inner sanctum, reemerged and made his way gloomily to a small table set close to a window.

"Lothario has been given the gate," announced Julia.

"Well, he certainly looks unhappy," said Sarah.

"Wouldn't you be?" said Julia, beginning a careful examination of her chosen entree, billed as Veal Rancho del Gato Blanco. "I hope this isn't dead white cat, but you never know."

Sarah had a sudden impulse. "Let's ask him to sit with us." How depressing to be dumped by your girlfriend in favor of the likes of Heinz Simmons.

"I should imagine it's Heinz Simmons doing the dumping. He probably wants to quiet Maria and keep things upscale, and it's obvious that the boyfriend is not on anyone's list of the top ten."

"So I'll ask him over? Besides being a kind thing to do, you know you're dying to find out about that scene on the lawn."

"So are you, Sarah. Don't pretend you're not."

So Sarah put her napkin next to her place and made her way to Blue Feather Romero's table where that person was staring morosely at an empty water glass. Sarah made her request, was stared at, and then without a visible sign of pleasure, Blue Feather hauled himself to his feet and made his way to Julia's larger table.

Introductions were exchanged, and Julia, blunt as usual, asked whether he was to be "Mr. Romero" or "Blue Feather" or was there something easier for all of them.

"Friends call me Blue," said Blue Feather. "I mean any friends I have. Not that I have any in this place."

Very sorry for himself, decided Sarah, but with Julia and Sarah taking turns at bat, they squeezed out the information that Blue was a sometime actor, had done bits in a western miniseries, had once met Robert Duvall on a set, had worked as a stuntman, and had done a riding sequence for a truck ad.

"As an Indian, a Navajo?" asked Julia.

Blue Feather, downing his third glass of wine—and he must have had a couple before he got here, thought Sarah—shook his head in a muzzy sort of way.

"Naw, just as a rancher. I used a blond wig. Hell, I'm not Indian, but I look like it and it's real useful sometimes. Like if I want to have continuing education or get a loan or say I want to do something for my tribe. If I had a tribe. I grew up in L.A.

My dad was an electrician in the old Warner Brothers outfit. His mother was half Mexican. From Texas."

"But you were named Blue Feather."

"I took the name when I went into the movies. I thought it might get me some western parts. Hasn't worked that good."

There was a pause while Blue did something uncoordinated with his chicken Kiev and then Sarah asked, "You're here for Christmas? With Miss Cornish?"

Blue drained his glass, looked at its bottom with suspicion, and reached for the wine bottle—a nice Graves that Julia had chosen with care and had hoped would last through dinner.

"Here for Christmas," repeated Blue. "I'll say I'm here for Christmas. But if I'm here with Maria, well, you better ask her." Blue made an expansive sweep with one hand and nailed the bread basket on the outer circle. "She's in there making out with Mr. Ranch Owner, who I could throw over my shoulder."

"I wouldn't if I were you," said Julia.

"Perhaps Miss Cornish is upset," said Sarah, getting down to it. "About what happened tonight." She thought, I'd better ask the question now while he's still able to talk.

"Tonight? What happened tonight?" and Sarah saw his eyes were almost entirely unfocused.

"The scream. Miss Cornish out there on the lawn," said Julia.

"Oh, that," said Blue. "That crap. That wasn't nothing. Nothing to get all hot about. Just a little old snake. Little old rubber snake in her bathtub. Little old black snake. Not real. Don't know any snake looks like that, all curly with its mouth open. Maria sure started yelling." Blue smiled in satisfaction. "Lucky she had some clothes on, running out like that."

"*Rubber* snake," said Sarah and Julia in one voice.

"Yeah. Rubber. Like those ones you can buy in the dime store to frighten people with. I mean it was a cheap one. They make a lot better ones than that. I was in a movie once and we had to fall down in a den of snakes and . . ."

Julia waved away the den of snakes. "You mean someone put a rubber snake in Maria Cornish's bathtub. As a joke?"

"Well, yeah, I guess it was a joke. I mean, what else was it? One of the maids maybe or someone who's got it in for her because she's a movie star. You shoulda seen Simmons pouring on the glop apologizing. Champagne, all that jazz." Blue reached over for his wineglass, found Sarah's, and drained it.

"Shit," he said sorrowfully, "Maria, hell, she just wants me to carry her fucking luggage around and find her sun-cream stuff and hold her horse while she gets on and has her picture taken."

Sarah saw a safety valve and went for it. "You like to ride, Mr. Romero?"

"I said call me Blue. Ever'one calls me Blue. Sure I ride. Didn't I tell you I did stunts? Fall down, roll over, play dead. Tha's me, down dog. Good ol' Blue."

The dinner wound up with Blue thankfully silent, too stunned by alcohol to contribute much more to the conversation. Julia had perked up with the introduction of the horse as a topic and had pried out the information that Maria didn't encourage Blue to go off on trail rides without her. Or even with her sometimes. She wanted Morty or Todd during her excursions on Diablo, but didn't like the thought that Blue might be enjoying himself riding out on the range with some of the younger female guests.

"Well, well," said Sarah after dinner, as she and her aunt made their way to the main lounge for coffee, detached from Blue Feather. "A rubber snake. I'll bet Blue put it there himself."

Julia sat down carefully on a large down sofa—a sofa in which it was possible to sink and never rise again. "He couldn't have pulled off those other stunts even if it's the sort of thing someone like Blue would do. He and Maria only got here yesterday."

But before the two women could speculate further, a large flowered woman wedged herself onto the end of the sofa, and three children clustered around the other end, and at the foot of the large Douglas fir tree, now blazing with ornaments and lights, Laddie Danforth struck a G-major chord on his guitar and the entire room launched raggedly into "God Rest You

Merry, Gentlemen, Let Nothing You Dismay."

"God save us everyone," said Julia loudly as the chorus died away. She hauled herself out of the cushions. "I'm going to bed. After all, back in the East it's almost midnight."

But Sarah, perhaps from curiosity, perhaps from a small surge of Christmas spirit, stayed the course, and for a full hour raised her voice in praise of peace on earth, goodwill toward men.

SEVEN

THE air on the next day, Friday, December 22, was almost frosty. It made it possible for Sarah to consider Christmas as a coming reality and to plan for a trip into Lodestone to do some shopping. This seemed a particularly sound idea when she climbed out of bed and found that her lower body felt as if it had been run over by a truck.

"I said you'd be stiff," said Julia as Sarah limped into the dining room to join her for breakfast. "Well, back in the saddle."

It took Sarah several minutes of persuasion to convince her aunt that postponing her date with Pokey until the afternoon would not jeopardize her equestrian career.

"I suppose there's a ranch bus that runs in and out of town."

"Don't be foolish, use my car. I'll sign you up for the afternoon ride. Now, I've just picked up my mail, and I've a letter from an old friend of mine, Laura Freebody. Inviting me to hunt with her, or rather with the Peeple's Valley Beagles."

"You're going to hunt beagles?"

"*With* beagles. On horses."

"I thought you hunted with foxhounds. For foxes."

"Actually they hunt jackrabbits with beagles—that's what Laura says—and very rarely catch any. Which is fine with me. I'd love to have a chance of getting out in a hunt field again. I went to school with Laura and we've kept up. I wrote her that I was coming to Arizona and I've been looking up Peeple's Valley. It's near Prescott, right around the corner."

"Isn't it dangerous? I mean aren't you pushing it?"

"You mean I'm old and brittle. Don't remind me. But Laura says she has a nice safe nag that will go over or through anything. It's to be a morning hunt on Christmas Eve day. I'll go up the night before and be back in the late afternoon. It will give you a chance to keep your detective hand in and find that poltergeist. I'm beginning to think there's a national practical joke convention quartered here and no one's told the management."

Sarah returned to her French toast only to become aware of Cookie Logan standing at their breakfast table.

Cookie smiled. "Is everything all right?" Her smile seemed pasted on and her eyes looked worried.

This was a routine question; often either Cookie or Judy went among the guests, greeting them and asking if all was well. So both Sarah and Julia politely allowed that it was.

"Any problems, please come to us directly," said Cookie.

"No problems, no rubber snake in my tub," said Julia.

Cookie acknowledged the joke with a bob of her head, but instead of answering or moving on to the next table, she bit her lip as if trying to think of a new topic.

"I think," said Sarah, "that you're trying to tell us something."

Cookie picked up a breakfast menu and, as if she were showing Julia an item, she leaned over the table and said in a low voice, "You wanted to know about those horses. Copper, and Pecos Bill, and Lollipop. Morty told me, but he doesn't want to get mixed up sending messages to guests. He needs his job. So do we all."

"You mean?" said Julia loudly.

"Voice down, please," said Cookie. She picked up Sarah's

menu and pointed out the waffle section. "I'm not supposed to talk but I just have to. The manager, the ranch accountant, and the ranch lawyer met with Mr. Simmons last night, and it's decided. They're really going to cull the riding horses. Cat Claw—that's my parents' ranch—is taking three, but the other three are going for dog food. The pickup's the day before Christmas."

"Morty McGuire must have given in to Simmons. We will have to do something immediately," said Julia in a decided voice.

"Don't think you can," said Cookie, "but I said I'd tell you."

"I even mentioned buying Lollipop," protested Julia, but Cookie was gone, bending over the guests at the next table, asking them if they were enjoying their stay.

"Mr. Simmons might not have wanted a guest to interfere in ranch operations," said Sarah. "And with everything that's been happening, it must be costing the ranch a wad of money to calm the guests. Maybe Maria Cornish is taking her pound of flesh, too. A rubber snake is probably worth big bucks to prevent a little lawsuit for mental anguish."

Julia poured herself a cup of coffee from the glass carafe on the table. "I need to think. So do you."

"I can't possibly think how to save three horses."

"Apply yourself. I think I'm going to make a personal appeal to Mr. Simmons. After all, we saved him a long hot walk yesterday. And those friends of his, too."

"But you're not to say that anyone told you about it, get Cookie or Morty in trouble."

"I shall be discreet. It's almost eight-thirty. I'll go over to his cottage and say I've fallen in love with Pecos Bill and I want Lollipop for a jumper and Copper for . . . well, I can't imagine what I want Copper for, but I'll think of something."

"He'll think you're out of your mind."

"I don't care, as long as he listens." Julia took a hasty bite of toast, another long draft of coffee, wiped her lips with her napkin, and departed looking like an elderly gladiator about to do in several lions.

On her shield or before it, thought Sarah.

She was back in twenty minutes. Sarah had lingered over breakfast and was still in place when Julia returned.

"Simmons's a real stinker," she announced, sitting down.

"He wouldn't?"

"All oil and sauce, but the upshot is that there's a rule about selling used equipment and horses to guests, to private individuals. Apparently there was a lawsuit once."

"Something you should know about, Aunt Julia. All those people you've sold horses to going around on crutches."

"Nonsense. Those were cases of complete mismanagement. Or accidents that couldn't be helped."

"Exactly," said Sarah. "And Mr. Simmons probably doesn't need some guest with a broken leg suing him because a horse the ranch sold acted up. I suppose he can sell horses to other ranches because they're incorporated, have liability coverage."

"Sarah, you're distracting me. Just listen. Mr. Simmons, with that Mr. Howell looking on and nodding approval, absolutely forbade selling to me. Said he was sure Morty will find a marvelous horse for me to ride—how about Rusty? Well, we'll have to think of something else."

"Call your friend Laura to come and rescue them by the dark of night," said Sarah. It was said lightly with an effort to show her aunt the impossibility of it all.

Instead, Julia Douglas stared at her niece with widening eyes. "We might just do that."

Sarah was alarmed. She knew that Julia, once in motion, was a force to be reckoned with, but kidnapping—or horsenapping—was too much. Wiser, younger heads must prevail.

"I was joking, Aunt Julia. I'm sorry, very sorry, but you know there's nothing much we can do. We can't buy horses they won't sell, and we can't disrupt the ranch."

"It's already been disrupted," her aunt reminded her.

"I know, but there's no reason for us to start playing games. Morty and Cookie have done all they can by letting us know what's happening. The staff people need their jobs, and they're not going to buck the rules." Sarah paused and took a sip of her now lukewarm tea. "I know I sound like some old school-marm, but isn't this all a bit, well, quixotic? I mean why these horses? You have barns full of horses and you're always buy-ing new ones. And getting rid of old ones. Are *you* sure your horses don't end up as dog food after a while?"

"I try to be very careful where my horses are placed," said Julia defensively.

"Yes, but you can't track them down forever. And these are western horses that have been used for guest trail rides. They're probably full of bad habits."

"I think," said Julia slowly, "that it's the principle of the thing. It's got my dander up. Copper is a perfectly ordinary western pleasure horse, Lollipop has potential, and Pecos Bill, he's good for me, and you know I had to put down Mickey Mantle last spring. I need a horse like Bill. I'm too rickety to school a young horse the way I used to. And now I have to think."

Julia sat at the table for a moment and then with new vigor pushed herself up: "I'll make a phone call and tell Laura I'd love to come for the hunt, and then I think I'll skip the morning ride and drive to Lodestone with you. Some shopping and then a little sight-seeing. I'll meet you at the car in half an hour."

Sarah should have been consoled that her aunt had opted for sense and reason and was planning a normal tourist morn-ing. But she remained uneasy. She remembered vividly several incidents involving her aunt, the Humane Society, and irate animal owners. There had been a winter night affair in which she, Sarah, had been recruited to help in the rescue of two mistreated Shetlands, and then there was the affair of Hazel the pig.

Sarah shuddered. She would have to keep a cold eye on her aunt's movements. She was not reassured when, as she was waiting by the car ready for the morning's shopping, she saw Julia come bustling up from the direction of the corral. But her aunt merely remarked that she had been signing both of them up for a nice afternoon ride. "Along Buzzard Creek. It's the creek that runs between the two ranches, this one and Cat Claw."

"Cat Claw," said Sarah. "Isn't that a plant?"

"Yes," said Julia, climbing into the driver's seat and reaching for the ignition key while Sarah hastily jumped in beside her. "It's a plant, catclaw, and a ranch, Cat Claw. Twin ranches once. Cat Claw and White Cat, owned by brothers way back when. White Cat sold out and went Spanish."

"Gato Blanco."

"Yes, and as you heard this morning Cat Claw is owned by Cookie Logan's family. I asked and found it's a working ranch that takes a few guests."

"No pool, tennis court, and golf course?"

"I don't know anything about Cat Claw," said Julia, whirling her car around an S-curve marked SLOW—GOLF CART CROSSING. "But we might make a little visit after shopping."

"Why?" said Sarah suspiciously.

"It's a guest ranch, my dear. If things keep falling apart at Gato Blanco, we may have to move."

And with this Sarah had to be satisfied.

Julia parked the car on a side street in the center of Lodestone by Parker's Western Saddlery, saying she always looked at tack shops, and Sarah went in search of presents for Alex and her parents. They met by arrangement an hour later, each with several packages.

Sarah climbed into the car and, keeping a package destined for Julia hidden, displayed her purchases. A silver bracelet for her mother ("They said it was Zuni but you never know"), flannel shirts cut western style for Alex and her father and brother. Julia indicated her parcels. "Very boring, just some horse things I couldn't resist."

"Don't you have everything you need at home? New England is stuffed with tack shops, isn't it? Show me what you bought."

But Julia shook her head. "I don't want to bore you. Now let's take a nice drive. There's a wildlife place, the Hassayampa River Preserve, though we could save that for Alex. And Oak Canyon up by Flagstaff, but it's quite a distance."

"Aunt Julia, you know you want to look at Cat Claw Ranch, so let's go there."

"If you want," said her aunt, starting the motor.

"No, *you* want, and I'm happy to go along." And Sarah climbed in beside her aunt and, after a distance of about six miles, Julia slowed the car and indicated an entrance over which hung a wooden sign with the name "Cat Claw Ranch" burned into the wood.

Sarah was much taken with Cat Claw Ranch. The complex, though not far from the road, gave a sense of privacy because of its many trees. There were a number of linked corrals and outbuildings, and beyond, a series of small cabins connected by sandy paths, each cabin surrounded by natural vegetation—sage, grasses, and cactus.

The two women made their way to a long, low lodge, nicely screened by three cottonwood trees, and were taken in hand by Mrs. Younger, a joint owner with her husband.

Mrs. Younger, a wiry, pleasant-faced woman—an older version of Cookie—took them on a tour. "We've a simple program," she explained. "Guests help with regular chores because we're a working ranch. But now we've a water problem and we're biting the bullet, drilling another well, and putting in a very small swimming pool. Guests expect it these days, and it *is* nice after a day on the trail."

"I hear," said Julia as they walked out onto the wide front porch and down the entrance path, "that you're getting some horses from Gato Blanco." She went on to explain that she and Sarah had heard this from Cookie Logan, who was, wasn't she, Mrs. Younger's daughter.

Mrs. Younger sighed. "Cookie leaned on me. I didn't think we could afford any more horses, but Cookie thought these were a bargain. She also wanted me to take three other horses due for the pet food place, but I said no, I could only take the three younger ones. I was sorry about Pecos Bill because he was ours once. We sold him about five years back. Of course, I know that Lollipop is young, but I've no time to fool with a difficult horse."

"I would love to see the corral," said Julia. "I always like to see where the horses are kept."

Sarah looked at her aunt with apprehension. Damn, maybe

Aunt Julia was planning to use Mrs. Younger or Cat Claw in some crazy rescue scheme.

Mrs. Younger was now giving details of the riding program. "We turn them out on their night range after the last afternoon ride, but we don't use them Sunday afternoons—the horses need a rest. And this Sunday is Christmas Eve, so we'll all be busy with a big buffet and helping to decorate the tree."

"What fun," said Julia. "I love Christmas. Perhaps Sarah and I can come as guests sometime." She shook hands with Mrs. Younger and walked back to the car with a look of satisfaction on her face.

"You look like the Cheshire cat," said Sarah. "And loving Christmas? What are you planning to do to that woman?"

"Nothing, Nothing whatsoever. I suggest, Sarah, that you spend your time worrying about rubber snakes and lost tennis nets. Now, it's quarter of one. Just time to make it back for lunch."

Sarah eyed her aunt. "Have you given up on saving the horses?"

"What," said Julia pathetically, "can one old woman do?"

"I trust you, dear aunt, as far as I can throw Pecos Bill and Copper and Lollipop."

"Sarah, what will be will be. The bottom line is that I'm a nonsentimental hardheaded realist."

"I'll grant the hard head," said Sarah as they drove through the wrought-iron gates of Rancho del Gato Blanco.

EIGHT

LUNCH at Gato Blanco was served on a tiled terrace near the swimming pool or, if weather turned inclement, in a sort of stucco pleasure dome that jutted off the central structure of the main lodge. Each glass-topped table sported an umbrella, and a number of lounge chairs were scattered around the rim for those who wished to recover from a surfeit of the luncheon buffet.

On one of these lounges Maria Cornish rested, her draperies about her, one creamy arm falling at her side, her hand wrapped about a ceramic pineapple from which a striped straw protruded.

Julia Douglas and Sarah staked out their table and then joined the buffet line. Sarah was staggered. A hundred salads, forty breads, and little hot dishes for dipping into or pouring onto pasta, toast points, shells, croissants. She sighed happily.

"Someone else's food is heaven—I really don't like to cook, though I keep buying cookbooks. In case I can catch the interest—like the plague."

Julia, who was rather indiscriminately heaping her plate, nodded. "Yes, I suppose it's quite good." She moved ahead to a tray loaded with melon slices, snatched off a slice of canta-loupe, and made for her table. Sarah followed and was sur-prised to see her aunt thump down her tray on the tabletop, turn around, and advance on Maria Cornish.

Sarah sat down to watch the action. First, Julia seemed to be expressing her joy at seeing again such a luminary. And Maria, from her smile, was graciously acknowledging the trib-ute. Then there was a certain amount of earnest conversation, which wound up with Maria doing a little sideways tip of her head as if agreeing to something.

Julia smiled and returned to Sarah. "Maria Cornish will be joining us for cocktails," she said. "I've asked all about her Paso Fino, said I'm interested in buying one."

Sarah looked up from her curried turkey salad. "Are you?"

"Who knows? I might be. Someday. And I think we'll have Blue join us for dinner again. Maria has been asked to dine with Mr. Simmons and the Howells for a second time. In their cottage."

"I wish," said Sarah, "that I could believe all of this came from a warm spring of human kindness."

But at this moment Julia's motives were shelved by the arrival in the luncheon arena of a broad-shouldered female with the face of an intelligent mule. She was followed by two men in dark business suits carrying briefcases. Sarah had just time to see the ranch van disappear around a distant curve and realized these must be the latest guests. They looked like a Mafia consortium, but perhaps it was just the black shoes.

At that moment a waitress appeared with a pitcher of iced tea, and Sarah indicated the new group. The waitress, on whose bosom was pinned a sign, "Sallie Summers," was only too happy to unload. "It's the senator. I mean it's the senator's aides. And his executive secretary, Miss Farnsworth, and ev-eryone's saying he's really running and is going to announce right here at the ranch. On Christmas night. The television people are coming in this afternoon. They're going to do back-ground shots of the ranch."

"Running?" asked Sarah when she could get a word in.

"The presidency," said Sallie Summers. "He made a big speech last night at an American Legion Hall in Tucson. All about ethics and good government from the top down."

"I wrote you he was here for Thanksgiving," said Julia.

"Senator Hopgood," said Sarah thoughtfully. "He's the one from Alaska who ran on a sort of oil-is-good-for-you ticket."

"You have it," said Julia.

"Why on earth," demanded Sarah, "would Senator Hopgood announce his candidacy from a ranch? A luxury resort ranch? I mean wouldn't you want to look like a man of the people?"

"Maybe it's more important to look like a man who knows people. Important people."

"Like the Simmonses and the Howells? Maria Cornish? Come on."

"Never mind Hopgood," said Julia. "We'll have enough of him later on. Imagine having Christmas compounded by a presidential candidate. Now, tell me about Patsy."

"What?" said Sarah, startled. "You mean my dog, Patsy?"

"I'm changing the subject. How is Patsy?"

"He's fine," said Sarah slowly. "Shouldn't he be? Have you had a message?" Her expression became alarmed. "Something you want to break to me gently?" Sarah put down her fork.

"No, no, relax. I was making conversation. I'm very fond of that big dog of yours."

"So am I," said Sarah.

"What I've never heard is how you and Patsy ever got together. The whole story. That time down in Texas."

"I must have told you. I'm always telling people."

"Just sort of an outline. You know how fond I am of animals, especially big ones like Patsy. An Irish wolfhound."

"Of course, I'm not sure he's a hundred percent Irish wolfhound. He was a stray, no collar, no ID at all."

"Tell me *all* about it."

Sarah studied her aunt's face for signs of guile and deception but could find nothing but expressed interest. "Well," she said, "it was like this. I was on a bus tour to a wildlife sanctuary because Alex thought the trip would distract me from all the horrible things that were going on. And just as I got there this huge dog came bounding out of nowhere, knocked me down, and began licking me . . ."

"And it was love at first sight."

"Almost. Love at first lick anyway." And through the cantaloupe course Sarah told her aunt about Patsy's status as an endangered stray and the possibility that he might have ended up in the pound on death row.

"You mean if you hadn't stepped in, he might have ended up being put to sleep, as they put it."

"Yes, so I took him over. I can't imagine not having Patsy."

"I see," said Aunt Julia, folding her napkin.

Sarah stood up, leaned on the table, and confronted her aunt. "So do I. This tender little story about Patsy is meant to warm me up to the idea of adopting a horse and hiding him under my bed."

Her aunt stood up and started down the path toward the Agave Cottage complex. "You're not ready for your own horse," she said as they departed. "Perhaps next year. For now we'll enjoy our trail ride, and Morty will give you a few more pointers."

"Not ready for owning a horse," said Sarah, "but perhaps for stealing one. My soft bleeding heart going pitter-patter as I lead Copper or Lollipop forth and ride off into the sunset."

"You must work today on keeping your heels down," said Aunt Julia, "and did I tell you that I asked Maria Cornish if Blue Feather could come on our ride? I think she views us as nonthreatening to her love life: I'm too old, and she looked you over and thought you were a nice little person."

"That should bloody well set me up for the day," said Sarah. "In case I was feeling fascinating."

"Fascinating isn't your type, Sarah. I'd say Blue likes them older with more flesh. And richer. But he's pulling at the leash. We can give him a chance to sound off and ventilate."

"Why? Why do you care whether Blue's pulling at Maria's leash? What on earth has it to do with us? I don't think you *like* Blue, and I don't see why you want to spend time with an overgrown baby who's sorry for himself."

For a moment Julia busied herself in pulling on her new cowboy boots, finding her woolen riding shirt—it was quite chilly—her Australian hat and dark glasses. Then she answered. "Blue may prove useful. As may Maria. Blue used to be a cowboy and Maria has a soft heart and owns a horse."

"Oh good Lord," was all Sarah could say.

They had a pleasant ride. Sarah on Pokey, Morty on Spider, Blue on a goose-rumped roan named Corky, and Mrs. Clancy mounted on the muscular bay called Rusty, as recommended by Mr. Simmons. Christy, the girl who had ridden Copper, had apparently gone home.

Not once did Julia refer to the missing Pecos Bill. Instead, after asking again if they could ride down by Buzzard Creek and over toward Cat Claw, she praised Rusty as a sensible horse with a steady forward-moving walk and a kind eye.

Sarah, looking at Rusty, decided the eye was not what she would call kind—more like shifty—but then, she didn't know much about horses' eyes. Pokey's for instance, when not entirely hidden by a thick forelock, were half closed much of the time.

They rode along peacefully for a short distance, and then as they came down to the creek bottom, Morty told Sarah it was time for her to try a lope. A short lope. This adventure took all of the space of fifty yards, and Sarah, thumping up and down in the saddle like a rag doll, felt that she would never ever enjoy riding. But when she slowed to a walk, she found she wanted to try it again. By the time they came in sight of the rooftops of Cat Claw Ranch, Sarah had loped three times and was still in the saddle.

Julia, through much of the ride, seemed preoccupied, barely noticing or commenting on Sarah's progress. Twice she rode alongside Blue—difficult on the narrow trail—and discussed landmarks with him, asking him if he'd done much desert riding.

When they returned to the ranch, Julia asked Morty if tomorrow morning's ride could take the same route. "With Blue if he can come. I think Sarah needs the confidence of repeating the same trail. Finding it familiar."

Sarah agreed. She felt if her riding skills were to advance, she and Pokey should cover the same territory.

At this Blue objected, but Julia took him aside and told him, as she reported later to Sarah, the facts of life. Blue was only released for a trail ride conditionally by Maria to certain company, and that certain company wished to repeat the Buzzard Creek trail. Blue was silenced. Then Julia reminded him that he was to join them again for dinner, and Blue—since he had few options, certainly not any to join a livelier or more swinging group—agreed.

Julia, satisfied, walked slowly back from the corral. "Things are moving right along."

"I'll bet," said Sarah, who had reached the point of hoping that they would all escape a felony charge and six months in the Lodestone jail.

"Look," said Julia, glad to avoid another argument. "The media has come." She gestured at the parking space below the lodge where several men in coveralls hovered about a white panel truck with an antenna rising from its roof like a small Eiffel Tower.

"An ill-omened bird," said Sarah. "What Christmas at the ranch doesn't need is media hype."

"Well said," agreed Julia. "But old man politics will just keep rolling along. We can just hope that Hopgood gets laryngitis and a tornado knocks out the television."

"I'm going in to have a shower," said Sarah.

"And I," announced Julia, "am going to find Mr. Blue Feather and see if I can stand him a drink."

"I wish somehow your plans didn't take in Blue Feather," said Sarah. "It gives me the creeps."

"The plans or Blue Feather?"

"Both."

"Blue Feather," said Julia, "knows how to sit a horse." And she turned and marched off in the direction of the Staghorn Bar.

Sarah had her shower, and then, deciding to check the desk for letters from family or friends, she walked over to the main lodge. Judy Steiner and Cookie Logan were at the desk and were confronted by the two men, now in light resort clothes, whom Sarah recognized as the two with briefcases said to be part of Senator Hopgood's party.

Seeing that a conference—or better, a noisy dispute—was in progress, Sarah sat down in a large sofa in a nearby alcove, prepared to wait her turn. She picked up the December issue of *Arizona Highways* from the table in front of her and began turning the pages. And stopped.

Voices from the desk were rising.

I must be invisible, she thought, and then realized that indeed she was. The sofa was tucked in just around an archway and turned with its high back to the office area—to give the sitter, she supposed, a wide view of the pool and patio.

Judy Steiner was trying for control. "I'm sorry, Mr. Yates, I just don't see how we can work it. That whole wing is taken. The senator has the suite on the Sombrero Wing, with the sitting room to use as an office. Miss Farnsworth has the next room, and Mr. Yates, you have the next double. Mr. Owen, we've had to put you in Ocotillo Cottage Two."

"Besides, Mr. Yates," said the voice of Cookie Logan, "you know the senator hasn't asked for a room for his family."

"Sweet Jesus, we know that," said the heavy bass voice with a western accent.

"But," said Mr. Owen, "he's damn well got to."

"Wife and kiddies by his side for the big moment," said Mr. Yates.

"You mean the senator *is* announcing he's a candidate?" said Cookie. "Right here at White Cat?" Sarah noticed that Cookie and Todd often slipped back into calling the ranch by its old name.

But the senator's aides had grown cautious. "We don't know the senator's final plans," said Mr. Yates. "But we're sure that he wants his wife and children here for Christmas. He just forgot to make the reservations. Please do all you can."

"Shall I call Mrs. Hopgood and confirm?" asked Judy.

"No," said both men at once.

"Let's surprise the senator," said Mr. Yates. "He's so wound up in that new land-use bill in the Senate he hardly knows it's

Christmas. Do your best. Haven't you got some guests who can double up?"

And there followed the sound of leather heels on a tile floor. Sarah saw the two men come across the archway and pause in front of the large sliding glass doors to the patio.

Mr. Yates, a short, stout, tanned man with sideburns, turned to Mr. Owen, a tall pale man with a potato nose, and shook his head.

"Well, shit, we gotta call her. We can't just scoop her and the kid up on a magic carpet and dump them down here."

"There is," said Mr. Owen succinctly, "going to be hell to pay no matter how you slice it." Then, as if aware that Sarah was easily in earshot, he smiled at her uneasily, and the two men followed each other out the sliding door to the pool patio.

It didn't take a Miss Marple, Sarah decided, to arrive at the conclusion that Senator Hopgood had not planned to have his loved ones by his side when he announced—if indeed he was going to—his candidacy for the presidency. And certainly the media thought so, with all that electronic gear and cables being dragged through various orifices of the main lodge. And she could see how his aides felt. Success in the political world usually demanded at least one presentable family member lurking in the background.

Sarah then remembered why she was waiting by the office. She rose and walked over to the desk to find Judy and Cookie engaged in a fever of erasing on a large reservation chart.

Judy looked up with interest. "Miss Deane, do you suppose you could possibly double with Mrs. Clancy? We have a real problem, something we didn't anticipate."

Sarah reminded them that Dr. McKenzie would be sharing her room and doubted whether her aunt would want to make a threesome.

"Certainly not," said Julia Clancy firmly, appearing suddenly at the desk. "What a terrible idea. Come along, Sarah. Maria Cornish will be coming to our room at five and I've got to pick up some ice." Then, as the two retreated toward Agave Four, Julia said, "You're right. Blue is on the creepy side, but I'm counting on Maria Cornish to be sentimental. Most theater people are. Sentimental and with egos that need transfusions. Sarah, you will please be an admiring audience, perhaps ask for an autograph."

"I don't even remember her movies," complained Sarah. "And that TV miniseries with the pirates in Shanghai was awful."

"For tonight you will have found her performance inspiring. Her last three movies were *Woman at Large, Fortune's Lady,* and *Down-Under Dame.* Mention the titles and I'm sure she'll do the rest. Remember, Sarah, you are essential to the plan."

"Along with Blue Feather and Maria? Well, God help us all."

"I'm sure He will. Now, I'll bring the ice if you'll go back to the cottage and start squeezing limes. How lucky that I have rum. Maria loves rum swizzles."

Sarah had to admire her aunt's management of Maria Cornish. It was as if Julia Clancy had spent her life nourishing the self-images of actresses. She admired, she flattered. She brought Sarah into play by saying that her niece was too shy to ask for an autograph. Here Sarah almost gagged, but her aunt shoved a pointed toe into her ankle, and Sarah reached for a second rum swizzle as the only form of relief in sight.

Julia, fixing her guest with a third jolt of rum, spoke of the affection of theater audiences—by theater she meant the *legitimate* theater—and was Maria thinking of going back on the stage? Julia then progressed to the triumphs of Maria's past films for which—what *was* the Academy thinking of?— she deserved not one but several Oscars.

And Maria lapped it up. Sarah couldn't believe it. No matter how heavy with syrup, how sticky the dose, Maria swallowed and asked for more. When three rum swizzles had gone safely down the hatch, Julia switched gears and brought up Paso Fino horses in general and Diablo, her own horse, in particular.

And Julia was right. Maria was sentimental—in fact, absolutely goofy on the subject of animals—and only too happy to go on about the merits of Paso Finos.

From this mélange, Julia extracted the fact that Maria was

the honorary chairperson of her local Humane Society chapter and had been last year a sponsor of a Save-the-Stray campaign in San Diego.

And Maria had her own rescue story. Julia and Sarah sat as if transfixed by the tale of Moussaka, her cat, and Barney, her dog, both saved by Maria from an unspeakable street life.

There was a pause while Maria's drink was "freshened," and then Julia leaned toward her guest in a confidential way and said, "We need your help."

Now comes it, thought Sarah. *We* indeed. She leaned back in her lawn chair and watched a pair of California quail scuttling back and forth in the mesquite beyond the patio. They provided a pleasant distraction from the war plans being outlined by her aunt.

The plans certainly didn't need Sarah's full attention, because she had all but guessed them in their entirety. As she had thought, Julia, Sarah, Maria, and Blue Feather were to seize Pecos Bill, Copper, and Lollipop, and ride off in the night. This to be done on Christmas Eve when everyone's head would be distracted by visions of sugarplums and probably by a heavy intake of alcohol. Alex, Julia assured them, would fortunately not be arriving at the ranch until ten o'clock Christmas Eve night. "When he gets here," she said, "it will all be a fait accompli. If he came earlier he might be quite troublesome."

Here Sarah agreed heartily. How she was going to present the scheme to Alex in a reasonable light was at the moment beyond her.

And Maria was all for it. Julia had inserted the word "publicity" early on in the narrative, and Maria was sitting up and taking notice.

"Too marvelous," she cried, lowering her black eyelashes and giving out with the famous Maria Cornish smile, a sort of angular half-smile meant to signify sex and enigma in equal proportions.

"You are simply the cornerstone of the whole operation," said Julia. "So you see you must come on our trail ride tomorrow. To go over the territory. During the operation, Maria will ride Pecos Bill, Blue will ride Lollipop—who can be difficult—and Sarah will ride Copper."

At this Sarah came to life.

"I can't ride. I haven't learned yet."

"Nonsense. You've been riding Pokey very nicely. Copper is a beginner's horse." And turning back to Maria, "We'll take some stills of you mounted. Sarah, you have a flash attachment don't you? Or fast film, because we don't want to frighten the horses."

"Heaven forbid," snapped Sarah.

"Photographs of Maria," persisted Julia. "Because you'll want to get hold of your agent as soon as possible. It will make such a good New Year's story."

"Oh, I do think so," crooned Maria.

"And Blue Feather. He'll go along? I've mentioned the project to him in a very general way."

"Blue," said Maria firmly, "will cooperate completely."

"Well, that's just fine," said Julia, putting down her drink. "Now, I'm afraid it's getting near dinnertime, and I know you're dining with Mr. Simmons."

"Blue," repeated Maria, rising unsteadily to her feet, "will cooperate or I'll blister his balls so he can't walk for a week."

Dinner with Blue Feather—he feeling absolutely no pain from his bar session with Julia and undoubtedly several subsequent dividends—cemented the plan.

Julia might have told Maria she was the cornerstone of the plan, but as the three worked their way through the main course it became obvious that Blue would serve that function. He was the stuntman, he knew horses, and, Sarah discovered, he was a lot happier talking about what amounted to simple horse stealing than about his work as Maria's personal assistant-cum-lover.

When Julia first proposed her plan, Blue had shown signs of wanting to manage the scheme, but Julia brought him to heel. Money, thought Sarah, had probably played a part in his acceptance of her control. Undoubtedly cash had been passed over in the bar and more was promised when the mission was completed.

"Okay, okay, I get it," said Blue.

"Let's go over it again," said Julia. "I gather from Cookie that the staff and guests all meet Christmas Eve for cocktails at five-thirty in the big lounge. Blue, Maria, and Sarah make their appearance at the party and then quietly slip out and go right down to the corral. Change to riding clothes in the bushes somewhere because there won't be time to go back to the cottage. The corral should be empty because of the party, but around seven that night the transport will be coming."

"But," objected Sarah, "will the transport people really be coming on Christmas Eve?"

"I have been busy," said her aunt. "I called every transport from around Phoenix and found that Southwest Horse Transport has a pickup order to take three horses from here to the Bonzo Pet Food factory. They've got four other deliveries to ranches in the area and didn't think they'd make it before seven. I thought of canceling the pickup order but decided that someone at the ranch office might be checking."

"Damn well they'll be checking," said Blue with his mouth full. "Place's full of spies."

"All the riding horses," said Julia, "will have been turned out on their night range. Except for the three who will be held at the corral to be picked up by the transport. If anyone turns up, just say you came with sugar for the horses because it's Christmas Eve. And, of course, Maria owns Diablo Bravo and has a perfect right to visit her horse. Then if anyone interrupts you, I've suggested that Blue, with your help, tie and gag him . . . or her. Or them. Don't let anyone see your faces. I've bought bandannas for masks. After the practical jokes this week no one is going to question anything. In fact, I'm counting on those golf and tennis net pranks to distract anyone from what we're doing."

"So," said Sarah, "after you've—what's the word?—neutralized the staff, you want us to take Pecos Bill, Copper, and Lollipop, and saddle them."

Julia was pleased. "Very good, Sarah. And it's most important to pick up the three horses' papers. They're on the corral office desk waiting for the transport people. Vaccination and blood test records. We'll need them for the shipping."

"Shipping!" exclaimed Sarah. "Where are they going?"

"Don't get ahead of the plan. It will be quite dark by the time you set off. Take flashlights. Get going. Down along Buzzard Creek toward Cat Claw."

"Piece of cake," said Blue in a blurred voice. Sarah saw Blue's eyes increasingly unfocused. Damn, she thought, I'll bet he's taking something more than alcohol. It's all we need, a druggie helping us steal horses. As the dessert arrived, she began reviewing steps in her aunt's plan. And almost immediately hit a major hole in the plan—more than a hole—a chasm.

"Aunt Julia," she said accusingly, "just where are *you* going to be when we're crashing around Buzzard Creek?"

"Yeah," said Blue. "This is your idea."

"Have you forgotten my invitation to go hunting with my old friend Laura?"

"I should hate to think you might have your day's hunting disturbed," said Sarah. "Will you be back in time to post bail?"

"No sarcasm, please. I have spoken to Laura, who will have three stalls ready. After we finish with the day's hunt, I'll borrow her truck and horse trailer and drive to Cat Claw Ranch. Their corral is quite close to the road, you remember. I shall back the trailer in a short way and be there by seven-thirty. You will, I hope, have arrived by then and be holding the horses in readiness."

"And Mr. and Mrs. Younger will of course risk their lives helping you load."

"You haven't paid attention. Mr. and Mrs. Younger and their guests will be trimming their tree and having their Christmas Eve buffet. We won't disturb them."

"My God," said Sarah.

"Leave God outta this," said Blue. "Things screw up when God messes into something."

"I'm a little concerned about Alex," continued Aunt Julia.

"When he arrives you must brief him completely. He'll have to back you up in what you were doing—or supposed to be doing—that evening. And Blue, no drinking, no drugs. Absolutely clean. Understand, my friend?"

At this, Blue Feather turned sulky; Julia was undoubtedly taking over the Maria Cornish role. "I'll do what I damn well please, and if I don't feel like riding around in the middle of the night on some killer horse called Lollipop, I won't."

Julia hastened to mollify. "Lollipop isn't a killer. She just needs someone like you who understands horses."

Blue subsided and the rest of the meal was finished in peace. After dinner Sarah noticed that Julia made a point of joining in the carol singing and later singled out Judy Steiner and Manager Fred Arco for conversation.

It was not until eleven that Julia and Sarah made their way back to Agave Cottage. "I've laid my groundwork," said Julia. "I told them I enjoyed my new horse, Rusty. And I asked whether they were worried about any more practical jokes. I said the jokes quite frightened me, that I was afraid there might be more."

"And they bought it?" said Sarah, thinking of her aunt's previous forceful public appearances.

"People want to think of old ladies as frightened because it reinforces their stereotypes and gives them a sense of power. Now, Sarah, I'm feeling quite up about this. The true meaning of Christmas, that's what we're expressing."

"The true meaning of horse thief, you mean," said Sarah. "And how I'm going to explain this to Alex is beyond me. Make it sound like good clean Christmas fun."

Julia paused by the door of Agave Four. "And that's exactly what it is," she said.

Sarah fell asleep that night as the laughter of the last guests making their way to the cottages had died away, and the only sounds that came from the surrounding desert were the yip-yips of circling coyotes coming down from the foothills and the occasional hoot of a visiting owl. For diurnal inhabitants it was a time of peace and rest, but toward morning Sarah turned restlessly in her bed and began a dream punctuated by scenes of riderless horses and Aunt Julia in a ringmaster costume cracking a whip at a group of circling guests, Sarah, Maria Cornish, and Blue Feather among them.

NINE

EARLY Saturday morning, two days before Christmas, found Sarah in an improved frame of mind. In fact, if it hadn't been for Julia's horse caper, Sarah could have felt herself remarkably happy. Alex was coming tomorrow night, she had learned how to climb on a horse, and Arizona, with its brown and purple mountains stretching and fading into blue beyond their cottage, beckoned invitingly. She reached for her sweater, a heavy rose wool that seemed just right for riding out on Pokey on a chilly morning, and headed for breakfast.

Julia, saying she had been up since five, was already into her oatmeal by the time Sarah joined her. "Me, a few coyotes, and Mr. Arco in his jogging suit, and birds, none of which I care to identify." She handed Sarah a slip of paper. "Final plan. Read it over and tear it up."

Sarah grimaced and scanned the paper. It was short and to the point involving repeat rides along Buzzard Creek and the timetable for Christmas Eve. Maria Cornish's particular assignment was to keep Blue under watchdog conditions during the idle hours.

"I think," said Julia with satisfaction, "that covers everything. Maria, for one, ought to be in heaven. It's a plot right out of one of her movies."

The morning trail ride along Buzzard Creek to the edge of Cat Claw Ranch went smoothly, and Sarah found that by keeping her mind off Aunt Julia's plan, periods of enjoyment were possible. The weather was crisp, the sun shone, and Maria Cornish, in a scarlet riding costume on Diablo, was an impressive figure. Even Blue seemed almost amiable, going as far during a halt to relate a questionable story having to do with varieties of horses' asses.

At noon the riding party returned and split up, Blue and Maria to their suite, Sarah to the office to make sure that the ranch van would meet Alex's plane on Christmas Eve, and Aunt Julia to pack. "Thank heaven I'll miss all the guests going on about being children at heart."

Aunt Julia would do well as the Grinch, Sarah decided as she made for the office. She herself clearly remembered the unbearable and joyful tension with which she hung her red flannel stocking to the fire screen on Christmas Eve. She hoped Aunt Julia would accept a Christmas present without snapping her head off.

The desk scene reminded Sarah of a war office. The senator's two aides stood by looking grim but satisfied. The woman with the mule's face looked as if she were about to throw hand grenades. Judy Steiner was expounding, and Cookie Logan was holding a room key and a bottle of wine by its neck.

"Miss Farnsworth, I can't tell you how sorry we are to move you," said Judy. "But the senator's aides were very insistent."

"I never would have come," said Miss Farnsworth in a loud voice. "I have my own family. I could have gone to them for Christmas. I thought Senator Hopgood needed secretarial and planning assistance. Not that he wanted a family love-in."

"I've explained," said the man Sarah had identified as Mr. Owen. "Please, Lily. This is crucial. If he does announce, well, you know, we have to have the family in the picture. I mean literally in the picture."

"And you'll be needed, Lily," said Mr. Yates. "Needed like you've never been needed before. CBS is here, NBC and CNN are coming. ABC and PBS tomorrow."

"Leo said he wouldn't do anything until after New Year's," said Miss Farnsworth. "He told me last weekend."

"Things have changed, the whole climate. We've got to jump," said Mr. Owen. Then, seeing Sarah, he paused, probably reflecting that this was the same young woman who had been on deck during their early planning and room-shifting scene. He eyed her suspiciously, then, undoubtedly thinking that anyone was a potential voter, he smiled and turned back to Judy. "I'll take the van in and meet Maud-Emma and Artie. And this good lady is waiting for you."

Sarah, in the guise of a good lady—later to be known as the horse thief—put in her bid for the ranch van to meet her friend, Dr. Alexander McKenzie. This was granted, and Judy Steiner reminded Sarah that after dinner there would be a special movie for guests, *Creatures of the Desert Night*.

Mr. Yates, still standing within earshot of the office desk, turned to Mr. Owen and nodded. "Good, a movie. Maybe that'll keep Artie Hopgood quiet. He's going to be a real pain in the butt."

And Sarah remembered. It was the son of the senator who was thought to be the one who cut all the girths. The poltergeist, except, of course, the boy had left the ranch after Thanksgiving. It might be an interesting evening at the ranch. Wife and son as a surprise to a husband who had not expected—wanted?—his family for Christmas. A husband who was thinking of announcing his candidacy *without* a family presence. Perhaps, she thought, Mrs. Hopgood was a liability. Or Artie so awful as to disgust the voting public.

Then, remembering that Aunt Julia was about to leave the scene of her machinations, Sarah hurried back to the Agave Cottage.

Julia had finished her packing and was just unwrapping the package from the tack store. She displayed the contents. "You see, I was thinking ahead. The bandannas, three halters, and three lead shanks. You'll need them if you get there ahead of me. Put on the halters—right over the bridles—and tie the horses to a fence by the corral. Use a quick-release knot. And here are three flashlights." For a moment Julia regarded her supplies with satisfaction and then nodded. "Now I really have to scoot. I want to get to Laura's in time to try out the mare she's lending me. There's no point in going out with a hunting field on an absolutely strange beast."

"Certainly not," said Sarah.

"Remember," said Julia, "Maria Cornish and Blue Feather are depending on you. Particularly Blue Feather, because there's cash in it for him, and I think he needs cash badly. I'm sure he has a drug habit." Julia went to the closet and pulled out her olive-drab oilcloth riding raincoat. "Sarah, could you just help me with my suitcase?"

Sarah reached for the worn canvas suitcase and shook her head. "I don't believe this. A movie star—or former star—a druggie, a schoolteacher, and a supposedly respectable senior citizen stealing horses."

Julia gave her a reproachful look. "Not stealing, rescuing. Saving three useful lives. A good and moral act. And I shall send the ranch a substantial check in payment." She opened the cottage door. "Goodbye, Sarah. Practice your riding over Buzzard Creek trail tomorrow. I'll be at Flying Horse Farm until tomorrow night. Did you know the animals are supposed to be able to talk on Christmas Eve? I wonder if it has to be at midnight."

"Fine," said Sarah, following her aunt out the door with the suitcase. "We can have a nice chat with all the horses. Do you suppose Diablo speaks Spanish?"

But Julia was already in the driver's seat. Sarah loaded the suitcase, Julia started the engine, and with a wave of the hand through the open window, swung the Chevy Corsica out and away.

Sarah felt more and more as if she had a one-way ticket on a fast train that made no stops and had no exits. Reluctantly, she joined Maria Cornish and Blue Feather for late afternoon drinks by the pool and found them both keyed up over what

Maria kept calling Operation Horse. Maria, having no confidence in Sarah's camera, had sent Blue Feather into town to buy an expensive-looking Nikon and a roll of fast film for night pictures. Blue seemed unnaturally cheerful—or high, thought Sarah—and equally committed to the plan. "We'll really shove it to them" were his words.

Here Sarah put in a last ditch suggestion that they hold it, put a call in to Julia, and try for some more legitimate way of saving the three horses. Maria topped her lines. Time was of the essence. Christmas Eve was the perfect moment. The transport truck was coming, they couldn't cancel it, the ranch would find out. And if Sarah was not interested, why, Maria and Blue would do it themselves. She, Maria, was an animal lover. Besides, she'd written her agent to stand by. "I've always wanted to do another western and there I'll be tomorrow, riding down the sunset trail."

Maria sounded exactly like Julia herself, Sarah decided. Julia had certainly done a brainwashing job on her. Sarah bowed her head in defeat. "Okay," she said. "I give in. Let's hope we don't end up in a four-man jail cell." She turned to Blue Feather. "Anyway, I'm glad a stuntman is going along on the rescue."

"This stunt," said Blue, "is kid stuff."

Sarah, feeling that somehow she should keep her finger on the pulse of the ranch, arrived at the main lounge for an announced cocktail party; this to be held at the expense of Gato Blanco—the ranch was still working to conciliate irritable guests. Here she found a crowd hovering over tables of hot hors d'oeuvres and a wide variety of cheeses. Then, in the middle of the clink of glasses and sounds of uneasy jollity, Sheriff Harvey Wallow arrived. In full uniform.

The sheriff stood for a moment in the archway that divided the main lounge from the lobby. At his side, looking as if he'd been bitten by something toxic, stood Fred Arco. Behind the two men, Heinz Simmons. For a minute the trio surveyed the territory, and then Fred Arco, shoulder-to-shoulder with the sheriff, strode toward the fireplace, and the guests parted like the waves on the Red Sea. Heinz Simmons, his face set like marble, followed.

The fireplace reached, Fred Arco waved his hands for silence, and as the murmurs died down, he said his piece. A statement no doubt rehearsed to give an equal balance between a happy holiday greeting and the serious matter that brought the forces of law and order to their hearth. The result was a rather garbled syntax.

"Sheriff Wallow's an old friend to lots of you," he said in conclusion. "And lots of us know that from time to time we need him to come and remind us that though everything's pretty near perfect here at Gato Blanco, sometimes there's some little thing happens, and we need Harvey Wallow to give us a hand."

At this, Harvey Wallow, a man built on the lines of a beer bottle with the face of a disillusioned turtle, stood forth and went straight to the point. He'd been called in by Mr. Simmons and Mr. Arco about some jokes going around here at the ranch, and he and Mr. Simmons and Mr. Arco wanted everyone to know that these jokes were in pretty lousy taste and they were going to stop. He and the sheriff's department were going to be keeping a pretty close eye on things at White Cat—"I mean Gato Blanco"—and the perpetrators would be punished. In fact, if any more jokes were perpetrated, the perpetrators— here Sheriff Wallow paused, struggling to dig himself out of a verbal pit—"if any perpetrators are found, well, they are sure in for a bad surprise." Lodestone was a law-abiding place and he would sure see it stayed that way. And, as an unwelcome afterthought, the sheriff grimaced and wished everyone a very merry Christmas from the sheriff's department in Lodestone.

Then Heinz Simmons stepped out of the background, shook Sheriff Wallow's hand, and hoped all were enjoying their cocktails: "Just a way we at the ranch can thank you beautiful people for sharing your holiday with us. We think we're pretty lucky to have you as part of the Gato Blanco family."

Here followed a few cries of "Hear, hear," and "Way to go" and then voices rose again in the familiar cocktail clamor.

And Sarah found her hand touched by Maria Cornish. "You

must let me eat at your table because I simply cannot eat by myself, too humiliating, and besides we need to talk. Blue Feather's in the bar, and I don't want to make a scene by going and getting him. And, my dear, I have news. Mrs. Senator Hopgood's arrived and she's simply steaming. I saw her practically dragged in by those aides of the senator's. And that dreadful boy of hers. If Hopgood's going to be elected again to anything, he'd better do something about young Artie. And Maud-Emma—that's her name; too, too southern—well, totally rumpled, in a poor shade of blue, and she needs real help with her hair, a much lighter rinse."

Here Sarah allowed herself to be ushered by Maria to Julia's table and, after settling herself, returned to the subject of Maud-Emma Hopgood. "Poor thing, no wonder she's looking rumpled. She was expecting to have Christmas in Alabama and was just sent here to make the senator look like a family man."

"Hush," said Maria, "here she comes. Making her entrance." And Maria flicked a braceleted hand in the direction of the dining room door where a complete hospitality team stood in deferential postures: the two senatorial aides, Manager Arco cradling a swaddled bottle of champagne, Judy Steiner with a gold-tasseled menu, and Heinz Simmons in his usual faultless dinner jacket extending his arm. Maud-Emma herself hesitated, then, disengaging the Simmons arm, she lifted her chin and stepped forward. She was rather stout and snugged into a layered dress of blue and apricot, probably chosen, Sarah thought, for an Alabama vacation. Nevertheless, as she proceeded across the dining room floor followed by her entourage and a discontented-looking boy with hair flopping across his eyes—Artie, no doubt—Sarah had to admit she was making the best of a bad situation. True, her expression suggested that she had been swallowing nails, but there was a certain determination, even a gutsy quality about her progress, that Sarah had to admire.

Maria apparently agreed. "Not bad, not bad at all. I'm surprised. More to the lady than I'd have thought. Entrances are so important because you can absolutely *lose* it if you botch them. Now, Sarah, I think we should just be ordinary guests tonight, watch that movie and sing Christmas carols. We don't want to attract attention by doing anything different."

Sarah thought that Maria couldn't inhale without attracting attention, but she agreed to the plan, and the after-dinner hour found the two of them escorted by Cookie Logan in her hostess capacity to the conference room for the nature movie. "Want to talk to you later," said Cookie from the side of her mouth, and then louder and brighter, "Enjoy the show."

The movie was poorly attended, as only those guests who felt strongly that it was time they learned *something* about Arizona were present.

Maria and Sarah had a large soft sofa to themselves, and Sarah, as soon as the lights went out, slipped into a half-sleep. She was aware that jackrabbits, javelinas, mule deer, and bobcats were flashing upon the screen while the presenter—a Professor someone—went on about the nocturnal wealth of the desert. And just as the speaker was explaining in detail how smaller mammals—ground squirrels and kangaroo rats— conserve water, Sarah passed out.

"It had its moments," said Maria. "From the point of view of cinematography."

Sarah pulled herself up and began smoothing her hair. "You liked it? All that stuff about little animals not losing moisture in nasal passages and managing their urine?"

"Not that, darling, the special effects, the cutting and past- ing. And people talk about actors manipulating scenes." She stood up, extended a lovely hand to the professor, who was packing up his film. "Thank you, Professor, so very stimulat- ing."

"I'll bet," said the professor, eyeing Maria. He departed, muttering to himself.

"You can't win them all," said Maria. "Now, I'm going to the lounge to sing Christmas carols, and there's Cookie Logan again with something on her mind. I think she wants you."

Cookie entered the conference room, waited for Maria to

pass, and then went directly up to Sarah. "Did your aunt understand what's happening? About Pecos Bill and the others? My message?"

"Yes, she does."

"And?"

"She's been thinking about it." Sarah paused and considered. Then plunged. "Look, Mrs. Logan."

"Cookie."

"Cookie. Look, Cookie. Aunt Julia's got it all worked out, but no one is supposed to know a thing about it. Not you or Morty or anyone. It will be worth all your jobs if you know. As it is, Aunt Julia and the rest of us will probably hang."

"The rest of you? Who are they?"

"It's better I don't tell you."

"I should know. So I can help in a pinch."

"Maria Cornish. Aunt Julia. And Blue Feather."

"Blue Feather drinks. And judging from what the maid found in his wastebasket, he's into drugs."

"Best Aunt Julia could do. Blue Feather was a stuntman. He rides and ropes and falls."

Cookie's freckled face in the dim light looked worried. "You're going to need more than that fake Indian. What can I do?"

Sarah ran over the plan in her mind. "Okay, two things. Try to see that the horse people—the cowboys and corral crew—aren't at the corral on Christmas Eve from five-thirty to about six-thirty. And, if you're over at your parents' ranch between seven and eight-thirty or so, do a lot of noisy carol singing."

"You're leaving those horses at Cat Claw? That'll ruin my folks. And it's the first place anyone would look."

"Not leaving them at Cat Claw. It's a way station. For as long as it takes to load three horses. Up by the road. And that's absolutely all I should tell you. You'll get into real trouble."

Cookie nodded soberly. "I can keep a secret." She hesitated as if to go on, but just then Maria Cornish reappeared in a state of excitement. "It's that senator. Hopgood. He's on television right now and everyone says he's going to announce."

I suppose, Sarah thought, I should get some sort of a line on the man. Especially if he's going to be served up as presidential fodder. Rather reluctantly she followed Maria and Cookie into the main lodge, where a large population circled about a television screen in the center of which the large smooth face of Senator Leo J. Hopgood shone like an illuminated egg.

Senator Hopgood, already in full flood, was on an ethics kick. Ethics in the halls of power, ethics in little towns and great ones. Ethics in the marketplace. Between nations. In personal life. Then the senator, gray hair fluffed, his wide brow glistening even with his makeup, leaned forward, angling his body so at least its eastern portion used a limp American flag as background.

"I haven't been perfect," thundered Senator Hopgood. "I've made mistakes. We've all made mistakes. I've made mistakes in judgment. Political mistakes. Personal, family mistakes. Let me tell you a little story. Something that happened to me today. Something that made me . . ."

"Oh Lord," said Sarah to Maria, "he's going to say a sadder and a wiser man."

"A sadder and a wiser man," said the senator in a sadder and wiser voice. "But a better man. A better father and husband."

"Well, shit," said Maria close to Sarah's ear.

"I'd planned a working Christmas vacation," went on the senator. "I sent my wife of thirty-six years, Maud-Emma, and my son, Arthur, to stay with Maud-Emma's folks. In Maud-Emma's beloved Talladega in the beautiful state of Alabama. I was going to hole up at a ranch to do some tall thinking about my future—and our country's future—with some of my good friends and my secretary."

"Lily Farnsworth—mad as a wet hen," said Cookie, who had sidled up to Sarah and Maria.

"Where have you put her?" whispered Sarah, remembering the scene at the front desk.

"Agave Annex. It's next to your cottage. We moved out all the folding cots and extra bedding and added flowers and wine."

Senator Hopgood now switched into his heavy-duty southern voice. ". . . and this afternoon when ah received the message that mah loved ones, Maud-Emma and mah boy, were going to be with me aftah all, well, y'all believe me, it's the best Christmas ah has evah had. There is no outside work—no matter how impo-tant it seems—that's worth bein' away from yo family."

"Darling, I may throw up," said Maria to Sarah.

"No," said Sarah, "it's perfect. We should freeze it."

The senator now leaned forward and the close-up cameras moved in so that his face, more like an egg than ever, filled half the screen, his voice back in its statesman groove. "I'm leveling with you now, as I will always level with you. The American people need the truth. The American people are smart, they know when you're not telling the truth. I intend to level with you about my whole life. I will give the American people an open book."

Suddenly Sarah became aware of a small vortex of movement in the corner of the listening crowd. Someone or someones taking the senator's proclamations to heart. The light was too dim, the crowd too large for Sarah to identify the source of the stirrings, but moving shoulders and bobbing heads suggested a certain agitation. "Let the chips fall where they may," said the senator, giving his chin an upheave. "The American people will forgive mistakes if they are acknowledged freely, and I will acknowledge now that I've made some mistakes. In judgment and in trust. But today is for me a new beginning. A clean slate. A fresh start."

"Sounds familiar," said Sarah to Maria.

"A new beginning with new hope and plans for our great nation," said Senator Hopgood. He paused and a smile creased his whole face. "And now, to you who hear and see me tonight, a joyous Hanukkah, a very merry Christmas. God bless you all."

"I need a very stiff drink," said Maria.

Sarah indicated a crush of people moving through the main lounge toward the Staghorn Bar. "You're not alone. Except not Mr. Simmons and party. They're above crass stimulation." She pointed as Fred Arco, the Howells, and Simmons moved toward the private dining room. "Perhaps," she added, "they're elevated by the idea of such a moral presence coming to the ranch for Christmas. Anyway, Hopgood didn't announce tonight."

"No, darling," said Maria, "he announced that he's going to announce."

Sarah yawned hugely. "Enough is enough is enough. Bedtime."

Maria looked disappointed. "The shank of the evening. No lighting of the Hanukkah candles, no Christmas carol singing? No Laddie Danforth and his magic guitar?"

"No," said Sarah firmly. "All I want is silent night." And she went forth to a sky full of stars and a full moon hanging in the heavens like a great translucent platter.

TEN

THE morning of Christmas Eve was clear and unexpectedly frosty, the thermometer standing at only thirty-eight degrees when Sarah went over for breakfast—a meal that was heavily invested with the seasonal spirit by the addition of cranberry muffins, kippers, and a steak and kidney pie. The chef's been reading Dickens, thought Sarah, who was sticking to toast.

"You're not going on the guest hayride, are you?" asked Cookie Logan when Sarah appeared at the desk to check her mail.

"Should I?" said Sarah. And then, "Even if I should, I can't. I've got to practice riding Pokey. Down that nice Buzzard Creek trail." This last was said in case Cookie feared that Sarah was having second thoughts about the evening's adventure. "Let's hope," she added a little nervously, "that no one comes along who wants to go into the mountains."

But going into the mountains is exactly what the rehearsal party did. Sarah—who had an honest fear of anything higher than a stepladder—was not able to stem the mountain enthusiasm of two ladies from Chicago. But Maria Cornish in a stage whisper told Sarah not to mind, and that she, Maria, was really psyched up and knew Buzzard Creek like the palm of her hand. Later, Maria drew her horse up to Sarah's at a scenic overlook into a gulch that sent spasms to Sarah's knees, and said, "No light colors. I'm wearing black with just a touch of purple. You do the same. You *do* have something black, don't you, darling?"

Sarah admitted to navy blue and Maria nodded her approval.

The ride being longer than usual, Maria, Sarah, and Blue Feather came late to lunch. This being so, Sarah thought it odd that the usual crowd was not pressing about the buffet table. She mentioned this to Cookie Logan, who was presiding over the two bowls of punch—one labeled "Adults Only," the other, "Nonalcoholic."

"Where are they all?" she asked Cookie.

"The morning hayride is late," said Cookie, and Sarah thought she said it with a certain satisfaction; in fact, so noticeable was her tone of voice that Sarah began having new ideas about Cookie. She remembered other times after the poltergeist had been at work when Cookie had not shown distress. And she remembered Cookie almost suggesting that morning that she not go on the hayride.

Sarah moved over to Maria, who was holding a full glass of punch. "I've got this idea about Cookie. I think she's quite happy about the hayride people being late. I think she wants something to happen. Or I should say, something more to happen."

At this moment a straggle of new arrivals, looking hot, disgruntled, and in two cases actually bandaged, came into the dining room and headed for the punch bowls.

Sarah joined the hayriders for a few moments, found them agitated and ready to talk. She returned to Maria and Blue Feather's table with the news.

"Wheel came off. Halfway out. Dumped half the wagon. Someone broke a wrist and has gone to the hospital, and two others—the ones with bandages—got cuts and bruises. One sprained ankle."

Maria nodded wisely. "Another of those funny little tricks. Only this time not so funny."

"Not funny at all. And Cookie looked pleased. In advance of the event, when she said the hayride was late."

"Darling, she'd probably heard about it before from one of the staff. The ranch van must have had to pick everyone up and someone had to arrange for the emergency room visit. You're wrong about Cookie. She and Judy just hold this place together."

"Yes," said Sarah slowly, "you have a point."

"It's probably a genuine accident," Maria said. "Wheels do come off. In movies all the time. And in life, too."

"Yes," said Sarah again. "They do. I wonder if Cookie was on the desk all morning. Never mind, I'm going to find out."

She returned chagrined. "Cookie," she said, "was on the desk at seven this morning. She worked late last evening in the lodge, and Judy spent the night at Cookie's house—Judy's cottage has been taken over by CBS. Anyway, even if Cookie fooled around with a wagon wheel, she couldn't have done all the tricks. They've happened all over the map and at all hours."

"I for one," said Maria, "am going with the poltergeist theory. Evil spirits. Trolls. Possessed bodies are very in."

"And I," said Blue Feather with thick truculence, "am going with the idea that this ranch is some fucked up."

With that remark, Sarah subsided, Maria glared at Blue Feather, and the three were well into dessert when Heinz Simmons rose in their midst.

It was Heinz Simmons at his smoothest. He was proud of what he could only call the good sportsmanship of his guests. Not guests, but friends. Real friends. Sometimes in life things do not run smoothly, but it takes sportsmanship to come up smiling. Now instead of the afternoon hayride there would be special games with prizes. Horseshoes, family races, and for the young and the young at heart, piñatas at three o'clock. Down at the old corral, just beyond the tennis courts.

Sarah turned to Cookie, who was going by with a clipboard. "Where's the old corral?" Sarah had had a sudden moment of panic, thinking that these games might encroach dangerously on their rescue plans, even run over into the witching hour itself.

"Between the new corral and the courts," said Cookie. "It's been paved over as a children's play area. I'm supposed to ask you if you want to play. Nice prizes. Mr. Arco just about cleaned out the gift shop after he heard about the hay wagon tipping over."

"Sounds like fun," said Sarah to Maria, as Cookie departed. "I suppose," she said to Maria, "we've got to go on pretending we're having a happy holiday. Not attract attention by being absent at fun and games."

"And," added Maria, "for the same reason, we'll be at the cocktail thing in our party best so no one will associate us with anything down at the corral. For ten minutes we can circulate like mad. Just like political candidates do."

Although the afternoon games had been scrambled together, the staff, Sarah decided, had done a creditable job. The ground crew, waitresses, Cookie Logan, and Judy Steiner had all been pressed into service, as had the cowboys—there being no trail riding that Sunday afternoon. Fred Arco presided over a long table heaped with packages wrapped in red paper and a long line of ribbons marked First, Second, and Third, and Maria Cornish graciously shook hands and gave out the prizes.

It was, Sarah thought as she wandered about from event to event, a real slice of Americana. A baseball toss, a basketball throw. A three-legged race for children, a water balloon relay. The horseshoes were won by Blue Feather, who threw his shoe with deadly accuracy. I'm certainly glad he's on our side, Sarah said to herself. What an arm.

"Quite a spread, isn't it?" said Cookie Logan, materializing again with an armful of Frisbees. "We only had two hours to put it together."

Sarah for a moment studied Cookie's face. That open, freckled face with a turned-up nose. A friendly face, the sort one thought of in connection with *Oklahoma!* Not a face to be involved with rubber snakes, loose golf balls, and wagon wheels.

But now Mr. Arco was calling the guests to order. It was piñata time. The manager climbed on a chair and explained. Fun for all ages. The higher piñatas were for the higher-up people (laughter). The medium piñatas were for the medium people, and the low ones were for the Munchkins (appreciative rustle among the parents). Fred Arco pointed overhead where Sarah could now see a collection of gaudy paper-covered animals hanging at different heights from a series of intersecting lines fastened from tree to tree. A frilled yellow dinosaur, a purple elephant, and a pink donkey for the little ones; a green horse, a blue pig, and an orange cow for those of medium reach; and highest of all for the long of reach and presumably the long of tooth, an enormous silver cow and a golden donkey.

Judy Steiner passed out the sticks and blindfolds, pressed parents into acting as guards, and the smallest children went to work and in a short time had battered their animals into pieces and been rewarded with a shower of wrapped candies and small toys.

The process was repeated for the older children—up to age twelve, Sarah thought—as they flayed about banging at the paper animals. Then it was time for those with the longest reach: youth and adults who were "the young at heart," as Heinz Simmons had put it. All ages went at it with a will, some with more energy than accuracy. But at last with a mighty swing Maud-Emma Hopgood connected with the silver cow, and one of the women Sarah recognized from her morning ride punctured the golden donkey.

And down came the shower. At first a trickle and then with several more connecting blows by other guests, a shower.

A shower of dark blue fluid that splattered and splashed on the upturned faces, on the shoulders and heads and arms of those who had not realized that candy and toys were not falling and continued to beat at the broken piñatas.

For a moment Sarah stared at the scene, and then quietly turned and made for her cottage, the shouts and cries of the blue-spattered guests sounding in their ears.

The room of Agave Three made a peaceful refuge: the white plaster walls reflecting the last of the late afternoon light, the mixed sounds of birds coming from the half-open patio window—these birds waiting, Sarah thought, for Alex to identify and log in his traveling bird diary. She walked to the window and remained for several minutes absorbed in the scene beyond. The Agave Cottage complex and its neighbor, Agave Annex, now home to Senator Hopgood's outraged secretary, were fortunate in being top-row end cottages and so had a splendid view not only of the undeveloped desert land that lay as a buffer between the residential sector and the fenced range, but of the connecting roads and the stable and corral buildings. There was, she thought, a sort of comfort in the mountain vista, the brown and purple shapes fading and merging with the darkening gray of the sky. And mountains themselves were satisfying. Barring a volcanic nature, they probably wouldn't fall down around one's feet for at least a millennium or so.

But now the patio lights and the lights along the main ranch road, Camino Rancho Grande, flickered to life, and with them Sarah's sense of comfort evaporated. Meanwhile, back at the ranch . . . it's like an old Marx Brothers movie, she decided. Or the Three Stooges. No, that wasn't quite right. How about Fawlty Towers, western style? Yes, that was it. Sarah shook herself and checked her watch. Quarter of five. Time to dress. Time to pack her riding equipment. Time to call Maria, get their act together.

Sarah walked to the phone and dialed Maria's room number. When Maria answered, her voice was heavy with annoyance. "That blue dye has absolutely ruined my suede skirt. You know suede, you have to treat it like a baby. It's an Yves Saint Laurent. I wore one like it in *Riders of the Lost Canyon.*

Sarah said what a wonderful role, Maria so magical, but hadn't they better coordinate?

And Maria, all business, coordinated. Leave party separately, change clothes, take separate paths to corral, she and Blue the low road, Sarah the one from the lodge, meet down there by quarter of six. She to keep a hand on Blue Feather at all times. "So he won't hit the booze, because he has absolutely no resistance. I'm going to tell his parole officer what a terrible burden he's been." And Maria hung up.

Well, how reassuring, Blue Feather with a parole officer, Sarah said to herself as she rolled up her blue jeans into a ball with her boots, a bandanna, a flashlight, and a jacket, and stuffed the collection into her swimming bag.

And now time was running short. Sarah slipped a blue wool dress over her head, wiggled it on, and fastened a rope of onyx beads around her neck. Then she hastily brushed her hair so the dark spikes lay flat, reached for her black sandals, and then stepped back to view the result in the bathroom mirror. Okay, a little like a character in a haunted house story; surely her eyes weren't quite that set-in and dark, her cheekbones that bony. Oh well, if they ever revived *The Addams Family*, she could try out. Draping a blue sweater over her swimming bag, she opened the cottage door and set out.

Sarah considered herself one of the world's experts on getting into, around, and out of a cocktail party in less than ten minutes. She hit the door at five-thirty and was glad to find that a considerable clutch of guests was already assembled, buzzing and gesticulating. Nothing like being splattered with dye to keep the conversation afloat, she thought as she prepared to take the plunge. Then, smiling brightly at no one in particular, she turned and started moving counterclockwise like a football player in slow motion. She twisted her way into the throng making sure she waved at Cookie Logan, nodded at Judy Steiner, was seen by a group including Maud-Emma Hopgood, Heinz Simmons, and Morty McGuire, and then slipped like a shadow out of the end of the room, through the library door, out to the terrace, doubled back to the coat room, and picked up her swimming bag at the back of the closet. On her way out, she tiptoed past the telephone booth, hoping the person encased there would not notice her departure. It was a person she recognized: Senator Hopgood's secretary, Lily Farnsworth, and her expression as she bent over the dial panel was one of pure rage. She's probably planning to booby-trap the senator, Sarah thought as she slid open a side door which opened toward the swimming pool.

The problem of an outdoor dressing room was solved by the discovery of an equipment shed with pool-cleaning apparatus. Five minutes later, her cocktail clothes hidden under a large plastic pail, at exactly sixteen minutes before six, she came up to the back of the corral to find Maria—in black and purple with silver studs and decorative hangings, the Nikon camera in one hand—and Blue Feather looking useful in jeans and a denim jacket.

And Cookie Logan.

Cookie incongruous in cocktail dress and high heels. "I had to come," she said. "Stevo was assigned to make sure the horses loaded okay on the transport, so I had to say I'd do it."

"But," said Sarah, "you can't be caught down here."

"I've got it figured," said Cookie. "I can handle the transport people, tell them we've taken the horses to Bosco's Pets ourselves in the ranch trailer and for them to bill the office. The office will think the horses are sold, and they won't find out for months when the dog food people don't pay. I'll think our way out of that when the time comes."

"Have you considered politics, Cookie?" said Sarah.

"Not after listening to the senator last night," said Cookie. "Look, I'm going to wait down at Corral Drive turnoff from the Rancho Grande Road and flag down the transport and turn them around. Here are the shipping papers, vaccination records, Coggins tests. The saddles are still hung up by the horses' names along with saddle blankets and bridles. Girths, too. I told Morty to leave 'em and ask no questions."

"Too many cooks mixed into this," murmured Sarah.

"A cast of thousands," said Maria. She looked very happy. "Blue's taken some stills of me next to the corral fence. And he's gone to bring out the three horses. They're being held in

107

that shed over there, aren't they?" Maria pointed to one of the larger sheds at the end of the corral fence. Cookie nodded and started down the road, her dress with its ruffled hem bouncing as she went.

And now it was quiet. Strangely quiet. Sarah, accustomed to the daily bustle of the corral, the farrier in his leather apron over in the corner shoeing a horse, the cowboys joking with guests, the business of saddling, adjusting stirrups, tightening girths, the horses behind the corral fence standing about switching their tails or, if it was close to their evening turning-out time, milling and bumping with each other. Now they were gone to their night range, the farrier's shed was closed, and not a cowboy was in sight. At least Sarah hoped there wasn't.

But there was little time for worrying. Blue Feather now returned, leading Copper. "I suppose you can't tack up by yourself," he growled. "Okay, I'll do it." And in seconds, Blue Feather had the saddle blanket in place on Copper's back, the saddle up, the girth cinched, and the bridle in place. "Okay," he said, "climb aboard and take him over by Maria. Don't dig him with your heels. Don't want a goddamn rodeo here."

Sarah agreed and succeeded in moving Copper over next to Maria, now mounted on Pecos Bill. She reached out over her saddle to Maria. "Here's your bandanna and flashlight."

Maria nodded, tied the bandanna around her neck, ready to slip over her face, and then they were joined by Blue Feather. He looked at Maria's costume with annoyance. "Christ, Maria, you'll shine like some damn reindeer. Let's get the hell out of here." And with that Blue Feather swung himself into Lollipop's saddle and tied on his bandanna.

"I'll go first," said Maria. "I've memorized the trail. It's positively boring. Sarah, you come behind me and then Blue on Lollipop can ride—what's it called?—shotgun?"

"I'll cover your ass, if that's what you're trying to say," said Blue rudely, and Sarah decided that Blue had managed to find some sort of stimulant. He was usually marginally polite to Maria, but not tonight. Sarah shivered in the cold evening air.

But then, as Blue swung Lollipop in behind Maria, the mare

flattened her ears and burst out in a series of bucks, humps, and crowhops and Blue proved conclusively that despite questionable sobriety, he had indeed spent time in the saddle as a stuntman. In no time Lollipop was pulled up, shaken out, collected, and then moved, snorting, in behind Pecos Bill.

"Nicely done, Blue," sang Maria, "but watch your lip, darling, or you're going to end up in some very nasty soup and I will be only too happy to stir the pot." And Maria pressed her leg into Pecos Bill's side and the three horse thieves moved at a sedate walk toward the gate and the road that led to the desert trails.

Blue Feather opened the gates, dismounting and mounting, and letting the others pass through until they lined out on the path that merged with the beginning of Buzzard Creek trail.

"Now all hell'll break loose," said Blue.

"What do you mean?" said Sarah, alarmed.

"Going past the night range. All our horses have buddies out there—they're herd bound, and one of them's gonna start hollerin' and then they'll all sound off."

Sarah had no time to ask what "herd bound" meant before there began an immediate demonstration of the word. Thundering to the wire fence, the entire Rancho del Gato Blanco company of horses stood neighing, stamping, calling. Answered in ear-piercing bellows by Pecos Bill, Copper, and Lollipop.

"My God," said Sarah, "someone will hear us. Or see us."

But no one came charging out from the corral shouting, "Cease! Desist!" and the riders by the dint of much heel and leg pressing made it past night-range boundary to the trail.

It was now so dark that it was a matter of squinting at the trail to see if they were truly on it and not wandering loose down some intersecting wash or narrow gulch.

"If we'd waited," said Sarah, "there'd be a full moon."

"If we'd waited," said Maria, "the horses would be dog food."

The air grew colder, the night darker, and as Sarah zipped her windbreaker close to her chin, she thought of the cowboys who even on Christmas Eve in states like Montana and Wyoming had to ride out in a whipping snowstorm to check their herd or bring in strays. She supposed she was lucky to be so comfortable. And Copper seemed surefooted and docile so that Sarah almost felt that being in a saddle—even in the dark—was a natural state of affairs. The rhythm of her horse's walk, the creak of leather, the small clink of a horse's hoof hitting a rock, all seemed increasingly reassuring.

Yet somehow travel in the dark to a destination which had been less than an hour away in the daylight seemed endless. Several times Pecos Bill and Maria on the lead left the path, and they had to circle around with flashlights looking for the trail.

"At least it's not raining," said Sarah as they headed down a small decline. We can see hoofprints."

"Goddamn right," said Blue from the rear. "Because if we lose the trail we could end up in some fucking canyon."

Blue Feather Romero, thought Sarah, sets my teeth on edge, but, she reminded herself, we'd be in real trouble without him, as Blue, now for the fifth time that night, picked up the trail.

Then at last, riding along a slight ridge, they saw below them the outline of Cat Claw Ranch, the windows of the main building blazing with light and a large fir tree by the front porch bright with red, yellow, and white Christmas bulbs.

"Gotta be careful," said Blue. "It'll be tricky coming down if their horses are close and start yellin'."

Sarah said that Mrs. Younger had told them the horses would be away on their night range.

"They got a dog?" demanded Blue.

Sarah tried to remember. Hadn't there been an orange and white presence on the porch, an old dog? "A collie, I think. An old one. Maybe he's inside. Collies usually bark."

"Cross your fingers," said Maria. "Go on, Blue."

They descended, loose stones rolling from the horses' hooves, sounding to Sarah's ears like bombs falling. But now the main Cat Claw lodge was close enough for her to hear singing. Sarah hoped Cookie was there by now, leading everyone in the noisiest carols.

And then the dog began. A loud staccato series of barks. The three travelers in one motion pulled their horses to a stop and held their breaths. But, blessedly, a door opened and closed on the lodge porch and the barking ceased abruptly.

They moved forward, and just as it seemed they might be riding onto the ranch front porch, the trail, now illuminated by a lamp fastened to the side of a shed, led them behind two linked corrals.

Maria, riding ahead of Sarah, gave out a long bubbling sigh. "I'm getting quite shaky and my stomach is really unsettled."

"Tough shit," came Blue's voice from behind Sarah.

But Sarah was trying to remember the layout. She studied the corrals, located the row of guest cabins, and nodded. "Okay," she said softly. "I know where we are. Just follow that path to the main road and hope to God Aunt Julia's there."

She was.

"Piece of cake," said Aunt Julia, emerging from the driver's seat of what looked to Sarah in the dark to be the section of an Amtrak passenger train. A silver body stretched for miles. "Six-horse van," she said. "Laura's four-horse was up for repairs. Now, we've got to load fast. You're almost forty minutes late. Take the saddles and bridles off and get those halters on. Who has the veterinary papers?"

Sarah, to whom the papers had been entrusted, handed them over, and Julia with Maria's help and Blue's strong arm began the process of unsaddling and loading three horses in the dark.

This finally accomplished—Lollipop having proved reluctant—Julia turned to her confederates. "I'll drop you off at the Corral Drive entrance, it runs off the main ranch road. Maria and Sarah can walk directly back to the ranch staying away from the regular ranch paths. They'll change their clothes and join the Christmas goings-on. Blue Feather, you must take care of the saddles and other gear. Be very careful, stay away from Corral Drive. If anyone's at the corral, lie low until you can get the tack back where it belongs. You'll have to make two trips."

"Christ," said Blue Feather. "You don't want much, do you? Busting my ass all night and then sneaking the tack back."

"Blue," said Julia, "you are very rude considering you are being adequately compensated for your trouble."

"Blue Feather," said Maria Cornish, "will bust his ass gratis. And now I need one or two quick photographs taken before we drive off. The van makes a good background."

It was almost eight forty-five when Julia Clancy slowed the six-horse van on Rancho Grande Road, turned into Corral Drive, and stopped. "Clockwork," she said triumphantly. "Smooth as silk."

In a matter of minutes Blue Feather, loaded with two of the saddles, a handful of bridles, and a saddle blanket, disappeared into the brush by the side of the road.

Julia started the engine and turned to Sarah and Maria. "Don't start out yet. Wait until Blue's been gone for five minutes." And then she added, "Turning this baby around is not that easy, but since no one's around I can take my time." They waited in silence and then Sarah and Maria stepped cautiously into the night.

"Someone *is* around," said Sarah. She pointed at the dark shape of a car pulled up on the verge of the main road some hundred yards behind them.

"Guests come for the Christmas Eve party, I suppose," said Julia, looking down from the cab of the van. "I'm blocking its way, but whoever it is can turn and go through the main entrance."

"Whoever it is may have been watching us," Sarah worried.

"No problem," said Aunt Julia. "No one has seen horses leaving, just the van arriving. And this van has no connection to us. It's Laura's Maryland farm trailer with a Maryland license. No one on Christmas Eve is going to start calling Maryland. Sarah, you are so very apprehensive. Now, start off, both of you."

Sarah and Maria watched the great horse van back and turn and back and do considerable damage to the vegetation at the edge of the road. Finally the vehicle made its circle and disappeared down the Camino Rancho Grande whence it had come. And in watching Julia disappear, the two women missed a good look at the impatient entrance of the waiting car, a dark car with an expensive profile. It swerved from the Rancho Grande Road, gunned into Corral Drive, ran a distance up the hill, slowed, and turned. A left turn, easily visible by the rising full moon.

"Right toward the corral," whispered Sarah. "My God, he'll catch Blue Feather."

"Blue Feather," said Maria in her penetrating whisper, the sort of whisper Sarah knew could reach all the way to the last row in the balcony, "Blue Feather is very sensitive to strangers. I gather from his parole officer that he was always remarkably difficult to jump. Now, we must get ready to slip into the lodge, one at a time as if we've been there for ages. I shall wear my red sheath with the amethyst choker."

Sarah fell in beside Maria and they began a slow traverse over rough ground toward the row of lighted cottages.

"I think," said Sarah, "that Aunt Julia could take elephants over the Alps and do it better than Hannibal, and I think you'd do a great job as Annie Oakley."

Maria squeezed her hand and they walked along in silence. Then, as they began their climb up the little side path that led to the Agave complex, Sarah pointed at the rising moon. "We could have used that tonight." And then, "Maria, do you believe the animals talk on Christmas Eve?"

"Darling, shall we? Go down to the corral and try our luck?"

But Sarah shook her head regretfully. "I suppose we'd better follow the plan. But what I'd really like to know is whether Blue Feather was caught by that man in the car."

"It was a Cadillac, dear. One of those little luxury ones. I'm really quite good about cars. And are you sure we shouldn't visit the animals? You could pat Pokey and I could say Feliz Navidad to Diablo."

Sarah hesitated, much tempted. The crowded hothouse holiday commotion of the lodge sounded more and more like something to be avoided. Then caution won out. Sarah detached herself from a piece of prickly vegetation and shook her head. "No, we'd better go right back and hit the Christmas crowd. Follow orders."

And following Julia's orders, Sarah reflected later, was something that she never afterward regretted.

ELEVEN

SARAH, checking her watch under the Agave Three porch light after picking up her clothes in the swimming bag, found that she had made it back to Agave Cottage Three a few minutes after nine-twenty. She opened the door and found two notes on the floor.

The first, incautiously signed "Cookie," said in a penciled scrawl: "OK, caught the transport and sent them off." The second was a sheet with the ranch logo at the top. It reminded guests that Christmas breakfast would begin an hour later than usual, nine o'clock, to allow members of the staff time with their families. For early risers a continental breakfast tray could be requested. Opening of stockings and distribution of the presents around the tree for everyone would begin at ten o'clock. The last sentence informed guests that Santa and his Christmas chuck wagon will arrive at the lodge at eleven-thirty with surprises for guests and staff.

Good Lord, Sarah thought, they're not trying another chuck wagon event. But then she remembered the wagon she and Julia had seen decorated with the sleigh bells. The ranch probably had a second and even a third chuck wagon standing ready. She put down the two notes and stepped toward the bedroom and immediately stumbled into a large duffel bag.

Good grief. Alex. She'd completely forgotten Alex. His plane had been due in Phoenix at seven-thirty and here he was. Or was he? She looked distractedly around the empty living room and then saw that the bedroom door was closed. She walked to it, opened it, and beheld Alex full length on the bed still in traveling dungarees and a heavy sweater.

For a full minute the fact of a sleeping and probably exhausted man overwhelmed Sarah's need to change her clothes and get back to the Christmas Eve party. And then a sense of urgency overtook compassion and she walked over and shook Alex's arm. He sat up immediately and immediately lay down again, extending a hand. "Sarah, where in God's name have you been? Kiss me hello. I'm so beat I just flopped down without taking off my shoes."

Sarah bent forward soberly, kissed Alex, and then perched on the edge of the bed. "Do you want the good news or the bad?"

"What the hell do you mean, bad news? I've just got here, how could there be bad news? The only bad news you could give me would be that I have to get up and go into that Christmas zoo I saw going on at the lodge. So give me the good news."

"The good news is I'm so happy you're here and I love you, and the bad news is as described. Get up, get dressed, and go to the party. We have to. At least I do and it will be easier with you."

Alex sat up again and Sarah saw his black hair disordered, his face creased with fatigue, and his rather grim mouth considerably grimmer. "The hell I will," he said.

Sarah didn't answer but struggled out of her jeans, grabbed her blue wool dress, now rather rumpled from its stint in the swimming bag, and pulled it over her head. Then she returned to the bed, took Alex's hand, and said very quietly, "Listen. It's hard to explain in five minutes, which is all I've got, but here's what happened and please, Alex, don't interrupt or swear. Just listen."

And Sarah in a tour de force of fast narrative told Alex of Julia Clancy's horse rescue plot, of the assistance of Blue Feather Romero and Maria Cornish, of Cookie Logan and the transport, and then roughed in the sequence of not-so-funny stunts that had had the ranch on its ear since the Christmas holidays had begun.

Alex looked not only as if he didn't believe his ears but that he didn't even want to make the effort.

"Jesus, Sarah, you are stark raving crazy. Riding three stolen horses over a trail at night. With a movie star and this thug Blue Feather. And Julia should be locked up."

"She probably will be. Maybe all of us. Now, please, Alex, I have to go and circulate. Won't you come?"

Alex rose slowly and, wearing the expression of someone about to strangle the nearest person at hand, walked over to his duffel bag and extracted a shirt, a tweed jacket, and a tie.

They reached the lodge at five minutes to ten, Alex not speaking and Sarah in a state of suspended anxiety. The lodge activities had plainly reached stage two: parents were busy rounding up tired and overexcited small children who, having hung their stockings along a clothesline stretched the length of the massive fireplace, now whimpered on their parents' laps or ran panting in decreasing circles around the room.

"The object," Sarah said through her teeth, "is not to be conspicuous."

"I," said Alex, "have no damn intention of being so."

Sarah pointed at the doorway. "That's Maria Cornish."

"She's conspicuous enough for both of us."

"Even if Maria wore a bag over her head," said Sarah, returning a wave and a kiss across the room, "she would still be conspicuous."

As promised, Maria, looking rather like an ancient Egyptian in her red sheath with the jeweled collar, floated across the room. She held a glass of champagne in one hand, in the other a cigarette holder without a cigarette. "For looks, darling," she explained, seeing Sarah eyeing the last item. "I've never smoked."

"And where," demanded Sarah after introductions had

117

taken place and Alex had remained scowling and silent, "is Chief Blue Feather?"

"Probably at the bar. After all, he's had a long day on a short leash. And I see that Mrs. Senator Hopgood is also without her other half. Over there by the tree."

Sarah looked around and saw Maud-Emma Hopgood in violet standing next to the senator's two aides. Maud-Emma's lower lip suggested a very unhappy frame of mind, but from time to time she shot a brave-looking smile at whoever was closest. Artie was nowhere in sight.

"Maud-Emma was imported," Sarah told Alex, "to make a togetherness-at-Christmas scene. He's probably just late. Or coming tomorrow morning. Senators who want to be president have a lot on their minds."

"Maud-Emma had better be one of the things on his mind," said Maria. "She's looking a little off-color. And where's the secretary, the one they shoved out into Agave Annex?"

But now Judy Steiner, in a red jumpsuit, came up. "Where have you been, Miss Deane? I know Mrs. Clancy's away but the waitress said you hadn't canceled dinner. I suppose you went down to Lodestone, but next time let us know in advance if you can."

Sarah struggled with the problem of claiming a restaurant in Lodestone and Maria saved her.

"Not Lodestone. I meant to cancel Miss Deane when I canceled Mr. Romero's and my dinner. We just had a tiny party in my suite. Food from such a nice little place in Lodestone. We took the phone right off the hook."

Judy departed and Sarah thanked Maria. "You did that awfully well," she said.

"Well, after all, darling, it's my job. If I can't turn up with a nice ad-lib lie at my time of life, I might just as well go to an actors' retirement home. Now, I must try and hunt up Blue Feather." And Maria moved off, an undulating figure in red, her champagne glass held high.

Sarah, followed by Alex, retreated to an alcove ostensibly to watch the windup of the Christmas Eve programs. The younger children had now been cleaned out and the older ones herded into the library room for a showing of *A Christmas Carol.*

"Keeping the troops happy," said Sarah. "No one *reads* it anymore, they just see different versions. Okay, Alex, one half hour more and then bed, okay?"

"Not okay. You've all taken leave of your senses and now you've made me an accomplice. Or some kind of damned adjunct." Alex glared at Sarah but just then a chord sounded from the fireplace.

"It's Laddie Danforth," she said. "He's going to sing."

"The man is drunk," said Alex irritably.

"Well, yes, he usually is—partly. But he can sing."

Laddie, dressed à la Roy Rogers, swayed slightly and struck a second chord.

"Stop being so cross," said Sarah. "We're going down the homestretch. Just flow with it."

So they flowed. Through "We Three Kings," "Angels from the Realms of Glory" (made into "Realmsh of Glory" by Laddie), and a tender and slightly off-key rendition of "Silent Night."

Walking back to their cottage, Sarah said, "No more recriminations, no more strictures. Just love. Christmas is a time of forgiveness, remember?"

"I wonder if this ranch is going to forgive the stealing of three horses."

"Save all that for Julia. She's our founder. I just buckled under. And Maria had an absolute ball."

"You don't seem to have struggled against it."

"Go find Blue Feather. You can both be disagreeable together."

"I came here to be agreeable with you."

"Then be so. The horse business is over and done. Look at all those guests who had blue dye splattered all over them. They weren't complaining. I told you it's a time of forgiveness."

"Which will last," said Alex, "for a couple of days or until they get their cleaning bills."

"Be quiet." Sarah reached over and tucked Alex's hand

under her arm. She walked a few steps, stopped, and examined the sky. Full moon and stars. "Remember Marcellus in the first act? About Christmas Eve?

". . . they say, no spirit dare stir abroad,
The nights are wholesome, then no planets strike,
No fairy takes nor witch hath power to charm,
So hallow'd and so gracious is the time."

"Except," said Alex, "after that things really went downhill in Denmark."

"Never mind. I think this evening was the absolutely perfect night to rescue three horses. Aunt Julia did the proper thing. Think kindly. It's almost Christmas."

Alex heaved an enormous sigh. "All right, I'm still sure you have rocks in your head, but, well . . ." He smiled down at her. "To all a good night."

Long after Sarah had fallen asleep, she half woke to the small crunch of tires from the parking lot that adjoined the Agave Cottage complex. Then a car door closing, determined footsteps, and the door of Agave Four opening and closing.

She turned sleepily on her pillow and nudged Alex. "Aunt Julia's made it home."

"Good for her," Alex mumbled, and rolled over.

At seven-thirty Christmas morning Sarah sat up. "She did make it home, didn't she? Or did I dream it?"

Alex yawned. "Go and look out."

Sarah, pulling on her kimono, made a cautious trip across the floor to the patio door, opened it, and returned. "She's back. Or her car is. Merry Christmas."

"The same to you, and many of them. And someone's at the door."

It was the continental breakfast. Two trays, brought by a sleepy-looking man in a white jacket. Coffee for Alex, tea for Sarah, a flagon of orange juice, and a basket of cinnamon buns.

"I called in the order last night," explained Alex. "Just before we went to bed. In the spirit of forgiveness. Coffee for me and tea for thee. And I have something for you. Before or after your shower? Or breakfast?"

"With breakfast, please. Not the big one at the lodge. Just our little event here."

After the orange juice and the first life-giving drafts of caffeine, Sarah presented Alex with his flannel shirt and a bolo tie with the turquoise and silver slide which featured the ranch brand, an interlocking *g* and *b*.

Alex gave thanks and presented Sarah with an incised silver bracelet. "Navajo design," he said. "I bought it at the airport."

"It almost matches the one I'm giving Aunt Julia. Lovely, because I was dying to keep it."

"Virtue is its own reward."

"No, a silver bracelet is." Sarah extended her arm and admired her present.

"Tell me about Julia," said Alex, buttering his roll. "Why is she so against Christmas? I mean abnormally so. We all hate the junk and tacky sales pitch, but she's really vehement."

"I don't think she's sentimental about holidays in general, but it's more than that. Uncle Tom—you know they didn't get married until Julia was over forty—well, Uncle Tom died suddenly about the twentieth of December, and I think Aunt Julia had a terrible time enduring other people's attempts to cheer her up and call up the Christmas spirit. Uncle Tom was an Irishman who lived for his horses, and it was a match made in heaven. As long as it lasted, twenty years or so. Though after last night, she may feel that she's rehabilitated Christmas."

"I suppose the real winner in this horse business," said Alex, "besides the horses, will be Maria Cornish. All the publicity, Senator Hopgood coming in, and every network in the country coiled around the place ready to strike. If Maria plays her cards right—and I can see she's a real pro—it will be seen as a great coup for the Save the Animals movement. People will write in offering to adopt every horse in the place and money will be put in envelopes addressed to Pecos Bill and Copper and Lollipop. We can siphon off some of the cash to take care of Julia's bail. And yours."

"Okay," said Sarah, "and now, assuming Aunt Julia is sleeping the sleep of the righteous, let's us dress and get some fresh air."

Alex agreed and they took a brisk trip, half jog, half fast walk, around the entire complex, noting as they went that the television network vans had moved closer to the front door and that cables stretched around the entrance as well as disappearing into the ranch building windows.

"Senator Hopgood must not have come last night," said Sarah as they made their way to the main lodge.

"Or he came in and they're waiting for him to make it to breakfast," said Alex. He pushed open the front door, waved at Judy at the desk, and walked into the Christmas morning bedlam of little children dragging stockings about the big living room and parents and staff chasing them down and crumpling colored paper and ribbon into waiting wastebaskets.

But Julia Clancy was not asleep; she was at the breakfast table, a plate heaped with scrambled eggs and bacon in front of her. She waved her fork at them. "I deserve cholesterol after last night, though I'm not as tired as I expected to be. All is well. I stayed to see the three beasts bedded down, stalls next to each other so they can hear familiar noises. I don't see Maria and Blue but I assume everything went like clockwork."

"A car did turn in toward the corral last night," said Sarah. "About the time Blue Feather was toting saddles to the corral."

"As long as he kept his head," said Julia. "Told whoever it was he was there patting horses. Or taking an evening ride. It's a little eccentric but probably lawful. Has the senator come, because I see the networks are at our throats?"

The question was answered by the arrival of Maud-Emma Hopgood and Artie coming from the breakfast buffet table. Artie appeared to be carrying a champagne cocktail.

"I don't see him, so I suppose Maud-Emma is still putting on what they call a brave face," said Sarah, indicating the uptilt of Mrs. Hopgood's nose. "Do you suppose the senator's standing her up?"

"Perhaps Hopgood's going to make a grand entrance, the kind Maria Cornish would approve of," said Julia.

"Yes," said Sarah. "He'll stride into the dining room—when it's packed, of course—hair flying, briefcase in hand, polo coat over his shoulders, and he'll sweep Maud-Emma into his arms, gather Artie to him, signal to the media, and then wish us all a very, very, very merry."

"Which is why you went into literature," said Julia. "Alex, it must be a thrill a day with Sarah."

"I have an overheated imagination," said Sarah. "Alex, are you going for a second breakfast?"

"Certainly," said Alex. "Eggs, pancakes, bacon, sausages, all the killer foods."

"Me, too," said Sarah.

At the finish of breakfast, Sarah presented her aunt with the silver bracelet and exhibited her own. Julia was gracious. "If I dress up—which I rarely do—I will certainly wear this." She folded her napkin and pushed back her chair. "Since there's no riding, what do you say to a walk? Yes, I know you've just had one, but you're young and I must keep my joints moving."

So they walked. Down to the golf course, where a foursome was teeing off, then around the tennis courts and children's playground, where Sarah saw in the sandy ground that a few dark blue stains still lingered. "Best to keep completely away from the corral," said Julia. "Never return to the scene of the crime."

Alex, binoculars at the ready, claimed a verdin and a distant Harris hawk and several jackrabbits. Which reminded Sarah, "How was your hunting, Aunt Julia? She was fox-hunting jackrabbits with a hunt, the Peeple's Valley Hounds, or something like that," Sarah explained to Alex.

"Sarah, you don't listen. It's the Peeple's Valley Beagles and they hunt only jackrabbits, not foxes, and it was perfectly splendid. Laura gave me one of her favorite mares, a thoroughbred. Named Mrs. Friska. She took every fence and gulch and heaven knows what else and I simply sat there. Great heavens, what's that?"

Julia pointed to a large open wagon hung with sleigh bells and drawn by two heavy-duty animals. At the reins, Santa Claus.

This vehicle, swaying heavily, rumbled up the road, and Santa as the horses drew abreast waved cheerily. "Ho, ho, ho!"

"Good grief, it's Morty McGuire," said Julia.

Santa adjusted his beard to facilitate speech. "I'm afraid so, Mrs. Clancy. Management is trying to make friends. Come along and see the fun, something for everyone."

"How awful," said Julia as Santa gave a flick of his whip and the horses moved on. Now the three watchers could see that the entire open wagon contained a huge brown sack from which protruded a mountain of Christmas-wrapped packages.

"Let's go, Aunt Julia," said Sarah. "Give Morty some support. After all, we're supposed to be normal fun-loving guests."

Julia grimaced. "All right, but it's been a long twenty-four hours. I think after this Santa nonsense I'll have a little lie-down and a nice read. The new Dick Francis."

What seemed like the entire guest population and staff had been herded onto the front portico of the lodge. Standing front and center in a command position, Fred Arco was flanked by Heinz Simmons. Behind them stood Esty Simmons and the Howells. On stage left, Cookie Logan stood beside her husband, Todd, and Stevo, the other cowboys, their wives and children, as well as Laddie Danforth. On stage right, stretching around the edge of the cactus garden, were the entire kitchen staff and the grounds crew, along with the golfing and tennis staff. Apparently there were to be presents for all.

"Bountiful Mr. Simmons," said Sarah.

Judy Steiner appeared at Sarah's elbow. "An old tradition. They had a Santa in the chuck wagon way back when it was White Cat Ranch. Presents for all the staff, mostly joke presents, and funny little souvenirs for the guests. Only about thirty guests and a small staff then, so it was easy."

"It's quite something now," said Sarah. "That huge sack."

Judy shrugged. "It's gotten a little out of hand, but Mr.

Simmons thinks it's good publicity. And this year, with all the goings-on and guests gunning for us, it's bound to ease things. Upgraded presents for guests and children. And Mr. Arco added a toy for each child under the tree this morning."

"Well, I certainly think you have to do something," said Julia. "I've just heard about the piñatas. There had jolly well better be good goods in those boxes."

But just then a television crew muscled its way forward, a man climbed to the wagon and fastened a microphone to Santa McGuire's chest, and Sarah heard a man in a blue coverall with ABC on the pocket say, "Jesus, we may as well shoot this Santa crap until Hopgood turns up. Get some background footage anyway."

The presentation began. First the guests. To each male, a bolo tie with the turquoise and silver slide, a twin to the one Sarah had given Alex. To each female a white enamel and silver pin in the shape of a cat. And then humorous presents which centered around long-standing jokes among the staff. Outsize aprons, chef hats, a stuffed owl, an outsize plush horse, a pair of tiny cowboy boots, a golf club with a shovel fastened to its end for golf pro Tommy Brass, a buggy whip for Judy Steiner, a megaphone for Laddie Danforth, and other items which, Alex reflected, if you happened to be privy to the inner workings of the ranch, might have been thought hilarious. The presentation seemed to go on forever, and Morty McGuire grew hoarse with his continued ho, ho, ho.

Midway into the presentation, Julia beat a retreat to Agave Four and Dick Francis. Sarah, pressed to the front of the crowd, lost sight of Alex, and just as she had decided that she had been acting the loyal guest far too long, Morty stood up and waved for silence. "That's about it, folks. Only one more present. Looks like a big one. Right at the bottom of Santa's bag."

"Bigger than this, Santa," shouted a man in a chef's cap. He held up a six-foot inflated plastic bottle labeled "Spice of the Old West" that he had just unwrapped.

"Bigger than that, Pete," said Morty, and Sarah knew the man must be the chef, Peter or Pierre Doubler.

Morty bent over his sack and fumbled into its bottom. Finally grunting, he said, "Gotta roll this one out." Suiting action to words, he took hold of the sack by its bottom and tried to shake the last present loose. "Christ almighty," Sarah heard Morty say entirely too loudly. "Give me a hand, Todd, will you?"

"Sure, Santa." And Tod Logan stepped forward and vaulted himself over the side of the wagon. Together they wrestled the object loose.

"Another bag of feed," grunted Santa. "I don't see a tag."

And then Todd stood up, pale, eyes wide. "Fred," he called. "Mr. Simmons. Come here." Then, "Judy, Cookie, get those people inside. Now. Pronto."

"What is it, Morty?" called Fred. "You're ruining the whole scene."

Morty stood up and pulled off his beard. His face was red over his tan. "I'm not what's ruining anything."

Fred Arco scrambled to the wagon, where Todd Logan was loosening the strings of the feed bags. He paused, bent over the wrapping, and then turned around and backed up. And threw up.

Senator Hopgood had arrived.

TWELVE

LATER, when Sarah had time to think about it, she decided the scene at the front portico was like one of those disaster drills conducted from time to time in small towns. Some people shout, some people try to move other people forward or backward, and no one listens to anyone else. The curious onlookers elbow the frightened out of the way, friends call "Over here," and clutch at each other and ask, "Is it really happening," and "Is it just another practice?"

In this case it was not a practice and it was really happening. The junior Republican senator from Alaska, Senator Leo J. Hopgood, had just been rolled out from the confinement of two poorly joined feed bags onto the bottom of the wagon through the combined efforts of Santa Claus, a.k.a. head wrangler Morty McGuire, and assistant head wrangler Todd Logan.

The senator was quite dead.

This was the considered opinion of Morty McGuire, Todd Logan, and Fred Arco, who, when he had recovered from his fit of nausea, returned to examine the remains. All three men had in their lifetime ample experience, one way or another, with death, and the senator's cold limbs, fixed eyes, and the two blood-soaked holes—one in the forehead, the other in the senator's gray silk shirt going directly through the monogram on the pocket—proved that Leo Hopgood was no more.

However, proper procedures must be followed. Clear the decks, call the police, get the doctor.

The decks took some time to clear and involved all the skilled herding talents of the corral staff, of Judy Steiner, Cookie, and chef Peter Doubler. Fred Arco, who might have been useful in this capacity, chose to conduct Maud-Emma and Artie to the swimming pool area and sent for Esty Simmons to act as comforter. Heinz Simmons went inside to call the police.

In the meantime, the general noise succeeded in flushing out those guests who had retired to the peace of the billiard room or to their cottages. These last included Aunt Julia, her half-glasses hanging around her neck, the new Dick Francis in one hand.

It was, in the words of Cookie Logan, a total zoo.

As for the call for a doctor, three physicians presented themselves. An ancient gentleman with a hearing aid, a young woman in an advanced state of pregnancy murmuring that she was a dermatologist, and Alex.

And of these, Alex was certainly the one most able to clamber aboard the chuck wagon without the possibility of adding yet another mishap to the growing list of Christmas misadventures.

This he did with dispatch. Taking a pull-up from Todd Logan, he swung himself into the wagon's seat, then over the seat into the main section of the wagon. But as he landed in the center of the wagon, the two paired horses, Samson and Goliath, grew agitated. What with the milling crowd, the general clamor, and the rising tide of television people now pressing forward, the great horses began to back and turn, throwing their heads and hauling the wagon sideways.

At which Aunt Julia, for whom all displays of horse temperament were her meat, stepped forward, stationed herself between the heads of both animals, took hold of their bridles, pulled down firmly on the gathered reins, and in a loud voice said, "Ho there, ho. I said, ho." And Samson and Goliath stopped cold.

"Someone," said Aunt Julia in her penetrating riding-ring voice, "should unharness these horses and take them back to the stable. They are becoming upset."

And Todd, seeing that Morty, Alex, and Fred Arco were quite sufficient to get on with the examination of Senator Hopgood, jumped lightly to the ground and began unhitching the pair.

Sirens sounded in the distance and Judy Steiner, having moved guests, returned and stood ready. Judy, decided Sarah, is the mortar holding the place together. If anything is holding it—a point that might be questioned. In fact, Sarah would not have been surprised to find the entire ranch complex break into chunks of adobe and tile and broken beams and go rolling off down the road into the desert. Sarah made her way to a set of wrought-iron garden chairs on the rim of the cactus garden and waited. But waiting for what? she asked herself, trying to shake off a creeping numbness that threatened to immobilize her forever on the hard chair. She felt just as if she had taken a solid bite out of a poisoned apple and its nerve-dulling venom was now seeping all the way to her fingertips and down through her ankles into her toes. And even her head felt heavy and her eyes cloudy, as if she not only saw through a glass darkly but was encased in some opaque substance that dulled sight and sound.

And that was something of a blessing, she reflected. Hear no evil, see no evil, feel no evil.

But bursting into this state of semiconsciousness came Maria Cornish. Alert and ready with exclamations.

"It's that senator," she said. "Quite dead. I heard Morty say so and I saw Alex shake his head. The television people are going absolutely mad."

Sarah gave herself a shake and made an effort to respond to her companion. Maria, as if dressed for the role of Cassandra, wore another of her Greco-Roman garments, all folds and drapes, and her dark hair was pulled back smoothly from her brow and held by a wreath of gold-leaf ivy. Sarah even wondered wildly if, on hearing that a body had turned up, Maria had rushed to her room, freshened her makeup, and changed her costume.

"The television people going mad?" Sarah repeated stupidly.

"Of course, darling. They're in hog heaven."

"You mean . . ."

"I mean what a godsend. Like Jack Ruby. On the spot. It only happens once in a lifetime, I suppose. A journalist's lifetime. Like that dirigible, the *Hindenburg* blowing up, or picking up survivors from the *Titanic*. The Berlin wall. Look at them."

Sarah looked. The media in motion. CBS crawling over an NBC camera, knocked to the ground, ABC and CNN and probably PBS and heaven knows who else were up and at 'em with a vengeance. The police hadn't come yet, and efforts of the staff to clear the area were met with a hostile resistance from the journalistic hordes. One enterprising man had vaulted into the wagon and was now bending over what must have been the senator's remains.

"Ghouls," said Sarah. "Bloody ghouls."

"Well, yes," said Maria. "But there it is. Life and death. Makes the world go round, doesn't it? Good copy, first spot on the evening news." She spread her hands in a gesture of hopelessness. "And really, darling, we can't do anything about it."

"I don't think we should lap up every detail of a tragedy," said Sarah crossly. "Encourage blood-and-gore journalism."

"You're a teacher, aren't you, Sarah? So, of course, you have these ideals, but the world doesn't work that way, darling. There's no use my pretending to be in a state of shock, because I'm not. I grew up on mean streets. Brooklyn. And of course, Hollywood can be absolutely bloodthirsty. The things that go on. To be honest, saving three horses strikes me as a lot more important than this senator being dead. From what I've heard he spent a lot of his time helping to pass legislation that actually *killed* animals—all those birds and dolphins and tundra moose or whatever they are. And he voted for single-hulled freighters and look at those dead otters just because of the Exxon spill."

Sarah looked at Maria. She sat composed, beautifully made up, her eyeliner particularly dark, her draperies artfully folded about her. She should be in Congress.

"Well," said Sarah slowly, "yes, I'm glad we saved the horses, but I'm damned if I want a body added to Christmas. And think of Artie, and poor Maud-Emma Hopgood trying to put on a good face about not being wanted by her husband, and then this happening."

"Think of Hopgood's secretary," added Maria. "She'll be hit hard, because I've heard things. Blue Feather was in the bar one night, and I gather that even if she was built like a mule she was a very hot item. At least the senator thought so."

"Then I'm sorry for the secretary, too," Sarah said.

Maria nibbled at a beautiful finger for a minute, frowning. "With all that's been going on, do you suppose Senator Hopgood is just the grand finale?"

Sarah shook her head. "I don't think you can put a dead senator in the same class as golf balls and tennis nets and squirting Aunt Julia with a hose."

"Loosening the wagon wheel wasn't very amusing. This may be the climax."

Sarah nodded. "We'll just have to wait and see, because the police will be crawling all over in another ten minutes, and I suppose that those so-called jokes will all be gone over."

"Police and then some," said Maria. "Probably the FBI."

Sarah was startled. "The FBI?"

"Sarah, my sweet, Senator Hopgood was on the Senate Armed Forces Committee . . . or subcommittee, wasn't he? And with that group that went to look at Albania. If he's been killed, I suppose the spooks will think it's Libya or Iraq. Or Panama."

"Spooks?"

"Spooks, agents, CIA, you know. Didn't you see my movie *Message from Moscow?* Very authentic. I played a Soviet ballerina who defected. The most adorable fur hats and lovely ballet scenes, though I had a stand-in for the onstage scenes. Oh, look, here come the police."

It was almost a relief. Sarah saw the flashing lights of three cars, one after another, just as they swung from the main road into the ranch entrance into the curving Rancho Grande Road that circled the ranch buildings. Beyond, far back on the main road, she now saw the white boxy shape of what must be the ambulance. Then a red truck. Then a series of dark sedans.

Maria bent close to her ear. "We've got to meet. Soon. Our story." Then, seeing Sarah's puzzled look, "My dear, we can't go to the police with fifty different accounts of what we were up to last night. That story, the real story, will come out later. It's a matter of timing. Now it's Senator Hopgood and whoever killed him that's important. Two o'clock, my room. The police won't get around to statements by then."

Sarah grasped at straws. "Perhaps he killed himself. Or died naturally."

"In the bottom of Santa's bag? When he was about to announce for the presidency? Darling!" And Maria rose, settled her draperies, and made her way gracefully to a point slightly nearer the scene of action.

It was amazing the difference made in the milling crowd by the forces of law and order. The ground by Santa's chuck wagon was cleared and roped off in a matter of minutes. Guests were ordered away from the area, the staff to their regular posts, the media to tennis and golf pro shops and the playground where they were to stay put. The corral whence the chuck wagon had come was cordoned off. Only escorted personnel were allowed there to tend the animals. All were reminded that no one was to leave the ranch complex until further orders. Statements would be taken, everyone would be as little inconvenienced as possible. It was now twelve-thirty; luncheon would be served at one o'clock. Guests were to eat at their usual tables and then return immediately to their rooms. Thank you.

Alex, freed by the arrival of the police and the laboratory crew, joined Sarah. "Sorry," he said.

"Sorry?"

"A general statement. Sorry for all concerned."

"It wasn't natural causes? Or an accident?"

"Not with two holes in him."

"Oh God."

"Exactly. It's going to be a long business. I think the FBI will be in on it. U.S. senator, internal security and all that."

"That's what Maria said. She's apparently an expert. Was in a spy movie. Very authentic."

"That woman hasn't an authentic hair on her head."

"Contrariwise. Underneath there's a steel breast and an iron foot. She wants us to get our stories straight. Her room at two."

"Stories? What stories?"

"Last night's adventure."

"You can't make up a story, you tell the truth."

"That isn't what Maria has in mind. She said it's a matter of timing. And if the police find out about the horses, well, I'm sure they'll be brought back and turned into dog food as planned."

"Certainly not, Sarah. What a negative view of things." It was Aunt Julia, her book still in her hand. "I've seen Maria. We meet at two. Her room."

"Tell the truth, Julia," said Alex. "Every word of it. Where you were, what you saw, what you heard. When and why."

"Alex, you're turning into a stuffed shirt. First, I'll have you know that when I saw that something had happened to Senator Hopgood, I went to the laundry pay phone to call Laura Freebody, and right now she is arranging to fly those three horses out today by cargo plane. She found slots on a carrier going to New York—race horses to Aqueduct. Patrick will met them with our van. Pecos Bill, Copper, and Lollipop should be arriving at the Phoenix airport any minute. Out of sight, out of mind, I say. Out of the police mind."

"The only reason I will meet at two with Maria," said Alex, "is to insist that you square with the police. Julia, Sarah, have either of you any idea what happens when you begin to freelance in a criminal case?"

"Certainly, dear," said Julia. "It confuses things. It prevents them from trying to trace my horses."

"The police probably don't give a damn about the horses. But someone shot, got that, shot, plugged, Senator Hopgood. He's dead and he's been murdered. If you play games with the police you're probably helping the murderer, or you may help put the blame on some innocent person."

"Alex," said Julia in a reasonable tone. "I'm sure we all want to tell the truth. But we want to tell the same truth, if you know what I mean. I was visiting Laura so I have no first-hand idea of what was going on. I got home very late—or early—five in the morning and went right to bed. My story is quite simple, but it should fit with the others. What we want to do is make sure that we don't irritate the police. I see no reason to load their plate with more information than they can handle. Information," she went on in her firmest voice, "that is entirely irrelevant."

"Aunt Julia," said Sarah, "if you think you can get the same truth from Maria and Blue Feather, you are dreaming."

"We'll talk it over at lunch," said Julia. "We must all try to think clearly. Alex, have you gone and helped that poor senator's wife? I imagine she must be in shock."

"Yes," said Alex. "I did, but I can't treat her without an Arizona license. She did have a tranquilizer in her bag and I suggested she take the dose her doctor prescribed. Her son, Artie, and Mrs. Simmons are with her now."

"You've done your best, then," said Julia. "Now, I'm a little worried about Cookie Logan. She's the one who told me about the horses. I've thought that she wasn't really unhappy about all these so-called practical jokes that have been taking place."

Sarah looked at her aunt. "I've had the same idea. Don't forget that her parents own Cat Claw Ranch."

"You two, stop that right now," said Alex as they moved into the crowd of guests lined up for the dining room door. "Don't start speculating, thinking you have to do something."

"Really," said Aunt Julia. "None of the younger generation can think or act positively. *Carpe diem,* that's my motto."

"But you, dear aunt," said Sarah, "you've gone and carped more than diem, you've carped three horses."

Considered as Christmas dinner, Sarah thought, this one was certainly in a class by itself.

Much of the table setting had obviously taken place before the arrival of the defunct Senator Hopgood at noon. Baskets of red- and green-wrapped candies stood at every place, and a cracker and a paper hat lay in the center of every red place mat.

And most of the feast itself was ready: the turkey and ham cooked and decorated, the cranberry salads in their little bowls, the chestnuts mashed, the sweet potatoes glazed, the rice pilafed, the peas and okra buttered, the onions creamed. But last-minute items had suffered: the corn bread was cold, the paella appeared without its seafood, the *buñuelos de plátano* were soggy, and the plum pudding was a depressing dark lump without flame or brandy.

Strangely enough, some of the guests appeared not to have heard the news. Sarah looked about in astonishment as a young couple and their three children happily pulled at their crackers, blew on their horns, and donned the paper hats. As did white-haired twin sisters who had arrived the night before.

"What can they be thinking of?" demanded Aunt Julia as she unfolded her napkin.

"They must not have heard," said Sarah.

"Slept late," suggested Alex.

"Through all that?" said Sarah.

"Certainly," said Aunt Julia. "When you're tired, you can sleep through anything. I suppose it's quite possible to come in the dining room from the back doors and not have a clue about Senator Hopgood." Aunt Julia indicated a large man and two women at a nearby table wearing gold paper crowns.

But bad news sometimes travels as fast as good, and by mid-meal it was clear that word had gotten round. Paper hats came off, voices were lowered, and a somber air hung over the dining room. At several tables, guests rather ostentatiously put down their knives and forks, folded their napkins, and departed, saying audibly they couldn't eat another bite.

Not so Julia. "I see no reason to skip lunch because of Senator Hopgood. I'm very sorry about it but one must keep one's strength up." Julia speared a piece of dark meat, added a lump of stuffing, and chomped down.

Alex, for whom meals were often events caught on the run between seeing patients, concurred. "I learned early on that my being starved wasn't going to help my patients."

To Sarah alone, a minority of one, was left the honor of finding food distasteful and making futile pushing movements with her fork. And then giving up the attempt.

"I know it's sensible to eat," she said, "but I can't. I do keep thinking about bodies in bags, and Maud-Emma, and the whole thing. And you know," she added to Julia, "this has happened before. Bodies, I mean. I have, Alex and I have, stumbled onto them, and I've hated it."

"So your mother told me," said Julia, moving on to a slice of mince pie. "It must be kismet. Well, since you and Alex have had all this experience, I'm expecting you to handle our horse affair and even help the police out like real professionals."

"Which we aren't," exclaimed Sarah with some vehemence, "though, of course, Alex is one of the local medical examiners at home so he knows what he's doing."

"But I'm not a forensic pathologist," said Alex, "and believe me, this affair *is* going to be handled by professionals."

Julia put down her fork. "I for one shall not muddy the investigative waters."

"Stay out of the investigative waters. Don't even get your feet wet, Julia," said Alex. "And don't encourage Maria, because here she comes with an escort."

Sarah looked up to see Maria twisting her way between tables, smiling down at occupants as if blessing them briefly with her presence. Blue Feather followed, he, too, smiling. And that smile, like almost nothing else besides the death of the senator, alarmed Sarah. It reminded her of crocodiles. Why should Blue Feather smile? Had Maria given him some new and signal mark of favor? In bed? Drugs, money?

But Sarah was denied any chance of finding out. At the very point of arrival at Julia's table, a man in a gray suit stepped swiftly forward, took hold of Maria's elbow and Blue Feather's shoulder. "I'm sorry, but we're asking that the guests stay at their own tables until they finish their meal and then go directly back to their rooms." And with a practiced hand he started the two on their return trip, Maria having just time for a sharp look at Julia and then at her own watch.

"Maria won't make it in the real CIA," observed Alex. He allowed himself a look at his own watch. "It's ten of two. We certainly can't go to our cottage and then back to Maria's, so we'd better hang around, have coffee, and go directly there."

"Won't they know we don't belong with Maria?" said Sarah.

"I doubt that they're that organized as yet. In another hour or so maybe they'll have a working list of who stays where, but right now they must be busy securing the exits, posting men, making sure no cars take off, and getting some sort of fix on the death details. It's probably safe."

So it proved. Sarah and Alex, by dint of rising with deliberation and nodding at the man by the dining room door who repeated the injunction, "To your rooms, please," set off as if they knew what they were doing and went down the long hall of the main lodge toward the southern wing and Maria's Desert Star Suite.

"Really, it's too James Bond," said Maria as she led the way to the patio—a large walled enclosure with six garden chairs and a table with a striped umbrella. "Little men in dark suits crawling around with walkie-talkies."

"I don't want to seem rude but let's make this short," said Alex. "We're supposed to be back at Agave."

But Julia was looking around in an admiring glance. "What a lovely amount of room."

Maria smiled complacently. "It *is* nice, but it's costing the earth. I've wired my agent for more money, and he'll have a seizure, but after all, if *he* can't send me money, who can? Now, darlings, what are we to tell the police?"

"The truth," said Alex shortly.

"If they ask for it," said Sarah, hedging.

"I always say," remarked Julia, settling herself in a chair, "that you answer questions put to you in the simplest possible way. The police don't want someone babbling on and on."

"What they *will* ask you is where were you at whatever time they decide Hopgood died," said Alex. "And if they say he died around nine-thirty last night in the corral, what will you say?"

"I for one," answered Julia, "will say I was not at the corral, I was driving a horse van for a friend in Peeple's Valley. Laura Freebody is all set to say what a help I've been."

"And Sarah?" said Alex.

"The truth," said Sarah. "Around nine-thirty I was finishing an evening hike with Maria Cornish up the road. I went to our cottage and she went along toward the lodge."

"We did see a Cadillac turn into the corral," Maria said. "But we didn't see who was driving."

Alex turned to Blue Feather, introduced himself, and then asked, "What about you, Mr. Romero? Sarah says you carried the saddles back to the corral."

"Two trips with all that stuff, but I didn't see a goddamn thing," said Blue Feather in an unusually agreeable voice.

"Sure?" said Alex.

"Hell yes. I didn't see any senator or any Cadillac. If a car turned into the corral road, it probably turned off again. I'll say I was just out for an evening ride on Diablo on account of I don't get a chance to ride him in the daytime because Maria's on him, and he's a hell of a better ride than the plugs this ranch has. And that's the truth."

Alex looked at Blue Feather with disfavor, and then said, "If you all went for a ride along Buzzard Creek, you'd better say so."

"Wait a minute." It was Cookie Logan. She came onto the patio and perched herself on the edge of a chair. "I took a chance and got over here. They've enough cops crawling over the place to hold in a riot. Look, I've thought it out. You're right, Dr. McKenzie. You three had better say you went riding. Say you all had this sort of urge to go out on Christmas Eve.

And that I brought in three horses for you. That I went into the night pasture and got them."

"That's a tricky job, isn't it?" said Alex. "Getting a rope on the right horses when it's almost dark."

"It wasn't all that dark and I've done it before."

"While actually you'd left the cocktail party and were down on the main road to flag down the transport," Sarah reminded her.

"Okay, say I cut out three horses from the herd and then walked back by Rancho Grande Road. I was tired of all the party life and I had a long evening ahead. Which is true."

"We didn't ride any three horses," objected Sarah. "I'm a beginner. I couldn't ride anything but a beginner horse."

"Okay," said Cookie again. "Pokey's easy to catch. Say Pokey, Patches, and Diablo. Patches is a pinto. I tied them up and you came down for your ride at a little after six and I went for my walk. Mr. Romero knows how to tack up a horse, so he can say he helped."

"I sure did help," said Blue Feather.

"You went for your ride," continued Cookie. "Along Buzzard Creek. Flashlights in case of trouble. You knew the trail, you've ridden it before. But listen. You didn't go down to Cat Claw. Nowhere near Cat Claw. We're leaving my folks out of this. Okay?"

Alex looked doubtful. "It's beginning to sound complicated."

"Alex, it's perfectly straightforward," said Julia. "Cookie, you've put it all together. The police certainly won't care what horses you rode. You can say you all came back to the corral at nine or so, since Blue Feather says he didn't see anything."

"Like this," said Blue Feather. "You dismounted and I stayed and unsaddled and turned the horses out and put away the tack and you went up and joined the Christmas Eve party stuff."

"That makes good sense," said Julia. "Now all of us must practice our stories. It's really the truth except for loading the horses at Cat Claw and being driven back to the ranch in Laura's van."

"Practice," repeated Maria. "Always be word perfect by the time the first scene is ready to shoot. Start off on the right foot with the director and then you can have your own way later."

"This," said Alex, "is no script. It's real, as in real life."

"We never said it wasn't, darling," said Maria.

And Julia and Sarah rose to leave, Cookie behind them, and Alex six steps back shaking his head. They made their way to the path that wound around the cactus garden toward the Agave cottages. And just as they came abreast of a remarkably large barrel cactus, Sarah came to an abrupt halt.

"That's it."

Julia and Alex, who were ahead, stopped and turned.

"The car," exclaimed Sarah. "That Cadillac. Over there parked by that cottage just below ours."

"That's Agave Annex," said Julia. "Didn't you say that that's where they put Hopgood's secretary?"

"I mean the car, not the cottage," said Sarah. "The one we saw turn in Corral Drive last night. Of course, I never know which kind of car is which unless there's a name or a little medal like BMW on it, but Maria said it was a Cadillac."

"Yes, that's a Cadillac," said Alex. "One Cadillac. There may be a dozen or more at this place."

"But it looks exactly the same shape," said Sarah. "And it's dark gray and that one looked dark."

"That would hardly hold up in a court of law," said Julia. "You have to know about bumper configurations and window shapes."

"Julia's right," said Alex. "You can't be sure this is the one you saw." He looked over his shoulder. "We have visitors."

"We are asking," said the arrival, a small bald man in a business suit, "that guests return to their rooms and cottages. What are your names, please?"

"This," said Julia, "is my niece Sarah Deane and Dr. McKenzie. We have adjoining rooms, Agave Three and Four."

"Dr. McKenzie?" said the man. "Dr. Alexander McKenzie?"

Alex said yes, Dr. Alexander McKenzie.

"You're wanted in the manager's office. The pathologist is here and they want to go over a few details with you. You examined the body when it was first discovered, didn't you?"

"Not examined," said Alex. "I saw that the man had been injured, that he wasn't breathing, there was no pulse or heart action, and rigor was well established. That's about it."

"That's enough," said the man. "You may come with me." The man produced a notebook, ran his fingers down a list, and said, "Mrs. Clancy, Ms. Deane, please go now to your rooms." And, followed by Alex, he turned and made his way toward a side entrance to the lodge, the front door still being roped off—subject to photography, measuring tapes, soil samples, wagon experts, and the like.

Sarah and Julia had just reached their cottage when Sarah again pointed at Agave Annex. "It really does look like the car we saw last night. You don't think Lily Farnsworth went off to have it out with the senator and . . ."

"What you're saying is that Miss Farnsworth, feeling scorned, went down to the corral and shot her boss, and I want to ask why would a secretary want to kill the goose who's laying the golden egg, a boss running for the White House? I think sex is vastly overrated in these cases, particularly if you compare it to sheer power, and for my money Senator Hopgood was into sheer power."

"Lily Farnsworth may have wanted both, sex and sheer power," said Sarah. "Maybe she didn't like sharing."

"Then she was stark raving mad," said Julia, "and you usually don't end up on the staff of a U.S. senator if you're stark raving mad. Now come in, Sarah, and we'll have a game of Scrabble. I've brought a board. It will settle your brains."

And Sarah had to admit that Scrabble sounded a great deal more palatable than the idea of a revengeful secretary pumping bullets into her boss.

THIRTEEN

ON his arrival at manager Fred Arco's office, Alex was met by
Sheriff Harvey Wallow in the role of timekeeper and usher.
Alex sensed that the sheriff was rather miffed at this degrada-
tion of his usual constabulary function, but since the arrival of
the big boys of the investigative world, he had to accept the
job or find himself relegated to checking automobile license
plates.

"You're McKenzie," said Harvey Wallow, looking at a clipboard. Harvey knew perfectly well it was McKenzie, since he
had stood shoulder-to-shoulder with him over the senator's
body in the wagon, but one had to start somewhere.

Alex agreed that he was McKenzie and was ushered into
Manager Arco's office, an oval chamber overlooking the swimming pool, its walls hung with western scenes involving steers
and bucking horses, and Chamber of Commerce placques testi-
fying to the managerial skills of Frederick G. Arco.

"Please sit down, Dr. McKenzie," said a blue-shirted man.

Alex sat down on a leather chair and studied the two men
facing, these now each consulting notebooks.

The blue-shirted man, who remained standing by the manager's desk, was short. Extremely short, about five foot four, with the shoulders and arms of a gymnastic gorilla, a thin body and legs, and a bullet-shaped head topped by curly gray-red hair. His craggy tanned face reminded Alex of a walnut. A man of the outdoors, Alex decided. He turned his attention to the second man, who sat behind the manager's desk. Expressionless. Black hair, tidy black mustache, white shirt, dark tie, wristwatch, the sort that tells the owner the time in London, Zurich, and Bombay. A pale-skinned man, an urban resident, perhaps, or one who came from northern sunless skies.

A New York accent, Alex decided when the second man spoke. It was an even voice, a cool one.

"I'm Douglas Jay. I've come out to help in the investigation. And this is Lieutenant Fox." He indicated the blue-shirted man. "From Phoenix. Homicide. He's going to ask you some routine questions and I'll listen."

Lieutenant Fox, known to friends as "Shorty," nodded at Alex. "Won't keep you long. Want to run over your findings when you examined the senator. Also we'll want some personal data. Should tell you we've called Maine for a check with the state police. A Sergeant Fitts says you've helped him out in a couple of cases, and that you're also one of the local medical examiners there, so this won't be new."

Alex agreed that this situation was not new, adding again that he had not examined the body thoroughly. Just determined that the man was dead, had been dead for some time.

"Okay, you can go over that with Dr. Jackson later. He's the chief medical examiner and forensic pathologist around here—Phoenix, that is. By tomorrow the Bureau's lab people will be on deck and we'll be coordinating with them."

Here he paused and looked at Douglas Jay for confirmation. Mr. Jay smiled faintly and said, "Correct. Full cooperation."

Lieutenant Fox turned back to Alex. "We're checking the whole ranch population twice at least. First a short session to get a scenario in place, then a longer one. Okay, what can you remember that seems important? Anything oddball since you've arrived, which I gather wasn't until last night?"

Alex did his best, described his short stay at the Christmas Eve festivities and finished with the arrival of Santa.

Lieutenant Fox made a short note and then observed that there had been some strange goings-on. "Things happening that shouldn't. Golf carts, a wagon wheel coming off. Has anyone talked to you about these?"

Alex said yes, he'd heard. "Bad practical jokes, perhaps."

Douglas Jay tapped his pen sharply on Mr. Arco's desk. "Not jokes," he said. "You're a doctor. Don't you consider someone falling out of a wagon and breaking a leg serious?"

"Wrist," corrected Lieutenant Fox.

"Certainly that's serious," said Alex, feeling his temper rise, "but I wasn't here, remember. But I'd say a broken wrist isn't quite in the class with bullet holes in a living body."

"How do you know the body was living when it was shot, and that death was the result of bullets?" demanded Mr. Jay.

"I don't," said Alex. "But that's what they looked like—I've seen bullet holes before—so I supposed they could have been."

Mr. Jay made what seemed to Alex a very lengthy note and then looked up. "We're not saying what the cause of death was, you understand, Doctor, and so we'd appreciate it if you would not circulate such a rumor among the guests."

Alex replied tersely that he was not in the habit of circulating rumors and could he leave?

Mr. Jay nodded agreement but Lieutenant Fox raised one finger and said, "Wait. Julia Clancy."

Now comes it, thought Alex.

"Oh yes," said Mr. Jay. "The ranch records tell us that Mrs. Clancy—a member of your party, I gather—is the longest guest resident here. She's been at the ranch since before Thanksgiving. We'll be running a background check on her, and on all the guests, but now we want to talk to her. She's an older woman. Do you feel she's a reliable and sensible witness?"

Alex thought quickly. As far as horses were concerned, Julia Clancy was a rock of good sense; about her dealings with the rest of the world, he wasn't too sure.

Douglas Jay frowned at Alex's pause. "What's wrong with Mrs. Clancy?"

"Nothing," said Alex hastily, thinking what the hell, Julia's a better witness than half the people here, if she'll just stick to some semblance of the truth. "She has a good memory, is observant, and has a kind heart, particularly where animals are concerned."

"We're not worrying about animals," said Lieutenant Fox. "We think it will be useful to talk to a guest who's been here over a period of time. Someone who might give us an idea of the ranch operation from a guest perspective."

"That," said Alex, "she can do."

"We'll be doing a lot of cross-checking," said Douglas Jay, who made it sound like a nasty power play across the blue line.

I'll bet you will, said Alex to himself as he stood up and turned to leave.

"Don't forget, Dr. McKenzie," said Lieutenant Fox, "Dr. Jackson wants a word with you. Come on back here at four."

"Full-court press," said Alex when he joined Julia and Sarah on the Agave Four patio. "The FBI has spread out like an oil slick all over the ranch. I suggested to that cold-fish special agent, Douglas Jay, that the senator may have died as the result of bullets going through him, and I was almost remanded on the spot."

"Alex, you *can* be touchy," said Julia complacently. "I make a point not to rise to every little provocation. I suppose they're just doing what they have to do."

"Julia, I told them you were reasonable, but now you're overdoing it," said Alex.

Julia sat up straight. "And why was *my* name bandied about?"

"Not to worry," said Alex. "Not yet at least. They just wanted the longest resident counting back from today. You've won the title. I assured them you were a miracle of sense and were extremely observant."

"Which she is," said Sarah, "if she's interested."

"I am quite ready to help the police in any way possible," said Julia. She adjusted her glasses and picked up last week's copy of *The Chronicle of the Horse*. "I see that one of my students has made a fool of herself," she said. "She's written a letter saying that it's not necessary for a horse who goes on the bit to always go on the bit. She doesn't say he should relax on a long rein, she actually suggests . . ."

"Aunt Julia, you're not making any sense," said Sarah.

"I will explain," said Julia, putting down the magazine. "Although it hurts to find one's own student actually in print saying things like that. You see, in collecting a horse . . ."

They never found out what angered Julia. From beyond the confines of Agave Four came a scream. A scream topped and overrun by a second scream. And then a series of short shrieks, as if the screamer had run short of air and could only manage a smaller noise. Then the screams formed into words. "Holy Mary, help me, help. Mother of God, Holy Mary and Jesus."

And then running, pounding feet.

At the first sound Sarah had bounded out of her chair, Julia had dropped her magazine, and Alex had reached the patio gate in two strides and flung it open.

The steps came closer and rounding the corner, almost flinging herself into Alex's arms, a woman. One of the ranch's maids, a towel still clutched in one hand. She looked up at him, not seeing him, but gasping, "Holy Mary, mother of God, she's dead, she's dead, she's dead."

Alex took hold of the woman's shoulders. "All right, steady. Come and sit down. What did you see? Is someone hurt?"

The maid allowed herself to be led to one of the patio chairs, where she collapsed, wild-eyed and panting. She was a thin black-haired woman in the regulation Gato Blanco maid's brown uniform with the name "Rosa Espíritu" in running script across her pocket.

"Sarah, go call the police in the manager's office," said Alex. "Now, Rosa, can you show me what's upset you?"

Rosa Espíritu got up. "The Annex," she gasped.

"You show me," said Alex as Sarah, followed by Julia, headed for the telephone.

It was a short walk. Agave Annex lay at an angle below the Agave Cottage complex. It was the only single cottage at the southern end of a long curving line of cottage units, and it lay closest to a curve of the main ranch drive, Camino Rancho Grande. Like the other cottage units, it featured a small patio and a parking space by its side door.

Rosa Espíritu now pulled at Alex's arm, pointed to the parking area and a dark gray car—the same car which Sarah had spotted earlier in the day. "In there, look in there, I swear to almighty God I got a shock. You go look in. I won't, you can't make me."

"Stay here," said Alex. He strode up the little path and confronted a compact Cadillac of that year's design. Empty.

He frowned and turned to Rosa Espíritu, and she made a pushing gesture with her hands. "On the seat. She's on the seat."

She was. Across the front seat, lying as if, suddenly overcome by the fatigue of a long journey, she had rolled from a sitting position to take a little nap. Except a woman with a hole through the side of her head doesn't take a little nap. She dies. Suddenly, explosively, in a spasm of violence.

Alex, who in an almost involuntary movement had opened the car's front door, now closed it. I can't do anything, he told himself. She's dead, and I'll just mess up the fingerprints. For a moment, he stood trying to take in what he had seen. A woman with a hole in her head lying along the front seat of the car, a gun in her hand. Or below her hand? Alex turned back to the car window. She had fallen on her left side, apparently from the passenger seat, across to the driver's side, twisting so that her right arm dangled down on the far side of the gearshift. And just below the curved fingers Alex could make out the outline of a gun.

He straightened and found Sarah and Julia at his shoulder, Rosa Espíritu behind them, the towel to her face, her shoulders heaving.

"The police will be right here," said Julia.

"What is it?" demanded Sarah. "Someone in that car?"

"Yes," said Alex shortly, "and you don't want to look. Besides, here come the police."

They turned to see three men in a gallop. Special Agent Jay in the lead, then Lieutenant Fox, and puffing in rolling gait like that of a bear in a hurry, Sheriff Harvey Wallow.

"All right, all right, let's see." Douglas Jay elbowed his way to the driver's side of the car, looked in, studied the interior for a good fifteen seconds, and then turned to Harvey Wallow. "Get Jackson down here pronto."

Lieutenant Fox turned to Alex. "Any sign of life when you got here?"

Alex shook his head and indicated Rosa Espíritu. "You'd better ask Rosa. She came and got us. But for what it's worth I'd say she's been dead for quite a while."

"Quite the physician on the spot, aren't you, Dr. McKenzie?" said Douglas Jay, making a quarter turn and giving Alex a hard look. "Suppose you and your inspection party go back to your cottage. No wandering around and finding any more bodies, we've got enough to do as it is." Then, as the three began to walk away, he called, "Which of you is Julia Clancy? Oh, you are," as Julia nodded. "Okay, I'll be tied up here for a while but then I want to see you in my office—we're taking over Primrose Cottage. It's three now. Say five-thirty. And you," he said to Rosa Espíritu, "stay here with Lieutenant Fox. Fox, I'll send men to isolate this area. Too bad we can't cordon off the entire ranch." And Agent Jay returned to his study of the scene from the driver's side window.

"I shall be quite stiff," said Julia as they reached her patio, "if I don't get some exercise. It's my arthritis. I'm going to walk behind my cottage, twenty paces each way. I recommend it to you. It will help the shock we've all had. That poor woman. Sarah, didn't you suggest that she shot the senator in a fit of jealousy?"

"And you told me that secretaries whose bosses were running for president didn't do that sort of thing. Besides, how could she have put him in feed bags and hoisted him into the chuck wagon?"

"She looked quite strong," said Julia. "I, in my prime, could hoist feed bags and pick up a newborn foal."

"But perhaps not feed bags stuffed with a full-grown senator," said Alex.

"This whole conversation makes me want to throw up," said Sarah. "I think Aunt Julia's right, we can't sit around and fester. Do you suppose the police will allow us out of the patio?"

"I'd like to see them stop me," said Julia, leaning over to retie the laces on her shoes. "It's essential to my health, and I have a doctor here to prove it."

"I wouldn't say that to our FBI friend," said Alex.

"Investigative people can be very difficult," said Julia. "I've had several friends in the CIA, and when they come out in the real world, they have no idea how to behave. Now, I suggest a steady walk with arms swinging."

"I'll jog," said Sarah. "The more tired the better."

Alex chose power walking, and for a while the three pounded, heel-and-toed, and strode up and down on the small sandy connecting road in the rear of the Agave Cottage unit. This road ran between the first row of cottages, hairpinned around the back of the next tier, and swung and turned through the third and last row. Each cottage unit had four accommodations, each with its own parking space connecting with a link that gave access at its north and south ends to the main road, Camino Rancho Grande.

Camino Rancho Grande, planted with huge agave plants not native to the immediate region, looped the entire ranch, passed the main lodge, and fed into the golf course (Links Lane), the tennis courts, the playground, and, of course, by way of Corral Drive, the stables, pastures, and corral.

Like a gigantic spiderweb, thought Sarah, on her third jog past. Every road has access to every other road. And then another feature of the land began to impress her. The ground behind the first row of cottages declined steeply to the next two rows so that anyone in the first row had an excellent view not only of the cottages below and the desert beyond but of any traffic running along the circular Camino Rancho Grande.

Interesting, Sarah told herself. She slowed and watched a dark green truck move along below them and turn off onto Corral Drive. Well, then, surely someone the night before in the upper cottage row must have seen that Cadillac coming along and turning into the Corral Road as clearly as they themselves had. Perhaps this person—or persons—had then seen the car and its occupant, Lily Farnsworth, return from Corral Drive and go up the hill and park at the Agave Annex, murder having been accomplished. Might, if that person had a window open in one of the nearest cottages, have even heard the shot with which the secretary finished her life. If indeed it was suicide.

Sarah caught up to Alex and shared this observation.

"Christmas Eve," puffed Alex. "Everyone up at the lodge. Don't talk now, I'm just getting into it."

So Sarah accelerated her jog to a run and finished twenty minutes later in a good sweat and sense of physical well-being, if not of an equally happy mental state.

When they had returned to the patio, Sarah forestalled the rush to the shower. "It's bothering me."

Alex was silent for a minute. "Okay," he conceded, "it's possible. Someone could have seen the Cadillac turn into Corral Drive and later notice it when it drove up to the Annex."

"I can't believe everyone went to the lodge last night," said Julia. "Sarah's right, someone may have seen the car."

"Okay," said Alex, "you saw the car driven by a live person, but that's about all. You can't identify the driver."

"Actually," said Julia, "I missed the car. I had the devil of a time turning the van around at the entrance and getting back on the main road. All I saw were headlights in my side-view mirror."

"You agreed to tell the truth. As far as possible, and if necessary the whole truth," said Alex. "Sarah and Maria will have to say they saw a Cadillac turn in at Corral Drive as they started back to their rooms. If they're asked exactly where they were when they saw the car, they tell the truth. Right?"

"But," put in Sarah, "if someone saw the Cadillac from one of the cottages, they could have seen something else."

"Yes, yes," interrupted Julia, "say what you mean, dear, because I want a nice long soak in the tub."

"If," Sarah persisted, "someone else saw the Cadillac, he or she could even more easily have seen a great big monster horse van backing and filling and even hear a lot of gear-grinding noise."

"I don't grind gears when I shift," said Julia, "but you have a point. A six-horse van is hard to miss." Julia rose and picked up her Dick Francis. And," she added, "I certainly chewed up the ground there, and it will be no time before those eager FBI beavers swarm all over the place making plaster casts of tire marks."

"You don't suppose," said Sarah, "that they'll assume a big horse van came in loaded with political hit men who ran up and shot the senator and then his secretary."

"I don't suppose at all," said Julia in a cross voice. "This is all giving me a headache. I prefer fiction to truth and that's why I want Dick Francis. The hero has just found out that the saddlecloths have been switched before the big hurdle race, the Cheltenham Gold Cup, and the favorite's saddlecloth—his name is Wooly Bear—has been impregnated with some awful compound. I shall be in my bath for at least an hour."

"You're supposed to go in and brief police on the ranch roster," said Alex. "At five-thirty, wasn't it?"

"Plenty of time, plenty of time," said Julia. "Shoot if you must this old gray head, but spare me my bath, march on, she said." And Julia disappeared into the recesses of Agave Four.

Alex looked at Sarah. "Sometimes I do have a very strong urge to shoot that old gray head." He looked at his watch. "May I have first shower? I've got to meet with that pathologist, Jackson, at four."

Sarah nodded and picked up a magazine, *Western Horseman,* compliments of the management, and began to read without comprehending one word in five why iron deficiency in foals is a source of anxiety to stockmen. And then an idea came to her, out of nowhere.

"Alex, I've thought of something. Something almost positive."

Alex, halfway out of his trousers, paused. "Okay, I could use a positive thought."

"It's the FBI and the homicide people from Phoenix. And the fact that it's a U.S. senator dead."

"Those are positive thoughts?"

"Listen. Remember those other murders in Texas, in Maine? On the islands, and in the college. Well, we were in the middle of it all. We knew the victims. And the murderers, it turned out. But now we don't know anyone here and no one will want more from Julia and me than where we were and when. We can relax, and when they let us go, we can get out and spend New Year's somewhere else and try and forget it. Take Aunt Julia with us."

"That's a nice thought, Sarah. But it doesn't quite jibe with this visit I'm making to the pathologist."

"Routine, Alex. Simply routine. Give them your medical opinion from your quick once-over of the bodies and then you're off the hook. It's all very sad, but it has absolutely nothing to do with us and there's nothing we can do to help. The professionals have it well in hand."

"And Aunt Julia and the three horses?"

"Marginal data of no use to anyone. We three report the Cadillac, say we enjoyed our Christmas Eve ride, and that's it."

"I hope you're right."

"For once I am. Go take your shower."

"Your track record on being right," Alex reminded her, "is a little suspect."

"Everyone has their off moments. Now I'm going to read about giving foals their iron—it's called Lixotonic—so they can grow up big and strong and shiny and buck the hell out of people like me."

FOURTEEN

ALEX, duly showered and dressed in a clean shirt, sweater, and lightweight flannels, made his way to the new police center in Primrose Cottage. A highly unsuitable name, he decided, for whatever morbid deliberations would be taking place in that space. As he came abreast of the center cottages he was surprised by two small girls who burst out of a door and ran down the front path and were hailed back to their door by a woman. Each child was dressed in velveteen with lace collars, and each cradled a large white teddy bear—obviously new—with a red tartan bow around its neck. Where was the party, wondered Alex, but then he remembered. It was Christmas Day. Almost four o'clock on Christmas Day, but Alex felt as if everyone at the ranch had been forced through a time accelerator and had landed somewhere on the other side of February. He looked at his watch and found that he had seven minutes to spare and so slowed his steps along the little stone path that wound around the cactus garden to Primrose Cottage.

Stopping at a display of rainbow cacti, he decided that Sarah was right. They would only be insignificant persons in a large crowd, while before, as Sarah had reminded him, as part of a small community, they had been closely involved in a very local crime.

Slightly cheered, he paused before the door of the Primrose Cottage complex, running over in his mind the few sentences with which he could describe what he had seen. He would make it brief and to the point and get back to Agave Three and Sarah and Julia. Perhaps they would be allowed out of their cottage and could drive to Lodestone for dinner, get away from the awful heavy sense of fatality that now hung over Rancho del Gato Blanco.

He lifted his hand to knock on Primrose One and found a plainclothesman opening the door and indicating the room inside. "Dr. McKenzie, isn't it? We've taken over all four units," the man said. "I'll tell Dr. Jackson you've arrived."

Alex thanked him and sat down on a couch which had been shoved against the wall to make room for two desks, several straight chairs, and a standing lamp. A number of heavy wires ran across the ceiling and disappeared through the walls. Two dark green file cabinets had been set up next to what in its other life must have been a picnic table.

They've done a job, thought Alex, and they only found the senator at noon. He studied the wires and decided that the cottage had probably been subjected to a crash course of wiring for computer capabilities and surveillance gadgets— after all, wasn't that what homicide bureaus and the FBI did? And by tomorrow he'd bet the whole place would look like an underground missile site.

Then the man who had met him appeared at the door, indicated its opening, and said, "Dr. Jackson's ready for you."

Alex stood up, walked to the door, entered, and faced a tall lean man with a neatly cut yellow beard. Dr. Jackson.

"Son of a bitch," said Dr. Jackson.

Alex stopped. And stared. "Solly?" he said. "God, is that you, Solly?"

"Christ, yes, it's me. Alex McKenzie, you old bastard, what in God's name are you doing lushing it up in this hole?"

"What I was doing just now," said Alex, advancing into the

154

room, "was congratulating myself that I was totally cut off from any of these damn goings on because I didn't know a soul here."

"You were wrong, weren't you?" said Dr. Jackson. "So pull up a chair and let's have a nice long chat about you know what." .

Alex, shaking his head, his mouth split in an unbelieving grimace, took the chair indicated and examined his long-ago friend, former medical school housemate, and fellow sufferer through first-year residency. Solomon Eisenberg Jackson, known informally as Solly, was built entirely of sinews and extended muscles. He had large hands, a long neck, now somewhat hidden by his beard, a beaky nose, a square head with a straw-colored thatch cut into bristles like a marine recruit's. The combination of fair hair, dark brows, and brown eyes— the gift of his maternal Eisenberg genes—gave the impression of two people accidentally mated in the same body.

"Well, Solly," said Alex, "last I heard you were in Alaska— Juneau, to be exact. About five years ago."

"I was in Juneau five years ago," said Dr. Jackson, looking at his watch as if allowing himself a few moments of social talk before business interfered. "Eight years ago I was in Buenos Aires. Ten years ago I was on a fellowship at Berkeley. But last year I rolled into Arizona. Don't you read your alumni bulletins?"

"Life as a medical rolling stone. I missed your switch to Arizona. I knew you'd gone in for pathology, but when the police gave me your name I didn't connect it. There must be thousands of Jacksons in medicine."

"How true," said Solly Jackson. "A universal name. So why are you at this tarted-up ranch finding dead bodies?"

Alex gave his old friend a quick summary of his life after residency and ended up saying, "I'm here on what looked like a harmless vacation, thanks to the aunt of my friend, Sarah Deane."

"Friend as in companion of the bedchamber, buddy, person of the opposite sex sharing living quarters?"

"That's right. We're getting married in the spring."

"About time," said Dr. Jackson with an approving nod. "I've had two wives and four children. Keeps me young and lively. And poor. I can't afford the likes of Rancho del Gato Blanco."

"Sarah and I are being 'kept' by Aunt Julia. We're really not in the resort class."

Solly Jackson rechecked his watch. "Back to the job, Alex. Maybe if I can get loose later, we can have a drink and I'll meet Sarah. And this Julia Clancy, whose name I see figures as a member of your party."

"You're working with the FBI and their lab people?"

"More like I'll be allowed to hold their jackets and shine their shoes. They're flying in a forensic team from Washington tomorrow morning, so then I'll just be the handyman."

"Did you know Hopgood in Alaska?" said Alex, settling back in his chair.

"By reputation. A colorful bastard, and if motive had anything to do with his being wiped out, I'd say it was through a combo of the Audubon and Wilderness societies, the Sierra Club, Greenpeace, and the World Wild Life Fund. He was worse than Mount Saint Helens and the *Valdez* oil spill put together. So half the country may be rejoicing, and I'll bet the other Republican candidates are dancing a jig. So tell me what you found. Hopgood first. Then Lily Farnsworth, late secretary to the late senator."

And Alex, considering his words with care, described the discovery of Senator Hopgood. "After all, he was stuffed into two bags, so I suppose you'd have to consider asphyxiation, but it didn't look like it from my quick once-over. I saw the hole in his forehead. It didn't look like a contact shot, but maybe done at fairly close range. I didn't search around for the point of exit. Hole through his shirt pocket, so he was plugged twice at least. Maybe more—you tell me. He'd been dead for a while, maybe twelve hours or so. Rigor established, but honestly, Solly, I didn't fool around with the body, it was so obviously a case for you people."

"Fair enough," said Solly Jackson. "We did the post at

about two this afternoon. Two bullet holes. Either one would have caused death, but the one to the head was first, negligible bleeding in the chest wound. Put into bags after death, held together by baling string and feet tied with someone's bolo tie—a black bolo tie like everyone's bolo tie. That's about it until the ballistics people finish. So how about Lily Farnsworth?"

"One visible point of entry, right temple. Didn't touch the body so don't know if or where the bullet exited. I'd guess she was sitting in the passenger seat and fell over toward the driver's seat after being shot. Some sort of weapon on the floor of the car. Below her hand. If this Lily Farnsworth had driven the car back to Agave Annex, why bother to switch seats to kill herself? You can shoot yourself from the driver's seat."

"More room, maybe, but I never figure out suicides—or murder—ahead of time. If you're interested, I can arrange a ringside seat at her post. Ten tonight at the Lodestone Community Hospital."

"Thanks, but no thanks. Our little holiday group is made up of noninvolved spectators who only ask to get away from the ranch for dinner tonight."

"Good luck on that. The place is sealed like a coffee can. Would you believe, even the horses need passes."

Alex sat up. "What do you mean by that?"

"Ah," said Solly Jackson, his triangular eyebrows rising, "horses interest you. Cowboy McKenzie, rider of the purple sage. If I were a homicide detective, which I'm not, I'd ask why the alert posture, the sudden interest in our equine friends."

Alex, cursing himself, subsided. "It's just the whole thing, when you said the place was sealed off, even the horses. Gives me claustrophobia. And what about the weapon, did you find any prints?" Get Solly back on the track, Alex thought.

"Fingerprints?" said Dr. Jackson, as if the word were new to him. "Don't rush us. Her body just turned up. Everything's being checked. It takes time. All those subtle problems of finger placement. The possibilities of someone wrapping a dead person's hand around a gun. Why was the gun dropped?

As you probably know, the victim can keep a tight grip because of cadaveric spasm. Hanging on to the weapon is often the sign of self-inflicted injury."

"Suicide," said Alex.

"Always possible, particularly in one of these husband-wife-and-other-woman scenes. But the boys have just begun to root around in the senator's life. And Lily Farnsworth's."

"So," said Alex, "that's about all you want from me."

"Give the boys a deposition. You can write it up or come in and tape it and sign a copy."

"I imagine," said Alex in a hard voice, "I'm already taped."

Solly Jackson grinned. "You're growing sophisticated in your old age. Never mind, the guys like things kosher. Write it up."

Alex stood up. "So no chance of a drink with you. Or a meal. You have to eat, don't you?"

Solly Jackson shoved back the desk chair. "I'll try, maybe after seven I can get loose. Now, don't be surprised if Shorty Fox and his merry men or the big boys from the Bureau call you in again. You know the song, 'Once I have found you I'll never let you go.' *South Pacific*, wasn't it?"

Alex, as he opened the door to Primrose Cottage One, gave his old friend a dark look, but Solly Jackson's bristled head was already bent over a folder.

After Alex had departed for his visit with the pathologist, Sarah and Julia, both showered and in fresh clothes, met on Julia's patio.

Sarah shivered slightly in the cooling late afternoon air and drew her wool cardigan around her shoulders. "May I mix you a drink, Auntie? Alex brought some of your favorite Scotch."

"No," said Julia firmly. "I have to see the police at five-thirty, so I'll stick to water. I need what few wits I have left in working order. Now I'm going to wheel the TV to the patio door. We need to keep up with the news."

"I'd like to forget the news from here."

"Don't be an ostrich, my dear. I want to see if some fool has

158

come out talking about seeing horse vans. Or horses coming and going around Buzzard Creek and Cat Claw Ranch." Julia sighed. "It's a little tricky. If I send the ranch a big payment check now as I'd planned, someone is sure to draw the wrong conclusion."

"The horses should be safe at your farm by now."

"They should be. I want to call Patrick and check. If there's even the slightest hint of trouble connected with my name, I'll send them along to a friend's stable."

"Well, then," said Sarah, "why don't you call?"

"Because of the telephone. I'm sure Agave Cottage phones go through the ranch switchboard, and that every single call going out since they found Senator Hopgood will be recorded. In fact, the whole place is probably bugged."

"Paranoia because of a bad conscience," said Sarah. "I'm going to make myself a rum swizzle to get me through the news."

The five o'clock news brought the outside world into Agave Cottage Four with a vengeance. And it brought the world of Rancho del Gato Blanco to the outside world with a similar bang. And somehow, Sarah thought, the senator's death announced on the tube made it real. Truth wasn't truth until it had been given this familiar public stamp of authenticity.

"Shock and outrage are echoing around the country, around the whole world," said the anchorman of NBC local news. "We bring you the latest update on the tragic shooting of Senator Hopgood from the little town of Lodestone."

"Why not direct from the ranch?" asked Sarah.

"Oh, the FBI has probably tied knots in all the network cables from here. After all, the newspeople are suspects, too."

"Later," said the anchorman, "we will bring you an interview with an eyewitness to the discovery of the senator's body, but for now we have a report just in. A reliable source has just reported that a second body—that's it, a second body—has been found at the ranch in a late-model car belonging to Senator Hopgood and has been identified as that of Lily Farnsworth, secretary to the senator for the past year. Cause of death at this point in time is unknown, but there is a rumor to the effect that Ms. Farnsworth may have taken her own life."

"And where did they get that?" demanded Julia.

"Someone here obviously leaked," said Sarah. "After all, look at those thousands of acres of rangeland around us. All anyone would have to do is to slip out through the mesquite and past the corral and walk or ride to town and spill the beans. You can't have perfect security in a place like this. Listen, now they're talking about those stunts."

For a moment both women listened to a garbled rehash of the untoward incidents that had plagued the ranch, and then Sarah turned to her aunt. "Speaking of all that, whatever happened about the idea that someone was out to get you? An old student who fell off one of your horses?"

"Didn't I tell you? I looked over the guest book this morning before you came in for breakfast, and I didn't recognize a single name in it. Perhaps the whole business is part of a publicity scheme and I was caught in the middle."

"Shooting Senator Hopgood and Lily Farnsworth is a publicity scheme?" said Alex, threading his way around the television set and walking onto the patio.

"I wouldn't be surprised," said Julia Clancy. "Turn off that TV machine, will you, Alex, and fix yourself a drink."

"The newspeople know about Lily Farnsworth," said Sarah. "They're suggesting suicide. Was it?"

"They'll do the autopsy tonight," said Alex. "Now here's my news. My old medical school buddy is the chief medical examiner in Phoenix. Solomon Eisenberg Jackson. We called him Solly."

Sarah stiffened. "And what does that delightful piece of news mean? You're involved?"

Alex shook his head. "Not so far. I asked him to have a drink or dinner with us, so he'll be here at seven."

"A visiting pathologist, how nice." Julia rose, smoothed her green skirt, and buttoned her matching jacket. "My best costume for the interview. It's almost five-thirty and I'm ready for them."

"It's not a contest, Julia," said Alex.

"Any meeting with people like that is a contest," said Julia. She marched out of the patio gate, and Sarah and Alex could hear her best dress shoes clicking down the walk toward the cactus garden.

FIFTEEN

JULIA Clancy paused at almost the same spot in the cactus garden where Alex an hour earlier had checked the time. She did the same and found she still had seven minutes. Good, she would arrive exactly on time and prove that she was an alert and mature person. Very mature, she thought without regret but with a certain sadness. So, with an eye to appear reasonably occupied, she bent low over the plant by her feet—the exhibits were lit at intervals by lamps embedded in the sandy soil.

The rainbow cactus, she read, "*Echinocereus pectinatus,* is found in the Sonoran and Chihuahuan deserts. This interesting cactus is ringed by colorful spines of pink, pale yellow, and gray, brown, and white. Its beautiful flowers appear through June and August." Julia moved on to the nearby display of tiny pincushion cacti and noted with interest its fishhook needles.

"Mrs. Clancy?" said a voice at her ear.

Julia straightened up so fast that she lost her balance and almost ended up as part of the pincushion exhibit had not a hand reached out and steadied her. It was Cookie Logan.

"You scared me to death," said Julia.

"Sorry, but I saw you from the lodge and had to talk."

"I've got to go, the police are waiting, but it's all right, Cookie. Everyone will say the same thing. They went for a ride last night and you helped saddle the horses. Their names were Patches—a pinto—Pokey, and Diablo."

Cookie sighed audibly but whether with relief Julia couldn't tell. Then she asked, "What if someone saw the horse van?"

"That bridge," said Julia with great firmness, "we will cross when we have to. You didn't have anything to do with the horse van, nor did your family. Now, I must go." Julia turned back to the path and hastened toward the Primrose Cottage unit, now lit up like an exhibit at a county fair, every window streaming with light.

"Right on time, Mrs. Clancy," said Harvey Wallow, opening the door.

"Thank you, officer," said Julia, determined to be the soul of courtesy. "A lovely night, isn't it?"

"That," said Sheriff Wallow, "depends on where you are."

Julia recalled to recent events, nodded soberly, and took the chair indicated.

"A five-minute wait, then they'll see you," said Harvey.

"Good," thought Julia. Time to psych myself up. She had been debating with herself about what facet of her personality to present to the investigators and had decided on that of an elderly woman who is shocked by events; a woman of good principles, a lover of the outdoors and of animals. She thought it would be clever to suggest a love of animals; it showed she had nothing to hide. Besides, any check on her background would show the police that she had two farms packed with horseflesh and at least seven dogs and cats without number. But most of all, Julia would try—it would be difficult—to show herself as a woman who depended on the judgment of men, and who did not initiate action but merely followed advice.

"Come in, come in, Mrs. Clancy," called Douglas Jay, rising to point out an armchair next to his desk—a desk, Julia decided, which had been lifted from the lodge library.

Julia sank down in the chair, annoyed to find that its cushions put her considerably lower than the chair used by Agent Jay. To the left of Mr. Jay sat the man that from Alex's description must be Lieutenant Fox of homicide, in a chair also higher than Julia's, so that she sat peering up at both men—a planned arrangement, she was sure. She folded her hands in her lap, placed her feet together in their neat black dress shoes, and waited.

Douglas Jay opened a folder, ran a forefinger down a page, and smiled pleasantly. "We have to check on everyone's background in a case like this, so suppose you tell me why you chose this ranch for such a long stay. Thanksgiving through January."

Julia, keeping her voice low, explained that the climate had been recommended for arthritis. A lengthy stay seemed indicated. "I have to limit my activity somewhat," she said.

Mr. Jay turned a page in his folder. "Do you call riding twice a day limiting your activity?"

"It's healthy exercise and not demanding. I'm following my doctor's advice to the letter."

"That's Dr. McKenzie, isn't it?" Mr. Jay and Lieutenant Fox exchanged a look, and then with a nod from the former, Fox took over the questioning.

"So give us your opinion, or make any comment you think useful in helping us understand the events or the people here. Judy Steiner—the chief clerk, or is she the assistant manager?"

"Both, I think," said Julia. "A very nice person, efficient, helps with the riding schedule and special events."

"And Miss Logan. Caroline Logan—they call her Cookie. Judy Steiner's assistant."

"She's just as helpful as Judy Steiner," said Julia, who was prepared to find all persons mentioned totally harmless.

This being the case, Julia was able to dispose with most of the staff known to guests in something less than ten minutes. Lieutenant Fox's expression grew grimmer with each paragraph of praise. "Manager Arco," he brought out without much hope.

"I don't know the manager well. But he's very considerate of the guests' comfort. He likes everything to run like clockwork."

"And has everything run like clockwork? Until the senator turned up, that is," asked Lieutenant Fox. He looked out the window in the direction of the golf course.

Julia felt something inside her ignite, but with an effort she increased the width of her helpful, placid smile. "Oh, you mean those jokes. That golf ball affair. The golf cart thing. I suppose it's one of the children, or some practical joker."

"You," said Shorty Fox, "were squirted with a hose on your patio and one of your chairs had a slashed seat. You came to the office and complained. You were pretty outspoken."

"Was I? Oh dear me. I've forgotten all about it."

Shorty Fox studied Julia, and she could almost hear him say under his breath, "The hell you have." Perhaps she'd better tone down the noncommittal approach. "Of course, it is unfortunate, all those things, and a broken wrist, too. I do hope when you've finished with this murder business you'll be able to find out who's behind it all. Cutting horses' girths could be hazardous."

"Could be!" said Mr. Jay, coming down hard on the words. "Mrs. Clancy, you know it is." He slapped his folder. "You are the owner of two large horse farms—High Hope Farm in Union, Maine, and Spring Hope Farm in Maryland. You breed horses, you've taken horses to shows all over the country. You race a few horses from your stable in Maryland, you bring horses into the country from a farm you own jointly with your late husband's brother in Ireland. His name is Michael Clancy."

Julia looked up as if this was all a wonderful surprise. "Why, of course, you're right. It's a tremendous burden. I'm so grateful for Patrick, that's my manager in Maine. And Luther, in Maryland. And Michael. I don't know what I'd do without them."

Julia looked at the two men in what she felt was a sensitive, docile way, the elderly woman with much too much on her hands.

Agent Jay looked infinitely weary, Lieutenant Fox studied the ceiling, and Julia thought she could see the wrinkle of a smile playing around the corners of his mouth. They're *not* buying it, she thought, and if they don't it's only a hop, skip, and a jump to deciding I'm quite capable of stealing three horses and driving a van. The whole business will go up in smoke. It's that senator, it's all his fault. If he'd been a better person, a better senator, this wouldn't . . . but here Julia stopped, brought to a halt by a wave of reason. After all, being a good person or a bad person, as history had so often demonstrated, had little to do with ending up in a feed sack.

Douglas Jay lifted a second folder from the table. "Amazing how fast records can arrive in an emergency. Think of the old days before we had computers and microfilms and fax systems. We don't have records yet for everyone here, but we thought you'd be valuable, because of your long stay here, so we put your name into the hopper along with the senator's, his family, and his staff."

"I should be flattered," snapped Julia, and then bit her tongue. Gently, gently, she told herself.

Lieutenant Fox looked pleased. "That's more like the Julia Clancy I've been reading about. So let's get down to it."

"I've got a call due from Washington," said Mr. Jay. "People getting antsy. Why don't you talk to Mrs. Clancy about the material that's come in? Then I'm sure she'll have more to tell us." Douglas Jay stood up, smoothed his black hair back along his temples, smiled a wintry smile at Julia, and left the room.

Lieutenant Fox wasted no time. He opened the folder and began reading off what might be called "highlights of a busy woman." Red Cross aide, France, 1944, Second World War; Joint MFH Union Valley Fox Hunt, 1958–63; Peace March, 1967, 1968, 1969, 1979; arrested, Boston, antiwar demonstration on the Esplanade, 1972; arrested, March on Washington, 1974; demonstration leader, Amnesty International, 1979; president, local chapter, Save the Whales, 1980; coordinator with her sister in a Save the Wild Horses program, 1984. "Shall I go on, Mrs. Clancy?" said Lieutenant Fox.

"No," said Julia. "What would be the point?"

"No point. The point was made. You're a busy lady, you get into things. Up to your neck. Okay, now, I'll run through again the same list of people, and what we want is an informed response. Okay, again, Manager Fred Arco?"

Julia gave a quick prayer: Save my horses, that's all I ask. And Cookie and Morty. And then, "Manager Arco is a snake. He ingratiates himself with the ritziest guests and chops his employees up for lunch. He knows he looks like Napoleon and he acts like a bully. A cowardly bully."

"Thank you, Mrs. Clancy. The tricks? Your view?"

"A poltergeist. Don't look at me like that. It's as good an explanation as any. My husband believed in ghosts, you know. Irish, of course. To be realistic, I'd say someone had it in for the ranch or for certain guests. I got hit twice."

"Yes, I know. Is there anyone staying here who might be a personal enemy?"

"No. I thought of that but I looked through the guest book. But you know, most of the incidents involved a great many people."

"It's a problem," admitted the lieutenant. "Now, how would you judge Maria Cornish?"

"Glamour star of old Hollywood, ageless. And gutsy, too. More than meets the eye. We had a few rides together."

"Blue Feather Romero."

"I think he's out for himself, but maybe he genuinely likes Maria. Difficult to tell. She's a little hard on him so he may be out of favor. He has a good seat on a horse."

"Mrs. Logan, Cookie?"

Julia kept her voice at exactly the same pitch. "Nice woman. Efficient, cares for the guests. She and Judy Steiner keep the place from coming apart."

"Mrs. Logan's parents own Cat Claw Ranch down the road from here. Did you know that?"

"Yes," said Julia firmly. "She told us the two ranches were once owned by two brothers."

"Yes, that's so. And Todd Logan, her husband?"

"I've only seen him in connection with the trail rides. Conscientious, knows his horses."

"Morty McGuire?"

"The same. Perhaps a little more outspoken than Todd, but then, he's the head wrangler."

"Morty's an old pro, he has every right to be outspoken. He taught me to handle a horse."

"Oh?" Julia looked up.

"Used to. Put myself through college and police academy. Jockey. Quarter-horse racing. What about Stevo?"

"The females like him and he must do his job, but I've never been on the trail with him . . . or anyone but Todd and Morty."

"Laddie Danforth?"

"Aging tenor and a lush, and a complete bore," said Julia, now shamelessly mixing information and prejudice.

"Senator Hopgood. His wife, his son?"

"I saw very little of the senator during Thanksgiving. I didn't make the effort because I know his record and deplore it. I don't know Mrs. Hopgood, but I thought she looked unhappy when she arrived. And the boy needs a strong hand."

"Probably he does. So tell me, Mrs. Clancy, for the record, where were you yesterday? And night?"

Though she had been prepared when she first sat down, now the question took her by surprise, and for a minute she stared at Shorty Fox as if she had never seen him before.

"Yesterday," he repeated.

Julia recovered. "I was taken up short, Lieutenant"—she smiled—"because I have nothing to say. I wasn't here." Shorty Fox frowned, and Julia decided that this piece of information had not yet made it into the folder. She warmed to her work, beginning with a short sketch of her friendship with Laura Freebody. Wear him out, she thought. But Lieutenant Fox showed remarkable patience. He endured her school days, her horse-related meetings with Laura, and a great many unnecessary details about her recent visit. She concluded saying she stayed far too long and hadn't gotten back to the ranch until early this morning, around five or so. "Too much Christmas cheer, I suppose," she said brightly.

"And did you see anyone out and around at five o'clock in

the morning? One of the staff? A guest? A car? Did you notice a car parked at the Agave Annex?"

Julia frowned. She had been concentrating so thoroughly on the horse rescue itself that she'd forgotten her return. She closed her eyes and tried to remember. A full moon, easy driving, but she'd been so tired, so very tired. In her mind she turned into the main gate, drove her car slowly up the Camino Rancho Grande, turned off at the top tier of cottages, parked the car in the Agave Four space, checked the time, and headed for bed. Had she seen someone? Yes, now she remembered. The same someone she saw every morning.

"I get up early every morning, habit, I guess," she said. "And I always see Manager Arco. Jogging. He jogs every morning around five. Or five-thirty. Over the whole place. I think he's checking on the grounds crew. I've seen him stop and take a note. Sometimes he waves to me."

"So he might remember seeing you this morning?"

"I doubt it. I certainly didn't wave, I was exhausted. I just tumbled into bed."

"Where was he?"

"Going toward the main lodge. At the beginning of the cactus garden."

"Was there a car parked at the Annex?"

Julia shook her head. "No, I didn't notice a car."

"Well, thank you, Mrs. Clancy, you can go for now," said Lieutenant Fox. And then when Julia was on her feet, he added, smiling, "If there's anything at all you feel we should know about, well, take my advice. Don't hold back. Tell us."

Julia arrived back in Agave Four in a state of mild agitation. "That man Fox thinks I'm hiding something."

"Well, you are," said Alex. "Now, what will you have? Scotch, whiskey, or a truth potion?"

"Scotch, thank you. Oh dear, I'm unnerved and so I'm talking too much. And I've got to call home." Julia accepted her glass from Alex and sank back into a chair. "You'd think the FBI would allow a call to a loved one without tapping the phone."

"Loved one, by which you mean Patrick?" said Sarah.

"Certainly. Patrick O'Reilly is my rod and my staff. And I think I'll go out late tonight and see if I can scuff up those tire marks from the horse van. Do you think I can find a rake?"

"Julia, you will do nothing of the sort," said Alex. "If anyone finds you out raking Corral Drive, you'll be in solitary before you can say horse."

"No landscaping, Aunt Julia," said Sarah. "Alex, I hope your old med school buddy won't linger over drinks. I'm hungry."

Solly Jackson did not linger. He arrived at their door at the stroke of seven, greeted Sarah and Julia, told the latter that he'd heard that Shorty Fox had enjoyed his interview with her, and downed a quick whiskey.

"What do you mean, enjoyed?" demanded Julia.

"Enjoyed, like he had a good time, thought you were an interesting lady. Hoped to chat with you again. Soon."

Here Sarah intervened. "How about dinner, everyone? Do you suppose we'll be allowed to go to Lodestone?"

"I've an announcement," said Solly. "This medical man has had a hard day. And will have a hard night. I've begged off a police dinner powwow and am cleared to take my new and old buddies—Alex, Sarah, and Mrs. Julia Clancy—out for a civilized bite in beautiful downtown Lodestone. I have guaranteed that none of you will hop a plane for Mexico City or defect to Estonia. Okay?"

It was okay. Very okay, Sarah thought. She had been dreading the schizophrenic dinner scene: Christmas decorations mixing in an indigestible way with the hushed voices and furtive looks of guests trying to grasp that one of the hidden extras of their holiday was a double death.

They left the ranch in Solly Jackson's battered Isuzu Trooper and stopped at the police roadblock that had been set up at the main ranch entrance. Sarah noticed that great care was taken in the examination of Dr. Jackson's credentials.

"Of course, short of bringing in the army," said the pathologist, "they can't keep this up, playing Checkpoint Charlie. People are starting to dribble out at the edges, and some of those business-type guests will decide soon they have to go home and watch the stock market. They'll make a few telephone calls to high places and take off. Now, tonight I'm suggesting a low-key place, Danny's Café. Pretty good food, sometimes a combo, a bar, and booths for privacy. The press boys will probably be hanging out at one of the trendy new bistros like La Hacienda or the Coyote Café."

Solly Jackson turned into the main highway and headed the Trooper for a cluster of lighted buildings that lay huddled south of the ranch, gunned through the main street, and swerved around Gemstones Unlimited. "God," he said, "the place has boutiques like smallpox."

However, Danny's Café had stood strong against the incoming New Wave and represented pretty much the old basic Lodestone bar. It was a log and board rectangle, the front room of which featured a long bar running down one side and a back or dining room circled by dark wooden booths. The decor ran to a number of mounted animal heads and photographs of citizens holding defunct animals, including two remarkable dead rattlesnakes. A crossed pick and shovel and a carbide miner's hat were fixed on the wall next to the door as a reminder that Lodestone had a long history of mining. In a bow to the season, loops of grizzled tinsel and sprays of plastic holly ran from one stuffed head to the next, and in the corner, a listless Christmas tree hung with a few dusty balls inclined toward the small scuffed dance floor. The air was blue with smoke; the No Smoking crusade had not reached Danny's Café.

Solly Jackson, having settled his party in one of the few empty booths, returned to the bar for drinks.

Since their booth had a clear view through the open archway of the bar, Sarah was able to see that in his predictions Dr. Jackson had scored one hit and one miss. The hit was the statement that people would be dribbling out of the ranch, and the miss was that they would seek out something other than Danny's Café.

Danny's was heavily infested with the press. At least six people standing at the bar Sarah, Julia, and Alex had last seen holding cameras or cables around the senator's bagged body.

In their midst, towering over his companions, the velvet voice of the West, Laddie Danforth. And, judging from ruffled hair and his expansive gestures, Laddie had a skinful.

"Drunk as a skunk," said Julia, eyeing the bar scene with distaste.

Solly Jackson arrived with a plastic tray, four glasses, a partly filled bottle of Seagram's V.O., and two cans of Coke. "Bartender's an old friend. Let us have a bottle so we don't have to keep jumping up. Me, I've got to stick to Coke and keep my head screwed on for the autopsy tonight." He sat down and pulled at the tab of the can. "Here's mud," he said, raising the can. "To old Alex and the good old days on twenty-four-hour shifts, to Sarah, and to Mrs. Clancy from the Auld Sod."

"Only by way of marriage," said Julia. "I'm just an old lady from Maine."

Solly waved in the direction of the bar. "The press. Sucking up to Laddie Danforth. The news boys can get all the backstairs gossip from old dimwit Laddie. I've heard he has a very big mouth. What guest sleeps with what guest's husband. Why Manager Arco hates everyone's guts. Who's shooting what kind of stuff, how he found out that Maria Cornish sleeps in the buff. How Heinz Simmons made his pile. About an ounce of truth per gallon."

"How *did* Heinz Simmons make his pile?" asked Sarah. "Is he one of those people who have resorts all over the country and own half of Las Vegas?"

"If you mean Mafia, I don't know. Doubt it. He's a big name in the West. Arizona, Colorado. And I hear in Montana. I don't follow high finance, but I hear it's something to do with mining interests, land in general, and resorts."

"On the up-and-up?" asked Sarah.

"Far as I know and I don't know nothin'," said Solly. He slid in next to Julia and picked up the menu.

They settled into their menus, placed their order to a grouchy-looking man in a striped apron who looked and sounded exactly like Ethel's husband, Fred Mertz. "Hi, Solly, long time, no see," he said.

"Hello, Danny. Things hoppin' tonight I see. The great American press."

Danny—presumably the Danny of Danny's Café—scowled. "I ain't responsible for what trash comes in the door. Just as long as they don't bust anything. And I could do without that dude Danforth." He sighed heavily. "But business is business."

They ordered and in a remarkably short time were served by Danny, who gestured at the bar and said that if it got any more crowded, the place would explode. "Christmastime is trouble time in my book," he said ominously.

Their dinner—beef in assorted shapes and guises—was good, well cooked, and more than ample. The baked potatoes were flaky, the yams well buttered, and the apple pie exceptional.

"See," said Solly, putting down his fork and reaching for his coffee. "Local food is good food. I know, I grew up here. Just a local boy who comes back when there's a crime wave."

"Dinner away from the ranch is very welcome," murmured Julia.

"I've just seen something come in that may not be welcome," said Alex. "Blue Feather Romero with a big black look on his face. Loaded for bear, I'd say."

"Or just loaded," said Sarah, craning her neck. It was indeed Blue Feather. Alone. He wore a tight, bib-fronted western shirt, jeans with a silver belt buckle as big as a tray, and he looked as if with any encouragement he would take the place apart.

The press corps, realizing that another primary source had arrived in their midst, hurried over and surrounded him. Laddie Danforth, suddenly deserted, sagged against the bar and glared at the newcomer.

Before Sarah had time to consider the implications of a Laddie–Blue Feather confrontation, a guitar strummed and the promised combo appeared at the end of the room. Two guitars, a fiddle, and a bass. Country music all the way. The dance floor filled, men in their best tight-fitting twill jeans and the women in jeans or ruffled skirts. Some women, having come alone, danced with each other; two young boys, flushed in the face, hopped up and down together; a couple of very senior citizens took to the floor and stepped rather uncertainly to the left and then the right.

Sarah, suddenly weary, felt out of place, overwhelmed by a great longing for her own pillow in Maine, even for the sound of snow and hail rattling on the roof. Alex and Solly Jackson were deep in recalling the good old days of their residency, and neither looked as if they wanted to call the evening quits. She looked over at her aunt and saw that Julia was looking old, gray, and drained, her blue eyes faded and watering—though this might be from the smoke.

Sarah reached over and touched her aunt's arm. "Time for bed, isn't it?"

Julia Clancy gave a sigh that rose from the floor and was audible over the music and the thumping feet. "Just a low moment, dear. And I must call Patrick because there wasn't time before dinner." And Julia rose suddenly, pushed herself out of the booth, and made for the bar.

Sarah explained that Julia was calling home, adding, "I think she's ready to call it a day. Me, too."

"No dancing?" said Solly. "I do a mean polka."

But Sarah was saved a reply. Blue Feather lumbered into the room, surveyed the dancing couples, discovered Alex, Sarah, and Solly Jackson, and walked—or rather rolled—over to their booth, seized both edges of the table as if he meant to haul it out by its roots, and leaned forward. Sarah, recoiling, saw that he looked not only drunk but extremely mean.

"Slumming?" he demanded.

"No," snapped Sarah, "are you?"

"Whadya mean? I don't belong up there at that fancy-ass ranch. I'm not a fancy-ass doctor or own a big snotty horse farm in the East or teach at a fancy-ass eastern college. I'm not a charter member of the Rancho del Gato Stinko."

"Aren't you?" said Sarah unpleasantly. "You couldn't prove it by me." Suddenly her fatigue, her homesickness, had loosened her temper. And her tongue. Right now she loathed Blue Feather Romero and wanted to tell him so. She shook off

Alex's restraining hand and said, "We're just leaving, Mr. Romero, so would you mind backing up a few steps and getting out of our way?"

"Little lily-livered Sarah on old Pokey riding into the night like you thought you were doing something for old mankind. Make that horsekind. Don't you be so high and mighty, you and your doctor buddy, and watch it 'cause I just might blow that whole ranch scene sky-high and let all you rich bastards blow with it."

And Sarah lost it completely. She stood up, her face inches from Blue Feather's. "Why, you goddamn rat," she started, but Solly Jackson got her by the arm.

"Easy," said Solly. "I wouldn't fool with that bird."

"Who'n hell you calling a bird?" said Blue Feather, angling in Solly's direction.

"Well, well, well," said another voice. It was Laddie Danforth and behind him several members of the press corps, all of them red of face and wet of lip.

Laddie seemed drunker than Blue Feather, and drink seemed to have moved him not to direct nastiness but to a heavy-handed satiric effort. "Well, well, well," he repeated. "It'sh Chief Pink Feather Romanceo. Pride of the tribe. Movie star Maria's pet Indian. She got a whistle for you, Pink Feather?" Here Laddie whistled and called, "Here li'l Indian, here li'l Indian." Then, obviously feeling that he could top this effort, he burst out in his trained though blurred tenor voice, "One li'l Indian, two li'l Indian, three li' Indian boys."

For a moment Blue Feather stood, still bent over Sarah's table, still clutching the edges. Then he slowly straightened and teetered forward. "You fucked-up gelding," he said, and stretched out his hands and went for Laddie Danforth's throat.

Sarah rose in her seat and was shoved down by Solly Jackson. Alex reached Blue Feather's arm, but Solly held him back. "Let them get it out of their systems," he said. And the two men rolled together on the floor, into the couples who gave way rather than stop dancing, and then thrashed along the edge of the booths. And all the while the little band played on, and the man with the fiddle began stamping his feet, beginning some sort of a reel. The press corps, to a man, edged back toward the bar entrance, willing to observe, and unwilling to mix it up. Sarah, watching the struggling figures, the flaying arms, the angled elbows, the booted feet, the two heads alternately banging on the floor, had a strong sense that both men might well kill each other before someone did something.

And someone did.

Julia Clancy, armed with the miner's shovel, took careful aim and banged the flat of the shovel down on Blue Feather's stomach as that section of him rolled into view. Then she repositioned the shovel and bounced it lightly off the back of Laddie Danforth's head.

The results were quite satisfactory. Laddie twitched, sat up, clutched his head, and groaned loudly; Blue Feather rolled to one side, holding his stomach and swearing.

"There," said Julia. "Enough of that sort of thing." She beckoned one of the larger members of the press corps. "Take those two men back to the ranch. Dr. McKenzie here and Dr. Jackson will check them over later. Come along, Sarah and Alex. If Dr. Jackson doesn't mind. I'm really quite done in. Such a busy day."

And Julia, her gray hair a bit tousled after her efforts with the shovel, reached for her coat, slipped it over her shoulders, and, stepping over the writhing form of Blue Feather, made her way toward the door.

SIXTEEN

"MRS. Clancy," said Solly Jackson as the four settled into his car. "I've investigated plenty of homicides, but I've never actually been present at an attempted one."

"Homicide, nonsense," said Julia sharply. "Just enough force to stop bad behavior."

"Have you considered what might have happened to you?" said Sarah. "Mixing up with those two characters."

"If I ever stopped to consider what would happen to me before I took action, I'd be long dead," said Julia. "If you have a thousand-pound horse acting up, you don't have time to weigh the consequences. You do something before it gets out of hand. I suppose," she added in a thoughtful voice, "I'm an action person. I solve problems directly without all that flim-flamming around, reviewing pros and cons."

"I'm certainly glad you're not working for the State Department," said Sarah.

"What," said Solly Jackson, "was that unsavory character, Blue Feather, talking about when he said he could blow the ranch scene sky-high? I thought he was Maria's boyfriend, or in Laddie Danforth's words, her pet Indian. Is he the guy behind these tricks?"

"I think he's just sounding off," said Sarah. "Straining at Maria's leash."

Alex, who had been silent during these remarks, came to. "Who had a better chance to put a rubber snake in Maria's bathtub? He's a stuntman. Maybe he took his profession seriously. If he was feeling 'kept,' all those tricks might give terrific relief."

"At this hour of the night," said Julia, "I cannot contemplate any further crimes. Or so-called tricks."

Dr. Jackson turned the Trooper in at the ranch entrance, saw that his companions were properly checked off by the sheriff's men, accelerated up the drive, and came to a halt before Agave Four. He turned to Julia. "But I don't want to contemplate a possible concussion or ruptured spleen on Laddie Danforth and Blue Feather, so watch with the shovel, won't you? In the future, that is."

Julia shrugged. "Blue Feather had Laddie by the throat."

"Repeat, no more shovels," said Solly Jackson. "Alex, do you want to come over and see the victims?"

"I don't want to," said Alex, "but I will. Sarah, please see that Julia has no lethal tools available when she goes to bed."

"Look, buddy," said Solly Jackson as they drove around to the main lodge entrance, "Shorty Fox—our homicide man—sort of thought that Julia during her interview was not exactly an open book. Initial attempt to appear ailing and aged, then a bit of circumlocution. What do you think?"

Alex hesitated. Just long enough.

"Okay," said Solly. "I see. You're in on it, too. Look, buddy, these FBI characters don't fool around. Everyone here is going to be pinpointed every minute of last night."

"Last night," said Alex, "Sarah, Maria, Blue Feather, all went for a nighttime ride. Along Buzzard Creek. Cookie saddled the horses. Apparently they thought it was an interesting thing to do. Julia came back early this morning. That's the truth."

"And nothing but? Look, I know you're a bunch of eccentrics, so that story doesn't throw me, but it might make old Shorty Fox sit up as well as Agent Jay, who probably doesn't know all that much about who rides when. I just wanted to say that the probe will be a long twisting one. Now, what's your idea about all these cute tricks that've been happening? Are you laughing?"

"I wasn't here, but from what I've heard, only the wagon wheel coming off was really dangerous."

"The police wonder if two deaths count as dangerous jokes."

Alex shrugged. "Wait and see if there're any more."

"Tricks or deaths?" said Solly Jackson. He pushed the door open and climbed out.

"Who knows?" Alex shrugged and followed his friend. "Laddie and Blue Feather have enough hate to do each other in."

"I suspect," said Solly thoughtfully, "that they're two of a kind. Both 'kept' men. And they hate it . . . and each other for it."

"Sarah thinks that Maria seemed to be distancing herself from Blue. Making remarks at his expense."

"So Blue Feather may be on his way out. Or has found another source of income. Another interested lady. Or a stash of nitroglycerin, with that talk of blowing up the place."

"Anything's possible," said Alex. "Now let's get the bedside visits over."

Successive calls to the rooms of the shovel victims found both sore, irritable, still half drunk, but not in any danger. Laddie was tracked to his apartment in an adobe building where a number of the staff had rooms. He was slumped in a chair and coherent enough to blame Blue Feather for the murder of Senator Hopgood.

Blue Feather was discovered in the small bedroom that led off from Maria's sitting room, Maria being elsewhere. He did not welcome them, and said he didn't need any asshole doctors hanging around. Alex and Solly Jackson left Blue Feather with that gentleman's last words ringing in their ears, something about certain people getting theirs in the very near future.

"Nice guy," observed Solly Jackson as they made their way to the main lodge front entrance.

"According to Julia and Sarah, he isn't always this nasty, and Julia admires his skill with a horse." And on that note Alex shook his friend's hand and they parted at the lodge door.

Alex found Sarah sitting in her cotton nightgown on the darkened patio. She had pulled a raincoat over her shoulders and was looking up into the darkened space.

"Stargazing?" said Alex.

"It's beautiful. Look at the sky. Stars, the Milky Way somewhere, galaxies, the whole bit. And not a corpse in sight."

Alex pulled a chair up beside her, leaned over, and kissed her on the cheek. "Good. So happy Christmas."

For a few minutes they sat watching and listening to the night. Once a coyote, quite close, barked twice and was followed by two other faraway yips, and then there was a near rustle in some of the bordering mesquite. Then absolute utter silence.

"As if someone was just inventing the night for the first time," said Sarah. "Trying out sounds and fixing the stars."

"A nice thought," said Alex. "But I have one nearer the bone. How are we going to keep Mrs. Thomas Clancy out of jail?"

"We don't even have five more minutes to look at the sky?"

"No. It's getting late and we've got to do some thinking. And some restraining."

"Have you ever tried to restrain Aunt Julia? I have. It doesn't work. This is a woman who schools very large-hoofed animals to jump over ghastly double fences."

"It's just a matter of time before she—I should say before all of you—are caught out on first base."

"Because of the horse trailer turning around."

"Among other things. But take the horse trailer. First, there were *two* horse trailers. The transport that was to take the three horses to the dog food factory that Cookie told to go away—that was at seven or so—and then Laura Freebody's big van coming in around nine. The police—which includes, no doubt, a very efficient FBI investigation team—will be scrambling over the neighborhood, Lodestone, and all the nearby ranches, and asking about people, vehicles, anything untoward. The horse transport outfit is probably well known, and a phone call to that company will let the police know that Cookie Logan stood at the road, flagged down the driver, and turned him around.

"So someone will ask why, and someone else will ask where are all the horses' vaccination documents—those Coggins' tests—if there was no pickup? And why was the pickup canceled? And then, my love—it must follow, as the night the day—someone will say, 'Where in hell *are* those horses?' And then the shit will hit the fan. At least for your particular little caper. Even if Todd and Morty McGuire don't want to guess what's happened—or know the horses have been rescued— they can't do much except scratch their heads and say the horses aren't around. And then it will be remembered that a group of three took a night ride."

"They won't guess we were on Copper, Pecos Bill, and Lollipop," protested Sarah.

"Oh sure, you'll try hard to establish that Pokey, Patches, and Diablo were the chosen animals. But then someone will recall that Julia Clancy—well-known horse person—was staying at a friend's in Peeple's Valley and came back early this morning."

"You mean they'll actually call up her friend?"

"Or call *on* her. With a big investigation like this, the death of a U.S. senator, they use the big net. Cast it wide and bring in whatever fish they can. Good fish, bad fish, smelly fish, and any flotsam and jetsam that get trapped. And then someone at Laura's stable will remember that her six-horse van went out last night with Ms. Freebody's old school pal, Julia Clancy, at the wheel, and that said school pal returned with three horses who had to be kept in isolation and then were loaded and delivered to the Phoenix Air Horse Transport bound for New York complete with all papers."

"But," said Sarah, "Laura Freebody, all the grooms, the whole place was sworn to silence."

"You cannot possibly keep something as elaborate as Julia's operation quiet. Human nature isn't intended for secrets. One or two people, yes. Maybe four or five. But this takes in friends and grooms, and stable hands, truck drivers, airport personnel. Laura Freebody's family. Plus the extras. These people aren't in the CIA or trained to keep their mouths shut. I'd say your Aunt Julia has about eight hours more of innocence before the dragnet is turned over and everything comes tumbling out. So you have to do some thinking. And I'm afraid some truth-saying."

Sarah stood up and moved in the dark to the low wall encircling the patio. The stars seemed farther away, cold, hard fragments of light, the air seemed sharp and inhospitable. She turned and faced Alex—or the dark shape that was Alex. "The saving of three horses from being slaughtered has nothing whatsoever to do with Senator Hopgood and his secretary."

"And the series of little not-so-nice tricks? Coincidence? Do you think the police are going to buy that? That three horses disappeared and the jokes and shootings all happened because Venus was in opposition to Scorpio, and Libra was crossed up by Aquarius, or the gods were having an extra exciting dice game? As your brother Tony might say, be real."

Sarah came back and leaned over his seat. "Let's give it one more day before we all go and confess. I know you're right, and I know they're going to start leaning on Cookie and the other staff members. And someone's going to crack. But let's see what we can figure out alone. Not the senator and his secretary, but the nasty tricks. I'm beginning to think we should have another session with Cookie. If we could separate the tricks from the murder, maybe we can convince the powers that be that the horse business was unrelated to anything else. And that yes, coincidences do happen. More often in life than in fiction. I'll try Cookie in the morning, after breakfast, or during. And I'd like a word with Maria Cornish. About Blue Feather. I wonder what's on his mind, that big talk."

"Stick to Cookie. Blue Feather Romero could be bad news."

"I'll start with Cookie anyway. Work up to Blue Feather."

"Not unless I'm standing behind you with a six-shooter."

"Men are so physical," said Sarah. "No subtlety, no diplomacy."

"That Blue Feather Romero," said Alex, opening the door into the cottage, "wouldn't know diplomacy if it bit him."

Cornering Cookie Logan did not prove easy. Sarah arrived at the main lodge at the stroke of eight on Tuesday morning hoping to catch Cookie by herself at the desk, but Judy was guarding it like an anxious vixen guarding her pups. Sarah decided that Judy had determined that though the ranch itself might fall into shambles, the office operation would keep going until the last trump. Sarah spent considerable time asking aimless questions about wildlife preserves before a buzzer sounded just behind the desk, and Judy said, "Oh dear, that's probably the police again. I'll take it in the office. And don't take any room reservations." And Judy bustled off into the back office.

"Judy's having fits," said Cookie. "People calling in for reservations and having to be put off. Seems like the murder has really turned this place into a freak show, a real tourist attraction. Listen, if you want to talk, I can't get loose for more than twenty minutes. Meet you at ten by the corral. The police are as thick as weevils. Everything's okay, isn't it?" she added anxiously. "About the horses, I mean."

"It's all right now, but it won't be a secret much longer," said Sarah. "Too many cooks. Two horse vans turning around. Never mind, we'll all probably survive the horse rescue. Aunt Julia will give Mr. Simmons a big check and Maria Cornish will go public about saving animals. But it's the whole thing. The tricks *and* the horse business. The senator *and* his secretary. The police will think it's all part of some huge plot."

"But the tricks are totally different. Aren't they? Not connected with the senator being shot and Lily Farnsworth being dead." Cookie paused, confused, and Judy Steiner returned.

"All set, Miss Deane?" she asked. Then, turning to Cookie, she said, "We're to get back into a modified routine as soon as everyone here has had a final statement taken. No one to leave ranch property without checking with the police. No solo trail rides or hiking trips. A green light for tennis and golf."

Sarah thanked them both and made her way into breakfast and found Julia, Alex, and Maria Cornish at their table.

They all looked a little worse for wear. Alex still had his Northeast hospital pallor, while Aunt Julia looked, well, Sarah supposed "weathered" was the kindest word. She was in a shirt and cardigan of a peculiar shade of blue better suited to the Air Corps, her nose looked pinched as if she had just recovered from a cold, her eyes were shadowed, and her wire-like gray hair was particularly unruly. And Maria Cornish had flunked makeup. Although her wine-colored shirt showed off her silver Navajo squash blossom necklace, it did nothing for the hastily assembled face. In fact, she had forgotten one eyelash system entirely, the eyeliner looked as if it had been applied with an unsure hand, the lipstick ended before the mouth did, and the nail polish had not been renewed.

Maria greeted Sarah. "Darling, I don't usually even think about moving until nine o'clock, but I had to catch Julia and all of you for some advice, and I know you eat breakfast at absolute daybreak. It's Blue Feather. Alex is just telling me that he was very bad last night. I mean really, darlings, pick on someone your own size, not that wretched Laddie Danforth. Well, Blue wasn't anywhere in our suite this morning. I even looked behind our sofa in case he'd passed out in an odd place. I suppose he may have gone hunting for Laddie. Blue has this idea about getting even."

"Perhaps he's gone out for a walk, to clear his head," said Alex. "Or to visit the stable, check on Diablo. We can look down there for you. He does see after Diablo, doesn't he?"

"Yes, yes, he does," said Maria faintly. She leaned back in her chair, closed her eyes, and brought her hands up over her face. Then lifted her head, gave it a little shake, and put on what Sarah could only call a brave little smile.

"It's just that I found this very strange note from him, and I do feel responsible for his being here."

"Strange note?" said Julia, looking at Maria from over the rim of her coffee cup. "Why didn't you say so before?"

"It wasn't like him at all. We've had our differences, but he isn't likely to be so, well, abrupt. Rude. As if he didn't even know who has been helping, been at his side all these months. Advising him with his career."

"The note?" said Alex.

Maria reached into some recess of her skirt and withdrew a folded piece of stationery, which she opened and smoothed on the table. Sarah could see the Gato Blanco logo at its top.

"I'll just read part," said Maria. "He says first he's sick of being tied down and that he'll be able to pay his own way after this, that he's getting another room. That he's got important business which he'll take care of himself. He ends—and this is really very hurtful—by saying, 'Don't think it hasn't been fun because it hasn't.' And then after he's signed it, 'B. F. Romero,' he says I can look after my own horse. See." Maria folded the paper so that the three could read the postscript. "You can look after your own bloody horse and get your hands as dirty as mine."

"That's certainly rude," said Sarah.

"And," said Maria plaintively, "he's left. Not that I think our relationship could go on much longer, because you see it wasn't supportive. Not mutually. I was doing the supporting and getting simply nothing back. But I never thought he'd begrudge me help with Diablo. He loves Diablo, and he's so good with horses."

"He can't go away," said Sarah. "The police aren't letting anyone out yet."

"As a matter of fact they are. That family from Houston, or was it Galveston, they left this morning. And Cookie told me that Blue Feather has just taken one of their rooms. Though how he's going to pay for it is beyond me. I'm certainly not going to."

Sarah sighed. Blue Feather, as a person of interest, receded even farther into the ranch woodwork. Except that he appeared to have come into money. Money not from Maria Cornish.

Alex pursued this idea. "Where is Blue Feather getting cash?"

Maria put down her coffee cup with a bang. No longer plaintive, she sounded furious. "I don't know and I don't care. For all I know he's picked up some poor woman and talked her into footing his bill. It's good riddance. Now, would you all like to go on an afternoon ride? I don't like to go out without someone I know and Diablo needs exercise."

Julia nodded. "Yes, I think our little riding party should continue to go out together as if it were perfectly natural."

Maria nodded and rose. "A tiny nap, I think. And then learning my lines. My statement, make sure it's memorized."

Alex looked up at her. "The time is fast approaching when you tell exactly what you were doing Christmas Eve."

Maria smiled. "Of course, darling. We went for a ride together by moonlight, or almost moonlight. The truth. I see no reason to ad-lib." And she swept down the aisle of the dining room, nodding here and there to grateful fans.

"That woman just goes around acting scenes," growled Alex.

Sarah put her hand on his. "Never mind, because what I want to do now with Aunt Julia and you is try to take a hard look at these so-called tricks. See if there's any pattern, so when I talk to Cookie, I'll have something to say. I know damn well she's involved, or she knows who is."

"Talk here in the dining room?" said Julia, looking around apprehensively.

"Yes, here," said Sarah. "For all we know they're bugging every cottage and here there's enough noise to cover what we say. I've brought paper so we can make notes."

"For all the good it's going to do," complained Julia.

Sarah looked at her aunt in some exasperation. "I'm trying to look at what's been happening. Three separate or three connected events. *We* know the horse-moving affair had nothing to do with shooting or the so-called tricks. But were the shootings the climax of the tricks? And were the tricks trying to destroy the ranch as a popular resort? Turn it back into White Cat? Get revenge for swallowing Buzzard Creek and most of the groundwater for miles around? Were the tricks part of a Cat Claw Ranch scheme?

Here Julia held up her hand. "Mrs. Younger of Cat Claw is a very unlikely agitator, or trick puller," she said.

"I agree, but Cookie, her daughter, is pretty sharp. And Cookie's husband, Todd. Who else? How many people here are related to the Logans and the Youngers? Lodestone is a small town."

"And small towns," put in Alex, "are noted for having complicated interconnected families, everyone a cousin or an aunt or uncle or grandson. Is that what you're saying?"

"Absolutely," said Sarah. "Now, Aunt Julia, here's where you come in. Go to the desk and say that you'll be leaving in a week or so, and since the staff has been so marvelous—lay it on with a trowel—you want to make sure you don't forget anyone when you make up your thank-you presents. Ask for a list of the staff."

Julia rose to her feet. "I'll try."

Left with Sarah, Alex shook his head. "The murder of Hopgood must be political. As for the secretary, maybe she knew what he knew, if he had hold of information someone wanted kept quiet."

Sarah objected. "You can't bet the murder is political. Not yet. And the whole affair may be part of Lily Farnsworth's revenge. Murder, then suicide. We don't know yet. But you can see why the police might put everything in one big pot. And until we tell the truth, we'll be in that pot, too. But first, research. I have a date at ten with Cookie, so let's get to it. Here's Aunt Julia back. Any luck?"

Julia waved a folder. "They make up a 'courtesy list' for people like me." She thumped down in her chair and passed the folder to Sarah.

Sarah went down the list. "There's a Younger in the kitchen, and the head landscape person is a Logan Younger."

"And Peter Doubler, the chef, is Cookie's cousin," put in Julia. "I remember being told that early on."

"And if you add Cookie and Todd, you've got a widespread crew. And there are probably others. Call it the Cat Claw connection."

"Let's see," said Alex. "With someone in the kitchen, someone on the grounds crew and in the corral, you've covered the waterfront. What was the first event, Julia? Something about girths being cut?"

Julia reached for another piece of toast and began loading it with marmalade. After several bites, she nodded. "It started with one girth. The children's Thanksgiving rodeo. Barrel racing was the main feature, and I must say that I do not think it safe for young children, because they don't wear hard hats. That wouldn't be allowed by pony clubs back home."

"Aunt Julia," said Sarah, "I've got to be out of here by ten."

"All right. One girth was cut first and everyone seemed to think it was young Artie Hopgood, but then the next day a great many girths were cut through. It's easy, string girths, not leather. The Hopgoods left the next morning and the general feeling was that Artie had done the works."

"But who better to slash them than someone who works at the corral?" said Sarah. "Todd Logan of the Cat Claw connection."

Julia shrugged. "You're pushing it, considering how easily we found our way into where the saddles and papers were kept. Why, anyone could have sliced them."

"But not everyone had equal opportunity," said Sarah. "Now, what comes next? Aunt Julia being sprinkled, wasn't it?" She poised her pencil. "Logan Younger is head of the landscaping."

Alex objected. "The grounds crew, all those maintenance people, they handle hoses and watering. I suppose Fred Arco and the desk staff know how the watering system works. And the maids who make up the rooms, they'd know how the hoses attach."

"Okay," said Sarah. "But let's just say that there is a Logan relative who works on the grounds. I'm writing down what's probable, not what's possible."

"What you're doing," said Alex, "is setting up a hypothesis and forcing facts to fit it."

"Logic doesn't always explain things," said Julia.

"Next," said Sarah. "The coffee with the dirt in it."

"Dirt, sand, I'm not sure which," said Julia. "I didn't taste it. That was the very same Saturday, December sixteenth."

"I'm writing down Peter Doubler, kitchen staff, cousin of Logans'," said Sarah. "Who served the cookout breakfast?"

"The waitresses and Cookie and Judy."

"Cookie again," said Sarah with satisfaction.

"I suppose she could have, if she had very fast fingers," said Julia. "I do know Fred Arco stayed back at the desk and Heinz Simmons hadn't arrived."

Alex shook his head. "I can't see either the manager or the owner trying to ruin the ranch—unless there's some arcane tax-loss gimmick involved. I think you can safely say that it's all part of a scheme to put the ranch out of business, and, if Sarah's idea about Cat Claw Ranch is any good, I suppose there are enough Youngers and Logans here to manage all of those pranks."

"Of course," said Julia, "it's anarchy."

"But I'll bet you approve," said Alex.

"No, I do not. If the ranch goes, all the horses might go for dog food. I just want to get rid of the golf course."

"Back to business," said Sarah. "My time is running out."

Julia put down her coffee cup. "I cannot nurse breakfast along anymore. Let's sit by the pool or in the cactus garden. Surely the police aren't hiding under water or behind a saguaro."

"Don't be too sure," said Sarah.

They rose and trooped out, greeted at the door to the swimming pool area by a young man in a gray suit who reminded them to remain on ranch property unless they had permission to leave.

"Really," said Julia. "I'm sure that if we all stay bottled up much longer, there will be further murder done."

"Hardly bottled," said Alex. "A luxury resort with pool and sports, a bar, and three meals a day. And your beds made for you."

"Well, let's get on with it." Julia dragged a poolside chair off next to a bush.

"I think we can wrap the rest up quickly," said Sarah. "There was the tennis and golf epidemic."

"Good clean fun," said Julia. "And since I'm up at dawn prowling around, I've seen the chef, Peter Doubler, head off for the golf course. Early, six or so."

"I'm entering Peter Doubler under the golf division," said Sarah. "And anyone could have swiped the tennis nets. Then there was Heinz Simmons's car breaking down at the airport, but that may not be related. Then there's Maria's snake. Anyone with access to a key to the cottage could have slipped it in her bathtub."

"Unless," said Julia, "that was Blue Feather at work."

"Next, the wheel on the wagon," said Sarah. "Easy, that's the corral crew. Todd Logan. The wagon was parked down at the corral next to the one Santa used. As for the piñata and the blue ink or whatever it was, easy again. Cookie and Judy put those together."

"Against your theory," said Alex, "is the fact that although there was always a Younger or Logan around, others could have been involved. An idiot can figure out how to loosen a wagon wheel and unplug a golf cart. Many of the staff had an opportunity sometime in the day or night to pull the tricks off."

"The how fits in with the why," said Sarah. "Rescue Cat Claw by cutting Gato Blanco down. Or cutting it back to size. My theory limits the stunts to just that, stunts. I can't believe the Younger and Logan families were so desperate that ruining the ranch included the murder of a U.S. senator. And his secretary."

"Do you think perhaps, just perhaps," said Alex, "that you're wrong about no connection to the murder? That doing in the senator was just part of the grand scheme? That the tricks were laid on to make the police go hunting down a bunch of crazy trails but really they're sideshows? That it was all planned since Thanksgiving? Since someone knew Hopgood was coming back at Christmas?"

Sarah stood up. "Possible. Maybe Lily Farnsworth is behind

it all: when I saw her last, she looked quite capable of burning the ranch to the ground with the senator in it."

Suddenly Judy Steiner was before them. She bent over Julia's chair and said, "Could you see the police in ten minutes? And Dr. McKenzie, Dr. Jackson wants to talk to you."

"Nothing for me?" said Sarah unwisely.

Judy smiled. "Not yet, but if you just happen to see Cookie, tell her I need her back in the office."

I wonder about Judy, thought Sarah. Judy knows everything that happens in every corner of the ranch, Judy works side by side with Cookie Logan. So Judy must know a lot. About the tricks anyway, maybe about the horse rescue operation. Perhaps even about the whole blessed shooting match— if "shooting match" was not too flippant a term to give to murder.

SEVENTEEN

Sarah made her way down to the corral, planning to tell any hovering police that she wanted to schedule her afternoon ride and then somehow work Cookie into a quiet corner for conversation.

But on arriving at the main tack room of the corral, she found Cookie already engaged. One of the now extended army of plainclothesmen that infested the ranch was taking Cookie along the saddle row. He had a notebook in his hand and the two moved from saddle to saddle, pausing at each while Cookie repeated the name of a horse and identified a saddle.

Sarah, ostensibly consulting the large scheduling board that stood just inside the tack room, tried to hear, and although the voices were low, Sarah heard enough to realize the questions had a thoroughly sinister aspect.

Then the man led Cookie to the door and said clearly, "You're missing saddles for, let me see, Diablo, Blaze, Patches, Sweetheart, and Bongo. Why is that?"

"Those saddles and bridles are kept separately so they won't be used for the everyday rides. Diablo belongs to Maria Cornish, Sweetheart and Bongo are Mr. Simmons's horses, and

Blaze and Patches were set aside for the Howells, Mr. Simmons's guests."

And Sarah, lingering in the background, felt a sinking followed by the absolute knowledge that, as they said in all good old crime novels, the game was up.

Cookie was released, came up to Sarah, smiling her professional staff smile, obviously unaware of what she had just said. "We can talk over by the corral, the far end. I can say I'm pointing out a more exciting horse than Pokey for you."

"Pokey for me is a thrill a minute, and wouldn't Morty or Todd do that?" said Sarah, falling into step with Cookie.

"It's okay. I've helped with the riding program before."

They reached the far end of the corral and sat down on a log bench fixed under a tree. Sarah decided to postpone the coming revelation, possibly coming to the matter by indirection.

"Why were you doing a tour of all the saddles?" she asked.

"Everything to do with the corral is being gone over, and the cowboys are all out on trail rides. But so far they haven't actually been into the corral to count horses and see if there's a horse for every saddle. Which there never is. They turn out horses that have been used for a while, rotate them, and use the same saddle and bridle for several horses."

"Why this fixation on saddles? Why not feed bags and wagons?"

"Listen, these guys are going through everything, the grain bins, hay bales, saddle soap, driving the farrier up the wall dumping his stuff out and sifting through nails and rasps. So far no one's said where's Pecos Bill, Copper, and Lollipop? The ranch staff assume they're dog food."

"I told the police I rode Pokey, Blue Feather rode Patches, and Maria was on Diablo."

"So?"

"You just told that man that Patches was one of the horses reserved for the Howells."

Cookie's face changed to stone. Then she opened her eyes very wide and said, "Oh my God!"

"Right."

Cookie scrambled. "You could say Blue Feather rode another horse, all the names sound alike. You don't know one horse from another."

Sarah shook her head. "The story's shot, Cookie. It's not just Patches. Pretty soon someone's going to say there were two horse transports around that night. We'd better come clean before they try to hang a murder—or two murders—on us."

But Cookie had regrouped. "Wait up. Like you said, the two transports will likely be found out. But they might have the murderer by then and no one will care about three missing horses. So don't jump the gun about a horse called Patches. Half the horses in the West—the pintos anyway—are called Patches." Suddenly Cookie grinned triumphantly. "But hey, we've got a Peaches. Big horse. Blue Feather can ride big horses. It's perfect. He just misunderstood the name."

"Okay," said Sarah. "Peaches, Patches, it's probably close enough. But what I'm worried about is all those stunts. I'm just damn sure you or Todd are behind them. Or masterminding them. Or know who is. I think you should come clean with the police because I'm sure they think the shootings were the featured attraction, everything leading up to Senator Hopgood in a bag."

Cookie's jaw set. "The police can think what they want. If they're dumb enough to think that, let them."

Sarah felt a wave of exasperation roll over her. "They don't have to be dumb. Because the whole affair, horse rescue and all, could look like one giant scheme to destroy the ranch. Because of Cat Claw losing the water."

"Cat Claw," said Cookie between clenched teeth, "can take care of itself. And what are you playing at? Lady cop? Miss Spy?"

"No," said Sarah, struggling with a reasonable tone, "but no one wants to be charged with murder. Or aiding and abetting murder. I'm sure the intent of the tricks was to embarrass Gato Blanco but not hurt anyone, and, damn it, Cookie, after a couple of interviews the police will see that for each of those blasted stunts, a Logan or a Younger was available while the others had alibis. It was a group effort. That's what I think, anyway."

But Cookie had also been working on self-control. And on imitating a brick wall. "Look, we're grateful for saving the horses. That took guts. But leave ranch affairs alone. What I am saying as politely as I possibly can, because I like you, is butt out. Keep the lid on the horse business as long as you can, hope that the three horses are safe in Maine, and hope that someone like Blue Feather Romero is hauled off to jail for a double murder before anyone asks where Copper, Lollipop, and Pecos Bill are."

And with this Sarah had to be content. Cookie marched off toward the lodge, and Sarah was left to reflect on the hardihood and self-assurance of certain western women. A role model for us all, she murmured to herself. Then, after signing up herself, Alex, Maria, and Aunt Julia for the afternoon ride, she walked back to Agave Three to find her companions ready for another session with the powers of law and order: Alex for a medical briefing with Solly Jackson and members of the FBI's forensic team; Julia, a second round with the police; and then Sarah herself, after Julia.

After telling them both that Cookie was hanging tough on all fronts, and that Blue Feather was supposed to have ridden a horse called Peaches, not Patches, on Christmas Eve, she subsided with a copy of *Arizona Highways* and its descriptions of glorious vacations and tranquil southwestern interludes— phenomena entirely missing from the Rancho del Gato Blanco experience.

Alex met Solly Jackson in one of the smaller rooms of the Primrose Cottage complex and was waved to a seat facing a metal desk. Looking about, he saw that the police decor of charts, wires, phones, and computers had completely overwhelmed the guest atmosphere, the single sad remnant of which was a table lamp shaped like a horse.

Solly Jackson was all business. "Okay. Alex, buddy, I'm going to fill you in on a few details and then Shorty Fox wants some of your time. First, time of death."

Alex held up his hand. "Wait up. I don't need to be filled in, do I? I'm just a quiet visitor who happened to spend a few minutes looking at a couple of bodies. Are you filling in the entire ranch staff in this openhanded way?"

Solly tapped the desk impatiently with his pencil. "Of course not, but you, Dr. McKenzie, are special. Not only doctor on the spot, but doctor who has been on similar spots before. You're being attached, in a low-grade, insignificant way, to the operation. The Bureau has called your home port and had words with the state police. So let's get on with it. If you have ideas, remember significant details, have suggestions, good. That's what we want."

Alex began a second objection only to be cut off by Solly. "Okay, I understand your reluctance, but you will participate. Lucky you. You can still be a guest, eat gourmet meals, have friends who take bizarre night rides, but you will help us when you can. Right? Right. Being low on the totem pole, I'm your liaison. We meet, we discuss, I pass along. Okay, here's what we have."

"Time of death," said Alex in a resigned voice.

"We judge the senator cashed in between nine and eleven o'clock Christmas Eve. Contents of stomach, state of digestion, and all that. Later we may pinpoint it better when we work out details of temperature inside feed bags that are stashed inside chuck wagons. Further lab reports pending."

"He was shot first and then put in the feed bags?"

"Right. Dead when he was stuffed into the bags. Then hoisted into the ranch wagon. The wagon with those jingle bells attached. The ranch has two wagons, but one was *hors de combat* because of the broken wheel."

"And the feed bags are sitting around waiting for bodies?"

"Empty grain feed bags, big babies. The empties are folded and stored and later reused. They're kept next to the grain bin in one of the equipment sheds along with buckets, bailing string, odd bits of wire, small tools, and so forth."

Alex considered for a moment the bulk of the dead senator. "Quite a job bagging the body, I'd say."

"Not that hard," said Solly. "Fasten the legs with that bolo tie, pull a bag over his legs, another over his arms and head, tie in the middle with baling twine. Rather like getting a small child into a snowsuit. More awkward than difficult. Lily Farnsworth could manage it."

"But into the wagon?"

"Ah, that takes some doing. Not just a man's job because lots of women around here, including little Cookie Logan, could hoist any number of dead bodies into any number of wagons. But our question is about Lily Farnsworth. Was *she* strong enough? She's not tall, about five six. Gives the appearance of a fair amount of strength, but after the autopsy I'd say her muscle mass is suspect. She was Hopgood's secretary and general helper, not a girl of the outdoors. Or of the indoor gym. Ninety percent of her time spent at the telephone or at the word processor."

"Or possibly in bed," put in Alex.

"Yes, that too. As we've been informed on all sides. The lady did double duty. But no matter how gymnastic her mattress life was, it doesn't seem to add up to the strength to hoist one-hundred-and-eighty-pound senators into wagons."

"How about equipment, levers, hoists, block and tackle?"

At this juncture Shorty Fox strode into the room, pulled up a chair, and joined the fray. "Alex is on target. There's a lot of odd equipment down at the corral including enough tackle to hoist the body. Cowboys have to hoist things, wagons and fallen animals. The real question may not be whether Lily Farnsworth could have loaded Hopgood, but why do such a weird thing? If she was bent on revenge and suicide, why not leave him where he was shot and then shoot herself? Or drive his dead body to Agave Annex for greater privacy and then do herself in?"

But Solly interrupted. "The whys are for you detective types. Pathologists do the hows. For my money I'd say Lily Farnsworth would have trouble doing the job by herself. So maybe she had help. So how did Senator Hopgood die? Answer, by a nine-millimeter pistol. Two shots. Distance: beyond contact range—circular holes with an abrasion collar without powder marking of the skin. Forehead wound—above the right supraorbital margin—suggests face-to-face confrontation with murderer."

"And Lily Farnsworth?" asked Alex.

"Weapon the same as the one that got Hopgood. Suicide, no. The prints weren't right. Fuzzy and misplaced. We guess the victim's right hand was wrapped around the gun, but clumsily. It's very tough to take a dead person's hand and force it into the position for grasping and firing the weapon and leave the prints looking natural. Very rarely we're helped in deciding on suicide by an instantaneous rigor—cadaveric spasm."

"Mighty rare," put in Shorty Fox. "I've only seen one case. The pistol was gripped so hard it took force to break it free."

"Okay," said Alex, "the gun wasn't in her hand at death, but was anything else? Strands of hair? A business card perhaps?"

"Zip in her hands, but bloodstains say she was killed in the passenger seat from someone standing next to the open car window, and fell forward. The lab came up with a lot of detritus from the car. From the driver's seat, tobacco, the senator's brand of cigarette. Spilled whiskey—we found the flask—bits of chocolate, and some soft navy-blue fuzz—a cotton-acrylic blend. The blend you get in sweatshirts, sweatpants. But the senator was wearing a gray suit."

"Nowadays," put in Shorty Fox, "you get that blend in everything, women's clothes, dressy things. My wife's favorite dress is made out of some sort of T-shirt stuff."

"Sadly true," said Solly. "We can't pin this on the campus jock. Calvin Klein probably uses the stuff. But lab reports are pending. The lady also had had a couple of belts before she died. Not to make her drunk, just feisty or mean as the mood took her."

"Can you tell if she was shot before the senator was? Or after?" asked Alex.

"Good question. All indications are for the deaths to be fairly close in time. Regular, not instantaneous, rigor develops differently in different people. Wait for the lab tests."

"The real problem," said Shorty, "is to figure out this crazy feed sack caper. I mean why get the senator out of the car, kill him—yes, he was shot on the corral ground, we found the bullets near the corral fence—then hunt up the empty feed bags, stuff him in, and hoist him in the wagon? Especially if you're going to make the effort to set up a suicide scenario with Lily's prints on the gun. And drive her, alive or dead, to the Annex—why, hell, it's plain loony."

Alex shook his head in disbelief. "If she was driven alive, she must have known or trusted the driver. Do you think we have two murderers?"

Shorty shrugged. "The Bureau boys are beginning to kick that one around. Two, maybe three murderers. A conspiracy. The FBI loves conspiracies. Particularly political ones. A conspiracy to get rid of the senator which came apart because Lily turned up."

"Shall I tell Alex why Lily turned up?" said Solly. "And how we know why? It was cute, real cute. Lily came down to the corral to have it out with Hopgood. Mad as hell. Wife and kid imported at Christmastime when only Lily was supposed to be sharing his stocking. She telephoned his car Christmas Eve from the lobby."

Alex nodded. "Sarah told me she saw her in the booth Christmas Eve."

"She didn't tell us that," said Shorty, reaching over and pulling out a pad of paper from a desk drawer.

"I suppose you didn't ask," said Alex mildly.

"Everything a murder victim does before she's murdered is important," said Shorty sharply. "Now, just why was Sarah loitering by the phone booth?"

"Not loitering. She was on the way to the Christmas Eve ride."

"Ah, yes. That trail ride," said Solly. "It does keep popping up. Perhaps the ranch will incorporate it into their holiday schedule."

"Okay," said Alex, holding on to his patience with difficulty, "suppose you tell me how you know Lily called Senator Hopgood."

Shorty Fox put down his pencil and nodded at Solly. "Like he said, it was cute. The management, for reasons we will be looking into, tape all outgoing phone calls from that so-called public phone booth. The excuse given is that there've been problems of security. So, lucky us, we have a tape of Lily making a date with Hopgood for a showdown at the corral at nine. To get things straight or she quits. Or blows the whistle. Her words. He said something like the hell you will. But then he got all soft and told her how great she was in bed, and he couldn't live without her and she should trust him. All that junk."

"She bought it?" said Alex.

"Her voice at the end of the call sounded a little less sour. So anyway we know why they were at the corral," said Shorty.

"A love tryst," said Solly.

"So Hopgood could have shot Lily, and then whoever listened to the tape could have shot him and bagged him and then drove Lily's body, fixed like suicide, to the Annex," said Alex.

"Listen, Alex," said Solly, "Mickey Mouse could have shot her and Donald Duck could have plugged him and Pluto could have stuffed the senator in the bags and put him in the wagon and Snow White and the Dwarfs could have driven her to Agave Annex. That's as likely as anything the police have right now, isn't it, Shorty?"

Shorty stood up, the interview plainly over. He turned to Alex. "The Disneyland solution isn't farfetched because the Bureau boys are playing with the idea—as I'm sure you've guessed—that the two murders are just Act Five to all those sweet little stunts. And that sweet little old lady, Julia Clancy, why two attacks? And Maria Cornish, why the snake? Those two are the only ones who got personal attention. Agent Jay is fascinated by the possibilities. I expect he's having a high old time with Aunt Julia right now."

Special Agent Douglas Jay certainly enjoyed himself more than his visitor, Julia Clancy. In fact, as the interview progressed, Julia—increasingly annoyed, uncomfortable, and finally agitated—decided the experience was not unlike being in the hands of a dedicated dentist. She found herself, her life, her interests, and her friends probed, explored, drilled, X-rayed, reexamined, and drilled again.

A feature of the interview, as Alex had been told, was Julia's role as victim of hose and chair. The guest book was gone over again, Julia's roster of friends exhumed, and finally, in triumph, it was established that in the long-ago days of boarding school, Julia had actually had a classmate—one Susan Davies—who was sister to Corla Howell, née Davies, who, along with her husband, Orvis Howell, was an honored guest of Heinz Simmons's. Further, Julia had once voted against Susan as riding team captain and Julia may have once met Corla on a visit to Susan.

"I cannot believe," said Julia, "that after fifty years Susan Davies's sister would spray me with a hose or cut my chair straps."

"No stone unturned," said Agent Jay, a remark that to Julia said, no tooth undrilled.

"Besides," said Julia, scoring a point at last, "Mrs. Howell didn't get to the ranch until Mr. Simmons did."

"True, but a niece of hers was here at Thanksgiving."

"The idea is ridiculous," said Julia firmly. "Unless Susan Davies has turned violent in her old age and has family members going around settling old scores. Susan and I used to meet at horse shows, and she was always perfectly civil."

"Well, we'll keep an eye on you and your party for your own safety," said Douglas Jay.

"Maria Cornish had a snake in her bathtub," Julia reminded him. "Surely no one is after her, too."

Agent Jay allowed himself a small negative gesture. "Maria Cornish is so well known that these types of jokes are almost expected. And by the way," he added, "I think you know that we will check with Mrs. Freebody about your visit. Routine questions. Now, describe again your return to the ranch after your visit to the Freebody facility."

And Julia, checking an impulse to fling her handbag at the agent's head, went over again her much-described return to the ranch at five o'clock Christmas morning, her sighting of

Fred Arco, and her own state of exhaustion. Again she denied seeing anything or anyone of a sinister nature. Certainly not a car arriving with or without a dead secretary in it.

"Just checking," said Douglas Jay. He reached across the table and held out his hand. "Now take care, Mrs. Clancy," he said. Julia shook his hand, noted the hard, unfriendly grip, and found herself escorted to the door.

Sarah, in what must once have been a dining alcove, was sitting in a folding metal chair outside Douglas Jay's office. The agent nodded at her and said it would be five minutes. He closed the door and left aunt and niece facing each other.

"Like a dentist," said Julia crossly. "Every cavity has been drilled. And the same old ground except for digging out the sister of Mrs. Howell, someone I knew back in the dark ages. He's going to have someone keep an eye on our party."

Sarah grimaced. "All we need, the FBI under our beds."

"Come in, Miss Deane, and sit down," said Douglas Jay in an iron voice, poking his head outside the door. "By my desk so I can see you. This isn't a social visit, you know. I mean business and I certainly hope you do."

While Sarah Deane settled into what promised to be an abrasive session, the investigative efforts of assorted homicide teams, laboratory teams, and secondary interrogatory teams were busy searching out the ways and means of Rancho del Gato Blanco, driving Manager Fred Arco closer to the brink of a breakdown. The Napoleonic façade, so carefully nurtured, had begun to show cracks with the occurrence of the first of the so-called stunts. Now cracks had become wide fissures, as that hapless gentleman found himself caught between the demands of guests wanting to leave, prospective guests wanting to arrive, the pleas of Judy Steiner for some sort of protocol, and the directives of the Federal Bureau of Investigation's field team. Fred Arco had become more and more the Napoleon of Saint Helena, and on this the day after Christmas he seemed to have shrunk into something resembling one of Napoleon's more unsuccessful generals.

"What about Primrose Cottage unit?" asked Judy. "Are the

police going to be there forever? We've got people booked there starting tomorrow."

"What about Agave Annex?" asked Cookie. "Lily Farnsworth's things are gone, so can we use it for guests? Or storage?"

"Fred, I can't handle the extra lunch and dinner guests from those bloody newspeople," complained chef Peter Doubler. "I'll have to beef up the menu. Can you get an okay for a double or even triple jump in the provisions orders?"

"How can I check the house staff," said Cookie, "if I'm spending half the time with the police giving my life history? I don't know where I was half of Christmas, the place was a madhouse. Even without the senator's murder."

"May we see your art supplies?" demanded one investigator, a Mr. Paulson, in a brief lull that morning.

Fred Arco, like an animal badgered beyond endurance, almost yelled, "What art supplies? We don't have art supplies, this is a resort. A triple-star resort."

"Yes, yes," soothed Judy Steiner, coming from the back office and standing by his elbow. "We have art supplies as part of our youth camp program." She turned to Mr. Paulson. "We run a youth program during school vacation periods."

"Right," said Mr. Paulson. "And now we want to go through the stuff being sent for laundry and cleaning. Guests and staff."

"Guest laundry and cleaning," said Mr. Arco irritably, "goes out today. The staff laundry and cleaning we do in our own facility at the ranch. It was cleaned and laundered yesterday. The staff must always have access to clean uniforms."

Mr. Paulson frowned. "You mean the staff stuff was cleaned? Never mind, we'll impound it anyway. The lab will have to do their best. And I want all the clothes, dirty or clean, identified as we collect them. Have guests and staff stand by." And Mr. Paulson departed, trailed by a distraught Fred Arco.

"Damn," said Cookie to Judy as the unhappy Fred Arco led the way to the laundry complex.

"What was that blue stuff in the piñatas?" asked Judy.

Cookie shrugged. "How should I know?"

"If *you* don't, who does?" returned Judy in a hard voice. "Listen, Cookie, I'll cover your tail just so far, but those guys aren't stupid. And don't tell me about the piñatas or anything else. I don't want to know. But Cookie Logan, do you and Todd want your jobs or not? And if you've decided to go into murder, well, why choose this place? God almighty, Cookie, think of the rest of us."

"Back off, Judy," said Cookie. "You don't understand."

"Here's what I understand," retorted Judy. "I want this job. Not forever, but right now. I'm socking every buck I make here away to buy my own place and fifty head of cattle and some good horses and start a damn good working guest ranch. In Montana, not in competition with Cat Claw. I'm Montana-born, and that's where I'll damn well die. And Morty's said he'll go along as head wrangler. He was born in Bozeman, and he'd like to raise his family there. You hear all this? Right now I'm going to hang in at this screwball Gato White Cat even if Heinz Simmons is Mafia and the Howells are godfathers and Fred Arco is a serial murderer and you, Cookie, and the whole Logan-Younger crew are ranch terrorists. I'll cover you just so far as it's safe for me. So be thinking up what you're going to say when the police zero in on some of the fun and games you've all been having."

Here Judy drew a deep breath, and then looking up and seeing Alex advancing across the lobby, asked if she could help him.

"I said I'd meet Sarah back here after she's finished with her interrogation. It's been over an hour and a half. And have you seen Julia Clancy?"

"No to Sarah Deane," said Judy as Cookie beat a retreat into the inner office. "Yes to Julia Clancy. She got a pass to drive to town—the police are easing up on guests who've had their statements taken. She said she'd meet you both at lunch here at twelve-thirty."

Alex thanked Judy and walked slowly out to the pool area, which commanded a distant view of the Primrose Police Cottage complex. Julia, he decided, had probably wanted to make an untapped phone call, another check with Patrick. He settled himself in a poolside chair, waved across to a terry-cloth-swathed Maria Cornish, and opened his paperback spy thriller to while away the prelunch waiting period. Sarah must be having the full treatment from Special Agent Jay.

The full treatment it was. Sarah had rarely spent a more uncomfortable hour. It was confrontation, argument, every question repeated, each of her answers challenged, picked apart, and tossed back in her lap. Sarah's chair became hard, her back stiff, and her brain increasingly numb. She had just described again the sequence of events leading to the Christmas Eve ride when Douglas Jay remarked that he planned to skip over the details of that particular event.

"Why?" said Sarah, her annoyance increasing. "You've had it twice before, why not try for a third run-through?"

"It's a curious thing about repeated stories," said Douglas Jay. "If they've been made up and memorized for a particular occasion, they usually come out the same. All the details in place, no additions or subtractions."

"What's that supposed to mean?" demanded Sarah.

"Just an observation from experience. Fabricated stories, if told by intelligent persons with decent memories, are pretty static. Same expressions, same pauses, same facts. Just like a part you've learned for a play. But accounts of real experiences are always changing. Each time the person recounts the event he—or she"—here Douglas Jay opened his eyes a millimeter more and fixed on the point between Sarah's eyes—"he or she remembers something new, a detail forgotten, the rest of what someone said, the fact that the mosquitoes were out, the temperature was over eighty. The stories get longer, they evolve. Earlier details are corrected, names are changed or recollected correctly, little nuances are recalled."

"Interesting," was Sarah's comment.

"I thought you might think so. I particularly admire the way your account of your Christmas Eve is so perfectly rendered. How well it jibes with Miss Cornish's, with Blue Feather Romero's. With Cookie Logan's account of her helping saddle your horses. Very nice of her, considering she must have been needed badly back at the ranch cocktail party. Even that confusion about riding Peaches, not Patches, because Patches was put aside for the use of Mr. Simmons's guests. Everyone telling me that all horses' names sound alike. That, Miss Deane, if you'll excuse me, is a lot of bull. When you are riding, your horse is important to your safety. You remember its name. Peaches, Patches, I don't buy the mix-up. I'll bet when you rent a car you remember whether it's a Chevy or a Ford or a Toyota. So we'll skip another letter-perfect recitation of your trip down Buzzard Creek. What none of you jokesters seem to believe—and I use the word 'jokesters' advisedly—is that this is a case of murder. Death, sudden death. Heart stopping, lungs not pumping, blood not moving. Dead. Senator Hopgood's dead. So is Lily Farnsworth, and everyone comes in here and gives me a lot of garbage about scenic night rides. Okay, answer me, when did Mrs. Julia Clancy make it home from her friend's place in Peeple's Valley?"

Sarah, her face increasingly red, her breath coming shorter, glared at Douglas Jay. Then she took two deep, slow breaths, fixed her gaze on Douglas Jay's left ear, and said, "I told you, I didn't look at the clock. I heard the car stop outside and her screen door close. I said to Alex, 'Aunt Julia's back,' and went to sleep."

"Did you have any idea that it was still night or early morning, or dawn?"

"I didn't open my eyes. I was still mostly asleep."

"So you couldn't say there was moonlight in the room? Or the sun was coming up? Or light from the patio lamp?"

"No, I couldn't."

"Has your Aunt Julia been known for her temper? For periods of anger, for irrational acts?"

Sarah hesitated just long enough and Douglas Jay said, "Thank you, you've answered my question."

"She's not dangerous," said Sarah, still hanging on to control. "It's just she doesn't suffer fools gladly."

"Neither do I," said Douglas Jay, "and now you may go." He turned to the side, selected a folder from a stack atop a file cabinet, and bent over it, leaving Sarah to stand, make her way to the door, and leave. The door slammed.

Slamming the door was an action she immediately regretted. She'd shown that he'd gotten her goat and been exactly right in some of his guesses—except about Aunt Julia, who surely was not given to temper tantrums to the point of murder.

And she, Sarah? What a gutless, softheaded wimp. Letting that FBI creature play drill sergeant. Sarah, boiling, stamped out of Primrose Cottage and, without paying much attention to direction, strode down the path behind the cottages until she came to a bench under a line of shade trees that commanded a distant view of one of the desert horse trails. She sat down, fixed her eyes on a distant line of spiny vegetation, and began to grapple with recent experience. And herself. Sarah the wimp.

She'd let herself be overborne by sarcasm, by an aggressive policeman. She remembered past periods of tearful reliance on male competence. And look at her now, afraid even of pokey old Pokey. Fie, fie, as one notable lady said to her lord. And, Sarah reminded herself, look at the notable ladies around you. Aunt Julia, who never quivered, unless on behalf of some horse who had taken a false step. Who shoulder-to-shoulder with Uncle Tom buffeted through life, and now without Uncle Tom kept right on buffeting. And Julia's mother, Grandmother Douglas. A woman of biblical force and relentless purpose. And look at Judy Steiner, at Cookie. At Maria Cornish. Iron maidens. I'll bet Douglas Jay didn't treat them like army recruits. But Sarah? An easy target. And even Alex, always the protective arm, the helping hand, the ready handkerchief. In fact, that's how the two of them had begun. She, Sarah, the nervous wreck, possessor of the murdered boyfriend, availing herself of Alex's shoulder. Why, she was a disgrace to the whole sisterhood.

Time to stand up. And start thinking. If it was murder that had to be reckoned with, well, then, time to reckon. Because if some progress wasn't made toward getting murder separated from lesser events, certain people might end up in a locked-up condition. Not for murder—the police weren't that foolish—but for editing their stories and giving tainted interviews. And the murders? Perhaps one of their riding party had seen something, had heard something. They had all been so preoccupied with their cover story that they may have missed what really happened. Blue Feather, for instance. Blue Feather swaggering, drinking, and picking fights. Leaving Maria Cornish, hinting at money in his pocket. Blue Feather had made two trips with saddles to the corral on Christmas Eve. What had he seen? A dead body? A smoking gun? A figure slipping into the mesquite? Lily Farnsworth slumped on the seat of the senator's Cadillac—the Cadillac the entire riding party had seen waiting for Julia to back and turn her horse van.

"Damnation," said Sarah aloud. "Time to see Blue Feather." Of course, the police had no doubt seen him several times, but Sarah had nothing but admiration for Blue Feather's ability to maneuver and just plain lie. Maria had lost her hold on him, and perhaps it was just a matter of time until he managed to implicate them all in something much less heartwarming than horse rescue.

And there was Maud-Emma Hopgood. Had anyone considered Maud-Emma in the light of a wronged and vengeful woman? Sarah remembered the determined tilt of her chin as she had entered the dining room. She looked at her watch. Twelve twenty-five. Time to meet for lunch. She braced her shoulders and made her way toward the lodge. Sarah, the woman with a purpose. Sarah, who was going to get a handle on some of these ranch goings-on, starting that afternoon with Blue Feather. Or with Mrs. Senator Maud-Emma Hopgood. Whoever first came within her reach. She began to think that her recent meeting with Douglas Jay had redeeming qualities: it had helped stiffen her spine and had served as a valuable—if humiliating—learning experience.

EIGHTEEN

SARAH, in the guise of the new strong-minded woman, met Alex and Julia in the lobby, whence they progressed to the luncheon buffet.

Settled, Sarah turned on her aunt. "Okay, what have you been up to? I've been bullied by that FBI man, and I'm not going to let it happen again."

Julia exclaimed and Alex frowned, but Sarah went on. "Never mind me. I've had a long talk with myself. Aunt Julia?"

Julia poked thoughtfully at a pasta salad and then said in a rather rueful voice, "Nothing more than that crazy connection to the Howells I told you about."

"As a matter of fact, I went to school with two Howells," said Sarah. "Cousins. Emma and Jennifer."

"But it hardly connects us with the murder of Senator Hopgood," said Julia.

"You forget the police mind," said Alex. "Give them a cobweb and they'll call it a rope and hang themselves—or you—with it. See how it works? Senator Hopgood is shot. Heinz Simmons and spouse are friends of Senator Hopgood's. The Howells are friends and guests of the Simmonses . Julia Clancy arrives at a ranch run by Heinz Simmons. Julia Clancy is the victim of two not so funny jokes. And you, Julia, went to school with Mrs. Howell's sister, who was not a friend. And Sarah, we now learn, went to school with not one but two Howells. Ergo, Julia Clancy and Sarah are connected to Senator Hopgood. People have been indicted for less."

"Well," said Sarah, "now that's established, what else have you done, Aunt Julia? Or said?"

"After the interview I drove to town and phoned."

"Phoned who?" demanded Sarah.

"Whom. Phoned whom. Accusative case. Really, Sarah, and you an English teacher. No wonder the country is flooded with illiterates. I called Laura Freebody. To alert her about police calls, but she says her end is holding steady. And, since Laura was at school with me, I asked if she knew the Howell family."

"And?"

"Laura does know the Howells. Various pieces of the family come out here for long stretches. Sometimes branches turn up at Gato Blanco. Like the present couple with the Simmonses. These Howells have quarts of money and fingers in real-estate pies. Big spreads like this one. Or retirement communities outside of Tucson and Phoenix. The Howells, both of them, and Simmons supported Hopgood, who voted for development and construction—all those bad words—and voted against saving the long-eared—or is it the short-nosed—vole or spotted owl or the mountain lion."

"Whatever," said Sarah.

"The point is that it would not be in Mr. Howell's interest to shoot the senator, who was very friendly to his projects."

"I suppose the same would go for Heinz Simmons," said Alex. "Why kill a helpful senator who's about to declare for the presidency? Or the senator's friendly secretary?"

"Listen," said Alex, "if Hopgood was going to declare his candidacy, he would have made damn sure that all his dirty laundry was clean. I'll bet he's been covering traces, hiding his evil relatives, putting his investments in blind trusts for months. You don't run for office these days unless you can open your closet doors and invite the press in to play hide-

and-seek. You'd better make sure that your school records are available, you didn't deflower the prom queen, you didn't mug a counselor at summer camp, and of course you haven't smoked pot for the past twenty years. Or been caught at it."

"Okay," said Sarah. "I thought maybe the senator had told the Howells and the Simmonses he wasn't going to be so friendly about their little projects in the future."

"The police hate speculation about motivation," said Alex. "What they love is hard evidence. Smoking guns, lipstick smears, hairs, fingernails, blood types, ballistic details—and that's what my session with Solly was about. Statistics. For your information Lily and Hopgood were murdered with the same type of gun. Lily Farnsworth probably didn't have the muscle to hoist Hopgood into the chuck wagon, both victims died in the same time period but there's no evidence yet about who was shot first."

"Maybe Lily was the number one target," said Sarah. "Has anyone even considered that Maud-Emma might have gone into action as the woman scorned?" Here Sarah raised her eyebrows and moved her head slightly in the direction of a table some fifty feet across from their own. Maud-Emma Hopgood seemed to have recovered. She was speaking with angry animation, gesturing with both hands at the senator's two political aides, who sat on each side of her.

"She looks alive," said Julia. "Not crushed but renovated."

"Stimulated anyway," said Sarah. "Or maybe mad. Or glad that someone's done in Lily and rotten husband Leo J. If he was a rotten husband."

"Aha," said Julia. "Motivation. You see."

"What I see," said Alex, putting down his fork, "is dessert. Day-old mince pie and other goodies. Let the murder rest for now. We're trail riding at two, right? And where's Maria? I thought she might turn up at lunch."

"She may be pining for Blue or making lunch with Heinz Simmons," said Sarah. "Or none of the above."

"None of the above, darling. A facial," said a voice over their shoulders. "Nothing like it. Restore, restore, that's what I say. If trouble troubles, go for a facial. And a complete massage. Tension just floats away." And Maria Cornish ducked under their umbrella and settled herself in a chair.

"Have you been grilled today?" asked Julia.

"An hour on the hot seat," said Maria, reaching across Alex and helping herself to a slab of corn bread. "But I didn't give an inch. Letter-perfect. And no, Sarah, I'm not pining for Blue Feather. Pining is not becoming, not at my age anyway. Besides, the more I think about him, the happier I am that he's moved off my turf. The whole thing was going stale, stale, and now it's over, and after the first nasty little shock, I'm glad. For lunch I'm going to have a salad and the nutritive shake they make up for me."

As Maria began a careful explanation of the protein and vitamin content of the shake, Sarah saw Maud-Emma leave the luncheon area, make her way to the front of the lodge, disappear for a moment, and then reappear at the lodge entrance at the wheel of a gray Ford Escort. Sarah put down her napkin, stood up, and before anyone could object, asked for the keys to Julia's car. "I've just remembered something I was supposed to do. Next semester. A book order. I think I'll go into town and call there. Some private class stuff, so I don't want the FBI doing heavy breathing during the call. Aunt Julia, may I have your pass? They won't check the name."

Alex started to rise, but Sarah put her hand firmly on his shoulder and told him she'd be right back. Go eat his mince pie.

Sarah was correct. The policeman at the gate only glanced at the date on the pass and the Gato Blanco sticker on the side of her windshield and waved her on. In fifteen minutes Sarah was at a Mobil station having Aunt Julia's car filled with gas, her car positioned at the opposite side of the pump to the gray Ford Escort driven by Maud-Emma. A boy sat beside her in the passenger seat, the egregious Artie, no doubt.

Sarah felt moderately pleased with herself. It had gone as planned. Acting on her aunt's favorite maxim, seize the day, she had flung herself into action at the sight of Maud-Emma in motion. And it was curious. Why was Maud-Emma in Lodestone getting gas like any commonplace citizen? Or did she, too, want out? A little freedom. Though in her case, considering a waiting blue sedan behind her, freedom from the police was just a matter of twenty yards. And why the choice of the self-service pump? Wouldn't the wife of a senator want the works, clean windshield, the oil checked? But as Sarah watched, Maud-Emma, packed into a pair of studded jeans and a flowing pink-checked shirt, climbed out of the car and began examining the pump, leaning over the instructions, adjusting her glasses. Why, it's a first, thought Sarah. This is the very first time she's filled an automobile tank. A historic occasion. This realization was enforced by a blue-suited man jumping from the waiting blue sedan and running up to the pump and seizing the hose. But Maud-Emma wrenched it back, said something, and the man retreated. Sarah, fascinated, watched as she might watch some creature emerging from a cocoon. Only this was an emerging woman taking her first tiny steps in the real world.

Then as Sarah saw her fumble the hose out of the car and replace it, a bit of sunlight caught her left hand, which was holding the tank cap. A flat gold ring. A familiar flat gold ring. The very same sort of ring that Aunt Julia wore from time to time, that her mother kept in a jewel box marked with a date, and that Sarah herself kept in the back of her underwear drawer. Was it possible? Sarah left the telephone booth and edged her way toward Mrs. Hopgood, who was now securing the fuel cap. Yes, the ring was familiar. The mark of an alumna of Miss Morton's Academy of Butler, Maryland. A flat gold ring with the dark initials *MMA* on the surface.

Sarah went into action. First, she pretended to be examining the four self-service gas pumps, then she gave a little cry of pleased surprise. She pointed at Maud-Emma's ring, said the magic words, "Miss Morton's," then added a few somber words of condolence on the subject of recent events, smiled at a sulky-looking Artie Hopgood, and identified herself as a fellow ranch guest.

The response was gratifying.

Maud-Emma, Sarah reflected later, must have been starved for companionship. Female companionship with some sort of common ground from which to find sympathy.

It was as if Sarah had opened a valve. As Sarah had guessed, it was the first time she had "evah in mah whole life" filled the gas tank of a car.

She went on to say in her southern accent that the late senator had not trusted her at the wheel of a car in the Washington traffic, so she had a driver, that in Talladega she always went for the full-service pumps, but now that she was on her own she was going to do a few things that everyone had prevented her from doing.

"Miss Morton's was surely supposed to teach a woman to be a whole woman," she went on, waving her credit card at Sarah, "but in my time that meant being a good mother and standing behind your man. Maybe going to college and getting a degree in art history, but never learning anything useful about how a car runs or how to do your income tax. Oh, I know, there are plenty of independent southern women, but I just bought the whole package. All I ever did was try to make myself attractive and remember names and give nice parties in Georgetown. Or go to barbecues in Texas and visit the museum in Juneau. Well, I have just had it. Up to here. I am sorry that Leo has been shot, just as sorry as I can be, but I am not just going to sit around weeping into a lace handkerchief."

"So you thought you'd drive into Lodestone today and get away?" said Sarah.

Maud-Emma waved a hand at the blue sedan. "How can anyone get away from them? It's a wonder they don't hide in my bathtub. Maybe they do. I thought I'd call Mother in Talladega without someone listening in on the ranch telephone. Tell her in my own words what's happening. And I am so glad you came right up and introduced yourself, because I don't know a soul at this ranch except for Leo's aides, and I do hate the very sight of them."

At this Sarah suggested coffee or tea. Some nearby eatery. Perhaps a sundae for Artie.

This was accepted, and Sarah collected her car, Maud-

Emma hers, and, followed by the blue sedan, they turned into a municipal parking space and settled themselves at the Lodestone Tea House, a building of vaguely Eastern design. Artie sat at a table apart with a double banana split, the two watchers from the blue sedan waited outside the door, and Maud-Emma ordered a strawberry parfait and Sarah a large Coke.

Maud-Emma continued the process of opening up, letting it all hang out. First came the good old days at Miss Morton's, and Sarah endured a disconnected series of incidents of a boarding school student of the early fifties. Fortunately some teachers that Sarah had remembered as octogenarians, Maud-Emma had known in their greener years, and she and Maud-Emma had both worked on the yearbook. Then, as a bit of frosting, Sarah told Maud-Emma that back at the ranch at this very moment was another Miss Morton alumna, Sarah's aunt, Julia Douglas Clancy, of the class of '42.

After exclamations and an expressed desire to meet Mrs. Clancy, floodgates now well open, Maud-Emma moved into the sphere of murder. A dead husband, his dead suspect secretary, a ruined future, a young son on the edge of hysteria.

Sarah, glancing over at Artie stuffing himself with whipped cream, did not think in his case hysteria was quite the right word, but she kept silent and made sympathetic noises. Eventually she steered the conversation to Maud-Emma's friends, Mr. and Mrs. Heinz Simmons and the Howells. So lucky to have their support in a time of such trouble.

A new explosion. Not her friends. Never her friends. Not the kind of support she needed. Here a tear welled up and trickled down one of Maud-Emma's well-powdered cheeks.

Sarah with a sidewise glance at her watch saw that they were perilously close to the projected trail-riding time of two o'clock and took a chance.

"You need a real change. Come riding with us. We're going out at two. Just my friend Alex, Aunt Julia, and Maria Cornish."

At first Maud-Emma seemed to hesitate, but with the addition of the name Maria Cornish, she sat up and took notice. "Why, yes, yes, it might be fun. But Artie."

"Bring him along," said Sarah recklessly.

And it was decided.

"They," said Maud-Emma, pointing at the silhouettes of the two men at the door, "will have to come."

"The more the merrier," said Sarah, swallowing hard. But after all, the police might even trust Morty to take the group out on a well-marked trail and so would stay well in the rear with walkie-talkies or whatever equipment they used in their profession.

Sarah was just pulling on her boots when Aunt Julia knocked at the door, pulled it open, and entered in one irritated motion.

"Really, Aunt Julia," said the new Sarah, "how did you know I wasn't rolling around in bed with Alex?"

Julia, taken aback, stopped and looked apologetic. "I shouldn't have done that, should I? But we're late for our ride."

Sarah stood up, picked up her straw Stetson, and informed her aunt of the additions to their riding party.

Julia began to protest but was stopped by Alex, who emerged from the bathroom. "Maud-Emma Hopgood!" he exclaimed. "And that miserable Artie. Are you out of your mind?" Then, seeing Sarah's lips tight, he added, "I see, it's the amateur detective at work. But damn it, you know the FBI have been through Mrs. Hopgood's life like a vacuum cleaner. The feds are thorough. They suck blood."

"Really, Alex," said Sarah. "I only want to cheer up that poor woman. And guess what, she went to Miss Morton's."

"Gracious heavens," said Aunt Julia with heavy sarcasm. "We'll just have to get together and sing the school song. Sarah, if you're so anxious to be Maud-Emma's friend, you can take on Artie, too. Alex and I can talk about the real things of this world."

"Like proper shoeing and laminitis," said Alex.

"Potomac horse fever," said Julia. "And strangles."

*   *   *

Maud-Emma was at the corral, already mounted on Noodle, a bay with one white sock, and Artie sat beside her on a small buckskin.

"Why can't I have a regular horse?" he complained to Morty. "It's not like I'm a beginner."

Morty looked at the boy. "Artie, if you don't gripe once during this ride, I'll put you on Montana tomorrow. Okay?"

And Artie, to everyone's surprise, probably including his own, said "Okay" and closed his lips tight.

At that juncture Maria Cornish arrived. Todd Logan brought out Diablo Bravo saddled and ready; Maria mounted and was ceremoniously introduced to Maud-Emma.

It was love—or at least admiration—at first sight. Maud-Emma was a fan, the only real fan in the group. The only one of the party who had actually seen fifteen of Maria's movies, had lasted through her miniseries, and valued her appearance on the talk show.

Maria glowed. Maud-Emma, to her, was, by way of her husband, someone from the corridors of power, and she was an almost central figure in a spectacular murder. And so for the next ten minutes, while Alex and Sarah were being mounted, Maria and Maud-Emma went at it. In fact, they were doing so well together that Sarah feared that her plan of having Maud-Emma to herself was going to founder on this developing mutual admiration society.

Fortunately Maud-Emma wanted the mountain trail, and Maria, like Sarah, expressed a horror of heights. The party split. Todd would take Maud-Emma and Artie up toward Coyote Canyon Pass, and Morty would take the others down their favorite trail, Buzzard Creek.

Sarah took a deep breath, remembered her vow to strike out as the new woman, and said that she was tired of riding on the flat and was dying—probably a good word for it—to take Coyote Canyon Pass. What fun. She and Maud-Emma could finish their reminiscences about good old Miss Morton's.

"Sarah," began Aunt Julia, while Alex's eyebrows disappeared into the shade of his hat brim.

"I'm sure," said Sarah, "that Artie would like to go with your group because he could go faster."

"Yeah," said Artie. "I like to gallop. Who wants to be stuck up on some mountainside where their horse could slip on a rock and go crashing down and get knocked into a bunch of bones?"

"Who indeed?" said Sarah, reining Pokey in beside Maud-Emma.

Sarah survived. Just. And only by closing her eyes at every hairpin turn, every move toward the edge of a drop-off. "Trust Pokey," Todd told her as he led them along the desert floor to a series of rocky foothills split by narrow trails, and then by degrees up toward the top rim of Coyote Canyon. It was amazing, thought Sarah, leaning forward and clinging to the saddle horn as Pokey strained, neck bent, into a curving, narrow uphill path that seemed to lead into thin air, that Maud-Emma, the tender flower of the South, submissive wife of the senator, seemed to have no qualms about being on a hoofed animal four feet off the ground and two feet away from a drop into space. Maud-Emma babbled on contentedly about early school days, her childhood in Talladega, her daddy the judge, her mother the secretary of the literary society, her brothers at the Citadel. Picnics, summer dances, all moonlight and roses until, apparently, the arrival of Prince Not So Charming Leo J. Hopgood.

"He was so, well, I just guess you'd say he was masterful. You know Texans. They can snow you right under."

"And you were snowed?" said Sarah as Pokey reached the top of the path and showed interest in looking over the canyon's edge. Here, dangerously, in her opinion, Todd Logan called a short halt.

"Yes, but it didn't last. As soon as Leo got me away from Alabama, I saw how I was going to spend my whole life. I did try. I was impressed at first by all the money and those important people coming round for dinner, and Leo's picture in the paper. But it wore off fast, and this Christmas, back in Talladega, I'd about decided to call it off when Leo's aides phoned and said I was to be here when he announced."

Sarah, keeping her eyes away from the canyon view, made sympathetic noises.

"Of course," Maud-Emma went on bitterly, "I thought Lily Farnsworth was as safe as Jesus, but now I have heard very differently. Of course, Leo was never a real family man, and, if you ask me, he must have gotten his hands into some dirty old mud pies to get himself killed. Well, he might have fooled me in bed, but I sure enough fooled him."

"You did what?" said Sarah, wondering if Maud-Emma was about to blossom as a bigamist or a member of NOW.

"Well, you know Leo just voted for development and just tons of military hardware. Business and armed forces people ate out of his palm. That's where his votes came from. So I joined, let me see, the Wilderness Society, the Nature Conservancy, the Sierra Club, the National Audubon Society, the Defenders of Wildlife, the National Wildlife Federation, and a whole bunch of Save organizations: Save the Whales, the Otters, the Dolphins, the Wolves. I've always just *loved* animals."

Sarah was incredulous. "As the senator's wife? He let you?"

A shadow of regret came over Maud-Emma's now rather dusty and perspiring face, its makeup lying in patches and streaks. "Well," she admitted, "I didn't use his name. My maiden name. Forrest. I used to be Maud-Emma Forrest."

"A perfectly good name."

"Yes, the Forrests are old Alabama people. A good Confederate name. The Hopgoods are upstarts. Originally carpetbaggers from Ohio. I used 'Forrest' for all those organizations, and sometimes I sent them extra money squeezed out of my entertainment budget."

But now Todd Logan called the two women to order. "Time to be moving on. We'll come along the rim for about a mile and then head down. Relax, Sarah, and ease up. You'll scare that pony by gripping your legs like you're going to strangle him. Give him his head. He knows what he's doing."

Sarah agreed that the last thing she would want to do was

scare Pokey, and they started along the canyon rim, Mrs. Hopgood's ever-present security guard to the rear. Even at the distance of fifty yards Sarah thought his face looked as green as she felt.

At last they reached the flat of a low wash and Maud-Emma rode up abreast of Sarah and began speculating on the desirability of retaking her maiden name of Forrest.

In this Sarah was encouraging, but added the caution that it might be a little soon. "You're still getting condolence calls from Washington, I suppose, and if you turned into Maud-Emma Forrest, you might become suspect number one."

Maud-Emma nodded, adding, "I'm feeling a lot better today. It certainly helps to talk."

They rode silently through the wash, joining an intersecting trail, and then, just as the corral gate came into view, Maud-Emma turned in her saddle and said, "Sarah, I've a favor. A great big favor. Can I ask you to do something?"

Sarah, surprised, pulled Pokey to a halt. "What is it?"

"My diaries. I've always kept diaries. Mama told me it was a good habit and I've done it all my life. And some very private letters. And papers. I've been hiding them in a sanitary-napkin box in my underwear drawer because, of course, our whole suite has been searched. I guessed that even the FBI wouldn't search a senator's wife's sanitary-napkin supply. I always keep a box with me even though I'm over fifty and haven't needed a napkin for years. But the box has been handy. Anything I didn't want Leo to see, why, I've hidden it there. But sooner or later the police will want to go over our things again. Will you take it for me? Hide it? No one would dream of looking into your things."

"Don't be too sure," said Sarah, thinking of her recent session with Agent Jay.

"Well, yes, a superficial search if the police are that desperate. But not into a Kotex box. Some things are sacred. Everything is under a layer of napkins. Say you'll take them."

Oh, what the hell, thought Sarah. Maud-Emma's diaries, even if they're as full of the senator's philandering ways and roving eye as of Maud-Emma's more intimate hopes and fears, can't do too much harm. And she, Sarah, could certainly sympathize with Maud-Emma's wish for privacy. "Okay," she said. "But how will we do it?"

"Broad daylight. We'll meet in Lodestone by a drugstore right after this ride. We'll both go in and buy something and I'll transfer the box to you at the door as we go out. You buy something bulky—in fact, buy a second box of Kotex, so you have a bag. And that Secret Service man won't come into the store. If he checks afterward to see if we've bought something, the clerk will say we have."

"I suppose it will work," said Sarah, thinking, why, Maud-Emma's as devious as Aunt Julia. Or Cookie—or Maria Cornish. As I am. We could have asked her to help save those horses and she would have been with us one hundred percent.

Maud-Emma appeared to read her mind. "You have to develop slippery ways if you deal with certain kinds of men. Bossy men with great big Texas-sized egos."

The sanitary napkin/diary plan went like clockwork. In the middle of the operation Sarah felt as if she and Maud-Emma were part of an experienced covert-operations team. Sarah even managed to convince those two skeptics of her party— Julia and Alex—that a second trip to Lodestone was necessary. The transfer itself was accomplished practically under the nose of the Secret Service man, the box being slipped from Maud-Emma's capacious canvas shopping bag to Sarah's plastic drugstore bag. Their apparently accidental meeting at the store was followed by the two women having a cup of tea at a nearby café, and plans for a second trail ride were made for the following morning.

"It's just been a nightmare since Leo was found in that feed bag," said Maud-Emma. "Artie's been so difficult, but I can't tell if he's grieved because he's lost a daddy or because there isn't a U.S. senator in the family. And the FBI people just won't leave me alone. They keep asking the same questions. Enemies Leo made. Business deals, his special friends."

"I can see why you want to get out on the trail," said Sarah.

"I need breathing space, so I will surely look forward to a morning ride tomorrow."

Sarah returned to Agave Three and managed to push Maud-Emma's boxed stash of letters and two bound diaries under a pile of her own underwear as suggested. Although she had accepted the assignment without too many qualms, she now began to feel queasy, rather as if she had taken possession of a bomb. On further and sober thought, the Kotex box might really conceal a bomb. Maud-Emma's diaries and letters, innocent though their author thought them, might just contain the one tiny link to some lethal clue, or person, or plan that would lead to a murderer. Or a conspiracy. And what if the police had no hesitancy in looking through the sanitary napkins of a suspect person? And suspect person, Sarah was beginning to feel, exactly fitted her own description.

"You look frazzled, Sarah," said Aunt Julia as she and Alex settled down on her patio for their predinner drink. "All that driving back and forth to Lodestone. Or is it something else?"

"You want to share?" said Alex.

"Maybe later," said Sarah. "I had a plan, or a plan to have a plan."

"You mean," said Julia, "you've decided to pump Mrs. Hopgood, who, if befriended, will come up with her husband and Lily Farnsworth's killer. Am I right?"

Sarah felt that her aunt was entirely too right, which was very annoying, so she simply said, "It's the pull of the old school tie. And Mrs. Hopgood wants to go trail riding with us again tomorrow. I really do feel sorry for her."

"Well," said Julia, "all right, though our trail riding is turning into a cavalry charge."

"Maybe we can detach Artie," said Sarah.

"As a matter of fact," said Julia, "he's my new project. He has a terrible personality but a natural seat for a horse. I gave him a few pointers, told him to stop being rude because he has real talent, and I said he could come with *me* tomorrow. At least we don't have to ride with Blue Feather. He seems to have evaporated."

"That creep," said Sarah succinctly, "would be more likely to combust. Originally I wanted to talk to him and find out what he knows about Christmas Eve at the corral, but the more I think of it, I'm sure he'd lie through his teeth about the whole thing. Or try and sell the information to us." Sarah put down her glass with a defiant thump. "So I certainly hope I never see the man again."

"Which means," said Julia, "as things usually work out, that there's a Blue Feather Romero in your future."

NINETEEN

SOLLY Jackson surfaced after dinner, found Alex, and ushered him into a small bedroom in the Ocotillo Wing.

"My home away from home," he said, kicking a chair in Alex's direction. "I am now officially in residence as local medical person in charge of almost nothing." Solly settled his length on the bed and pulled the pillow under his head. "I have news from the world of laundry and cleaning. Also news about you and yours."

Alex grimaced. "Let's start with laundry and cleaning."

"Certainly. Laundry bonanza. Man is a greedy animal, he wants for free. When Arco offered free cleaning and washing to staff and guests after the piñata affair, everyone reached down to the bottom of their hampers."

"Not just blue-dye-stained clothes?"

"The works. And it wasn't blue dye, it was tempera. Mixed from a powder. The sort of paint used in the vacation camp program run by the ranch. Point is the staff stuff got cleaned or washed right away and the lab so far hasn't come up with anything. Guest laundry has yielded nothing, not even from Julia Clancy and party."

"Be serious."

"Never more so. Interesting, however, that Arco, Simmons, and the Howells, as well as Cookie and Todd, sent full hampers, but you can't arrest anyone because he wants clean clothes."

Alex nodded and then bit the bullet. "Solly, speaking of laundry, it's time for the Julia Clancy party to come clean."

Solly shook his head. "Hold it. How about an after-dinner beer? No? Keeps the arteries young." He rose, headed for the small refrigerator that served as a unit with a small writing desk, extracted a Molson Lite, flipped open the top, sat down, and hoisted the can. "Here's to coming clean. Want it on tape?"

"Let me rough it in first. You can be official later."

"Wait up. Let me steal your thunder and tell you what the police, the FBI, the whole apparatus, have found out about you."

"Okay, then," said Alex, settling back with a sigh. "Shoot."

"An unfortunate expression," said Solly. "We know the following. Julia Clancy visited Laura Freebody December twenty-third and twenty-fourth. She came home sometime early Christmas morning. In between she was a very busy lady, driving big vehicles, playing horse hide-and-seek." Here Solly paused and took a long sip of beer, and then seeing Alex nodding agreement, went on. "We know three horses didn't make it to Bonzo's Pet Food, that three horses were vanned to Phoenix in a carrier with a Maryland license plate and flown to New York City and then were sent on to the Northeast. What the hell, we know the little Christmas Eve riding party—which included that scum ball, Blue Feather Romero—did the first part of the delivery and turned up in the horse van at the entrance to Corral Drive around nine o'clock, which is close to the time that the senator and Lily were being perforated. Now the next is the part you don't know about. The FBI thinks big."

"Big?" said Alex. "How do you mean, big?"

"Big like big. Conspiracy. The word 'terrorist' has surfaced."

"Don't be ridiculous."

"Who's being ridiculous? Terrorism is the buzzword of the decade. Big-time senator murdered just before he announces for the presidency. His confidential secretary ditto. Series of so-called jokes seem to lead up to this, because—now get this—even the senator's murder is disguised as a joke. *Another* joke. Black humor, stuffing Hopgood into feed sacks. And kidnaping three horses? A diversionary tactic, a related group of jokers? Alex, use your head. Why wouldn't the police tie the whole schmear together? So let me show you the official mind at work."

"Okay, if you must," said Alex, "but now you *can* get me a beer. Crap like this crap is making me thirsty."

Solly stood up, produced a second can of beer, and handed it to Alex. "Not crap," he said. "At least not all crap. Perhaps a misinterpretation of the facts. We'll give everyone a chance tomorrow to set the record straight. Right now the FBI is happily engaged in trying to prove that Julia Clancy's husband, Tom Clancy, was an Irish nationalist and probably had links to the IRA. He points out that Julia maintains a farm in Ireland and has been heard to make sympathetic remarks about conditions in Ireland."

"Oh Christ, Solly, everyone makes sympathetic remarks about the conditions in Ireland. Tom Clancy and Julia were and are horse people. Living and breathing horse. Horse, horse, horse."

"I'm just demonstrating the police mind. They have this idea that Julia, arriving here, found vast discontent among the Younger-Logan folk, found they were all into destroying Gato Blanco . . ."

Alex held his beer can aloft. "Whoa. Whoa up. Julia was victim number one of those stunts. Hit twice."

"Sure. And when the Logan-Youngers found what a feisty dame she was, how angry about the golf course, they took her on as a comrade-in-arms. Julia Clancy's been here since before Thanksgiving, so she's had a chance to get to know the staff and about grievances on behalf of Cat Claw. Douglas Jay is floating out the idea that Julia et al. joined forces to scandalize guests, to terrorize them with murder and as a sort of bonus eliminate a high-profile senator. A senator who hasn't an environmental hair on his head and who's made several speeches calling the Irish hopeless."

"He did?" said Alex. "I didn't know that."

"He went on a fact-finding trip to Dublin and made enemies left and right. A Baptist Texan in a land of Roman Catholics."

"I'm sure Julia doesn't know a thing about it. She's only Irish by marriage and keeps a small breeding and hunting stable there. With Julia, to repeat, the world is made up of horses and farms. Land of the Houyhnhnms. So for God's sake, Solly, tell that FBI bird the truth. Julia saved three horses. They were going for dog meat. Sarah helped because—" Here Alex paused and ran a hand through his black hair. "Sarah helped because it was easier than not to give in to Julia, and Maria Cornish is an animal lover—and Blue Feather was a Maria lover. Julia intended to pay for the value of the horses when she was sure they were safe. End of story. No funny business. No terrorist activity. No working with any group."

Solly nodded. "I could believe you, and Shorty could, too. It's the crazy sort of thing people do. Douglas Jay, I don't know. For a starter, I think he's about to pull Cookie Logan in. She's the link. She was at the corral Christmas Eve, *and* she knew the senator planned to meet Lily Farnsworth down at the corral."

"What's that?"

"Sure, remember I told you? The ranch office had a tap on the public telephone. A light went on in the clerk's office and in Arco's when a call went through. Cookie was undoubtedly around the office during part of Christmas Eve."

"But so was Judy Steiner. And Arco himself. And probably Heinz Simmons, and God knows who else. The office was probably open and anyone could wander in."

"But only the office people knew the telephone was bugged."

"I think," said Alex, "that you all have screws loose in your various heads. Julia and Cookie are not political. They have their little ways and means but it's local. Animals with Julia, and revenge for Cat Claw probably for Cookie and her family. Forget them, because the murder must be political."

"Terrorist action. Destroy popular resort ranch, symbol of capitalist America, and toss in a dead senator and his ladyfriend for good measure. No, I don't have screws in my head, I'm just giving you a light into the murky official brain."

"Brain isn't what I'd call it."

"Look, Alex, they're here to solve something. They're trying to find answers fast. Cookie and her tribe make nice targets because they sure as hell have been fooling around. So has Julia. The public wants answers, the media people are asking questions. The police need suspects so everyone will think they're doing their job. Julia's riding party and the Logan-Younger team fill a need. Later on, if they find Blue Feather went on a shooting rampage or that Laddie Danforth wanted Hopgood's Senate seat, well, the law boys will swing in another direction."

Alex rose to his feet, eyed his friend, and then tossed the empty beer at Solly's head. "Go back to pathology and stop being the FBI's aide-de-camp. Slicing up a corpse is a lot more wholesome. And if you need any of the conspirators tomorrow morning, they'll be out on the trail planning their next hit."

"No, they won't," said Solly. "They'll be writing out statements tomorrow morning. But they all can ride in the P.M. and get some wholesome air into their deceitful bodies."

Alex arrived back at Agave Three to find Sarah sitting up in bed with the latest copy of *Arizona Highways*. "I'm thinking," she said, "of submitting an article called 'Low Life on a Ranch.' "

Alex sat down on a bedroom chair and began untying his shoes. "The game is up," he said.

"Game, what game?"

"Aunt Julia's rescue league is unmasked."

Sarah pushed *Arizona Highways* off the bed and sighed heavily. "It was bound to happen. What now?"

"Damage control. Convince the police that you're not all some version of a fun-loving terrorist group specializing in horse stealing, stunt pulling, and shooting. Aunt Julia's Irish connections are being looked at with a doubtful eye."

Sarah sat up in bed. "You're crazy. They're crazy."

"My very words. But Solly said the Bureau thinks like that. Irish connections means IRA and that means trouble and trouble is what this ranch has in spades."

"Aunt Julia hasn't a political hair on her head," fumed Sarah.

"Right, so let's not waste energy on ridiculous ideas. Tomorrow A.M. you'll be given a chance to tell the police exactly how crazy they are." Alex pulled off his shirt and reached into a drawer of their shared bureau.

Sarah stiffened against her pillow. "That's my underwear drawer."

"You've got a lot of underwear, it's crammed full," said Alex, but he pulled open a lower drawer and withdrew flannel pajamas.

Sarah subsided, but the image of Maud-Emma's diaries and letters spilling out on the floor stayed in her head, and that night as she fell asleep she could almost see the whole collection increasing, swelling, multiplying into a thousand sheets, photographs, documents, check stubs, until she was smothered in a deluge of incriminating evidence.

When Sarah woke the next morning to brilliant sunshine, the notion that the police could for a moment conceive of Aunt Julia as an Irish terrorist was so idiotic as to be laughable. She sat up in bed and gave a sort of strangled chuckle. "We should submit this whole business to a joke magazine."

"Good," said Alex. "Aunt Julia can write an introduction. But this morning you're going to write a little essay entitled 'How I Spent Christmas Eve.' Unfortunately whatever you say isn't going to help Cookie." And Alex went on to tell Sarah that Cookie might well have heard Lily Farnsworth talking to Senator Hopgood on the office tap. "They know she was at the corral helping saddle horses, and that she didn't go right back to the cocktail party, that she stood down at the road and waved off the dog food transport. What they're asking themselves is why not linger a little longer, hide behind a bale of hay, and do in the senator and his secretary?"

"They think Cookie was carrying a gun?" said Sarah in disbelief. "In that little cocktail dress?"

"Guns have been hidden in—or down—cocktail dresses before this," said Alex. "Now, let's get this morning over with."

It was a long morning. Shorty Fox appeared at Agave Three and Four at exactly nine and presented Sarah and Julia with pads and papers. "Write it all down, how you were making the world safe for old horses. Time and place as best you can. No collaboration. One of our men will be standing by ready to take it when you finish."

"How thoughtful," murmured Julia.

"You may think this is pretty low-tech," said Shorty, "no taping and all that, but not to worry. We'll go over your written statements and then get you on tape."

"And probably video," said Sarah.

"You name it," said Shorty cheerfully.

Sarah couldn't stand it. "Are you arresting Cookie, because I'm absolutely sure . . ." She paused, and Shorty held up a restraining hand. "Write it down. Anything you're absolutely sure about, we'd like to know. So long."

Sarah and Julia retired to their designated writing areas and sat down to write. Each had her particular approach to the events of Christmas Eve.

Julia Clancy warmed up to her description with an attack on cruelty to animals in general and horses in particular and ended with a few terse sentences on the vanning of the three horses, their subsequent flight to safety—final destination not named.

Sarah, deciding to omit matters involving emotion, cause, and justification, turned in an arid description of the event. She reverted to the English teacher and concentrated on paragraph sequence, parallel construction, and coherence.

By twelve-thirty the Agave party, augmented now by Maria Cornish, Maud-Emma Hopgood, and Artie, joined together for lunch. At one o'clock, in the middle of dessert, Sarah espied from the luncheon patio two distant equestrian figures making their way against the skyline, and behind them on an oblique path, a third. It was a sign, she decided, that at least the horse program was back to normal. She wondered briefly why anyone was riding at the lunch hour but then remembered that some of the staff chose odd hours between regular guest riding times for their exercise.

At two o'clock, what Sarah began in later days to think of as the "last ride" left the corral.

The trail party broke naturally into two groups. Morty McGuire led the way, followed by Maria Cornish on Diablo and Alex on a dark bay called Boxer. Then came Julia Clancy with her newest victim, a subdued and almost attentive Artie Hopgood, newly promoted to the large black gelding, Montana. Bringing up the rear, Sarah on the trusty Pokey, followed by Maud-Emma Hopgood on Noodle. Behind both, at a discreet distance, sitting uneasily on a rawboned Appaloosa, the ever-present Secret Service man.

"Noodle is an absolute sweetie," said Maud-Emma as they left the corral gate and turned toward the foothills of Buzzard Mountain. "The sort that would help you up if you fell off."

Sarah thought this was unlikely; her memory of horse incidents was full of riders splatted on the ground while a wildly galloping horse, reins flying, disappeared in the distance. But she nodded agreement, and for some time the trail party alternately walked and jogged on a winding trail that led toward gradually rising ground punctuated by small gullies and sudden rock outcroppings.

And then, by a freak in the terrain, a huge thimble-shaped boulder rose past a curve in the path and the riding party disappeared one by one around the rise of the rock, and then some few minutes later, one by one reappeared on a downward slope toward a narrow wash. As each horse and rider emerged, Sarah was again struck how this and certain other scenes at the ranch had seemed to be part of a cinematic sequence. This one perhaps more than all.

First came Morty, the quintessential wrangler. Brown Stetson, bandanna, short bowie knife at his waist, worn leather chaps, boots with roweled spurs, silver-studded embossed saddle, rope hanging from the saddle horn. Morty sat upright, his body always in tune with the motion of his horse. Morty McGuire, turning from time to time to check on his followers, then squinting ahead to judge the going, keeping alert for a rattler coiled by the edge of the trail or a deer that could leap up suddenly in front of them to spook the horses.

Then came Maria Cornish, the girl of the lost golden West, the West of the Hollywood stars, the West of the East's imagination. Maria in her butternut suede fringed skirt, long western boots, turquoise silk shirt, suede jacket, black hat with a chin tie, oversize dark glasses. Maria on the beautiful Paso Fino, Diablo Bravo. Sarah, the fan of old movies, could almost hear the lilt of Jeanette MacDonald and the answering baritone of Nelson Eddy and half expected to see a Royal Canadian Mounted Policeman come loping over the horizon.

Then Julia Clancy, the sturdy elderly woman, everyone's western auntie, the one who meets the raiding Apache with her rifle raised, who flips flapjacks by the side of the chuck wagon, one hand on her horse's bridle, ready to mount and ride if the alarm is given. And Alex, the hero, with the red bandanna around his neck and wearing the hero's pale gray Stetson. Alex, strong and silent, chin and shoulders square, facing rustlers and thieves and revenge-minded Indians with unblinking courage. And Artie Hopgood as the Kid. For what is a western movie without some freckle-faced kid riding along with his family? Sarah had a brief qualm about allowing Artie into her perfect scenario, but his expression for once showed nothing but pleasure as he neck-reined his big horse around the end of the boulder, so, okay, Artie could be the Kid. Later, perhaps, kidnapped by the bad guys. And never seen again.

Next, Maud-Emma Hopgood, the widow. The widow, in her yellow checkered flannel shirt, her pink bandanna, who, facing the death—by shooting no less—of her husband, the loss of her mortgage, the rustling of her cattle, bravely rides forth with the town posse in search of the same bad guys who have grabbed her son, the Kid.

And following the widow, Sarah. The heroine. Of course.

Sarah, who manages with the slightest movement of her body to restrain the prancings and buckings of her mettlesome horse, Pokey. Pokey? How about Thunder or Stormy? Or Wildfire?

And last, shadowing them, the Mystery Man. Because Sarah found the Secret Service man a disturbing presence, no expression, no light chat, nothing. Riding along some fifty yards behind them in his black jeans, his dark blue shirt, his gray hat, he seemed positively sinister. But perfect for her movie—call him the Man from Dead Man's Peak. That would do nicely. Later on in the movie he could come to life, shoot something, tear a bar apart, perhaps rescue or seize the widow.

And suddenly Sarah found herself alone. She had unconsciously reined in Pokey while watching the passing parade riding out from behind the boulder and now realized that the entire party had moved almost out of sight, down into the wash beyond the rock. And Pokey, finding his rider's attention elsewhere, had seized the opportunity to munch on some overhanging vegetation.

So Sarah did exactly what inexperienced riders are told never to do. She jerked Pokey's head, loosened the reins, called "Giddap, Pokey," in a loud voice, raised both her legs, and gave Pokey a resounding thump on his sides. And Pokey, just as if he were really the horse hero of Sarah's western cinema, giddapped. To be exact, Pokey lifted his head with a surprised snort, whirled, snorted again, and took off.

Down a side wash below the boulder, down an intersecting trail, up a rocky incline, and across a flat stretch of desert sand on a good sound gallop. In fact, there was absolutely nothing pokey about Pokey for the next five minutes. Sarah lost both stirrups in the first whirl-round, hung desperately to the saddle horn, and called "Whoa, Pokey," and "Stop, Pokey," to absolutely no effect. Until, just as Sarah tilted to the pony's off side and had begun an inexorable slide under his belly, Pokey came to a stop as sudden as his start. Sarah banged to the ground and Pokey, like the well-trained pony that he was, stood beside her, flanks heaving. For an instant he hung his head over her as if puzzled at her position, then he moved slightly aside and began grazing on a thatch of range grass.

And Sarah sat up, her head thumping, her back sending messages of pain, and cursed. Cursed Pokey, trail rides, Aunt Julia, Morty McGuire, Senator Hopgood, the blue Arizona sky, and then finally, and correctly, her own stupidity.

Holding her echoing head and remembering Aunt Julia's strictures on the fact that western riding habits did not include hard hats, Sarah got unsteadily to her feet.

Well, first things first. Despite an apparent heaving of the ground, Sarah made her way to the grazing Pokey, took charge of his drooping reins, looped them over one arm, and sat down on a flat rock by his side. Now at least she had transportation. She looked at Pokey and, seeing that he appeared his usual reliable and mild self, felt a small measure of reassurance. What to do? Mount and try to find the trail and catch up with the others? Or mount and try to make it back to the corral? Or, in view of her dizziness and the generally unstable condition of her still shaking limbs, stay put? Yes, stay put and be found. Maud-Emma and her Secret Service follower would certainly have alerted the front party, and Morty McGuire, the good shepherd, must at this very moment be leading his troops to find her. All Sarah had to do was hang on to Pokey, nurse her throbbing head, massage her sore back, and sit tight. And from time to time give out with a shout or whatever was the western equivalent of a tallyho.

She found that she had ended in a sheltered area of mesquite, brush, cactus, and other desert shrubbery at the end of the long stretch of desert over which Pokey had so recently galloped. So after checking the immediate area for snakes and scorpions, she settled back on her rock. For a full ten minutes, there was nothing but silence, interrupted by the buzzing sound of a cactus wren and the varied notes of assorted desert thrashers—none of which Sarah, without the help of Alex, could possibly identify. Then, becoming impatient, and taking a good grip on Pokey's reins, she tried a tentative shout of "Hello there," followed by a resounding "Yooo-hoo." Pokey raised his head, stamped a hoof, and then settled back to his munching. And then, just as if the cinema director had called, "Ready, action, roll it," came the distant *clop-click* of a horse's hooves.

One horse. So where were the others? Or had Morty told them all to stay where they were, dismount, and wait, and had come himself to look for her?

The hoof sounds came closer and Sarah heard the rhythm change from the three-beat lope to the four-beat trot. Odd, they seemed to be coming toward her through a small gap in the brush ahead. However, she supposed what with all the trails that ran through the ranch property, Morty had chosen one as a shortcut down to where he had heard her call.

Now the hoofbeats slowed to a slower regular crunching of a walk, and Sarah imagined Morty and Spider picking their way through the mesquite. She stood up eagerly, called again, cupping her hands, and giving out with a sustained "Hello, hello, hello."

And was answered by a screech. A high, sustained screeching scream. Then a heavy thump, followed immediately by the accelerating thud of pounding hooves, and out of the brush, eyes rolling, nostrils wide, reins loose, stirrups slapping against the girth of the empty saddle, galloped that "perfect sweetie" of a horse, Noodle. Riderless, wild-eyed Noodle on a dead gallop. He swerved as he came upon the astonished Sarah holding Pokey, he snorted, swerved again, and took off down the open stretch of desert behind Sarah. And Pokey, for the second time that afternoon, demonstrated that Pokey was only a sometime name. As Noodle swerved the second time, Pokey started, flattened his ears, reared, yanked the reins out of Sarah's hands, turned, and thundered after Noodle.

TWENTY

THE sound of the two galloping horses faded to a distant drumming, and Sarah stood blinking, quite alone. Or was she? That scream. It must have been Maud-Emma Hopgood, rider—or former rider—of Noodle. But what had happened? Had Noodle shied, and Maud-Emma, feeling herself falling, screamed? Sarah reviewed her own recent unseating and found that a gasp and a squeak were about all that had been possible as she bounced off the horse and slammed into the ground. So perhaps the scream came before the fall, the result of fright. Or afterward because of extreme pain. Well, damn, she'd better hurry and find Maud-Emma.

But, despite a rising sense of an emergency, Sarah found that running, jogging, or even a fast walk made her head bang like a percussion instrument, and she had to make her way ahead through the brush with a soft and careful step. Her back, too, protested any effective knee action, so that her progress was slow. Further, although the vegetation was not really dense, it was necessary for her to pick her way carefully around the plants, since thorns and prickers of assorted cacti lay ready at every side to clutch at clothing, stab at exposed flesh. All this while trying to find and follow the print of Noodle's hooves. And then of course, there were creatures. Pressing forward cautiously, Sarah kept a wary eye out for anything that seemed likely to crawl or coil. She decided to make a lot of noise and not surprise anything lurking. And—she'd almost forgotten—she should call out for help. Surely Morty McGuire would be on the hunt by now. She shouted Maud-Emma's name loudly twice and each time heard faint returning echoes bouncing off a distant rise of rock.

Nothing. Not even an answering groan. The ground now rose sharply, and something resembling a trail crossed ten feet or more at about the level of Sarah's ear. She labored up the incline, squinted ahead at the trail, now shadowed by over-hanging rocks, and she saw it.

An outflung arm. An arm covered by a yellow checkered flannel sleeve. Maud-Emma. Sarah followed the arm to the shoulder, to the neck, the neck to the head. The back of the head, its blond hair disordered, the face down as if nuzzling the sandy ground. Maud-Emma sprawled half across the narrow trail as if she'd been flung down by some monster hand.

"Oh my God," said Sarah aloud. Forgetting racketing head and hurting back, she rushed forward the last few feet and knelt beside Maud-Emma. And even as she did so she could hear a deep sighing sound. Alive.

Sarah felt a shudder of relief. Maud-Emma was at least breathing. She sat back on her heels and thought. What had Alex said? She remembered another victim of a fall in Maine. Alex had been with her and he had said something about ABC. "A" for airway. Okay, Maud-Emma was breathing quite regularly and strongly, so she must have air. "B" was for blood. Or was it breathing? And what was "C" for? Sarah ran over a list of possible C's. Color, clotting, contusion, coronary. Circulation? Was her blood moving around? Was she pale or red-faced? It was hard to tell with that face pushed into the sand. She remembered a little rhyme from a first-aid class: "Face is red, Raise the head; Face is pale, Raise the tail." Sarah leaned farther over, studying what she could see of Maud-Emma's face. The color, camouflaged as it was by sand and dirt, seemed pretty normal. Not blue anyway. Or white.

Back to blood. Sarah ran her eyes over Maud-Emma's body. Except for a strangely twisted foot and a nasty-looking scrape on her right wrist, there didn't seem to be any amount of bleeding. How about her head? Sarah kneeled forward again and examined the back of the head and saw that there was a wet mark staining the hair somewhere near the back of the skull. Bloody but not flowing or spurting blood. But what about Maud-Emma's front? Could all her injuries be on her front side, a smashed forehead, a perforated gut, a lacerated throat? God, she thought, I can't move her or turn her over, she might have some spinal injury or some internal bone sticking into something.

For a minute more she studied Maud-Emma's unmoving body, not daring to touch or move, and then she remembered. The Secret Service man. Richard somebody. Well, where in hell was he when he was needed? Why hadn't he followed Maud-Emma and why wasn't he standing right here taking care of the emergency and calling in on his wrist radio or his walkie-talkie? For a helicopter, or a doctor drop. Sarah pictured a low-flying plane plopping an emergency physician complete with rescue kit at her feet.

"Oh Lord, oh Lord, I am so hurt."

Maud-Emma. She was awake. Conscious and talking.

Sarah leaned close to her face. "Don't talk, just lie still. We're getting help." Which was at the moment an absolute lie.

"Sarah, Sarah, that you?"

Maud-Emma was not only conscious, she was aware.

"It's okay," whispered Sarah. "Just stay quiet. Don't move."

"What happened? Why am I on the ground?"

"The trail ride," said Sarah.

"What trail ride?" Maud-Emma gave a half-groan. Then, in a thick voice, "All right, we were going on a trail ride. We started out, what happened?"

"You were riding Noodle."

"Sweetheart," murmured Maud-Emma. "Noodle's a sweetie."

"Something must have scared him. You fell off," said Sarah. "Now, please don't move. Morty or your Secret Service man will be along any minute."

For a moment Maud-Emma was quiet. Then she licked her lips. "I'm so thirsty, I want a drink. Something to drink?"

Sarah shook her head and then told her once again to lie still. "You don't want to make anything worse."

The merest shadow of a smile flickered across Maud-Emma's lips. "No, I surely don't want to make anything worse." Then, "Where are we? Did you fall off, too?"

"I don't know exactly where we are, off the trail somewhere, and yes, I fell off Pokey, and it was my own fault."

"Listen," said Maud-Emma. "I've got to say something."

"Please," said Sarah, "wait until the doctor comes. You've got a bad bump on your head. And your foot looks funny."

"They'll take me to the hospital," said Maud-Emma, her voice stronger and more insistent. "I hurt like very hell. Listen, before someone comes, you've got to listen. That box I gave you."

"The Kotex box with the letters and diaries," said Sarah.

"Yes. You keep it, Sarah. Not let anyone see it. Don't give it to anyone. Not the Senate or the police. No one. For Artie's sake. Leo, he's dead now. No point raking that stuff up."

"What stuff? You said . . ."

"Listen, Sarah. My diaries, two of them, those papers. Who cares? Artie needs to think his father was okay. Not a bad guy. Nothing in that box will help. Promise? Keep the box. Okay, Sarah? I feel dizzy, all mixed up and sick. I think I'm going to throw up. Promise? No one?"

"Please," said Sarah desperately. "Stop talking. I know someone will come any minute."

"Promise?" said Maud-Emma in a throttled voice. And tilting her head slightly, she vomited into the sand. Sarah reached for her bandanna to wipe Maud-Emma's lips and heard once again, just a whisper. "Promise. No one."

Sarah bent lower and tucked her hand under Maud-Emma's

cheek to cushion her head from the sand and rock. "Okay, I promise."

"See for yourself, read the papers. You'll see. For Artie. For my mother, Granny Forrest. Oh my Lord, I am so sick. Where is that stupid Richard? Always there when I don't want him." Maud-Emma's words were now slurred, her voice infinitely weary.

"Shh," said Sarah soothingly. "Close your eyes."

And then he came. Not Richard Secret Service rescuer riding down the trail at a lope, but Richard clinging to the back of Morty's saddle, bouncing like some department store dummy.

Morty. Thank God. And then Alex, coming up behind them fast, pulling his horse down and dismounting.

In a minute Morty and Alex were off their horses and were kneeling beside Maud-Emma, and the Secret Service man was doing something with a little transmitter.

Sarah held the reins of Spider and Boxer, Alex's horse, and watched, more and more aware of her own thumping head, but feeling such a small matter shouldn't interfere with Maud-Emma's major injury. There was no time for explanations, and after a few minutes, Morty took both horses and tied them to an overhanging tree limb so that Sarah was free to settle back on the ground and watch the proceedings.

Instead, a sort of restlessness overtook her, a sense of irritation combined with her aching head and sore back, and she found herself limping past the two men, still huddled over Maud-Emma—she with eyes now closed.

Unnoticed, with the vague notion of seeing if Maud-Emma had dropped something when she fell, or to discover why she fell, Sarah made her way up the trail. What had so spooked Noodle—the bombproof horse—that he had dumped his rider?

She looked behind her. Nothing but brush, cactus, mesquite, rock walls. Ahead. A blank, slightly overgrown trail. To the right. Nothing but more of the same. To the left. Nothing. She took three more steps and stopped. Looked up. And saw it.

A shadow. A long, humpbacked shadow. A shadow moving, twisting ever so slightly in the small breeze that ruffled through the dry vegetation.

But shadows don't exist by themselves. Something casts a shadow. Something solid, long, and turning slightly, cast this shadow and made a twin of it. With a sickening sense of horror Sarah followed the shadow to its source.

Hanging: a long round-shouldered, slack-headed figure, arms behind its back, ankles crossed and tied, its face a peculiar shade of blue-purple-gray, one eye half closed, the other staring. A familiar face. A face Sarah had confronted across the dinner table, a figure she had seen sitting easily, arrogantly, on the back of a horse. A face and figure to remember when living. A face and figure never to forget when dead.

Blue Feather Romero, sometime lover of Maria Cornish, occasional stuntman in low-budget movies, fellow rescuer of endangered horses, and most recently brawler in Danny's Café. Dead. Hung. Swinging just over Sarah's head. A sight to spook the sweetest and gentlest of horses.

Sarah's past responses to sudden horror had been denial—an immediate skid away from what had happened, off into safer byways in which she imagined the victim was walking and breathing and going about his or her usual daily business.

Now it was different. Blue Feather Romero as a corpse, a dangling swollen-faced corpse, seemed, ghastly as was his appearance, to have achieved an inevitable, almost natural transformation. A consummation, if not devoutly to be wished by his associates, at least to be often thought of.

For a few stunned seconds Sarah stood under the slowly revolving corpse, then, throbbing head and sore back forgotten, she stumbled down the incline and reached the rescue group, still huddled over Maud-Emma, before anyone had realized she was gone. But when it came to explaining what she had seen, Sarah found her throat had turned rebel, and she panted out the news to Alex, Richard, and Morty McGuire in a voice gone hoarse. Then, alarm given, she sank down on flat rock next to Maud-Emma, took Maud-Emma's hand gently into her own, and waited.

It happened all over again. Men running, orders given, radio transmissions, responses. The sound of rotor blades, the hovering helicopter, the lowering of rescue persons, the packaging of Maud-Emma, who, rolled like a hot dog in a bun, disappeared in a horizontal state up the path, along the trail, and in a sort of basket vanished skyward into the maw of the helicopter.

Morty left to rejoin his riders and to look for Pokey and Noodle, and Richard remained to guard the still dangling remains of Blue Feather Romero and await forensic reinforcements. Alex, now that Maud-Emma had been turned over to higher medical powers, suddenly noticed that Sarah seemed to be spending an unusual amount of time holding her head.

"I fell off," she explained. "My fault."

"Never mind that. Did you hit your head?"

"I'm afraid so. It's made me light-headed. And my back feels like I've been in a rugby game."

Alex became the concerned physician, examined his patient, ran his fingers over Sarah's skull, gently probed her back. The upshot being that two hours later, at about six that evening, Sarah found herself in the emergency room of the Lodestone Community Hospital.

"You're pretty lucky," said the doctor in charge. "Those rocks can really dent a head. Take it easy for a couple of days. Stay off horses."

"Gladly," said Sarah.

"Give your back a rest. No heavy lifting. Okay?"

"Okay," said Sarah, and, not to miss the chance, asked how Mrs. Hopgood was.

"Nasty fall," said the doctor. "Got a bunch of government types hovering over her. Neurosurgeon brought in. But they don't tell me nothin'."

"She'll be all right?"

"Guess so," said the doctor, "but don't quote me. She's not my patient now."

"Alex," said Sarah urgently as they climbed back into Aunt Julia's car, "I've got to do something pretty unethical and I'll need your help."

"If you're intending to sneak around with a banged-up head and a sprained back looking for the person who strung up Blue

Feather, forget it. Home is where you stay . . . Agave Cottage Three."

"That's where I'm going to do something unethical."

Alex frowned. "Does it involve anything that's happened today?"

"Yes. But it's an extension of something sort of unethical that happened earlier. Something you don't know about. I promised not to tell, but I'm worried. I need you to fend off Aunt Julia."

"Swear to stay put and if you find something earthshaking, even if unethical, let me in on it. Promises made under stress don't have to be kept. If it's a matter for the police, we go to the police. Right?"

Sarah looked out the window as Alex swung the car in the main gate, identified himself to the now familiar guard, and drove toward the Agave Cottage row. Then she nodded. "It's a deal. But you've got to siphon off Aunt Julia. If she gets into this, well, it's like having a bulldozer perform eye surgery. I've got to be careful. I'm dealing—I think I'm dealing—with a bomb."

Alex brought the car to a complete halt. "A bomb? What the hell do you mean, a bomb?"

"No, not really. Not an actual bomb. Something that might be, well, in its consequences, a little explosive."

"There's no such thing as a 'little explosive.' "

"Start the car. I'm speaking figuratively. I've just enough energy to do this tonight. I'll send in for room service for something to eat, something light. My head is affecting my stomach."

"Then leave this explosive research until tomorrow."

"It won't wait, but give me space. You and Aunt Julia can have dinner together. Tell her I'm going to bed early and that I've made a New Year's resolution. I resolve never to fall off again because I'll never ride again."

"You will, too," said Alex, who knew Sarah's resolutions. "Besides, you love Pokey."

"Yes," sighed Sarah. "I do love Pokey. As seen from the ground."

It went as planned. Julia, full of maxims on the subject of riders who cause horses to throw them, went off with Alex to dinner. Sarah, watching, saw the two work their way through a now augmented police presence to the lighted lodge, and then she returned to her bedroom.

For almost twenty minutes Sarah lingered over soup and rolls, putting off the unsavory business of searching through Maud-Emma's papers. Then, at last, fearing that Julia and Alex would make a prompt dinner, she went to the drawer, burrowed under a pile of underpants and bras, brought forth the Kotex box, and opened it.

It was remarkably full. Maud-Emma must be quite a diary and letter writer, Sarah decided as she upended the box on the yellow counterpane of the queen-sized bed.

There were indeed two diaries, green-covered volumes stamped "Daily Reminder" on the front cover. Then there were letters. And copies of answers to letters. A small bundle tied with string, the topmost addressed to the Legal Department, Defenders of Wildlife, 1233 19th Street, N.W., Washington, D.C. 20036. And under these, two folders stuffed and rolled into cylinders and held by stout rubber bands.

Sarah breathed a deep breath and pulled a chair up to the end of the bed. For a moment she wondered if she should wear gloves, but remembering that the only gloves she had were her winter ones, bulky and awkward, she decided not to worry about fingerprints. After all, she was acting on the specific orders of the diary writer, who, *in extremis*, trusted her, Sarah, to the hoard.

She started with what might be called Maud-Emma's "Wildlife Series," putting off the intrusion into the diaries until later. This group of copies and answers were all pretty much of a kind, and were of a sufficiently damaging nature—damaging to the senator—to have warranted his throttling his wife for sedition. Maud-Emma warned of upcoming committee votes reported the opinions—from direct knowledge of her husband's affairs—of certain swing senators on various environmental issues, and gave alarm of the senator's anti-environmental moves and ploys, his meetings with legal advisors, lobbies, and businesses. At times Maud-Emma went as far as to give the names and telephone numbers of congressional aides who might be persuaded to modify the senator's opinions. She had in the name of M. E. Forrest apparently signed petitions, supported congressmen with an environmental bent, sent contributions to assorted groups, and all in all been as busy as any mole in any clandestine operation.

Folding the last of this packet, Sarah shook her head. How on earth had Maud-Emma gotten away with it? Perhaps by the not so simple job of playing the perfect southern helpmate and decorative wife—the senator being too full of his own ego and dubious machinations to believe he harbored a subversive wife.

Sarah turned to the first of the two diaries and found it wasn't a diary. She had expected the usual notations of weather, family minutiae, visits, and plans, and perhaps an outpouring of personal grief, worry, or triumph as the case required. Nothing of the sort. The diary was a compendium of dates, times, and cryptic cross-references. Sometimes there were references to some mysterious land sale or acquisition— acreage given; cost, in millions—frequently with a question mark. Often after each little squib of information came initials, in clumps or alone: *HJL, SJH, SE, HO, HC,* and *FL.* Usually when *HJL* appeared, the initials *FL* followed. Each item was given a Roman numeral and an alphabet letter. The second diary featured more of the same.

Well, it didn't take much brain to see that Maud-Emma wouldn't qualify as a cryptologist; she had simply reversed her husband's initials and probably the others. *HJL* was Leo J. Hopgood, *FL* was the faithful Lily Farnsworth, and the rest were equally obvious. Sarah looked at her watch. Alex and Julia would be turning up any minute. She'd let the other initials go for the moment and hit the manila folders.

She unrolled the first of the folders and found a number of news clippings, some brown and dry with age, some alone, some clipped to a file card, but each marked with a Roman numeral and alphabet letter. Simple enough. Match the letters, the numerals to the diary entries and initials, and you had the story. But the story of what? Sarah could see that as a secret agent Maud-Emma was in kindergarten—a gutsy lady, no doubt, but a naïve one. Or perhaps she hadn't taken the trouble to encode her information with more sophistication because she trusted to the secrecy of the Kotex box. Heaven knows, the hideaway had worked up to now.

Sarah opened the second of the manila folders and found a collection of newspaper articles published in a paper she had never heard of, the *Arapaho Post-Times*, by a reporter named Enoch Harden—obviously a pseudonym. And therein lay the bombshell.

Because Sarah knew—even if she did not immediately understand the complexity of the scheme—a bombshell when she saw it. What it amounted to was that certain friends of Senator Leo J. Hopgood's, friends whose names matched the initials, had had their sticky fingers in the federal till and would have kept them there if the senator had not ended up in Santa Claus's wagon.

Sarah heard footsteps outside the front door of Agave Three, slammed the folder closed, stuffed the papers and diaries back into the box, jumped up and jammed it into her underwear drawer, and was reclining on the bed with her copy of *Arizona Highways* when Alex's key turned in the lock.

He came in alone. "Julia's off to bed. Going reluctantly because she says she knows something's afoot, and that she didn't ask you to be a detective here at her expense. She wants in. As in 'in the know.' What do you say?"

"Absolutely not," said Sarah.

"How about me?" said Alex, closing the bedroom door.

Sarah sat up. "I don't know. I just don't know. But it was a bomb. At least I think it's a bomb. Or would have been. The kind of bomb that might have caused a murder."

Alex sat down on the end of the bed. "Are you saying no one knew about this so-called bomb?"

"Maud-Emma seemed to think no one knew about her collection."

"Let's you start by sharing. With me."

"But I did promise to keep it quiet. It's Maud-Emma's bomb."

"Is the information going to hurt her, ruin her life? Her son's life? Does it bear on the murder?"

"I think it's going to change her life, and Artie's And a lot of people who trusted her, friends of the senator's, are going to think she's a rat. But I'll also bet there'll be Maud-Emma Forrest fan clubs springing up all over the country."

"Forrest?"

"Maiden name. It's her *nom de guerre*. Someday you may find her heading up the Wilderness Society—that is, if she stays out of the clutches of Hopgood's aides. Okay, Alex, I'll let you in if you swear in blood not to tell Julia and think very hard about telling the police. We'll have to go over the material together."

"Your head, you fell off your horse," Alex reminded her. "How about tomorrow?"

"No way. Tonight. If you think it's police stuff, we can stay away from the FBI and call in that Shorty Fox. And your friend, Solly. Those two are at least human."

"Somewhat human," agreed Alex. "Okay, open up."

Sarah waited for the count of a minute. She thought of promises, one's sacred word to an injured woman. Then she thought about murder—three murders. And murder came out ahead. She jumped off the bed, wrenched open her underwear drawer, pulled out the Kotex box, and for the second time upended the contents in the middle of the big bed.

Alex proved a fast study. He digested the wildlife support papers, remarking that it was lucky that Maud-Emma hadn't ended up in a feed bag with her husband. The diaries caused little difficulty; the initials reversed revealed themselves as members of the Hopgood inner circle and included the Howells—Orvis and Corla were *HO* and *HC*—Heinz J. Simmons, *SJH*, and his wife, Esty, *SE*, as well as Lily Farnsworth and a few notations indicating faithful manager and sycophant, Fred Arco. From the diary it was a cross-court step to the more complex bundle of information in the two envelopes. Dates had to be matched with articles, copies of the *Congressional Record,* copies of interoffice memos and personal letters apparently lifted by light-fingered Maud-Emma.

"She's the one who should be working for the Bureau," remarked Alex. "But I still don't follow this thing to the end. What was she trying to prove? That her husband was skating close to illegal thin ice, that he had friends in high finance?"

"More like he was planning for his future comfort and helping his friends to federal real estate. I don't follow the twists and turns, but it all adds up to Hopgood alive was valuable and useful. Dead, Simmonses and Howells lose their man in Washington."

"I agree, nothing here, odorous as it is, leads to someone shooting someone else. And this stuff"—Alex pounded the heap of papers—"isn't in order. It's not set up as a case against Hopgood and his buddies because it's more suggestive than conclusive. But I say it's time to call in the troops."

Sarah saw Maud-Emma's battered but reproachful face rise before her. "We have to?"

"As we decided, Solly and Fox. A team of two. I'll call now . . . no, I'll do it in person. Calls go through the police machinery. Hang in here, I'll be right back."

Sarah followed him to the door, opened it, and looked out toward the illuminated cactus garden. Several shapes stood, fence-post still, at the outer verges. She made a small sound of disgust, closed the door behind Alex, and returned to the contemplation of Maud-Emma's collected works spread across the bed. She had just picked up one of the diaries for a review when she was jolted by a rapping on her door. Alex? Back so soon? Had he forgotten the key?

Sarah turned and made her way to the door, and jerked it open, saying at the same time, "Okay, Alex, what did you forget?"

"Not a thing, Miss Deane." And a man in a light gray suit stepped over the threshold followed immediately by another in dark brown.

Senator Hopgood's aides. Sarah recognized them immediately even as one turned and pulled the door closed behind them, the other striding into the living room.

Mr. Yates and Mr. Owen. Uninvited guests.

TWENTY-ONE

FOR just the flash of a second Sarah struggled between confrontation and a polite effort at dismissal. The latter approach won out and she advanced into the little sitting room and switched on a lamp.

"I'm sorry not to be friendly but I'm very tired. Maybe you've come into the wrong cottage."

"We know where we are, Miss Deane," said the short, stout, puff-faced Yates. "Take it easy. We just want to find something." He lifted up the cushion on a small wood-framed chair.

"We're Senator Hopgood's aides," said the taller thinner Owen, "and we think you can show us something." He moved his right hand in a sweeping circular motion that took in the room.

Sarah remained standing, her back to the bedroom door, sheltering, she hoped, the view of the bed in its heaped-up condition. If she could stall the pair with confused protests and questions, then Alex should make it back with reinforcements. Because suddenly she wanted the police, any number of them being preferable to this sudden visitation by Senator Hopgood's aides.

"Show you what?" said Sarah. "Would you please leave, because I've never even met Senator Hopgood."

Mr. Yates looked up from sorting through a pile of magazines on a coffee table. "You've sure enough met his wife."

"Buddy-buddy," put in Mr. Owen. "Going riding, going shopping. Women talk."

"Yes, I've met Mrs. Hopgood," said Sarah in an austere voice. "I've enjoyed her company."

"Enjoyed her little secrets," said Mr. Yates. "Little whispers in your ear."

"Mrs. Hopgood and I are casual acquaintances," said Sarah.

"Come off it, Miss Deane," said Mr. Owen. He kicked over the end of the Navajo-type rug at the sliding doors to the patio, scowled at the floor underneath, and looked severely at Sarah. "Look, let's be up front, shall we? Open."

"Like open and aboveboard," put in Mr. Yates, shaking out the pages of a magazine.

"It's like this," said Mr. Owen. He moved over to a little cabinet filled with glasses and an ice bucket, pulled it open, and inspected the interior with an air of disappointment. "It's like this," he repeated. "We've been to see her."

"Maud-Emma," explained Mr. Yates. "In the hospital. She's leaving the critical-care unit tomorrow if everything goes okay. She's conscious most of the time."

"I'm glad to hear it," said Sarah.

"Thought you might be," said Mr. Owen. "Trouble seems to be she's a little bit confused. You know, falling like that, hitting her head. Can't remember much about it. But remembers you. Couple of times while we were looking in on her, she kept talking about you. Seemed to think you were standing right there."

"Oh," said Sarah. "I'm glad she remembers me."

"What she remembers," said Mr. Yates, "is giving you some stuff. Papers, diaries. She's worried."

"Plenty worried," said Mr. Owen.

They were, thought Sarah, with a shiver of apprehension, like some awful comedy team in a Pinter play who were going to make jokes until they pulled out knives or ropes and finished you off.

Mr. Yates perched on the edge of the sofa, balancing his bulk awkwardly so that he had to teeter back and forth to keep his seat. "Maud-Emma Hopgood is afraid the police might find these papers. Personal stuff. Wants to make sure you don't tell anyone. Which we surely hope you haven't."

"We surely hope not," said Mr. Owen, nodding vigorously.

"Okay, Owen," said Mr. Yates. "If Miss Deane doesn't know what we're talking about, why don't we just take a look in the bedroom? For my money, ladies always hide interesting items in the bedroom. Under pillows, in their toilet article case."

"Someplace intimate," said Mr. Owen unpleasantly. "Okay, come on with us to the bedroom, Miss Deane. Don't worry, we don't want anything funny. No bed games, nothing like that. Just papers, diaries. Whatever Maud-Emma is all heated up about." He turned to Mr. Yates. "Joe, slip the bolt on the front door. And the chain. I'll lock the patio. We don't want Miss Deane's boyfriend bothering us. Or the old granny."

Mr. Yates referred to a small notebook. "That's Mrs. Julia Clancy," he said. "Agave Four. So let's keep the noise down. If the telephone rings, Miss Deane, answer it just like you would normally. We'll be right here with you."

There was no help for it. Sarah preceded the two men into the bedroom and there they were: the Maud-Emma Forrest archives.

And the two men fell to, ruffling pages, reading bits here, pieces there. Exclaiming, and then, picking up the stack of wildlife correspondence, Mr. Owen blew a long whistling breath.

"Christ almighty, that Maud-Emma. Look here."

Yates peered over his shoulders and exhaled in his turn. "That bitch. All that soft talk and molasses. Why, she was sticking it to him every day and he never knew."

"More'n that," said Owen. "She was going to blow him right out of the water."

"All we worked for," said Yates. Then, remembering Sarah, "Okay, Miss Deane, we're going to pack up this stuff and take care of it. You may be into real hot water. Hiding things from the police, concealing evidence. The FBI doesn't fool around. They'll eat you up. Indictment. Grand jury. The works."

"Congressional investigating committee," added Own. "You name it, you'll get it. And so will your doctor friend if you've let him in on this. Federal prison. Big fine. God knows what all."

"But since you're such a nice lady," said Owen, "we can give you a deal, a special deal. We'll take care of all this. Save Maud-Emma's reputation. Save the senator's reputation. Save Artie from being humiliated every day of his life. We'll do that if you shut up about this. Shove it right out of your mind."

Yates began pushing the papers into piles. He looked up at Sarah. A long look. "Like Mr. Owen says, shove it out of your mind. Or. Or we won't answer for the consequences. The consequences Yates here has just told you about. Your life, your family's life, well, believe me, I know what happens when someone gets caught in congressional cross fire."

"Credit rating, insurance dropped." Owen smiled, a bleak smile. "You understand? Okay, you understand? This is for everyone's good. Yours, ours, Maud-Emma's, Artie's. Forget what you've seen. And read. Or it's hardball. Okay?"

Sarah, backed up to the wall, gave an imperceptible nod. She was outnumbered, outbullied, and could only hope for Alex and the police. She wondered if Owen and Yates were armed. Probably. Aides *and* bodyguards no doubt. And if Alex didn't come, why, in another three minutes the evidence would be gathered up and lost. And what she would tell anyone would become hearsay. As for Maud-Emma, the fear of God and veiled threats to the safety and health of Artie would probably take care of her silence.

Someone at the door. Sarah could hear the key turning, the bolt clicking back, the door opening the two inches allowed by the heavy security chain. And Alex's voice.

"Sarah, open up."

She looked at Owen and Yates.

"Go slow," said Yates. "We'll make it out the back." He grabbed a pillow, slipped off the case, and with a sweep of the arm, pushed the folders, papers, the diaries into the opening. "Slow, now," he repeated. "And zip up your lip, Miss Deane."

"Or else," said Owen. And the two men, bent double, scurried like some kind of giant armadillos out past the front door, to the living room. Sarah heard the patio doors slide open, close. And then silence. Except for Alex.

"Sarah, open up. Hey, Sarah. Unfasten the chain."

And Sarah did. Alex stood aside, and Solly, all six foot six of him, and five-foot-four Lieutenant Fox stepped in.

And Sarah did not zip her lip. She spilled the beans. Pointed, exclaimed, and gesticulated.

Solly shot out through the living room, out the patio door, and Shorty Fox, like a small torpedo, propelled himself through the front door.

Sarah sank onto the now denuded bed. "Did I ever blow it, letting them in. I thought it was you. Coming back for something."

Alex looked at her anxiously. "Okay? They didn't touch you?"

"Only verbally. Threats about concealing evidence and then took off with Maud-Emma's stuff for the good of us all."

Alex reached over and took her hand. "Sorry."

"And," Sarah went on, "for all I know, Owen and Yates—those are their names—may be right. It might be for the good of everyone if they deep-sixed the whole blasted collection."

"Wait and see. Ours not to decide. Besides, truth will out."

"Not always, Dr. Pangloss. Sometimes only the smoke, not the fire. Or bits and pieces. Sort of distortions. Hints and innuendos and everyone gets hurt."

"Very, very shortly this will be out of our hands."

"How do you know?"

"Because I have just seen a struggling group round the corner by our window. The front door will now open."

It did.

Solly entered with a Yates under one long arm, an Owen underneath the other. Followed by Lieutenant Fox, who carried at right angles to his body a small firearm. Smears of dirt and sand mixed with wet covered Solly's front section.

"Messy," said Solly. "It's raining and I haven't tackled anyone since high school. Now, where shall we stow these characters?"

"Coat closet," said Shorty Fox promptly. "For the time. Put a chair under the handle. Alex, a necktie. Or a bolo."

"Tie up their busy little hands," said Solly.

Sarah watched as Alex, the sailor born, and Shorty, the cowboy-jockey, did an expert job with two ties and Sarah's Christmas present to Alex—the bolo. Then taking the two now restricted aides, Owen with a bloody nose that caused him to snuffle, Solly shoved them into the bedroom closet, securing the door with a leaning chair.

"Not quite proper treatment," said Shorty Fox. "Did I read them their rights?"

"They're here voluntarily," said Solly. "Making a social visit to Miss Deane and Dr. McKenzie. I don't think they'll press charges. Okay, now let's look at the loot."

Solly disappeared again through the living room, the patio, and returned holding a soggy pillowcase. "Our special-agent friend, Douglas Jay, would kill to see this," he said.

"He will see it," said Shorty. "But not right now. Time the local homicide department got a look-in. Okay, Solly, dump it out."

It was not until almost an hour later, when Shorty Fox and Solly had finished reading and sorting Maud-Emma's treasure trove, that the group in the bedroom became aware of increasing rumbles, kicks, and muffled expletives coming from the bedroom closet.

"Okay," said Shorty. "I'll let the buggers out and pack them off. They've had time to think about blackmailing innocent guests."

"If that describes Sarah," put in Alex, but now Solly was removing the chair from the door. He reached one arm in, removed it, holding Yates by the collar, and Shorty Fox took hold of the elbow of Owen. Both, after a short struggle and much profanity, were escorted to the cottage door and pushed out into the night.

"Good riddance," said Solly. He returned to the papers on the bed. "It's a real paradox, an oxymoron. The older liberated southern woman. Maud-Emma as tiger lady."

"There've been plenty of liberated southern women," objected Sarah.

"Yeah," said Shorty, "but I wouldn't have figured Maud-Emma as one of them."

And Sarah had to agree. But now it was time for thinking. Solly sank into a bedroom chair, Alex sat on his duffel bag, Shorty leaned against the wall, and Sarah propped herself at the head of the bed and stared at the blank television screen that stood on a small table near the foot of the bed. It was one of the "extra amenities" at the ranch: two television sets, one for the living room, one in the bedroom. Almost five minutes passed. Then, to everyone's surprise, Sarah's contemplation of the empty screen brought forth fruit. Or light. For all at once she stiffened.

"Television," she said in an excited voice. "That's it. I've an idea. And if it's right, it's a motive for murder."

"I don't know what you mean about television," said Shorty, "but motivation doesn't fit any of the folk here. At least not the senator's aides and friends. Simmons and the Howells needed Hopgood alive and helpful and in the White House."

"No," said Sarah. "Not in the White House. The Senate, yes. But not in the White House."

"I don't get it," said Alex.

"The day before Christmas Eve," said Sarah. "Television."

"Okay, television," said Shorty, "but you know I don't hold that much with motives. With juicy public figures like a senator there are thousands of motives for doing them in."

"Thousands of motives among the people at the ranch?" asked Sarah.

"Spit it out," said Solly. "Tell us why someone here at Gato White Catto wanted Hopgood with a hole in his head."

Sarah gestured at the television set. "Did you hear that speech he made on the twenty-third? I did, I was standing next to Cookie making remarks. I didn't really listen at first, because all political speeches sound alike, the same old dreary rhetoric. But Hopgood's speech took a different turn. He talked about running for president. *And* talked about letting it all hang out."

"What do you mean?" demanded Solly. "I heard the speech. Routine."

"No, it wasn't," said Sarah. "Think back. Among all that trite verbiage, those slogans, that stuff about a strong, proud America, we had promises."

"That's not new," said Shorty.

"Promises of coming clean. Going on about making mistakes in the past, that he was going to start with a bright new slate. He was going to tell all. Throw himself on the mercy of the wonderful American people. I tell you, I've suddenly had another view of Leo J. Hopgood. He was actually trying something new. Something Johnson never did with Vietnam, something Nixon never did with Watergate, something Carter never did with that fouled-up Iranian rescue mission, something Reagan never dreamed of doing—or maybe didn't remember—with Iran-amok, and something Bush couldn't even imagine doing."

"Okay, okay," said Solly. "Get on with it."

"It's something only John F. Kennedy did. In small part. Take blame. Kennedy took blame for the Cuba mess. Said the buck stopped there or something like that. Didn't take blame for much else, but he's been much admired for that tiny bit of candidness. Leo J. Hopgood must have figured out that confession endears the public. The public loves to forgive. They love people who tell all and say, sorry I was wrong, please love me. Please forgive me, I'll do better. It's something that warms the public heart. The old prodigal son motif. It works. It really does work."

Alex nodded. "You may have something. And it is a different approach to being elected."

"Yes," said Sarah, pushing herself back on the bed and settling the pillow behind her. "Instead of waiting until some nosy newsperson snooped out all his wheelings and dealings, Hopgood was going to beat them to it. Remember all those other presidential candidates being nailed by the press and having to drop out? I'll bet a bundle Hopgood was going to give with a fairly comprehensive hangout, and guess who was going to be hung out along with him. In fact, more hung out."

Shorty Fox came away from the wall with a jerk. "All his cronies, Simmons, the Howells. Maybe even Arco."

"Yes, yes," said Sarah excitedly. "And I remember that after the senator's TV speech almost everyone headed for the bar—everyone except Arco, the Simmonses, and the Howells. They went right off into some private room. Probably a war party meeting."

"Arco is small meat," observed Solly.

"But not the others," said Sarah. "Those four figure—as initials—in most of the transactions Maud-Emma took notes on."

"Only one thing wrong," said Shorty. "The murder scenario goes like this. Someone shot Hopgood between nine and eleven. Between then the Howells are accounted for—plenty of witnesses. So is Arco. Simmons could have done it in a hurry between nine and nine-thirty. That's the only time slot he's not pegged for. But unless he has wings, he couldn't have shot Hopgood *and* had time to tuck him into feed bags and hidden him. That took hoisting, climbing up on the chuck wagon, stuffing the body down to the bottom of the wagon, rearranging all those presents—some were already in place. And that doesn't allow for the few minutes it took to do in Lily Farnsworth. There just wasn't enough time. Besides, hear this. Lily Farnsworth was driven—we think—back to Agave Annex at about three in the morning of Christmas Day. A mother in Agave Two, up with a sick child, saw a car pull in there."

"And Simmons and the Howells are accounted for then?" asked Alex.

"Afraid so. Unless the whole guesthouse staff and night watchmen and Mrs. Simmons and Mrs. Howell are lying, no one, repeat, no one left those two cottages that night. Not at three in the morning. In fact, no one is reported out of place around the lodge or owner house and guesthouse complex.

Simmons has a guard full-time on these digs. Always has. Standard operating procedure."

"Arco was seen," put in Alex.

"Yeah," said Shorty. "At five in the morning. Doing his usual jog around the place. Mrs. Clancy saw him when she drove in from her horsenapping toot. But Arco is accounted for one hundred percent during the nine-to-eleven murder period. He was at the lodge in sight of at least thirty people. He never left."

Silence.

A knock at the door. The connecting door between Agave Three and Agave Four which stood at the far bedroom wall.

Aunt Julia.

"Open up. I've heard nothing but commotion. Something's going on and you're all holding out on me."

Alex heaved a sigh, raised his eyes at Shorty, and received a short nod as he pulled a blanket over Maud-Emma's pile of papers.

Aunt Julia stood in the doorway, gray hair spiking up wire-like on her head, her ancient wool dressing gown wrapped around her, the sheepskin slippers on her feet. At the sight of Shorty Fox and Solly she stopped and retreated one step.

"Oh dear. Alex, Sarah, you have guests."

"Not exactly guests, Mrs. Clancy," said Shorty. "Come in. See if you have any ideas about confession being good for the soul. A U.S. senator's confession. Live on TV."

"Aren't you sleepy?" said Sarah. "Perhaps tomorrow."

"Yes, and I'm still having trouble with time," said Julia. "I should be asleep because although it's only eleven here, it's one in the morning at home and I never really adjust."

Sarah nodded absently, stopped, and then stared at her aunt, her eyes opening wide. "One in the morning," she exclaimed.

"Yes," said Aunt Julia. "It's a two-hour difference."

"Two watches," said Sarah. "You wear two watches."

"But not to bed," said Julia.

"Christmas morning, did you wear them both?" demanded Sarah.

"Two watches?" said Solly.

"Yes," said Julia. "It helps keep me in touch with home. In Maine. One is eastern standard time, the other is mountain time."

"Christmas," repeated Sarah. "Both watches?"

Julia looked from Sarah to Alex. Then around to Solly sitting bolt upright in his chair, to Shorty Fox leaning forward.

"Why, yes, dear," she said slowly. "I always wear two watches. When I'm out of the eastern time zone."

Again, complete silence. Julia stood looking from one to the other, a puzzled expression. "I don't understand," she said.

"Aunt Julia," said Sarah, "you have just helped us to a murderer. Or an accomplice. To something we didn't know before."

"Welcome, Julia Clancy," said Solly. "You have untied a knot. A Gordian knot. There are others, but this starts the unraveling. Come in and sit down." And Solly rose, went over to Julia, and settled her in his chair. "It's a place of honor," he told her. "And you're entitled to it."

Julia, bewildered, subsided into the chair and looked about her. Sarah thought perhaps it was one of the few times her aunt had been without a retort or a command.

"I don't understand," she murmured again. "I always keep track of home time." Then, more sharply, "It's certainly not against the law to wear two watches, so I don't see why the police are here, almost the middle of the night. And Sarah, after that fall I think you should be resting and I . . ."

She was interrupted by Lieutenant Fox. "You can wear as many watches as your arm can hold, Mrs. Clancy. What we want to know is whether early Christmas morning you really did wear two watches."

Julia answered with vigor, and Sarah could see that her aunt was getting back into the groove. "Weren't you listening, Lieutenant, because I just told you I always do."

"Which arm?"

"My left. Both always on my left."

"And on Christmas morning which one did you look at?"

Julia paused, then went on, less certainly, "Why, the western one. I think it was."

"Your statement said you were tired."

"Well, yes, I was. Exhausted. All that driving back and forth in that big transport. The worry of it all."

"Stealing is always exhausting," put in Solly, and received a dark look from Shorty Fox for the remark.

"Which watch is closest to your wrist?"

"The western one. I keep the eastern time one closest to my heart. To remember which is which. Because of that old saying, 'Home is where the heart is.' "

"Touching," murmured Solly.

Shorty Fox scowled again at Solly and then said to Julia, "Could you see both? Or just the western watch?"

Julia frowned, screwing her face up with the effort of memory. "I don't know, I just read the time. The dial is luminous."

"On both watches?"

Julia stopped cold. Sarah could almost see her aunt's mind backing up, examining previous statements, and then saw a look of dismay travel across her face. Then, slowly, "The eastern time watch has the luminous dial. It's my good watch. The western one is a cheap Timex. I bought it for this trip."

"So chances are you saw the eastern time watch."

Julia looked from Solly to Shorty Fox, took a deep breath, and exhaled softly. "I suppose," she said, "you could be right."

"So you could have seen Fred Arco jogging at three in the morning, but because you looked at your good watch with the luminous numbers, you thought it was five in the morning. You said in your statement that there was moonlight, but we thought you'd made a mistake, confusing ranch lights with moonlight. Because at five in the morning, no moon, but at three, yes, still moonlight. Right?"

"Yes," said Julia very softly.

"And Mr. Arco was jogging toward the lodge, toward the cactus garden? And he was the only one you saw?"

"Yes."

"Could he have been coming from Agave Annex?"

"I didn't think about *where* he was coming from. I thought he was on his usual rounds. But, yes, he could have been coming from the path of Agave Annex."

"What was he wearing, do you remember?"

"Oh, what he always wears jogging. A sort of dark suit, navy or black, I think. The kind joggers wear, sweatpants and top."

Solly turned to Shorty Fox. "I think we've found the origin of those navy-blue fuzz bits from Hopgood's car seat." Solly walked over and joined Alex on the other end of the duffel bag. "And," he said, "I think we may have found Lily Farnsworth's chauffeur. Or the chauffeur of her body."

"But not her murderer," said Sarah.

"What? What did you say?" said Julia, startled.

"We'll explain later," said Shorty Fox. "For now you've been very helpful."

"And you'd like me to go back to bed, is that it?" said Julia with annoyance.

"Not yet. We've got a scenario to work through. Maybe you can contribute," said Shorty. He turned to Solly. "Think we should call in the Bureau?"

"Aw shucks," said Solly. "Give 'em a rest. Let's give all our fishes—present company excluded, of course—a little more play before we send in for the net and gaff. Let's see if we can't bring this thing close to shore all by ourselves with the help of these good interfering non-law-abiding visitors."

"My sentiments," said Shorty, "on the nose. Okay, since Arco may have driven Lucy Farnsworth to Agave Annex at three A.M. but wasn't down at the corral between nine and eleven to do the shooting, well, what do we have?"

"We have Simmons," said Solly. "And the Howells."

"You said Simmons didn't have the time to shoot two people and also bag and hoist the senator," Alex reminded the room at large. "You also said the mysterious Howells are accounted for."

"And that," said Aunt Julia, now wide awake, "leaves . . ."

"Blue Feather Romero," finished Sarah.

"Or Cookie Logan," said Shorty Fox.

"Let's go for Romero," said Alex. "He was down at the corral putting away saddles and bridles at the right time. Nine o'clock on. Knowing that character, he may have decided to stick around for a while and see what a Cadillac, a senator, and a secretary were doing at the corral."

Shorty Fox, who had been rummaging in a back pocket of his trousers, now extended a closed fist. "Guess what was found this afternoon in Blue Feather's pocket by yours truly. I took charge of the hanging scene first, since the FBI doesn't automatically have jurisdiction on this case."

"They'll grab it anyway," put in Solly, "and try and tie it in with the other stuff."

"For now," said Shorty, "it's our case, but I'll show the Bureau any goodies that turn up. Like this." He opened his hand and held up a triangular bolo tie slide. Turquoise and silver, the turquoise serving as background for the inset silver logo of Rancho del Gato Blanco. "Look familiar?" he asked the company about him.

It did.

"Everybody has one," said Sarah. "I bought one for Alex for Christmas. They sell them in the gift shop."

"I know," said Shorty, "but was it in Blue Feather's pocket because he was just another tourist buying souvenirs?"

"No," said Sarah. "Blue Feather Romero never wore anything like that. At night he wore a scarf tied around his neck. I never saw him in a bolo tie, and he was always making snide remarks about the ranch, so I don't think he'd have worn anything with the ranch logo."

"Really an unpleasant young man," said Julia, "but he could certainly sit a horse. He handled Lollipop perfectly."

"Consider this," said Solly. "Our fake Indian friend found this tie slide where it didn't oughter be. Like on the ground or near a murdered senator, and was using it as blackmail bait."

"I'll buy blackmail," said Sarah, "because I'm sure that he was hiding something, the way he was acting after Christmas Eve, talking about blowing the ranch apart, having cash coming in."

Julia stood up abruptly. "Bedtime. For everyone, I should think. I'm very sorry if I misled you about my seeing Mr. Arco and I hope it all can be straightened out. Good night."

To Sarah's surprise, both Solly and Shorty Fox seemed to take this dismissal seriously. Both rose and wished Julia a good-night as she retreated through the connecting door.

"A question," said Sarah as the two men moved to the door. "Did Senator Hopgood wear a bolo tie with that kind of slide?"

"You mean could Blue Feather have shot the senator? Or could he have swiped the bolo slide?"

"Both, I suppose," said Sarah. "Though why do either?"

"To answer question one," said Shorty. "Hopgood usually wore a bolo tie of some sort. According to Mrs. Hopgood, he had quite a few, silver ones in the shapes of buffalo skulls, longhorns, eagles, and so forth, plus several in the shapes of Alaska and Texas. Nothing around his neck when he was found in the feed bag. But, as we've said, a tie—a braided leather one—without a slide was wrapped around his ankles. Making him more portable, I suppose."

Sarah shook her head, now heavy with fatigue. "Aunt Julia's right. Bedtime. Good night, give my best to Maud-Emma and please don't tell her you're impounding her diaries. I did promise."

"We will keep them very, very safe," said Shorty. "There may be enough in here to make Simmons and Howell queasy, but it'll take some doing to fit them into the corral shooting. And how can we pin the murders on Blue Feather, because then who killed Blue Feather?"

"We will sleep on it," said Alex, opening the door to the cottage.

"I don't want to sleep on it," said Sarah as she kicked off her shoes. "I just want to sleep."

And she did. If Sarah dreamed, it was the floating, muddling kind of dream that mixed place and person and event into a harmless jumble that is immediately forgotten upon awakening.

TWENTY-TWO

BUT nothing about the three murders seemed clearer in the morning. Alex, up at dawn for a long walk, came back and reported that he'd run into Shorty Fox on a similar exercise and been told that Maria Cornish reported that Blue Feather never carried a gun, nor to her knowledge owned a gun, that he believed a hunting knife or his fists were adequate for personal affront or challenge.

"I believe it," said Sarah. "But I like the blackmail idea. It's just the sort of thing he'd do. Easy money. Maybe he thought the bolo tie slide would prove the murderer had left it at the scene, not realizing that half the people at the ranch wear them. It could have been that the senator's own tie clasp came off, not the murderer's, and Blue Feather found it and drew wrong conclusions."

"I wonder," said Alex, "if Blue Feather was shot with the same sort of gun that got Senator Hopgood."

"But he was hung," objected Sarah.

"Shot and then hung, according to Solly. Shot through the ear and probably still alive but unconscious when he was strung up. The necktie party was just a little cosmetic extra."

Sarah grimaced. "God, how awful."

"It's all awful. When we can, we'll get away from here as fast as we can. Find a quiet little ranch. Or go home. I think Julia may be ready for that."

"Very ready," agreed Sarah. "She wants to see to her stolen horses."

At breakfast Sarah found herself counting bolo ties. As far as neckwear went, they appeared on almost thirty percent of the male population and about ten percent of the female. A small number were of the type sold by the gift shop—the ranch logo in either coral or turquoise set into a silver triangle. But none that Sarah counted was like the one she'd seen in Shorty Fox's hand, the silver logo set into turquoise. Perhaps these were sold out. Other bolos in sight showed the usual variety of western and Indian motifs. Sarah presented her findings to Alex and Julia in the middle of the oatmeal and pancake course.

"Wait until dinner," counseled Aunt Julia. "Then you'll see the ties come out."

"But the police can hardly make an announcement about a lost bolo slide found in the pocket of a hanging corpse and ask the owner to please step up," said Alex.

Julia looked up from her oatmeal. "Never mind the bolo slide, they're all over the place. What worries me is that stupid mistake I made about seeing Mr. Arco at five A.M. when it was really three. I wonder if he saw me, my car coming in. He should be worried if he thought I recognized him."

"He certainly should," said Sarah, "so perhaps we'd better keep an eye on you, although I'd think that with three days gone by since Christmas Eve he'd be thinking he'd gotten away with it."

"Manager Arco may well have been on some legitimate errand," Alex reminded her. "The ranch was on its ear with all the goings-on. But Sarah's right, let's stick together. We're already associated with Blue Feather by the police, perhaps by the murderers, not to mention Sarah's involvement with Maud-Emma's paper collection."

Julia Clancy returned to her oatmeal, took a mouthful, and

then said, "I hate uncertainty. All this going in circles when a few simple answers to a few simple questions would take care of the whole mess. Now I wonder if I saw someone else, not Mr. Arco?"

"We'll give you truth serum and find out that you saw a lost horse," said Sarah lightly. She looked around the dining room and then moved her elbow toward one of the window tables. "Hopgood's aides are here and one of them has a Band-Aid on his nose."

"Stear clear of those birds," said Alex.

"Really," grumbled Julia, "if this goes on, we won't be able to associate with anyone here."

"Except me, darling." It was Maria Cornish. She pulled up a chair and sat down. "They've given up not having guests consort with each other," she explained, picking up the breakfast menu. Maria was dressed in a subdued costume of gray suede with a blue-gray vest and a soft black sweater. With one beautifully polished nail—gray polish, Sarah noticed—she touched the neck of the sweater. "For Blue Feather. About all he deserves, one day of mourning, because really, my dears, I'm shocked but not surprised. I've felt ever since Christmas that he was going to end up dead. No, I don't want to speculate how or why, but I suppose he was messing around with the Hopgood murder. Or did it himself and someone killed him in his turn. Disgraceful, the whole business." And Maria whipped her napkin into her lap.

Sarah, listening to Maria, did not immediately notice that Julia had left the table. She looked around, saw Alex half out of his chair and looking toward the lobby.

"Shall I go after her?" she asked. "Remember what we said about sticking together."

Alex subsided into his chair. "She can't get herself in trouble in the lodge during breakfast, and she hasn't finished her oatmeal or her coffee."

"Ladies' room," put in Maria. "Older women have to go a lot. I know because I've worked with some very talented senior actors, and you wouldn't believe how much time they spend in the loo."

"I'll go look," said Sarah. "Just to be sure."

But Julia wasn't in the ladies' room. Or in the lodge library, the drawing room, the telephone booth, or the lobby. Sarah advanced on the desk and was met by Judy Steiner—who was wearing somber rust brown. It was, Sarah decided, another gesture, like Maria's costume, at recognizing the events of the past week. Judy today wore around her shirt collar the bolo tie with the ranch logo slide. Sarah was about to add another mark to her score pad when she squinted again at the bolo slide. Something wasn't right. But Judy smiled her guest smile and asked how she could help.

Sarah, recalled, asked for Aunt Julia.

"I've just come back from breakfast," said Judy. "But I think I saw her come into the lobby ahead of me. I'll ask Cookie."

Sarah nodded and then took another hard look at Judy's tie. "That tie slide," she said. "I haven't seen many exactly like that, with the silver logo set in the turquoise. It's from the gift shop, isn't it?"

Judy looked down, ran her hand over the surface of the slide as if to check on what she was wearing. Then, "Oh no, this is a staff bolo. The gift shop sells silver with the turquoise or coral logo. This is just like it but the turquoise is the background and the logo is silver. These are much more expensive."

Sarah felt a cold hand pass down the length of her spine. "The whole staff?" she repeated.

"Well, the management staff: Todd Logan, Morty, Cookie, me, Manager Arco, Peter Doubler, and of course, the Simmonses have them. I think maybe the golf and tennis pros, too. Sometimes a VIP is given one. The Howells, for instance. Senator Hopgood refused one, wanted the regular tourist type. Maybe he was being political and wanted to look like a man of the people."

Sarah asked the next question almost breathlessly. "Has one like yours been reported missing?"

"Not that I know of," said Judy. "Have you found one?"

Before Sarah could answer, Cookie joined her at the desk.

"Fred wants you to take his calls," she said. "He said he's needed outside, that he'll be tied up for a while."

"Aunt Julia," said Sarah. "Have you seen her, Cookie?"

"Why, yes," said Cookie. "She came in here a minute ago and asked to see Manager Arco right away. I said he was busy and then the phone rang, and when I turned around she was gone."

"Just like that," said Sarah in a hollow voice.

"Yes," said Cookie cheerfully. "She must have gone back and finished her breakfast. She said she'd left it in the middle because she wanted to ask Fred something. I don't know . . ."

But Sarah didn't wait to hear what Cookie didn't know. She ran full tilt back to the table, gave the news to Alex and Maria.

"She wouldn't," said Alex. And then, "Would she?"

"You don't know Aunt Julia," said Sarah grimly. "She believes in direct action. Crops, spurs, and a tight rein."

"Guts, real guts," said Maria in admiring voice.

"Damn fool," said Alex. "I'll go and find Shorty Fox and call out the troops."

Sarah nodded. "And I'll check back at the desk and then look around by the cottages and then the corral." Sarah laughed nervously and added, "She may just have had an uncontrollable urge to pat a horse."

"And I," said Maria, "will do the pool, the tennis court, and the golf pro shop and check at the gate."

Sarah returned at a fast walk to the front desk. "Please," she asked Judy, "will you go into Mr. Arco's office and see if anyone's in there?"

Without argument, Judy went into the rear of the office, opened a door, disappeared, and returned almost immediately. "Empty. Mr. Arco is out—Cookie said so, remember? His office has outside doors connecting to the patio."

Sarah didn't wait. She sprinted for the front door, pounded along the path by the cactus garden, and arrived breathless at the door of Agave Four. "Please, please," she gasped aloud as she wrenched open the screen door, "let Aunt Julia be in her cottage."

But she wasn't.

Sarah stood fixed for a full minute to the flagstones at the entrance to Aunt Julia's cottage. Then, without much hope, she turned and walked to the side gate leading to the patio. Perhaps Aunt Julia, having missed Fred Arco, was lying on the chaise longue, taking a short nap, deaf to Sarah's calls. Sarah could close her eyes and almost see the short stubby figure of her aunt at rest, her beloved *Chronicle of the Horse* spread over her stomach. But the patio, too, was empty. And past the patio and the lower tier of cottages, beyond the bright green of the golf course, stretched only desert sand, rock, and brush, and in the distance the rising shapes of the mountains. Not a breath of wind this morning and not a soul moving, not a bird calling. An absolutely empty landscape.

No, not empty. Not the usual ranch service truck, or a morning hiker, but advancing at a sober pace on the main circular road that led to Corral Drive, a lone golf cart. A golf cart with a striped brown awning. A cart freighted with people. Certainly overloaded, Sarah thought. And where on earth was it going? The golf course had its own winding paths and the route back to the pro shop never went along the main Camino Rancho Grande.

The sight was so unusual that Sarah felt she had to see more. She turned, jumped over the small wall dividing Agave Three from Agave Four, wrenched open the patio door, and found Alex's binoculars on the living room coffee table. She snatched them, ran back to the patio, and focused in at the now disappearing cart.

Three persons mashed together in the cart plus luggage. Navy-blue and red lumps of luggage packed into the rear of the cart, a space usually reserved for two large golf bags.

Was this a new entertainment feature of the ranch? Rides around the perimeter of the ranch, rides on the unimproved roads and dirt trails? Sarah was not a golfer, but she had from time to time enjoyed going out with her father and riding in his cart. It was a satisfying activity, bouncing quietly over the ground, rather like riding in the bumper cars found at amuse-

270

ment parks. But why suitcases? And why three people on a seat designed for two?

But then Sarah realized that the contemplation of an errant, overloaded golf cart had nothing to do with finding Aunt Julia, and she vaulted lightly over the wall of the patio and began a fast descending cross-country passage in the direction of the corral and the stables. If the golf cart turned up there, well and good, she would have her curiosity satisfied. But *her* business was to find Aunt Julia. If Alex had been able to goose the police into motion, they would be spreading out now, and she hoped her own little expedition would be simply an exercise in . . . well, exercise.

The corral was almost empty. Apparently the death of Blue Feather and the accident to Maud-Emma Hopgood had put a frost on trail riding. Only Morty McGuire was present, over in the corner, conferring with the ever-present farrier about a large piebald, the front hoof of which was being filed.

A quick questioning of Morty told her that Aunt Julia had not turned up that morning. At least not in sight of Morty, but Sarah then remembered that her aunt had enjoyed standing at the fenced enclosure and looking over the horses, examining them for good and bad points, speculating about gaits and temperament.

Sarah made her way to the fenced day corral that lay just beyond the tack house and farrier's shed. She walked around it, calling her aunt's name softly. Nothing. She swung back and toured in the opposite direction, noticing as she went that Pokey and Noodle were among those present. And Morty's big roan, Spider. But no Aunt Julia. Then, just as she was wondering if her aunt might have decided to visit the night range, she became aware of a change in the horses who had up to then been at rest, chewing on flanks, whisking tails, moving slowly about the compound. Now heads came up, snorts sounded, and several animals moved restlessly, turning, stopping, and turning again, pawing the ground.

Then Sarah heard it. The distant metallic insectlike *tock-tock* of an airplane. No, not an airplane. A helicopter, a tiny dark speck against clear colorless sky. A speck coming imperceptibly closer. And closer.

The agitation of the horses increased. Several whirled and began trotting up and down by the corral fence, nostrils wide, ears pricked forward.

And then the golf cart. To her astonishment, Sarah, standing now just behind the farrier's shed near the gate of the corral, saw the golf cart shoot into the open space between the tack shed and a roofed enclosure holding a utility car and small tractor. It hesitated, turned slowly as if uncertain of direction, and then bumped forward over the dirt ground and, increasing speed, bucked off past the corral and toward an open stretch of unfenced range.

Its passage from entrance to exit, Sarah thought, couldn't have taken more than thirty seconds, but in that time she identified those two honored guests of Heinz Simmons's, the Howells, Mrs. Howell in the middle clinging to the arm of Mr. Howell, and on the other side, Esty Simmons hanging on to the small stanchion on the side of the cart. In the rear of the cart bounced the pile of luggage, secured, Sarah now saw, by a tangle of rope.

Her first impulse had been to shout and then run after the cart, but again she checked herself. She was looking for Aunt Julia, who certainly was not on the overburdened golf cart. She turned toward Morty, thinking to enlist him in the search, and saw that, rooted to the ground, he was staring with amazement, and she was close enough to hear him say, "For Christ's sake," and then saw him run toward the corral, concern and anger mixed on his face.

Sarah saw the reason. With the increasing noise, the horses had gone from an agitated milling herd to a whinnying, snorting, stamping mass. The word "stampede" forced itself into Sarah's brain, and she turned toward the corral and saw Morty shoving a third and higher rail into slots above the gate itself.

Uncertain whether to get out of the way or to offer help, Sarah came around the end of the farrier's shed with the intention of signaling to Morty when a second golf cart whirled into the space, ground to a stop, then angled off toward the open range.

Heinz Simmons. And more luggage piled on the seat and behind. Simmons at the wheel, his usually smooth blond hair ruffled, his face rigid. The golf cart, like its preceding twin, bounced out in the direction of the range, taking a route so close to the farrier's shed that Sarah could have reached out and touched it.

Everything converged at once. The helicopter noise increased, the churning fearful horses broke into faster movement—short gallops, squealing, rearing—and the farrier, who had grabbed at the lead shank attached to the halter of the piebald he was shoeing, now found himself dragged across the ground almost to Sarah's feet. Then the animal went up into the air, front hooves high, plunged, twisted, and took off down the main corral road, lead shank dragging. In an instinctive move to take cover, Sarah backed up to the wall of the farrier's shed, then, looking out toward the range, saw and heard—the racket was horrible—the helicopter hovering, its blade twirling just over the ground so that a storm of brush and sand funneled into the air.

Then steps were lowered, three human shapes moved into the mouth of the machine, the second golf cart came into sight, shot around a boulder, rose in the air, jounced, tipped, flipped, and spewed out the driver with a cascade of luggage. Sarah, rigid, clutching the edge of the farrier's shed, watched like someone at some awful improvised "happening." For a moment, the driver lay flat, arms wide like some stricken desert crawler, then slowly, painfully stood up, started to run forward, arms waving. But the helicopter, its rotors whirring faster, climbed, tilted, and began a full-engine ascent toward the distant rise of the mountains.

The helicopter moved higher and higher, but the waving man continued his efforts as if by this display of energy he could call it back. Then slowly, with a certain purposefulness, the figure let his arms fall to his side, and one hand moved into his jeans pocket. He turned and strode in the direction of the corral.

Heinz Simmons. Black dungarees patched with dust, a torn red shirt with silver buttons. Heinz Simmons, iron-faced, walked without urgency, but lost no time in looking about. He headed directly for the corral. Sarah's last coherent thought was that here comes a man who knows exactly where he's going. He's missed his ride but he has a plan. Sarah, confused, fearful of the still circling, snorting horses who might any minute break out of their corral, pressed her back hard against the farrier's shed. There she hesitated, not knowing whether to dash out or to stay put.

And this indecision probably saved her life.

Because at exactly the same time—as if planned by someone holding a stopwatch—down from the corral road, tires screeching, blue lights flashing, came the forces of law and order. The modern-day posse. The Lodestone police and the FBI, Sarah supposed, in several unmarked cars. The works.

They came to a tire-wrenching stop: uniformed men and plainclothesmen erupted, guns in hand, and splayed out, running, crouching, in all directions—to the tack shed, to the equipment shed, behind one of the standing chuck wagons. Sarah saw two men zigzag toward the corral as if already dodging bullets and shoulder Morty out of the way and shove him to the ground.

The horses, many of whom had begun to slow their milling with the fading of the helicopter noise, now began again to whirl, to rear, to squeal.

And cutting across the end of the tack shed and into this police-car-jammed space walked Heinz Simmons. He seemed oblivious of danger, out of it, as if the most everyday thing in the world was to walk toward a crowd of emptied police cars. Sarah heard a shout from someplace ahead of her. Something about holding fire, for Simmons to put his hands on top of his head. And then with amazing agility, Heinz Simmons dodged around a squad car, doubled back around the farrier's shed, pushed past Sarah without seeing her, and twisting and turning flung himself behind the second chuck wagon . . . perhaps the very chuck wagon in which Senator

Hopgood made his last and most impressive public appearance.

And then the shots. Rapid-fire. An explosion from three sides, an uninterrupted *boom, boom, boom.* From the fourth side, behind the chuck wagon, returning shots. Of course, he's armed, thought Sarah. Everyone here is. Weapons for every hand.

Sarah crouched, holding her ears, seeing little explosions of dust when a bullet slammed into the ground. And then all at once Heinz sprinted out from behind the chuck wagon. Straight for the corral gate. Straight for the cover of a herd of frightened horses. He must have taken the watchers by surprise because for almost four seconds not a shot. And four seconds was long enough for Heinz Simmons to propel himself under the lowest corral rail and disappear in the melee of plunging fear-crazy horses.

Morty stood up. Shouting and yelling.

"Hold your fire. Hold your fire. Those are my horses. Hold it, hold it. I said damn you, I'll blow your hides off if you fire into that corral." Then pulling himself up on the gate so that he stood several heads higher than anyone watching, he shouted again. "You fire, damn you, I won't answer. Those horses can't hold much longer. They've gone loco with all the noise. They'll stampede. All over you and the whole goddamn ranch."

But it was too late. Along one side of the corral fence came a cracking noise, a smashing of wood, of rails splintering and falling, and like a huge moving tide, as if flogged forward by some giant whip, the horses moved, shoved, plunged over the broken fence. For a moment Sarah thought the herd would swerve back toward the waiting police, but Morty ran out, his arms windmilling, and the lead horse, a great leopard Appaloosa, eyes wild, nostrils flared, rammed in his hooves, threw up his head, reared, turned, and with the fifty horses at his tail, stampeded down the trail toward the main ranch road, pounded past the turnoff to Corral Drive, and turned the bobbing, galloping, sweating, neighing herd directly toward the tenth fairway.

And Heinz Simmons?

He lay on the ground by the broken rails, sprawled, a flattened red-shirted sawdust shape, one trampled hand stretched in the direction taken by the departing helicopter.

TWENTY-THREE

TIME stopped dead. Dead as Heinz Simmons. In fact, Sarah thought, the shape pressed by those pounding hooves into the dust of the corral could never have been alive. Too flat. Too still. The thing lying out there in the empty corral was no more than some large and strangely shaped puppet left by some careless child. The puppet had no relation to the man known as Heinz Simmons—the man who in faultless evening dress had made his entrances into the dining room with Maria Cornish on his arm.

The police, some with weapons still raised, some still in a crouch behind open squad car doors, froze in place as if held by the sudden quiet. Then time cranked itself up and moved with jerks forward. The police and plainclothesmen gesturing, organizing. Radiotelephone calls. The ambulance. The photographers. The media. The body bag. Sarah, Morty McGuire, and the farrier rounded up. Statements taken. Descriptions of the helicopter collected.

And then Morty, shaking off a police arm, demanded his freedom. His horses were at risk. So were some of the ranch guests. He had his job to do. Mercifully, Shorty Fox arrived and released Morty, who strode over to the vehicle standing in the tractor shed, climbed in, started the motor, and hightailed it out the corral road in the direction taken by his maddened horses.

Sarah stood about in a sort of after-shock daze, dry-mouthed, hands unaccountably trembling. She was in that curious state in which everything seems either hilariously funny—the fact that Morty was driving a Ford Bronco—or completely tragic—Heinz Simmons's horrible death. Three times by three different officials she was asked for her name, her address, her status as a ranch guest, and three times someone demanded to know what she thought she was doing down by the corral. From these interrogations she was rescued by Shorty Fox.

"She was looking for a missing person, her aunt," said Shorty to the third uniformed man. "She's got nothing to do with this affair. It's just coincidence she turned up. Let her go."

"It *was* a coincidence, wasn't it?" asked Shorty as he walked Sarah out of the corral area.

Sarah, now feeling the beginning throb of a headache, found not only that her mouth was dry but that her voice apparatus seemed again to have rusted in place. However, she croaked out that the search for Aunt Julia had propelled her to the corral and that the golf cart–helicopter scene had been only a sideshow.

"A god-awful sideshow," she concluded.

"Can say that again," agreed Shorty. He came to a halt and pointed up the long slope to the cottage rows. "Okay," he said. "On your way. Stay put at your cottage. We'll be in touch. We'll keep you posted about your Aunt Julia."

"Is Mr. Arco still missing?" Sarah had to ask.

"Yep. We've issued an all-points. For both of them. But," he added, "we've no real proof they're together."

Sarah shook her head sadly. "Don't I wish. But Aunt Julia was last seen . . ." and here her voice cracked again.

Shorty shook his head. "Last seen doesn't always add up. From what I've noticed of Mrs. Clancy she's just as likely to

278

have gone bear hunting or hang gliding. Look, worry about Fred Arco—she's probably got him roped and tied by now." He smiled to indicate sympathy and then at a last effort at reassurance said, "Anyway, all the witnesses, you included, said she wasn't one of the ones boarding the helicopter."

With that Shorty Fox turned and walked back in the direction of the corral. But Sarah, remembering the hasty business of loading, now asked herself whether Aunt Julia, although she hadn't been seen boarding, may, in fact, have been loaded as luggage. In pieces.

This gruesome idea she relayed to Alex and Maria Cornish, both of whom she found on the patio of Agave Four. Alex was pacing restlessly back and forth in the small enclosure and Maria reclined on the chaise longue.

Alex stopped his pacing, took one hard look at Sarah's blanched face, stepped into the cottage, and returned with a blanket and a full glass of water. He pointed out a chair. "Sit, Sarah, and wrap up, it's chilly out here. Try and relax, because your circuits must be overloaded." He settled Sarah in a chair and solicitously tucked the blanket about her knees while Sarah alternately sipped her water and shuddered.

"We heard all the racket, dear," said Maria. "It sounded like the first day of Gettysburg. I did a film on that once . . . just a short. I was a grieving widow."

Alex sat down beside Sarah. "Shorty gave me a call, said you were on your way, that you'd been caught smack in the middle of a very rough scene. I'll send out for lunch, we can eat here. And your Aunt Julia would never let anyone chop her into pieces."

Sarah took a last long gulp of water and sank back in the chair. "That's what Shorty Fox said. But she's sixty-seven, you know, and Mr. Arco is in his prime."

"Darling," said Maria, reaching over and patting Sarah's arm—a generous gesture considering that Sarah's shirt-sleeve arm was covered with a layer of corral dust. "Darling, I can read people, I really can. Mr. Fred Arco may look like Napoleon, but it's all false front. Mark my words, the man is a total jelly."

"I hope you're right," was all Sarah could say. Then she added, "But with the corral scene, everything that's going on, well, I can't believe Aunt Julia is the police's number one concern."

"Maybe not," said Alex, "but Fred Arco may be. Now, how about telling us what happened? If you can bear it, because it might be better to spill it all out."

And Sarah spilled. The golf carts, the helicopter, Heinz Simmons tipping over, the shooting, and Heinz Simmons acting the part of the lone renegade. "I couldn't believe it," she said. "He walked almost into the middle of all those police cars as if he was on auto. He must have been so busy thinking about his next move that he didn't even see or hear the police come slamming in there. Of course, the helicopter was making a monster racket and the horses were going bananas." Sarah stopped and bit her lip. The scene was still right there banging in her head so that she could close her eyes and see and hear it all again.

"You don't have to go on," said Alex sympathetically.

"No, it's okay. Nothing much more. There was a sort of gun storm, Mr. Simmons jumped into the corral, maybe for cover, maybe because there was no place else to go, and Morty stood up and stopped the firing. But the horses did the rest, they went completely crazy. Broke out and took off. Just like wild horses."

"Horses are wild, basically," said Alex. "They're herd animals; if they're frightened, they run."

"They ran over Heinz Simmons," said Sarah. "It was terrible."

"If it makes you feel better, it was probably over fast. He'd have been killed at once."

There was a long pause and then Maria pursed her lips, shook her shapely head. "So Heinz Simmons is the villain. I thought there was something about him, all that smooth talk, wanting me to have dinner with him. I was better off with Blue Feather."

"I think, said Sarah, "there are multiple villains. And," she added, frowning, "I'm not sure who did what when. How do the Howells fit in? And Blue Feather and Fred Arco?"

Maria sat up. She looked, to Sarah, as bright-eyed as she had on Christmas morning when the senator's body had been discovered. In fact, she positively glowed.

"Darlings, it will all be sorted out. There'll be some frantically ghastly dénouement. But think of it. Too theater of the absurd. Imagine escaping by golf cart and leaving by helicopter, all those designer suitcases, and the police charging down. And a shoot-out in a corral. I mean, really. Where do you suppose they've all gone, the Howells and Mrs. Simmons? If I were writing the script I'd send them to Mexico. Over the border. Have them crash somewhere and be captured by *bandidos*. Do you suppose the police have little pursuit planes, Stealth fighters?"

"I did wonder when I saw the golf carts," said Sarah, "but I thought the ranch might have used them for exploration tours. And the first cart with the Howells just went along quite slowly. It didn't rev up until it got to the corral."

"A golf cart is a good choice," said Alex. "It's pretty much an all-terrain vehicle. No one would think of it as an escape car while that red Porsche belonging to Simmons would have been spotted right away."

"Golf carts are junior Jeeps," said a voice. Solly. He pushed open the patio gate and perched himself on the edge of the stone wall. "All the conspirators here, I see. Sarah, I've been told to check on your health." He nodded, satisfied. "You seem to be okay."

"She will be after some lunch and some peace and quiet," said Alex. "I'll call in now." And without waiting for an answer he disappeared inside the cottage.

Maria turned to Solly. "I can't believe there's been a shoot-out, a real shoot-out at the corral. What shall we call it? 'The Shoot-out at Gato Blanco'? No, that doesn't work. How about 'Shoot-out at the White Cat Corral'?"

"Charming," said Solly. "Just like you, Ms. Cornish."

" 'Maria' to you, Doctor," said Maria, lowering her eyes.

"Aunt Julia," interrupted Sarah impatiently. She had about had it with Maria's zest for turning life into cinema. And it was contagious, because she, Sarah, had been doing the same, all those imagined western scenarios—life imitating art.

"No word on Julia," said Solly, "but the police are on it."

But Sarah was in forward gear. "How can you sit here," she accused Solly, "when Esty Simmons and the Howells are in a helicopter on the way to Mexico or someplace like it? Why isn't someone chasing them? You're sitting here talking and they've escaped."

"I'm just a poor pathologist," said Solly. "And the police can't just take off and start shooting down unidentified helicopters. They're tracking it, but don't hold your breath. That chopper had a fair head start. Those guys could land and climb into cars, other planes, covered wagons, rockets. Who knows?"

"Anyway," persisted Sarah, "what I care about is Aunt Julia. She may be with Fred Arco, and he's probably one of this gang of killers. So I'm going to go on looking." She stood up abruptly.

Alex reappeared and put out a restraining hand. "Lunch is coming. Take it easy. You can't do anything."

Sarah shook off his hand. "I can try. I can start looking in places the police wouldn't. Or go to Lodestone. Or something."

Solly got into the act. "Alex is right. Honestly, Sarah. We can't have you steaming all over the place, distracting the police, endangering yourself. We're not sure that Fred Arco was really working with Simmons. We don't know exactly where he fits in."

Sarah smoldered. "Are you worried about Arco's civil rights, or will the police wait until Aunt Julia's body is found under a cactus and then you'll say, 'Ah, yes, Fred Arco was implicated in several murders, but unfortunately we couldn't harass a citizen without evidence'?"

"Fred Arco," said Solly, "is being looked for just as urgently as your Aunt Julia. Be sensible. Have lunch, stoke up, and then if you and Alex and Maria here want to make safe little trips together between here and the lodge calling out her name—and go nowhere else, mind you—okay, go for it."

Sarah gritted her teeth and subsided. It was infuriating for them to be treated as if they were curious children who might trot about keeping busy and out of harm. All right, she thought, I'll eat the blasted lunch—after all, she was beginning to feel the first hunger twinges—and then I'll go looking again. With Alex and Maria. Or without them. On foot or by car. And then, suddenly, she had a thought. "Her car? Aunt Julia's car."

"Right where it should be," said Alex. "By the side of her cottage."

"And Fred Arco's car," persisted Sarah.

Solly looked rueful. "Gone. But listen, don't get excited. Someone from the staff may have borrowed it. There's no proof your aunt climbed in the car—actually it's a Jeep—with Arco."

"I'll bet he made her. With a gun," said Sarah.

"Don't trouble trouble," said Maria. "And now, loves, I think it's time for a before-lunch lie-down. If anything really stirring happens or you find Julia, leave word at the office." And Maria rose, smiled at Solly, lowered a green and gold eyelid at Alex, pressed Sarah's hand, and swept out of the patio gate.

"Me, too," said Solly. "Back to work. Blue Feather's autopsy report. Probably have to help with the post on what's left of Simmons. Sarah, I promise to keep an ear out for news of Julia and Arco and will keep in touch."

And Solly was gone.

Leaving Sarah with the newly arrived lunch tray, which was spread out on the patio by a pale and worried-looking maid. She uncovered a bowl of soup. "Chicken noodle," she said.

"What the doctor ordered," said Alex.

For a while Sarah worked on lunch and then, pushing her bowl aside, she confronted Alex.

"I am now going to look for Aunt Julia."

Alex scowled. "To the lodge and back. No free-lancing."

"You want to leave it to the police?" Sarah said accusingly.

"I do. They probably have a full dossier on Arco and can guess where he might have gone."

"With Aunt Julia?"

"Maybe yes, maybe no," said Alex.

"Look," said Sarah, "I won't go into Lodestone. Not yet anyway. But I will try some ranch highways and byways. Arco may have gone somewhere into the desert. One of the ranges, or a feed station. Or one of the campfire places with shelters."

"No," said Alex. "You'd be putting your neck on the block. Besides, we don't have a Jeep. Or an ATV."

"No, but I've an idea," said Sarah. "What did Solly call it, a junior Jeep. A golf cart."

"Forget it. Golf carts are by now black-listed. No one will let you go near a golf cart to cruise around the ranch."

"Unless," said Sarah slowly, "we play golf. We could take off from the golf course."

"We don't play golf," said Alex.

"But we can play at playing golf. Get some clubs, dress the part, talk it up. Can you hit a golf ball? I mean well enough to start us off the first tee?"

"I played in college. For a year or so. Gave it up. Took too much time."

"And I've watched my father. We can fake it."

"And if I say no, don't, stay here, stop it, what then?"

"Lone Ranger," said Sarah, moving toward the living room door.

"Damn it to hell," said Alex, rising in his turn. Then he grinned. "If these were the good old days, I'd take you by the hair and haul you into my cave and sit on you."

"Happily," said Sarah, "these are not the good old days. Women have risen up and gone hunting."

"But not in golf carts," said Alex, letting the living room door slam behind them.

Sarah, in the closest approximation to a golfing costume that she could manage—slacks, pale blue sweater, hiking shoes—and Alex in something similar, together made their way in purposeful steps to the golf course.

"I've brought a map of the ranch. It's got trails and cookout spots marked," said Sarah. Then as they reached the door of the pro shop, she added, "I suppose we have to sign up or something."

"Yes," said Alex, "get a starting time, rent a cart. But I don't see anyone around except on the putting green." He pointed out a contorted figure bending over his putter on the smooth green oval by the pro shop.

"Of course," said Sarah, "there's the matter of golf clubs."

"We may have to try a snatch."

"You mean steal?"

"Lift, borrow, appropriate. I'll go into the men's locker room and see if there's a bag that hasn't been put away. You try the ladies' locker room. Meet you back here in five minutes."

It took Alex two minutes. He emerged from the locker room with a golf bag bristling with clubs slung over his shoulder. Sarah, due to initial hesitations, lingered two minutes longer in the ladies' locker room, but a locker hung open and Sarah took a deep breath, reached for a bag, shouldered it, and scuttled out.

They compared notes. Both locker rooms had been deserted.

"I wonder why," said Alex. "From my experience, nothing short of an active hurricane or total war would frighten off a golfer."

At which Tommy Brass, the golf pro, materialized. "It's that stampede. Horses all over the back nine. The cowboys are rounding them up but no one can play those holes—fairways are a mess, the greens are trampled, hoofprints all over. Anyway, only one foursome has gone out since it happened. Most people won't settle for less than eighteen holes. But you can lift your ball out of a hoofprint without penalty."

"I'll remember," said Alex, "and nine holes is just fine."

"A cart," said Tommy Brass helpfully.

"Great," said Alex, accepting the proffered sign-up pad and pencil. He leaned over and signed in in a firm hand, "Mr. and Mrs. Robert W. Service, Agave Three."

"You might just as well have written Dan McGrew and the Lady that's known as Lou," said Sarah as they rolled toward the first tee in their cart.

"I'm being half honest," said Alex. "The room number is okay so we'll get the bill." He brought the cart into place by the first tee, jumped out, and handed Sarah a long club with a wooden head. "Driver. To drive a ball with. Just watch me swing and hit and you do the same. From the ladies' tee, it's a few feet closer to the pin."

"How kind of the men," said Sarah.

"It's body build, not discrimination," said Alex, flexing the head of his driver.

Sarah studied the teeing up of the ball, the setting of the feet, the final waggle of the club. Alex then bent his head, swung his club, and distinguished himself with a long looping drive that rolled into a patch of rough at the edge of the fairway. Then Sarah stepped up and took a swing that almost pulled her off her feet.

"Shorter," said Alex. "You're going too far around and losing your balance. Just keep your eye on the ball."

Sarah gripped her club harder, lifted it, and swiped. And was rewarded with a sharp click. To her utter amazement she saw the ball rise in a graceful arc, bounce in the middle of the fairway, and roll a healthy distance in the direction of the pin.

"Have you considered golf as a substitute for detective work?" said Alex as they bumped decorously along in their cart toward their balls.

"Never, but I'd like a golf cart. They're fun." And Sarah, at the wheel, accelerated and made a circling turn around her ball. She took out a five wood, dribbled twice, and then hit another shot straight and true while Alex with great energy drove his ball directly into a growth of ornamental cactus at the green's edge.

And so it went, Sarah occasionally connecting but more often flubbing, and Alex alternating a slice with a hook, and both keeping an eye out for other golfers.

At the green of the third hole, Sarah poked Alex. "Okay, let's go for it."

"Dump the clubs," said Alex. "They rattle and the weight slows us down." He climbed down from the cart, unstrapped the two bags, and shoved them under the bench by the edge of the third tee.

The sun was bright, a cactus wren rattled from a nearby growth, and for a minute Sarah could almost believe they were on one of Alex's bird-watching excursions. Then she shook herself and opened her map. "Okay, that way, there's a path— it's called the Saguaro Nature Trail, all marked—and it goes past the place the ranch has their big cookouts. Aunt Julia told me it was where the sand was in the coffee. Arco might have taken Aunt Julia there."

"I still don't follow. Why wouldn't he drive her out of town and then take action? Why stay on the ranchland?"

"I've thought about that. But if it's true they've sent out an all-points, there'll be roadblocks all over the place. Arco would know that. But with a Jeep on the desert he could take the trails, to one of those sheds or feed stations, and hole up somewhere. I think it went like this. Aunt Julia must have decided to bomb right into his office this morning and clear up the business of his jogging at three A.M. She hates not knowing things, absolutely bullheaded . . ."

"You do make a nice pair," Alex said softly.

"I'll never be in the same class with Julia Clancy, but sometimes I wish I had her starch. Never mind, my idea is that Arco will want to know what she knows, may think she knows more than she does and will try to get it out of her. And he'll take her someplace where he can try. I can't be-lieve he'd kill her. Not right off. Oh, Alex," Sarah said almost in anguish, "it's all I can do . . . we can do. We can't just sit back at the cottage wondering if the police are making a decent job of searching."

Alex didn't answer; he simply pointed ahead to a turn in the trail where the top of a small building was visible.

Sarah nodded and then went on urgently, "Aunt Julia may be bullheaded, but she's not dumb. She'd take a risk but a limited one. I've seen her with big horses. Here's what I think. I'd say she'd play for time, lead Arco on."

But no Julia was at the cookout grounds. The shed was

empty, there were no tire tracks, only days-old foot- and hoofprints.

"There's a feed station beyond," said Alex, examining the map.

They bumped to the feed station, the wide cart tires sometimes slewing in the soft sand. But the feed station when reached was simply a wide-roofed structure partly filled with packed bales of hay, covered by a hanging tarpaulin. And no Aunt Julia.

"Damn it," said Sarah, and she stamped on the accelerator and turned the wheel viciously and they bounced off down the trail.

"Easy, easy," said Alex. "Let's not us end up as statistics."

"Got to hurry," muttered Sarah, "before it's too late. Try the rodeo corral. The trail goes between these rocks, hold your hat." She accelerated again and turned sharply.

"Whoa," said Alex. "We don't want to make so much noise that we'll flush them out, and Arco will panic and do something." He pointed ahead. "There's the rodeo corral. See the bleachers."

Sarah turned the wheel again, missed the trail curve, overcorrected, and the cart bounced, hit a rock, swiveled, and came to an abrupt stop in heavy sand beside the boulder wall.

She almost cried. Instead, "Oh shit. Oh shit."

"On foot," said Alex. "We'll walk quietly in, keeping low behind things, and if we see anything, anyone at all, we take cover, lie low, and go back for help. Okay?"

Sarah was about to answer when in total unbelief she pointed. "My God, there, look there."

Alex looked there. To one side of the small bleachers stood a Jeep. A dark gray Jeep. And just dimly—the sun was directly in her eyes—Sarah thought she could make out two heads, two heads set on two shoulders behind the Jeep's tinted windshield.

Trying to fight a rising sense of terror, Sarah squinted, tilting her head for a better focus. Yes, the head and shoulders in the driver's seat seemed marginally higher than those of the passenger. The passenger must then be shorter than the driver, or slumped down in the seat.

"Look," whispered Sarah. "In the passenger's seat. Do you think it's Aunt Julia? Or," she faltered, "her body? Or"—this more hopefully—"she's unconscious?"

"Get down," instructed Alex. "If you can see them, they can probably see you. Well enough to take a potshot at. And remember, Fred Arco's about the same height as Julia . . . Napoleon size. So maybe he's in the passenger seat. Had a seizure or something. No, I'm not joking"—as Sarah stared at him—"it's possible. And now we need a battle plan. Something fast."

But no battle plan was necessary. There sounded a grinding noise, a motor throbbing. The Jeep hopped forward, stalled, started again and accelerated, and rolled directly at Sarah and Alex, turning at the last minute so that the driver's window had a good view of the golf cart.

And the driver? Aunt Julia. She was frowning, leaning forward gripping the wheel with both hands. Beside her, in a declining posture, the top third of Napoleon, a.k.a. Fred Arco.

Sarah and Alex jumped up at once, calling, waving.

The Jeep jerked, stalled, and came to rest against a tangle of mesquite.

The window on the driver's side of the Jeep rolled down. Aunt Julia leaned out. "Don't do that. Waving and shouting. You startled me and I'm not used to this Jeep yet. I might have gone right off the road, and Fred here isn't feeling a bit well."

Sarah and Alex, unable to speak, could only stand and gulp.

Aunt Julia started the Jeep again, backed abruptly into a large rock, cranked the wheel, and leaned out again.

"I see that you've wrecked a golf cart. Have you taken up the game or have you stolen it? Really, out here horses are much more suitable. I can't give you a ride back because Fred and I have a few more things to settle and we need privacy.

But I'll send help." Aunt Julia gave a gracious twirl of her hand—a gesture often used with effect by Britain's Queen Mother—and the Jeep bounced off down the path in the direction of the ranch.

TWENTY-FOUR

SARAH and Alex spent the better part of that afternoon in a state of burning and unsatisfied curiosity. Aunt Julia had driven back to the ranch and parked the Jeep by temporary police headquarters in the Primrose Cottage complex. She had debarked and escorted a drooping Fred Arco into the jaws of Lieutenant Detective Shorty Fox. She had then become the guest of the police and Special Agent Douglas Jay of the Federal Bureau of Investigation and at four-thirty she was still sequestered.

Cookie Logan, on one of Sarah's repeated trips to the front desk to ask about her aunt, told her that five luncheon trays had been delivered to Primrose Cottage, so it could be assumed that everyone therein was in good health. Sarah also used these meetings with Cookie to have several short but productive conversations.

"Aunt Julia is the living end," she complained back at Agave Three on the patio with a rum swizzle. "Let's never ever go anywhere with her again. She's taken years off my life. I thought she was dead, or mangled. Or raped. Or strung up like

Blue Feather. And there she was, big as life, driving that Jeep, I mean the gall of it. The nerve. You name it."

"Oddly enough," observed Alex in a mild voice, "you, Sarah, my love, have sometimes caused me to say exactly the same things about you. It must be in the genes. The genetic capability of causing extreme anxiety and exasperation in the significant other."

"Ah, children," said a now familiar voice. Solly again. He vaulted over the wall, no easy task for someone whose legs in Sarah's estimation were at least five feet long.

"Have they finished with Aunt Julia?" demanded Sarah.

"Almost. Your aunt is going strong and is coming over in a minute to join us for drinks. Then we're all going out for dinner. On me. I'm going to toast the lady and then see if we can't clone her in the lab. Not, mind you, that I ever want to spend a vacation in the company of anyone like her."

"I know what you mean," said Sarah.

Alex poured himself a stiff Scotch on the rocks. "I'd choose the ER on New Year's Eve to a quiet holiday with Julia Clancy."

"You should see Fred Arco," said Solly. "He may need a complete course of psychotherapy. In prison." Solly sank back in his chair and balanced his feet on the top of the patio's stone wall. "But you know, Shorty Fox is beginning to think that Julia's approach to suspects has something going for it. Julia said she just treated Fred like a badly broken horse, lot of faults and needs a strong and definite hand."

"That's right," said Julia, opening the little gate to the patio and stepping in. She had a large glass of a dark amber fluid in one hand. She stepped to an empty chair and plumped herself in the middle. "Patience, discipline, and let them know who's boss." She lifted her glass. "Well, dears, I'm quite done in. It's been a long day and I'm an old woman." She looked about and shook her head sadly, repeating, "An old, old woman."

"No tears from me, Julia Clancy," said Solly. "I'm the one who needs sympathy, a long night ahead with the Simmons autopsy set for eleven. So, everyone, we'll eat early."

"And you, Aunt Julia, despite fatigue, old age, arthritis, or whatever," said Sarah, swiveling on her aunt, "will tell all."

"And," said Alex to Solly, "you will tell the rest of all."

Julia Clancy was allowed a full hour for a restorative bath and a second belt of whiskey and then Solly bundled his party into his damaged Isuzu Trooper and drove to Lodestone.

"We'll skip Danny's tonight," he said as they shot through the main street of Lodestone. "There's a little barbecued-ribs mom-and-pop operation around the corner, low-key and closes down at ten-thirty. I'd say it was just our style."

"Whatever our style is," murmured Sarah, leaning back against the seat and closing her eyes. She wondered if she'd have the strength to chew anything tonight. Perhaps stewed vegetables.

Not so Julia Clancy. "I haven't had barbecued ribs in ages. I think it's just what will pull me together."

"Good, because you've got a hell of a lot of explaining to do, my dear aunt," said Sarah as the four climbed out of the car and made their way to a log-cabin-style building set back from a patch of weedy grass. A single sign on the window said DRAFT BEER and on the door a notice written in hand, WELCOME TO DINGLE'S FAMILY RESTAURANT—CASH ONLY. NO CREDIT CARDS OR CHECKS.

"Sensible," remarked Solly, holding open the door. "That's how to stay solvent. Trust no one. In with you all. I've reserved one of the back rooms. Intimate, all of ten feet square."

The first half hour in the small dimly lit chamber was devoted to ordering and receiving plates of smoking-hot ribs, coleslaw, and Italian bread, and a pitcher of draft beer. Then after a period of munching and cutting, it was time.

"Okay, Mrs. Clancy," said Sarah, putting down her fork. "You are on. Start with this morning at breakfast and do not pass Go until you get to Fred Arco being driven by you in his own Jeep."

Julia took a long sip of beer, speared a piece of bread, rotated it in the barbecue sauce, chomped down, chewed, swallowed, and began. "I can't stand not knowing something that I can find out just by asking. Fred Arco seemed to be the key to part of this whole stupid affair because he wasn't where

I thought he was at the time it was supposed to be on Christmas morning. And since everyone said Fred wasn't down at the corral during the time the senator was shot, it wasn't as if I was going to confront a killer."

"Since when has Mr. Arco turned into your buddy Fred?" demanded Sarah. "And he isn't cleared for Blue Feather's murder."

Julia with a gesture of her fork waved away Blue Feather's murder. "Fred Arco and I are on a first-name basis because we have spent a long period of time together in his Jeep. It's important for people to be at ease with each other in delicate situations."

"So," said Alex, "you left us at breakfast and went stomping into his office—scaring us half to death."

"It couldn't be helped," said Julia. "There we all were entangled in this affair, and I felt if I could just get a handle on Fred Arco you other super-sleuths could clear up the rest. For instance, the nasty tricks. Fred Arco had nothing to do with trying to destroy the ranch."

"That's true," Sarah admitted. "I pinned Cookie down this afternoon when I was asking about you. But go on, Aunt Julia, I'll explain about those later, how they worked—or didn't work."

"Well, I took Fred by surprise. His nerves must have been pretty well shot, but he tried to bluster, and I could see that unless I was really overbearing, he might win the round."

"Overbearing is descriptive," said Sarah.

"And," put in Alex, "his winning the round might have landed you in the morgue."

"No, no. Fred isn't a murderer. He's an accomplice. As Maria Cornish might put it, a second banana. A spear holder, an extra. It's written all over him. He does his bully act with the staff because they can't talk back, but bring in the big guns—Simmons, the Howells, the police—and you have Mr. Lily Liver."

"And you, Julia, are a big gun?" asked Alex.

"Fred is a bully, and I know about bullies. Sarah, remember

that big sixteen-hand chestnut 'Konker' of your Uncle Tom's? No? Well, he was a bully . . ."

"Aunt Julia," said Sarah impatiently. "Go on. You went into Mr. Arco's office . . ."

"And he may thank me in the end."

"Why," said Alex grimly, "should he thank you?"

"The police are thanking her," said Solly. "Not liking her but thanking her. But they'll never tell her so."

"Well," said Julia, "it's like this. I threatened and demanded, but then I saw we'd get nowhere in his office because those macho western scenes, the desk on a platform, the whole setting, worked as Fred's power base. I suggested we take a drive, and I suppose he even thought at first he'd dump me, but it just isn't in the man. By the time we drove out into the desert he was trembling and sweating. I had to take over the wheel, and I parked where you found us. We took a long walk, I settled him down, told him what was in his best interest, his chance for not being charged with first-degree murder, and he buckled. Just like I knew he would." Julia gave a triumphant smile and took a long drink of beer.

"But Arco wasn't going to be charged with first degree," said Solly. "Not for the Farnsworth and Hopgood murders, anyway. You knew he had a complete alibi for the whole murder period."

"*He* didn't know that because he didn't know exactly how and when those murders took place. And he was near enough to the Blue Feather shooting and hanging that he was feeling quite ill on that score. Blue Feather had arranged a meeting with Heinz Simmons out on the trail—expecting a payoff—and Fred had orders to follow them. Simmons shot Blue Feather, but Fred was made to help with the stringing up."

"Oh," said Sarah suddenly. "I remember. During lunch. I saw two horses going out and then another following."

"Fred Arco was a stooge," said Julia. "Heinz Simmons's stooge. It was Simmons who had Fred drive Lily Farnsworth's body in the senator's car up to Agave Annex and park it there at around three in the morning. Just about when I saw him walking or jogging. He told me Simmons took him aside Christmas Eve and said there'd been a terrible accident to the senator and Miss Farnsworth, a murder-suicide, and there'd be a scandal if the bodies were found at the corral, that the ranch staff might be implicated. Simmons's story to Fred was that Lily must have had a lover's fight and had shot the senator by the end of the farrier's shed, then climbed into the car and shot herself. Said the gun belonged to Lily. To avoid more bad publicity for the ranch, Fred was to load Hopgood's and Lily's bodies into the Cadillac, drive them to the Annex and arrange the senator in the driver's seat and Lily in the passenger seat with the gun in her hand, and leave it all for the police to find in the morning."

"Whoa up, Julia," said Solly. "Only Lily's body was in the car next to the Annex. With a revolver shoved into her hand by someone wearing gloves—we've checked for fingerprints."

"Yes, Fred told me. He couldn't find the senator's body. Fred didn't have a clue, then or now, why Hopgood's body turned up in the feed sack at the bottom of the chuck wagon. Fred said Simmons was furious his murder-suicide scene couldn't be put together and really horribly upset about the body being missing."

"So," said Sarah, "it looks like Heinz Simmons shot Hopgood."

"And for good measure, Lily Farnsworth," said Alex.

"Lily was the prime mover," said Solly. "Oh, it was going to happen sometime, putting Hopgood on ice, but Lily with that call on the tapped public telephone let the office people know that Hopgood and his secretary had set up a meeting."

"Yes," said Julia. "Fred listened to the tape and told Simmons, because Simmons had said he wanted to know exactly when Hopgood was arriving at the ranch."

"Faithful Fred," said Solly. "And now, presto! There was Hopgood driving right into the Simmons trap. Down to the corral after dark on Christmas Eve when no one would be around. Perfect for murder. Lily might have been a problem but Simmons saw she could be useful. Kill her, too, and fake the suicide-murder. Actually Simmons was pretty lucky, because after Sarah and Maria came back from the horse rescue they sneaked back to the lodge and missed the murders. But Blue Feather didn't. He had to put those saddles away and he must have been the uninvited guest at the murders. Or turned up just after the murders. Oh sure, Cookie was in the area, but what the hell, Cookie wasn't into rough stuff and Shorty Fox's been trying to tell the Bureau men so. Her husband, Todd, might have tried that sort of stunt, but he and the whole Younger-Logan tribe are accounted for during the shooting period. But Blue Feather was right there on the spot."

"Are you saying," demanded Sarah, "that Blue Feather, not Simmons, did it?"

"No, Sarah," said Solly patiently. "Listen to your Aunt Julia. All the fake information about the so-called murder-suicide came from Heinz Simmons to Fred. Yes, it could have been the other way round, Blue Feather doing the shooting and Simmons finding the bodies and arranging the transportation to the Annex for the reasons given, except that the weapon belonged to Simmons and . . ."

"And," said Sarah, "Blue Feather's dead and shot by Simmons. Blue Feather was only an opportunist. He must have kept his head down, heard some of the goings-on, found the senator's body and the special silver and turquoise bolo slide lying around—dropped, I suppose, by Simmons—pocketed it as a trophy, and began having dreams of glory. But what about the two bodies? What did he have to do with them?"

"We're betting that Blue Feather didn't see Lily's body in the car, probably she was slumped over. But what if he did see the senator's body lying by the farrier's shed and decided on a joke?"

"A joke?" demanded Aunt Julia angrily.

"Or a ploy. Or something. Who knows? Say Blue Feather ties the feet together with the leather bolo tie—left along with the slide by Simmons—stuffs him into the feed bags, and heaves the body into Santa's chuck wagon. He had the strength for it. Maybe Sarah's right, the blackmail idea hit him then. Maybe he got hold of Simmons that night, said something like, 'I've found this little silver and turquoise slide, and I've hidden a body.

What's it worth to you?' We can never prove that Blue Feather bagged Hopgood, but no one else had the opportunity, and every member of the ranch staff—excepting Cookie, whom we can discount—has been accounted for that night. The only corral arrival is Fred Arco on his body-moving mission, and he couldn't find Hopgood's body. Why? Because it was already in the wagon."

"Blue Feather's certainly the wild card in all this," said Sarah. "But what if someone from outside the ranch complex could have come in and hoisted the body into the wagon?"

"Yes," said Solly, "anything's possible, but in the annals of crime the mysterious stranger usually turns out to be the old familiar figure." He looked up abruptly from his plate and indicated a stout woman in an apron approaching the table.

"Dessert? You want dessert?" said the woman.

Dessert was denied by all, coffee was ordered, and Sarah saw that her aunt, now that her big moment was past, was drooping on her vine. In fact, Solly and Alex now in the dim sepia light of the little back room appeared considerably worse for wear, Solly's long hound's face lined with fatigue, Alex, black hair untidy, shadows under his eyes, his mouth a slash across his face. Their whole group, with the dusky brown and shadowed yellows of the pine walls, looked like a genre oil painting of an unsuccessful supper party over which too many layers of varnish had been laid.

Mid-coffee, Julia put down her cup. "My friends, I have had it and I want my bed. Sarah, you can tell me about the Logan-Younger business later. You and Alex find out why on earth the senator was shot, won't you? I don't even want to hear about anything until tomorrow after breakfast. I've had my moment in the sun."

"Which luckily," said Solly, "was not your last. Okay, troops, up and out. I'll brief Sarah and Alex on the main events when we get back to the ranch. Your arm, madam." Solly rose and with elaborate dignity bowed low over Julia's chair, extended his arm, and assisted her to her feet.

And for once Julia neither shook him off nor complained that she was perfectly fine and to stop the nonsense.

298

TWENTY-FIVE

AUNT Julia having left the field, Alex and Sarah stood by the wall at the end of their cottage patio looking out into the night. The air that evening had done a turnabout and become warmer and moist with a soft south breeze. Solly, a blurred elongated figure under the single yellow patio lantern, held up a spectral hand, pointed toward the south, and predicted rain.

"Tomorrow will be overcast, warm, wet, and messy," he said. Then he turned and stretched himself out on a patio chaise longue, put his hands behind his head, and added, "Sit down and I'll fill you folks in on what you deserve to hear."

"We deserve to hear a lot, especially Sarah," said Alex.

Sarah arranged herself on the second chair, tucked up her feet, pulled her jacket close. "So now we know the bad guys," she said. "After reading through Maud-Emma's papers, it's easy to see that Hopgood was working to make life pleasant for Simmons."

"And the Howells," Solly reminded her. "The big scene. Condos, ranches, tax shelters here, tax deductions there. Federal property turned over to private investors for mineral rights. Mineral rights developed. Sort of. Then, hocus-pocus, lands turn into resorts. More big bucks and less cash outlay in resorts. Ski. Ranch. Fat farms, health spas."

Alex pulled himself up on the patio wall and faced Solly and Sarah. His voice was grim. "And our government in the person of Leo J. Hopgood and his tame little subcommittee members turned the other way. I can just hear them all bleating softly and Leo J. riding herd and talking about free enterprise."

"Yeah," said Solly, "lots of senatorial bobbing and weaving."

"But the Howells?" put in Sarah. "Where do they fit in?"

"The Howells," said Solly, "are real money. I mean real *real* money. Oh, Hopgood had some nice bits of capital stashed away in not so blind trusts, but more important there must have been promises for the senator's future comfort and security. The Howells were big-time. Their finger men, their messenger boys, bought up, raided, consolidated, played fast ball. Takeovers by dummy companies held by dummy corporations, and at the center of the web, Howells. Little Howells, Grandma and Grandpa Howell—never mind that apparently some of the old Howells are in nursing homes, having given away power of attorney, and that some of the corporate officers are under twelve years old. Hell, the FBI, the police, the U.S. Senate, all the king's horses and all the king's men, will spend the next year sorting it out. We can't even begin to guess how it all worked, the nitty-gritty details. So soon there'll be paper chases, fox and geese through Wall Street and obscure foreign banks and God knows where else. As for now, thanks to Maud-Emma's stuff, they've just been given a nice nauseating whiff of mess."

"And to think they got away," said Sarah.

"Didn't I tell you?" said Solly. "No, maybe I didn't. The Howell magic carpet alias the helicopter with Mrs. Simmons, developed engine trouble just north of the Mexican border near Sasabe. Welcome-committee arrangements are under way."

"Good," said Sarah, "though I suppose it will take thirty months to even hit the courts. But what I don't understand is that if everything was working on little greased wheels, why did Hopgood go and upset the cart with that speech about letting it all hang out? Truth at all costs. 'The American people want honesty' theme? I know we thought it was a new gimmick to get elected—telling the truth—but it chopped off his future security blanket."

"Is that a pun?" said Solly.

"Never mind puns," said Alex. "To me that speech made no sense. Hopgood had set himself up for a happy old age and then he blew it. He must have known that Simmons and the Howells would be running scared—away from him. What possessed him?"

Sarah sat forward suddenly. "Hey, that's it. 'Possessed' is right. He was bitten. Potomac fever. Presidential virus. Chief executive flu. Suddenly he wanted to be president, stand there in the door of *Air Force One* listening to 'Hail to the Chief.' Simmons and the Howells were expendable if, by telling the truth—or part of it—and humbly asking for forgiveness, he could be elected. Future cash suddenly wasn't that important anymore. He wanted to be numero uno in this 'great land of ours.' Am I on track?"

"On track, on the button," said Solly. "At least we figure it that way. Me, the police, his aides, and most important, Maud-Emma. According to these folk, Hopgood bought the idea of truth-telling when he began studying mistakes of past presidential candidates—the police have dug up a memo on the subject from Hopgood's briefcase. Hopgood, he wanted to be president. He wanted it bad. Future money took second place. But of course the Howells had come into the business on the understanding that Simmons had a cooperative Senator Hopgood in his pocket. It was a nice arrangement. Howells the basic funding, Simmons the wheeler and dealer, Hopgood the government safety man. And then whambo, smashed to bits."

"But who was behind Hopgood running for president?" demanded Sarah. "Was that his own ego trip, or the state of Alaska wanting a man in the White House, or the Howells-Simmons consortium?"

"I'd guess all of the above," said Solly. "Ego is easy. Leo J. was Mr. Ego. Alaska wouldn't mind their junior senator in a high place, and Simmons and the Howells probably thought, hot dog, now we'll have Hopgood where we can really use him."

"But," said Sarah, "could Hopgood have been elected on this truth platform? Or even get the nomination? After all, he had a record in the Senate and in Texas and Alaska of being the developer's favorite legislator, and a lot of people must know that he did some sleight of hand with his subcommittee in those federal land grabs. Alex, you said any candidate had to be squeaky clean, all the dirty laundry washed and shining."

"His own money picture was pretty clean," said Solly. "After all, he'd been working for *future* handouts. But I suppose he was going to shrug off his connections with Simmons and the Howells, say he'd been deceived by greedy business interests. He was going to screen his associates from now on, be a purer, better person. Ad nauseam, ad vomitum. Would it have worked, would the voters have bought it? Who knows, but after all, huge numbers of voters never vote at all and those that do have a very short attention span, so he might have pulled it off."

"Except for the murder team in waiting."

Solly rose, stretched, extended his wrist to the light, and examined his watch. "Ten-thirty. Here's the moral: Never cross up them what's backed you, paid you, bought you, own you. Rules of the game. Howells probably told Simmons to 'take care of the matter.' Mr. and Mrs. Howell kept their hands clean. Simmons to do the job, Arco the cleanup. Blue Feather was the accident. Who had to be terminated."

"No chance Blue Feather was on the Howell-Simmons payroll?" asked Sarah.

"Doubt it," said Solly. "We think he was your basic sleaze. In it for what he can get and not too bright about methods. Blackmailers usually end up in the muck. Hell, Simmons wouldn't use a meathead with a temper and a prison record. Not even as a hit man. No, Blue Feather was the surprise package. I suppose the picturesque hanging stunt out there in the desert was supposed to be a sort of warning. And so, Best

Beloveds, I go to inspect the remains of the late Heinz Simmons and give my opinion that yes, indeed, said victim was trampled by many horses, and death resulted."

Left alone, Sarah stood up and with Alex turned again to face the darkness that rose beyond the patio wall, Sarah almost imagining she could see the mountains moving, undulating across the night sky. For a moment they stood in silence savoring the moisture, the forgiving currents of air.

"And so to bed?" said Alex.

"Of course," said Sarah, reaching over and taking his hand. "Bed, bed, beautiful bed. We don't even need a jug of wine and a loaf of bread. Just thou."

"Amen," said Alex into the night.

Julia Clancy, Alex McKenzie, Sarah Deane, and Maria Cornish met for the last time over breakfast. The breakfast menu was not diminished, despite the fact that the ranch operation was in shatters, its owner dead, the manager in custody, and the sum of dead bodies now stood at four. True, the general atmosphere was sober, the guests depleted in number—the early morning had been marked by multiple departures—and those remaining conversed in subdued rumbles. But the oatmeal was hot, the French toast plump and brown, the bacon crisp, the breads yeasty and warm, and the coffee well brewed.

"How on earth do they do it?" wondered Sarah.

"Judy Steiner," said Julia, who, fully recovered from her efforts of yesterday, was making a good breakfast. "Judy's been the real engine here. Fred was so much bombast, and Simmons obviously had other things on his mind. Judy even kept things going during all those tricks you're going to tell us about."

"Yes, Sarah dear, do fill us in," said Maria Cornish, beautifully made up and wearing tangerine cashmere, a return to normality after yesterday's mourning costume.

"Yes," said Julia, "spit it out. Was it as we all guessed? The Cat Claw gang at work."

"More or less," said Sarah. "I got it all out of Cookie yesterday when I was trying to find out whether Aunt Julia had been kidnapped. I don't think Cookie or her husband had the idea when they first came here to work. It was just a job and paid well. But when they found Peter Doubler working as the chef, and several Younger-Logan cousins working on the grounds, it all came together. Gato Blanco was sucking the jointly owned creek dry with its golf course, and the whole resort scene bothered the hell out of them. They began after Thanksgiving to orchestrate a series of stunts, hoping to drive the ranch out of business. Cookie said they got the idea when Artie Hopgood slashed that girth in the kids' Thanksgiving rodeo. It was pretty naïve, but it almost worked. Everything they did made someone or whole groups furious. And Fred Arco was ruining the budget trying to make up to guests, buy presents, have parties, give free golf carts. Gato Blanco began to have the reputation of a bad-news facility. Especially when that damaged wagon wheel ended in someone being hurt. No wonder the police thought perhaps the murders were the climax to the whole scheme, with the senator in a bag as the biggest joke of all."

"Now, just stop there," said Aunt Julia. "I understand the golf balls and golf cart business—really, those were quite amusing—but why was I singled out with the water and the cut chair, and Maria here with the snake in her tub? Otherwise it was whole groups who were bothered. Why us?"

Sarah grinned at her. And at Maria Cornish. "I think you can figure it out, both of you. What two guests would you choose to make a maximum fuss if they had some nasty practical joke pulled on them? What two guests could really sound off?"

Aunt Julia was silent for a minute and turned quite red, but Maria Cornish smiled a smile of satisfaction. "But darlings," she said, "of course. Everyone knows I lead a high-profile life. I have to. It's business. If someone's going to fool around with me, I'm going to come right back and make a scene, let everyone know I won't stand for it. And Julia . . ."

"Julia," said Julia, recovering, "is not ever going to stand for outrage at a place where she has paid good money to make her comfortable."

"Nothing," said Maria Cornish, who was almost purring with pleasure, "is lost. Last night I jotted down the notes about our little animal rescue affair and faxed them to my agent, and this morning he called to say they're doing a big publicity release on the whole business—lots of the stills with Diablo and me, and he's talking a six-episode mini. We're trying to find a really big name for the Blue Feather part. Sylvester Stallone if he's free."

Sarah looked up. "Are we in it? The miniseries, I mean."

Maria shook her head regretfully. "I know you'll understand, dear, but it *works* so much better with just a *tiny* cast, so much more dramatic tension. Not that I wouldn't have been absolutely *thrilled.*"

Sarah said she did understand, that she and Alex had jobs, and neither of them could act to save their lives, and Julia had her farm to tend to.

Julia agreed and said she looked forward to the series, and where were they going to get the horses?

"All Paso Finos," said Maria happily. "And the character I'm playing is going to rope them—I have a very good double— and load them on the van. It will be set near Frisco and then I'll be driving the horse van when we have an earthquake, six point five on the Richter scale."

"Fantastic," said Sarah. And then, frowning, "Maud-Emma? How is she? I hope we can see her before we leave. She's really the key to the whole Simmons-Hopgood affair."

"One of the keys, anyway," said Julia. She reached into a jacket pocket, opened it, and produced a notebook. "Our schedule," she explained to Alex and Sarah. "We'll stop in and see Maud-Emma on the way to the airport. Judy Steiner says she's doing very well and has said that perhaps now her life will take an upturn. Maud-Emma has true southern grit. Anyway, we'll fly from Phoenix at eleven. Straight to Chicago, change for Boston, and Patrick—my stable manager," she explained to Maria, "will meet us there. Home late tonight."

Sarah, standing behind Julia and shoulder-to-shoulder with Alex in the departure area at the Phoenix airport, had a question. It concerned the future of Rancho del Gato Blanco. "Do you think it will go back to nature, the golf course and the whole complex? Or change back to the original White Cat low-profile ranch? The creek all filled up again?"

"You," said Alex, "are a dreamer. Just before I left I heard Judy Steiner—who's off to a ranch in Montana with Morty McGuire as head wrangler—I heard Judy say to Cookie that some big development outfit had put in a bid for Gato Blanco and were planning another eighteen-hole golf course—a championship one that could be used for the pro tours. Golf courses aren't ripped up; they grow, they metastasize."

"Oh," said Sarah in a small voice.

"Sarah," said Aunt Julia, turning around. "I've been thinking about which of my horses you should start your lessons on. I think Charlie, my little bay crossbred."

Sarah looked at her aunt. "No, no, no. Never. I've had my day in the saddle. And out of it. No more."

"Want to bet?" said Alex, looking over at Julia.

"I believe," said Julia, "I could work you in Wednesday evenings and Saturday mornings. That's when I take my beginners. And Sarah, dear, I've been thinking that you and Alex can have your wedding at my farm. So much space. In May. Just before the summer show season cranks up. We can use the indoor arena for the reception if it rains."

"Aunt Julia," began Sarah, "You cannot arrange . . . ."

Julia smiled and waved Sarah away with her boarding pass. "No dear, not a word. You don't have to thank me. It will be great fun and save your parents a world of trouble. Leave it to me."

Sarah rolled her eyes at Alex, who shrugged and pointed ahead. "We're boarding," he said. "Relax, Sarah, maybe Julia will be sucked out in an updraft or we'll be hijacked and she'll be taken hostage."

Sarah nodded. "We can hope, can't we?"